Praise for Lexi Blake and Mercenaries.

"I can always trust Lexi Blake's Dominants to leave me breathless...and in love. If you want sensual, exciting BDSM wrapped in an awesome love story, then look for a Lexi Blake book."

~Cherise Sinclair USA Today Bestselling author

"Lexi Blake's MASTERS AND MERCENARIES series is beautifully written and deliciously hot. She's got a real way with both action and sex. I also love the way Blake writes her gorgeous Dom heroes--they make me want to do bad, bad things. Her heroines are intelligent and gutsy ladies whose taste for submission definitely does not make them dish rags. Can't wait for the next book!"

~Angela Knight, New York Times Bestselling author

"A Dom is Forever is action packed, both in the bedroom and out. Expect agents, spies, guns, killing and lots of kink as Liam goes after the mysterious Mr. Black and finds his past and his future… The action and espionage keep this story moving along quickly while the sex and kink provides a totally different type of interest. Everything is very well balanced and flows together wonderfully."

~A Night Owl "Top Pick", Terri, Night Owl Erotica

"A Dom Is Forever is everything that is good in erotic romance. The story was fast-paced and suspenseful, the characters were flawed but made me root for them every step of the way, and the hotness factor was off the charts mostly due to a bad boy Dom with a penchant for dirty talk."

~Rho, The Romance Reviews

"A good read that kept me on my toes, guessing until the big reveal, and thinking survival skills should be a must for all men."

~Chris, Night Owl Reviews

The Men with the Golden Cuffs

Other Books by Lexi Blake

ROMANTIC SUSPENSE

Masters And Mercenaries
The Dom Who Loved Me
The Men With The Golden Cuffs
A Dom is Forever
On Her Master's Secret Service
Sanctum: A Masters and Mercenaries Novella
Love and Let Die
Unconditional: A Masters and Mercenaries Novella
Dungeon Royale
Dungeon Games: A Masters and Mercenaries Novella
A View to a Thrill
Cherished: A Masters and Mercenaries Novella
You Only Love Twice
Luscious: Masters and Mercenaries~Topped
Adored: A Masters and Mercenaries Novella
Master No
Just One Taste: Masters and Mercenaries~Topped 2
From Sanctum with Love
Devoted: A Masters and Mercenaries Novella
Dominance Never Dies
Submission is Not Enough
Master Bits and Mercenary Bites~The Secret Recipes of Topped
Perfectly Paired: Masters and Mercenaries~Topped 3
For His Eyes Only
Arranged: A Masters and Mercenaries Novella
Love Another Day
At Your Service: Masters and Mercenaries~Topped 4
Master Bits and Mercenary Bites~Girls Night
Nobody Does It Better
Close Cover
Protected, Coming July 31, 2018

Masters and Mercenaries: The Forgotten
Memento Mori, Coming August 28, 2018

Lawless
Ruthless
Satisfaction
Revenge

Courting Justice
Order of Protection, Coming June 5, 2018

Masters Of Ménage (by Shayla Black and Lexi Blake)
Their Virgin Captive
Their Virgin's Secret
Their Virgin Concubine
Their Virgin Princess
Their Virgin Hostage
Their Virgin Secretary
Their Virgin Mistress

The Perfect Gentlemen (by Shayla Black and Lexi Blake)
Scandal Never Sleeps
Seduction in Session
Big Easy Temptation
Smoke and Sin
At the Pleasure of the President, Coming Fall 2018

URBAN FANTASY

Thieves
Steal the Light
Steal the Day
Steal the Moon
Steal the Sun
Steal the Night
Ripper
Addict
Sleeper
Outcast, Coming 2018

LEXI BLAKE WRITING AS SOPHIE OAK

Small Town Siren
Siren in the City
Away From Me
Three to Ride
Siren Enslaved
Two to Love
Siren Beloved
One to Keep, Coming August 7, 2018

The Men with the Golden Cuffs

☐

Masters and Mercenaries, Book 2

Lexi Blake

The Men with the Golden Cuffs
Masters and Mercenaries, Book 2
Lexi Blake

Published by DLZ Entertainment LLC

Copyright 2012 DLZ Entertainment LLC
Edited by Chloe Vale and Kasi Alexander
ISBN: 978-1-937608-93-4

McKay-Taggart logo design by Charity Hendry

This is a work of fiction. Names, places, characters and incidents are the product of the author's imagination and are fictitious. Any resemblance to actual persons, living or dead, events or establishments is solely coincidental.

Sign up for Lexi Blake's newsletter
and be entered to win a $25 gift certificate
to the bookseller of your choice.

Join us for news, fun, and exclusive content
including free short stories.

There's a new contest every month!

Go to www.LexiBlake.net to subscribe.

Chapter One

"What brings you to McKay-Taggart today, Miss?" Adam forced himself to ask the question when all he really wanted to do was tug the curvy brunette into his arms and promise her everything would be all right.

From the moment Jake had shown her in his door and dumped her at his desk, Adam had wanted to put a hand on her. It was an instinct. She was exactly his type, and she seemed to be in trouble. He was a sucker for a woman in trouble.

Luckily there was a desk between them or he might prove he was completely unprofessional.

"It's Serena Brooks. That's my real name." Her hands fluttered nervously before she forced them into her lap. "Please call me Serena. Everyone does. Well, my friends do. I actually have a couple of names. Did I offend the first guy?"

Interesting. Adam found himself leaning forward. He caught the faintest whiff of something citrusy. Serena Brooks was a sweet-looking thing. Golden-brown hair escaped from the bun on the back of her head in soft wisps that framed a lovely face. She had on a slightly too big green sweater and jeans. She wore a very professional-looking pair of glasses that she toyed with from time to time. She looked like a sweet librarian.

Fuck, it had been way too long since he'd gotten laid. He usually at least had a full conversation with a woman before he decided to lay her out, strip her down and sink into her.

"Jake? No, you didn't offend him. He's odd. I'm sure he had something important to do."

Jake had a lot of explaining to do. Apparently, he hadn't even introduced himself to Serena. He'd simply walked her across the hall and dumped her, mumbling something about some research he had to do, and ran out, leaving Adam with more questions than he could answer and one very lovely damsel in distress. At least she could answer a few questions.

"Why do you have more than one name?" Maybe he should back off a bit. Adam knew that sometimes the softest packages could explode in his face. He had the scars to prove it. Ten years of security work including five years serving his country with the Green Berets should have taught him not to take anything at face value. Unfortunately his dick hadn't gotten the message.

He glanced at the clock, wondering how long Jacob Dean was going to take. They rarely worked apart. Even during something as simple as a client referral meeting, he preferred to have Jake at his side. Jake so often caught things Adam didn't.

"Oh, you think I have assumed names. Aliases." She laughed. It was a throaty, sexy laugh. It went straight to Adam's cock.

"That would be the very definition of a name that isn't your own." He was utterly fascinated with the way her eyes lit up when she laughed. Even from behind her glasses, he could see her eyes were a lovely shade of green.

She smiled and leaned forward. She probably had no idea that when she leaned forward, her sweater opened and he could see a creamy expanse of breast. He bet she was at least a C cup. Maybe a small D. She would fill his hands. Those breasts would more than likely look beautiful with rope surrounding them, forcing them to stand up and show off.

"I like the idea of an alias, Mr. Miles. It makes me sound far more interesting than I really am. I have a pen name. Amber Rose."

"You're a writer." That fit. He could see her hunched over a notepad writing out innocent romances. He wondered if she blushed when she wrote the kissing scenes. If he told her how he liked to take a woman, she would probably run the other way.

The question was would he chase her down?

The door to his office opened, and Jake strode in. "Sorry. I had a few things to deal with including one very pushy receptionist who likes to put her overly cute nose into everyone's business." He turned to the client, and Adam noticed his double take. Yeah. They had the same taste in women, which was good since they liked to share. "I'm Jake Dean. It's a pleasure to meet you."

"Serena Brooks." She held out her hand, and Jake hesitated only for the slightest second before enveloping it in his own.

Adam understood his hesitation. The woman in front of them was lovely and potentially submissive. It was there in the way she held herself, in the soft way she spoke and the pleasure she obviously took when she thought she'd pleased someone. She might not know or understand it, but Adam had been in the lifestyle long enough to recognize all the signs. Jake was far more invested in being a Dom, but Adam always backed him up.

"That's a beautiful name, Serena," Adam said, wanting to see if his hunch was correct.

She flushed and looked down. "Thank you."

Yep. Score one for the team.

Jake looked at him, shaking his head slightly. Adam could almost read his mind.

Client. Stay away.

He smiled back, a slight uptick of his lips to give Jake his response. *No way. No how.*

He certainly wasn't going to back away. They hadn't even taken the case yet, and there was no certainty that they would. It was very difficult to believe the woman in front of him had gotten herself in enough trouble that she would actually need their services. More than likely she wanted to check out a cheating boyfriend. McKay-Taggart didn't provide those types of services. Adam could happily refer her to a private investigator, and then in a few months, he could call her up and offer her a little solace—ménage style.

Jake looked at her, his eyes fastened to her face. "I didn't have a reminder about your appointment. I apologize for being late."

Bastard. He knew damn well she didn't have an appointment. Jake was pushing her to see if she would lie. Adam sighed. Jake was good at playing bad cop.

Serena didn't even try to lie. She flushed and stammered a little. "I didn't have an appointment. I kind of walked in. I'm sorry if I'm inconveniencing you. I really should have made an appointment, but my agent thought it would be okay." She started to stand.

Jake's voice deepened, proving to Adam beyond a shadow of a doubt that he'd picked up on the same signs. He only used that voice on submissives they picked up in the clubs. "Sit down, Serena."

She settled in again.

"We're not upset. I was simply apologizing for not being here at the start of the meeting. Adam and I are a team. We work together. We usually meet clients together." Jake leaned on the side of the desk. "We don't usually have clients who simply walk in off the street. McKay-Taggart doesn't advertise."

McKay-Taggart Security worked for a very select clientele.

"I know. I had never heard of you." She nodded and sank her hand into what seemed like a never-ending handbag. Adam was pretty sure she could have fit the contents of a small house in that bag. She apologized as she searched through it, finally coming up with a small business card. She passed it to Jake. "My agent sent me. I guess she's worked with you guys before."

Jake looked at it and then passed it to Adam.

Anderson Literary Agency
Lara Anderson, Agent

There was an address and phone numbers, but he didn't recognize the name. It didn't really matter. He would look her up as soon as the client was gone, and he would know the woman right down to what she'd had for lunch. He was damn good. It wouldn't matter if they took the case or not. He was interested in whoever thought to send clients their way. Usually the government or wealthy corporations were more their style, but he was intrigued at the idea of a single client in need of help.

"So what brings you in today?" He tried to come up with any reason for someone so obviously harmless to need a security company of McKay-Taggart's level. They wouldn't come cheap.

She took a deep breath, as though steeling herself to get through the next few moments. "I have a stalker. Sometimes fans joke about stalking an author, but this one is serious."

Jake's arms crossed over his chest. "Have you talked to the police?"

"On several occasions. I have the police reports right here." She shoved her glasses back up her nose before delving into her bag. She came up with several papers, each one slightly wrinkled. She put them down on the desk, attempting to smooth them out. "Sorry. I'm not the most organized of people. My friends keep telling me to get a personal assistant."

Jake snatched the paperwork before Adam could get a hand on it. His fingers tapped along the desk. He knocked twice and swept his fingers toward Serena. It was his signal for Adam to keep the client talking while he reviewed the data.

Adam was the soft touch, and Jake the hard hand. Adam was all right with that. It usually meant that he got to play first.

"Do you know the identity of this man? Is he an ex?" Adam asked, allowing his voice to go soft and sympathetic.

She shook her head. "No. I don't know. What I mean is I have no idea who this guy is. I'm divorced, but I can't imagine Doyle would do this to me. He's an asshole, but he's really upfront about it."

Adam wasn't convinced. When a woman was being systematically stalked, the proper place to start was with an ex. "Your divorce was acrimonious?"

The little huff that came out of her mouth told Adam all he needed to know. "My divorce was started by my ex-husband. He blindsided me. I thought we were happy. We've been divorced for almost three years. He's not interested in me physically. Believe me, he made that plain. And this guy seems very interested, if you know what I mean."

But Adam didn't buy that her ex was completely uninterested. If he was male and had working parts and the right bent, he would be interested. Adam let it go for now. "Fine. Tell me what happened."

"It started really simply. I have a Facebook fan page. Uhm, it's nothing special, just a place where I talk to fans and post excerpts. But a couple of months ago I got a friend request from someone named Joshua Lake. I thought it was kind of cool because he's one of my most popular characters. I thought it was cute. It was fine at first. And then it got weird."

"What do you mean by weird?"

Her face flushed. There was no doubt in Adam's mind that this woman truly believed she was in danger. "He started to send me private messages. I'll be honest. At first I thought it was a woman. Most men don't read romance novels."

"I would assume you don't have a lot of male fans. Do you often have men who try to friend you?" The internet was full of predators. Social networks often made ripe picking grounds.

"Usually they're in the business. I know a lot of cover models, agents, editors. It's people like that. I knew the minute I got the request that this was a fan. He knew too much about my work. This is a person who has read all my books."

Adam was definitely interested. "You said it got weird? What were his private messages like?"

"At first I thought he was just role-playing."

Jake pulled out his phone. He pushed off the desk. "Yes, I'd like to talk to Lieutenant Brighton. Please let him know it's Jake Dean."

Serena shook her head. "Oh, the officer assigned to my case was named Chitwood."

Adam waved her off as Jake stepped away, talking quietly on the phone. "I'm sure they assigned someone very junior to your case. We know Lieutenant Brighton from our Army days. He's sort of our liaison when we have cases involving the local police. I'm sure Jake would just like to get his hands on the source material. I take it the police have transcripts of all the conversations?"

"Yes. Apparently the network kept the conversations on file even after I unfriended him. I blocked him as well."

Adam could guess what happened next. "And he simply changed his name and came back."

"Yes. And he was angry. He laid low for a few weeks and then told me that I wouldn't be able to get rid of him. He called me arrogant for even thinking that I could brush him aside. I blocked him again. That was when he showed up on my personal page."

Adam frowned. This man seemed very determined. Usually the trollers gave up after the first rejection and went on to find easier prey. "How well known are you?"

"As Amber Rose? I have a following. I make my living this way. I sell tens of thousands of downloads every quarter. But I could be in a room with two hundred people and the likelihood of someone knowing me is very small. Even a successful author isn't very famous. I've never hit the *Times*. I probably won't, but I have some crazy fan girls. I didn't get really worried until he sent a friend request to me as Serena Brooks."

Adam didn't like the sound of that. "How closely do you guard your name?"

Her hands threaded together in her lap, a sure sign that she was very nervous about the whole situation. "I've tried to keep it out of everything. Obviously my publisher, my agent and editor know my real name, but no one else does."

"Not even your friends?" If this woman didn't have a few deeply close friends, he would shoot himself. He would bet a lot on the fact that she developed intimate relationships. Perhaps not with many people, but there would be a few who would know all of her secrets.

Her eyes went wide. "Yes. I have two friends who know what I do. Bridget and Chris. But they're writers, too. We all write romance. They would never give up my name. Bridget has been through the same thing. She's had some guys write her letters from prison saying they were coming after her when they got out."

"Is that normal?" It sounded horrible. She wrote romances. The worst she should have to deal with was some fan asking her when the next one would come out.

She shrugged. "It happens more than you would think."

"And what have the police said?" He could guess. They wouldn't do a whole hell of a lot. Even with stalking laws in place, unless they knew who the guy was, they couldn't do much.

"He uses public access to computers. Everything has come from

17

a library, and apparently he has several fake names."

Adam was pretty sure he could do better than that. *Damn it*. He was going to have to take her case. She actually needed the firm, and not just the firm, but him especially. He was a computer expert. He'd been his unit's communications expert in the Green Berets. He'd taken that to another level in the civilian world. He considered himself an excellent hacker. If this asshole was out there, Adam was sure he could find him.

"What has he threatened to do to you?" Adam was pretty sure he didn't want to know, but he had to ask.

Her hands twisted in her lap. He wanted to hold one in his while Jake enveloped the other, the two of them providing a bulwark against the myriad of dangers she faced.

"He hates me. He says I tempt him, and I'm ruining his life. He says I'm dirty, and I should go to hell. He says he's the one to send me there. It's odd, really. It's changed over time. At first it was about the characters. He thought one of my characters should be with someone else. It was fairly typical fan stuff. He said he was coming after me if I didn't get Melissa and Dan together. He claims they were supposed to be together, but I never intended for those two to get together. Dan is very immature."

She got animated as she talked about her work. He thought it was adorable, but they were getting off topic. Adam had to bring her back in line. "You said he changed?"

Her eyes widened as though she had to pull herself out of her own thoughts. "Oh, yes. Uhm, the online stalking stayed the same, but then the calls started and the e-mails. Those were about how evil I am. It's weird. I don't understand how this person can be invested in my books when he obviously thinks they're pornographic."

Adam sighed. "He's obviously not right in the head. Our resident profiler could explain it better. He's crazy. That's all I've got." Adam got out of his chair, unwilling to sit any longer. He walked around his desk and sank to one knee, sliding his hand over hers. He could practically feel her relax. "It's going to be okay. Let me look into this."

There was the low sound of someone clearing his throat. Adam looked up, and Jake stood in the doorway, a frown on his face.

Fuck. He wouldn't like what Adam had just said.

"Ms. Brooks, what Adam is trying to say is that we'll bring this case in front of the group. We don't have the authority to take the case. It has to go up for review." Jake stared down at them, a forbidding presence.

Adam wondered what the hell had put that look on his face.

Serena pulled her hand back, retreating as effectively as if she'd walked across the room. Her face went blank and polite. "Of course. I appreciate you listening to me. I suppose you have the police reports?"

Jake nodded, but there was a coldness to his stance that Adam didn't like. "I do. I think we have everything we need. We'll get back to you."

She stood, careful to avoid touching Adam. "I'm sure you will."

There was a defeated slant to her shoulders as though she was sure everything Jake was saying was mere lip service.

"We'll be in touch very soon, Serena." Adam barely restrained himself from reaching for her. "I promise. I will call you tonight."

"Sure." She turned her head, not making eye contact. "Thank you both for your time."

She walked out of the room without looking back. The door closed with a quiet click.

"What the fuck was that about?" Adam turned on his partner.

Jake's face shut down. "It's about putting the horse way before the cart here. I just talked to Brighton. Everyone at the DPD thinks this is a marital squabble. Her ex-husband recently decided to sue her for a portion of her income. This could really help her case."

"She told us it couldn't be him." Adam could already see Jake's brain turning. Jake had been hurt before—on a fundamental level. The scars on Jake's soul ran deep, and no one had been able to make a dent in them yet.

"And yet she gave the cops clues that led them straight to her ex's door. This is an angry woman, Adam. I get that she's beautiful, but we need to take a look at this before we get involved. I can already see that you're in way too deep. Even if we decide to take her case, I think it would be best if we passed it off to Liam or Alex or someone who isn't going to get emotional."

Maybe he'd read Jake wrong. For the last ten years, he'd shared everything with Jacob Dean, including women. Jake was the brother he wished he'd had and the friend he couldn't imagine living without. He couldn't believe that Jake wasn't attracted to the woman who had just walked out the door.

"I want to see those reports. And even then I don't think I can turn her away. She was scared. If you can't see that then you weren't looking at her and you're not who I thought you were."

Jake shook his head. "Look at that. She's already causing problems. I knew that woman was trouble the minute Grace walked her into the room. I knew you would react this way. And this is precisely why we're not taking this case. I left the file with Grace. You can review it. We present to the group in the morning."

Adam felt his fists clench. "And if this asshole kills her before then?"

"You know the likelihood of that happening is next to none." Jake leaned in. "Buddy, you have to learn to protect yourself."

"And you have to learn that not every woman is Jennifer." There. He'd said it. The name dropped like a lodestone between them. Adam could practically feel the room's temperature drop.

Jake turned on his heels. "I'm heading out. I'm going to the club tonight. Are you coming with me?"

He didn't wait for an answer, simply left Adam standing there wondering if Jennifer Kelly was going to haunt them forever.

Chapter Two

Serena forced herself not to run out of the office. Tears blurred her eyes as she rushed past the pregnant receptionist. The woman had been very kind. There was something about Grace Taggart that made Serena want to confide in her.

Unfortunately, Grace wasn't an investigator, and the men of the company didn't want to have anything to do with her case. Maybe she needed to find a female private investigator. She would feel more comfortable. And she probably wouldn't make an idiot of herself by drooling over a female PI.

She should never have come. It had been a stupid idea.

"What happened? We expected you to take a little longer." Chris stood in the middle of the elegantly decorated hallway with a cup of coffee in his hand.

"They were assholes, weren't they?" Bridget asked. She had a diet soda. She was almost never without a diet soda. She pointed a finger at Chris. "I told you. No one takes this shit seriously. I'm buying a gun."

Chris's light blue eyes went wide. "Oh, no you're not, sweetness. You would have one hormonal day and the lives of anyone who annoyed you would be over. As a person who annoys you on a regular basis, I claim the right to live."

Serena ignored her best friends' banter and strode to the elevator. She pressed the button, praying it would get here soon and she could put this whole thing behind her.

She had no illusions that they would actually take her case. She'd seen it in Jake Dean's dark eyes. He didn't believe her any more than the police had. The police had actually asked if she was making it up as a publicity stunt. At least the investigators at McKay-Taggart had been more polite.

She would have to tell the freaking press for that ploy to work. She'd done her best to keep it quiet. And besides, she wasn't big enough to make the news. Given the nature of her work, she likely would be told by everyone that she had asked for it.

It was brutally unfair, but she'd be judged and sentenced and no one would even have read what she wrote. They would take one look at the covers and call her work smut. She'd seen it time and time again.

"Honey, I'm sorry." Chris's arm slid around her shoulder. He leaned over and kissed her forehead.

Her gay husband had proven so much more loving and affectionate than her real husband. She leaned into him, grateful for his strength.

"I want to know what happened in there. Do I need to go talk to someone?" Bridget asked.

Bridget was the sister she'd never had. The scourge of lazy retail clerks, snooty waiters, and bad drivers everywhere, Bridget was always the first one to kick a little ass.

Serena doubted Bridget could handle Jake Dean. Adam Miles was another story.

"No. It just didn't work out. It's not a big deal." She brushed away a stray tear as the elevator opened. "None of this is a big deal."

It couldn't be. It was someone's idea of a sick joke, and when she refused to respond, they would give up. Nothing physical had happened. She would be fine.

Chris followed her into the elevator, a frown on his handsome face. Chris Roberts was six feet two with a crown of blond hair and an angelic face. It was a crime to women everywhere that he preferred men. "It's not nothing. I'm moving in."

She had to avoid that at all costs. "No, you're not. You just moved in with Jeremy. You can't leave him. You're happy. And before you say anything, you're not coming over, either. Your boyfriend already hates my guts, Bridge."

"Only because he's an asshole." Bridget's pretty face screwed up in a look of pain. "I don't know why I'm still with him."

Because she'd been with him so long she wasn't sure how to not be with him. Serena knew the feeling. She was over her ex in every way imaginable, and yet she still woke up at night feeling alone. It couldn't help that Bridget had watched how amazing Serena's dating life was. Nonexistent. Nothing. A big fat zero. She had no time to even think about dating. She only had her work.

The door to the elevator opened, and she walked out, forcing her feet to move. She let her friends lead her to Bridget's Nissan, and she snapped her seatbelt on like a zombie. They started talking, but she felt far away.

She hadn't loved Doyle in a long time. She kind of actively hated him now. Their marriage had been over forever and yet the man could still make her feel like she was nothing.

And so could Jake Dean. When she'd first walked into his office, she'd felt an instant connection to the man. His eyes had been warm, and she'd sized him up immediately. She did that a lot. She'd seen big, strong Jake and immediately started building a character around him. And then he'd shoved her at Adam, and her brain had gone on overload.

Two gorgeous men. Partners. Jake would be the deadly predator and Adam the tender warrior. They would function as a team, as halves of a whole. They just needed the right heroine to bring them both to life.

Yeah, that was going to happen.

You're sick, Serena. You're perverted. It's just wrong what you wrote. It would be wrong if you wanted one man to tie you up and spank you, but no, Serena Brooks has to go for two. I never would have married you if I had known just how depraved you are. No smart man is going to want a woman like you.

She still could hear her husband's words as he'd blown up six years of marriage. She'd made the horrible mistake of showing him one of her stories. She'd written in private for so long. But he'd utterly rejected her when he'd read one of her books. She'd supported him as he'd tried to write, but he'd dumped her because her work wasn't intellectual. Because her work was embarrassing.

Of course, once he'd figured out how much money she was making, the asshole had changed his tune.

Her cell phone rang. She looked down. Her agent. She let her eyes close. She didn't really want to talk to Lara, but she owed her. "Hello."

Lara's voice came across the line with the force of a bullet. Several bullets. Lara spoke in a rapid-fire manner, peppering her with questions. "Are you out? Is everything done? How do you feel now? So, who did Ian assign to you? I know he can't take it himself, but I expect someone good."

Lara had been the one to send her to McKay-Taggart. She would not be pleased that Serena had been turned down. Serena ignored the first questions. Lara would only really be interested in the answer to her last question. "Sorry. I don't think they're going to take the case."

She was silent for a moment. Lara Anderson was a bitch and a half. It worked for her as an agent. It sometimes scared the crap out of Serena.

"I will handle this." The phone clicked off.

"Is über-bitch on the case? Goddamn it! What are you doing in the fast lane, idiot? Seriously? Do more than twenty miles a fucking hour!" The horn blared, and the small vehicle in front of them obediently moved to the right lane. Bridget was the very definition of road rage.

"She's going to try, but I don't think these guys go down easy. And, honestly, I don't think I want them on the case. If Lara forces them to take it, they won't be serious about it." And they would charge her out the ass. A pissed-off guardian probably wasn't the best guardian.

But when she'd first met Adam Miles, she'd felt like he liked her. He'd smiled and been friendly. There had been genuine concern on his face. She'd felt safe with him. But it meant nothing since Jake Dean seemed so damn willing to shove her to the side.

But the truth was neither one of them would accept her if they read her work. That would sink her. Jake had probably run her pen name. That was why he'd rejected her.

"Sweetie, we're home. Let's go inside." Chris got out of the car. He opened the back door and held out his hand. Bridget ran around the car and stood beside him.

Serena was enveloped in their arms as she got out of the car. Tears pricked her eyes. No matter what her ex said, she was loved. Even if she only had these two people beside her, she was blessed beyond measure.

Serena wrapped her arms around them. Whatever happened, she would be all right.

"Okay, sweets," Chris said, squaring his shoulders. "Let's do this thing."

She sniffled a little. It seemed wrong that she now had security protocols for walking into her own house. It seemed like a bit of overkill, but Chris and Bridget insisted on it. And it really did make her feel better.

Her two newest purchases had been all about safety. The alarm trilled as she entered her house. And her dog panted and wagged his massive tail.

"Hey there Mojo!" She turned off the alarm and got to one knee, the big mutt licking every inch of her face.

"Yes, Mojo is such a guard dog. Are you going to love the stalker to death? Yes, you are. You're going to take him down by humping his leg!" Bridget rubbed a hand down the dog's back. "You couldn't have gotten a pit bull?"

She tightened her arms around Mojo's neck. "I went in to get a killer, but they were going to put him down. He's so sweet. I had to save him. And he's big enough that he should make people think twice."

Chris stood looking at them, shaking his head. There was a baseball bat in his hand. He'd bought it right after the first death threat and placed it just inside her front door. "You two stay here until I get back."

He walked off, doing his normal perimeter sweep. She had gone with him a few times since he'd decided on this particular protocol. He would walk through each room, checking her closets and even looking under the beds.

Bridget walked to her answering machine. She frowned at the blinking light. "What's the bet?"

"I'm not betting. We both know who it is. I need to change my number." Serena filled Mojo's bowl with his favorite kibble.

Bridget pushed the button and Doyle's voice came over the line. Cool and crisp, he was every inch the pretentious professor, even in a voice mail message.

"All right, Serena. I got your latest little legal form. My lawyer is looking over it right now. I don't think anyone with half a mind will buy it. You wrote that smut while I was supporting you with a legitimate, respectable job. You wrote that filth on my dime. I want half. I'm not going away until you start paying me. Do you understand?" Then an angry click.

Bridget's face was bright red. "I am going to cut his balls off with a really crappy pair of scissors. I want him to feel every single moment of pain. After I cut his balls off, I'm going to stomp on them with my best shoes and then feed them to my cat. Wait. I'm not feeding my cat anything fatty and full of itself. She's on a strict diet. I'll feed them to that little yippee dog next door. That thing could use the cholesterol. That way I kill two obnoxious birds with one stone."

"Doyle?" Chris asked, a dark look on his face.

Serena nodded. "I think he just figured out I'm not going to write him a check."

Bridget shook her head. "And you shouldn't. He did nothing to help you. He divorced you over those books. He can't come back now and expect to get half the money. The divorce is final."

But according to her lawyer, Doyle had the right to file the claim. He seemed to think he could change the law. He wouldn't win, but he could make her life difficult. Her lawyer thought they were after a quick settlement to make them go away, but Serena wasn't going to give that man a dime. She would go to court and watch the judge throw out his case.

It all made her ridiculously tired.

She hugged her friends and said good-bye, promising to call if she needed anything. She set the alarm the minute the door closed, sealing herself in for the rest of the day. It was only afternoon, but she would stay here, locked in.

The cops said the stalker hadn't done anything to her yet. They didn't get that this man had already changed her life for the worse. She was isolated, utterly alone, and vulnerable.

Her cell phone trilled. Another message. Probably more threats from Doyle.

She pulled up the text.

You can't tease a person and expect God to forgive you.

She sank to her knees. He had her private cell. She brushed away her tears and called the police. They would tell her the same thing. He hadn't specifically threatened her. He hadn't shown up at her house. He used disposable, untraceable cell phones.

There was nothing they could do but make a report.

But by god, she would have her report. Jake Dean and Adam Miles might not choose to take her case, but she would find someone who would. She wouldn't stop. She wouldn't lay down for this asshole. She wouldn't let him take her life. She wouldn't stop writing because she was scared. She wasn't giving him an inch.

She was going to fight. Alone if she had to.

Chapter Three

Jacob Dean watched a pretty blonde give him the eye. She wore very little clothing, but that was the nature of Club Sanctum. No one wore much. He was in his leathers and a pair of boots. The blonde—he thought her name was Kallie—wore a leather bustier, thong, and no shoes. The bare feet marked her as a submissive. The tray in her hand marked her as working.

But that never stopped a good Dom. If he wanted, he could play with her. She had a lovely figure, very fashionable. She was slender with graceful breasts and slim hips. Her makeup was perfect and not a strand of platinum blonde hair was out of place.

So why was he thinking about a messy brunette?

He shook his head slightly to let Kallie know he had no interest. She shrugged and moved on.

He knew why he was thinking about Serena Brooks. Because she was far softer than Kallie. She was an adorable mess, with big green love-me-take-me-protect-me eyes. He'd taken a single look at Serena and wanted to take her into his arms and feel her soften against him. He'd wanted to get her in between him and Adam and not stop until one of them was buried in her pussy and the other in her ass.

And he didn't trust that feeling.

"What has crawled up Adam's ass and died a horrible death?" Liam's musical accent brought Jake out of his thoughts.

"He's pissed at me." That was an understatement. Adam hadn't talked to him all afternoon. Adam had shoved him out of his office and locked the door. Adam was having the grown man equivalent of a temper tantrum.

"Yeah, I got that. I asked where you were and he nearly bit my head off. He's still at the office. What's going on with that? He never works late."

Liam was right. Adam was great on a case, but when they were in between, the man liked to play. That was the problem. Adam was already on a case. It didn't matter that the group hadn't taken the case yet. It only mattered that Adam was already engaged.

Damn it.

Adam fell too hard and too fast. No matter how many women they had tried and failed to connect with, Adam was still trying to find 'the one.' After the Grace debacle of six months before, Jake had been happy Adam had taken some time off from his search. But the minute he'd seen Serena, he'd known that Adam's time off from his love search was at an end.

Sure enough, he'd been right. The minute Jake had walked into that room and seen the way Adam looked at Serena, his gut had clenched.

Couldn't Adam see that there wasn't one perfect woman for both of them? Women would play at ménage, but there wasn't a woman in the world who would actually live the lifestyle they wanted. They had tried living with a couple of women, and they always left.

Or they utterly betrayed them. Like Jennifer. She'd wrecked their careers in the military just to get a step up. And she'd laughed while she did it. He'd asked her to marry him, and she'd told him he was a freak. No one would want him, she'd said, because he was only half a man.

No one would ever understand how much he needed Adam. And lately he was thinking that it was time to let that dream go. Maybe it was better to be half a man and have a wife then it was to feel complete when the whole of society thought they were wrong. And then Serena walked in the door and he'd just known he was going to get his heart ripped up all over again. He'd managed to stay out of the thing with Grace. He'd known she loved Sean Taggart, but Serena was a different story.

Eve St. James strode into the bar area, a frustrated look on her face. She carried her briefcase in hand. She was still dressed in a chic business suit, her hair perfect. "Does anyone know what the hell this is about?"

"What?" Jake wondered why half his team was here, but no one was dressed for play.

"You haven't checked your cell?" Eve asked.

He hadn't. He'd gotten to the club with every plan to find a sub and settle in for the night—with or without Adam. But he couldn't get Serena out of his head. And he couldn't stop thinking about her case.

The cops were wrong. He felt it deep in his gut. The cursory information led him to believe this was a jerk who liked to feel powerful. He hadn't done anything beyond harass her on a social networking site and send her e-mails. But he would.

He would get sick of being ignored, and he would escalate.

Jake's gut churned, acid building. He wasn't going to be able to turn her away.

Adam walked into the bar. He'd ditched his tie, but he hadn't put on his leathers. Alex was right behind him, carrying his briefcase. The gang was all here, it seemed.

"Did everyone get that terse message from Ian?" Liam asked.

Jake found his phone and noticed the text. It was simple. Ian Taggart, his boss, told him to be at Sanctum at eight pm.

What the hell was going on?

"Do you know anything about this?" Jake asked, looking at Adam. "Did you go to Ian about Serena?"

Adam's jaw firmed, a sure sign that he was irritated. "No. I wouldn't go behind your back. I worked on the presentation of her case. Grace put it on the board for tomorrow's morning meeting. I'll convince everyone then. I'll even convince you."

Jake pulled him aside as everyone started talking amongst

themselves. "You don't have to convince me. I'll recommend that we take the case."

Adam's whole body sagged in obvious relief. "Thank god. She's in trouble. I can feel it. What did Brighton say? Did he convince you?"

Brighton had been a little dismissive. "No. The cops are sure this is a ploy for attention. Even if they believed her, they couldn't do a lot."

"Why would she make this up?"

It was a question that had been bothering him, too. "Publicity. Although if she wanted publicity, I don't see why she's kept it so quiet. And then there's the fact that all of this started just as her ex-husband decided to go after her income. Brighton says Serena is very smart and incredibly creative. Apparently she wrote a book where something similar to this happened. Right down to the author's stalker posing as one of her characters."

Adam grimaced. "I just can't see her doing this."

Jake's instincts told him she was innocent, but he'd been wrong before. "I think the best way to figure this out is to get close to her, but Adam, I think someone else should do it."

"No." Adam's head shook. "We're the best at close coverage. And this guy is using a computer. No one is better with communications than me. It has to be us."

He was being put in a corner, and Jake didn't like the feeling. "Tell me you're going to keep your hands off her."

Adam put on what Jake liked to call his "What, me? I would never do that" face. Adam usually had that look just before he did something stupid. "I know she's the client. Am I attracted to her? Yes. But I'm more concerned for her safety than getting her into bed. Come on, man. We've worked hundreds of corporate cases. This is a woman who needs us. This is an actual person in real danger."

"Fine. We'll talk to Ian in the morning about it."

"You'll talk to Ian right now." Ian Taggart strode into the room, a fierce frown on his face. The boss was six and a half feet of pure alpha male. Even though they had left the Army behind long ago, when Ian Taggart barked at Jake, Jake stood a little taller.

Sometimes he still missed the Army. "Everyone in the conference room now."

"There's a conference room?" Adam asked.

Jake had to admit it was an odd place to have a business meeting. He could hear scenes going on in the dungeon. Moans and the snick of a whip floated into the bar.

Ian strode right past them, not looking back. The boss was pissed off.

Alex, Ian's infinitely—to Jake's mind—more reasonable partner, shook his head. "You two are in serious trouble."

Thank god someone knew something. "What the hell did we do?"

Alex sighed and shook his head. "You pissed off someone important. Lara Anderson is a personal friend of Ian's. She sent you a client today, a woman named Serena Brooks, and the client went home in tears. Lara's brother served in Ian's unit. He saved Ian's life and died while doing it. He feels like he owes her. She's never asked for anything before. She asks him to handle one fucking case for her—to protect one of her writers—and you two send her away."

Fuck a duck. Yeah, he was in trouble, but there were a few problems with Alex's accusations. "I didn't send her away. I can't take a case on my own. It has to go through the group. Why didn't Ian tell us about this?"

"He didn't think she was coming in until tomorrow. He's distracted. He got a line on Mr. Black, and it didn't pan out."

Ian Taggart had a hard-on for bringing down one man. Eli Nelson, also known as Mr. Black, was a rogue CIA agent who had nearly killed Grace Taggart a few months back. Ian had vowed revenge. Jake thought Ian was looking for the man so hard for the simple fact that he didn't want his brother to go after him. Sean Taggart had gotten out of the business. Jake was pretty sure Ian was happy about that. What he wasn't happy about was the fact that Sean no longer spoke to him. It was obvious their little feud continued as Sean blew right past his brother. He was with his wife, Grace, who stopped and talked to Ian, but Sean didn't seem to want to.

Sean held out a hand. "So, big brother's finally done it. He's moved his whole business into the dungeon. Well, I can't say it's surprising. He's always felt more comfortable here. I just wish he would remember that his sister-in-law is pregnant and can use her rest."

Grace stepped up, playfully slapping her husband. "Don't put words in my mouth. I'm happy to be here."

Sean's eyes got hard. "Do you forget where we are, little one?"

Grace's eyes slid submissively to the floor. "I am sorry, Master. I would get on my knees, but I might never get back up."

"Forgiven, love." He sank one hand in her hair and his other went to the swell of her belly. He leaned in, their connection palpable. "You know why we haven't been here. I'm worried about the baby and you. I'll talk to friends while you deal with my brother. And maybe we can walk the dungeon when you get out."

Grace's face lit up. "Thank you, Master."

Sean took her hand in his. It was obvious he wasn't going anywhere until he absolutely had to. Jake wondered what it felt like to be that connected to a woman. Grace wore Sean's ring, and a delicate gold chain around her neck marked her as his submissive. What would it be like to have a woman trust him the way Grace trusted Sean?

He must be getting old. He tried to get his brain back in work mode since it seemed he wouldn't be playing tonight. Jake turned to Grace.

"Who is this Serena person?" Jake asked. He didn't want to walk into that room without knowing a thing or two. Grace had been the one to bring her to his office, the unholy gleam of a matchmaker in her eyes.

Grace shrugged. "I don't know. Ian sent me a message this afternoon that I should prepare the VIP treatment for her, but she'd already come and gone by then. I tried calling her place and leaving a message asking her to come back, but I got voice mail."

Alex, Eve, and Liam walked past them, filing into what seemed to be the conference room.

Adam stayed behind. "What do you know about her? She said she was a writer. Have you heard of Amber Rose? I didn't get a chance to look her up yet. She said she writes romances."

Jake hadn't had time to look at her work either, but he could bet they were sweet little books about true love where the couple consummated their union with a simple kiss. Amber Rose would never go for what they wanted. She would be shocked and horrified. It was their burden to bear that a woman like Serena was exactly what they wanted and exactly the type who couldn't handle them.

Grace stopped and looked like she was about to hyperventilate. Her face flushed, and her mouth dropped open. "Serena Brooks is Amber Rose? Are you kidding me? Oh, my god! I have all her books."

Sean's brows rose on his face. "Amber Rose—as in *Texas Sweethearts*?"

Even the title was sugary sweet. "She writes a series called *Texas Sweethearts*? Is it an old-fashioned western?"

Grace shook her head. "No. It's amazing. I've read them all at least four times. *Sweetheart in Chains* is my favorite. I've heard that *Their Sweetheart Slave* is coming out soon. I can't wait. It's Alexa, Caden, and Duke's story. I've been waiting for it forever."

"What?" Adam said, leaning in. "Are you telling me that sweet little woman who was in my office this afternoon writes porn?"

Sean winced. "Dear god, don't call it porn."

Grace frowned, a single finger pointed straight at Adam. "It isn't porn. It's erotic romance. There is a huge difference. Amber Rose writes hot love stories. And if you can't handle it, then I don't care. I love her books, and I wish I had known who she was when I met her. Erotic romance helped me figure out what I wanted."

Jake shook his head. Grace read some rough stuff. He'd never actually read them himself, but he'd glanced through them when Grace had been under investigation. "Are you serious? Those books you read are all about BDSM."

It was a little incomprehensible, but according to Grace there was a whole category of books that claimed to be BDSM romances. Female fantasies about bondage and pussy Doms who fell to their knees and let their subs walk all over them. Yeah, Jake hadn't read those.

Grace nodded. "Yes, they have BDSM elements." A little smile crept over her face. "And she also writes a lot of ménage."

Sean laughed. "I forgot about that. Wow. That's interesting."

"You've read these books?" Jake asked. Ménage? There was no way. This was a joke.

Sean shrugged, his face flushing slightly. "I wanted to know what my wife reads. I will admit Amber Rose's books are actually kind of good. There are several of those authors who write some pretty hot stuff. It's very different from what I imagined. Not my bag or anything, but the books have actual plots and stuff. Along with some pretty freaky sex…loving, freaky sex." He grunted as his wife elbowed him. "You are going to get so tied up after this baby is born. I'm keeping a running tab of all your punishments."

Grace smiled brightly at her husband. "I look forward to it."

"Get in here now!" Ian's bark resounded through the bar. Jake could have sworn every sub in a mile radius hit her knees, though Grace managed to stay standing.

Adam frowned. "I think we fucked this one up royally, brother."

Jake followed Adam and Grace into the conference room. He thought about telling Adam that it hadn't been his fault, but the truth was they had both mishandled the situation. Adam, in his own way, had come on far too strong. And Jake had pulled away too hard. Jake had misread the situation.

Ian Taggart stood in the center of the room, his arms across his massive chest. He might have let his hair grow out, but he still looked every inch the Lieutenant Commander of a Green Beret team. He hadn't been in command of Jake and Adam's team. That had been his brother, Sean, but there was enough military discipline ingrained into Jake's brain that Ian's stance had him at attention.

"What's up, chief?" Adam had always had a bit of trouble with authority. Where Ian's anger would make Jake more professional, it would bring out Adam's sarcasm.

Jake sent Adam a stare. It was Jake's "let me handle this" look. "I take it this is about the Serena Brooks case? We were planning on presenting it to the group in the morning."

It was nothing less than the truth. He had all the notes on his laptop. He'd intended to go over everything later in the evening after he'd burned off some of his anger. He'd intended to run all of Serena's information and have a perfectly polished PowerPoint presentation for the morning meeting. He'd planned on recommending that they take the case and then have Liam handle the whole thing.

He hated getting blindsided.

"Derek Anderson saved my life and the lives of three of my men, giving his own in the process. He was under my charge in Afghanistan. He was my responsibility. His sister was his only family. I owe her. She has asked me to do one thing in ten years. One fucking thing. She asked me to take care of her client who is being stalked and harassed. She asked me to take care of a single female in a professional fashion. Do you want to explain to me what the problem is?" No one in the whole world could ice over words the way Ian Taggart could.

"She did come in early," Eve pointed out. "Not a one of us knew what was going on. You might have at least let Grace in on the situation."

"I sent her an e-mail."

Grace frowned, obviously not allowing Ian's tone to intimidate her in the least. "Which I got about thirty minutes after Serena Brooks ran out of the office. Don't you try to pin this one on me. I handled it the best way I knew how. The minute I found out she was dealing with a stalker, I called in Jake and Adam. They're the close contact guys. They're the only ones here who can do twenty-four seven since you put Liam on the Black case."

Ian's mouth turned down. "Well, the last information I have is that the bastard is in Europe. Liam has better contacts there than anyone else."

"And I've contacted them. Now all we can do is be patient. But the big bastard here doesn't do patient well. I can handle more than one case at a time. Especially when all I'm really required to do is keep my ear to the ground," Liam complained.

Alex sat back in his chair, his hand scrubbing across his face. "I can handle it, especially if Liam can back me up."

"Not the way we can," Adam interjected. "And you have that corporate case you're working on."

Ian held out a hand and everyone shut up. "I always meant to put Jake and Adam on the case. Jake and Adam handle close contact, Eve profiles the asshole, and Liam can be the backup. From what I can tell, the cops assume this is a domestic dispute and are trying to stay out of it."

Eve sat forward. The former FBI profiler pinned Ian with a stare. "Why do they think her husband is involved? Is there a history of violence? Do we have a file on him?"

Alexander McKay passed her a file folder. "I pulled together what I could after I talked to Ian. I knew you would be interested in this particular case. This is personal, more up your alley."

Her warm brown eyes turned to her ex-husband. Jake didn't know why the couple had broken up, but there was no doubting that they still cared. There was also no doubt that there was a wall between them. As Eve's hand went for the file, she carefully avoided contact.

"What was your take on the husband?" Eve asked, her eyes sliding away from Alex's.

Alex cleared his throat and sat up straighter, his usual professionalism back in full form. "I'm not half the profiler you are. I would rather you formed your own opinions. And he's her ex-husband. They divorced years ago. He filed. She didn't contest it."

She started to flip through the file. "Then why would he start harassing her now? Especially if he's the one who decided to leave?"

"That's what's thrown the cops off." Ian finally took the seat at the head of the table. "Look, according to the cops, she's somewhat suspicious."

"Bullshit," Adam said. "There was nothing suspicious about her."

Jake thought about strangling his partner. He never knew when to shut up. He could practically hear Ian's thoughts before he put them into words.

"Adam, don't make me regret giving this to you. She is the client. Actually, she's not the client. Lara Anderson is the client. Serena Brooks or Amber Rose or whatever you want to call her is to be handled carefully, and part of her handling is going to be figuring out what's the truth and what's complete fiction. She should know a little bit about fiction. She writes a bunch of it."

"Are you trying to say she's not trustworthy because she's a writer? That's ridiculous." Grace looked ready to defend the author.

Ian held out a hand to stop her. "I'm saying she's incredibly ambitious. The woman went from working part time at a retail store to publishing fifteen books in a two-year period. She learned the business very quickly. Lara said she's never had a writer quite as prolific as Serena. She's worked the whole e-publishing business to spectacular advantage, building a devoted following in a short period of time. A woman like that could use the publicity. Tell me, Grace, what is she known for? What types of books does she write? We all know it's erotic, but there's something more, isn't there?"

Grace's flushed face told Jake that Ian was right.

Ian shook his head in a brief arc. He wasn't going to take silence for an answer. Ian rarely asked questions for which he wasn't pretty damn sure of what the answer would be. "And what types of plots does she write?"

"Suspense." Grace sighed. "She's known for writing great suspense plots. Damn it, Ian, that doesn't mean she's making this up."

"Has she ever written a stalker book?"

Grace's head shook, but her words told the truth. "*Three Riders, One Love.* The heroine was being stalked. She ran to a small town and found her lovers there. But she's also written serial killer books and books that feature Russian mafia hit men. They haven't shown up in her life."

Ian's fingers drummed against the desk. "She's very creative. This would make a great story. Aren't all writers looking for a little publicity?"

"Then why hasn't she publicized it?" Jake was a little surprised he'd said the words out loud. He'd intended to stay completely neutral, but those big green eyes were haunting him. Now that everyone else was leveling accusations, he felt a need to defend her a little.

Ian's shoulder came up in a negligent shrug. "Maybe she's waiting for the right time. I'm sure she has a book that will launch sometime soon."

"Two weeks," Grace said.

Eve looked Grace's way. "Could you give me a list of her

books? You can tell a lot about a writer from her work. Writers can be…unstable. They can also be wonderfully sane. Rather like the rest of the world. The good thing about writers is they usually give you a view of their soul, right there on paper. Well, in her case, on an e-reader."

Ian frowned. "Just buy the books and expense it. That's going to look great on our tax forms. Mommy Porn."

"It's not porn." Grace practically fumed.

"You know what they say about porn, you know it when you see it." Ian slapped his hand against the desk, a sure sign that they would be dismissed. "Start tonight, you two. And bring her into the office to meet with Eve tomorrow afternoon. And Adam, try not to sleep with her until we figure out whether or not she's fooling us all."

Adam gave him a snappy salute. "I will try, chief."

Ian sighed as though he knew Adam wouldn't try very hard. "Don't fuck up."

Jake sighed. At least he had his marching orders. Don't fuck up. If only he hadn't fucked up so brutally in the past, he might actually look forward to the assignment.

Chapter Four

Adam couldn't help the thrill of excitement he felt as Jake pulled the SUV into Serena Brooks' drive. He hadn't expected to see her again so soon—maybe not at all. He'd felt a connection to her the moment he'd seen her. He didn't even want to deny it. He was naturally optimistic. The thing with Grace hadn't worked out. She was happy with Sean. Adam was happy for her. Now it was his and Jake's time to find what they needed. He had the strangest feeling Serena Brooks was it.

Her house was a neat little ranch-style house in a fashionable section of Dallas. It wasn't Highland Park, but it was certainly upper middle class. According to his records, this wasn't the home she'd shared with her husband.

Her yard was lush and green, the house set back amidst a small copse of old trees. There was a small patio at the front of the house with a little fountain. It was hidden by Spanish style walls and a gated entry that wouldn't keep a three-year-old out. It was a lovely house, but tactically it was a bit of a nightmare.

"Fuck," Jake said as he put the SUV in park. "I hope her backyard is bare."

"Probably not. It's more than likely as much of a nightmare as the front." Adam knew what Jake objected to. There were far too many places to hide in that front yard. It wouldn't be difficult at all to conceal a body in any number of places. The trees were huge. The porch itself was surrounded by lovely brick walls, covered in ivy. Adam was sure it was beautiful in the daylight, but in the gloom of night, all he could think was how easy it would be to hide there and attack the lovely homeowner as she searched for her keys.

"She parks in the driveway. That means she has to walk all the way across the yard. Anyone could walk right up to her and force her to let him in the house." Jake's low, angry voice gave Adam a tiny bit of hope. He wouldn't be this upset if Serena Brooks hadn't moved him in some way.

"We'll obviously have to talk to her about some security protocols. She needs to park in the garage. Well, if she has a garage door opener. God, I hope she has one. And an alarm system." Adam snapped the hold on his seatbelt. "That is if she doesn't slam the door in our faces. What time is it anyway?"

"Almost ten. I doubt she's gone to bed, but I intend to lecture her if she actually answers the door."

"And if she doesn't?"

Jake shrugged. "Then I'll praise her for being smart after we've broken in and proven to her she doesn't have enough security." Even in the dark shadows, Adam could see that Jake's face was set in stark lines. It was a bad sign. Adam knew his partner. Jake could be dangerous when he was on the edge.

Adam kept his tone light and easy, not wanting to feed Jake's beast. "Come on. Hasn't she been through enough? Shouldn't we go a little easy on her?"

"I doubt this stalker, if there is one, will go easy on her. And if she's playing us all, then it might do her some good to get a little scared."

He was so fucking frustrating. Adam took a deep breath. How long was this going to go on? It had been over a year since they'd tried a long-term relationship. Adam had known almost immediately that Lila wouldn't work out, but he'd been so sick of one-night stands that he'd held on for four months. "You know not every woman in the world is out to screw you."

Jake turned back, his mouth a flat line. "And not every woman in the world is trustworthy. Can we figure out which one Serena Brooks is before we sacrifice another career for a woman?"

"Don't you blame me for Jennifer. You found her. I didn't even particularly like her." He slammed the SUV door, hoping it would give the poor woman some warning that they were here.

Jennifer had been the reason they got their asses kicked out of the Army. Jennifer was the reason his family no longer spoke to him. He'd lost as much as Jake. It had been years, and the bitterness had faded. He still didn't talk to his father or his brothers. He was still the first Miles in four generations to get kicked out of the Army. But he wasn't going to give up on life.

Jake walked down to the end of the yard. He looked up and down the quiet street. There were cars in the driveways and at the curbs. No one would probably notice someone parked and watching.

"I bet she doesn't know her neighbors past the ones on either side," Adam commented. The world didn't work like that anymore. Especially in an upscale neighborhood. These were two-income, highly ambitious families. They sent their kids to private schools and worked twelve-hour days.

"If she even knows those." Jake pointed down the street. "Those lights are out. I wonder why they haven't been fixed."

"I'll call the city tomorrow." It would be first on a list of things he was going to have to do to make her home safer.

"And she doesn't have motion sensor lights. We've been standing out here for five minutes. She should have called the cops by now." Jake's head shook in disappointment.

Adam looked back at the house. The shades had been drawn in the front. The house looked neat and tidily shut up. He strode up to the door. The gate opened, creaking slightly, but there was no movement inside the house. No one opened a shade to check outside. If she was listening, she hadn't heard him. Her porch light was off, the small enclosed space locked in gloom. Even if she looked out the peephole, she wouldn't be able to see the person requesting entry to her home. He sighed and rang the bell.

"I don't hear anything," he said after a moment or two. He tried again but nothing. "Maybe she's not here. Maybe she's staying with a friend."

"Not according to Ian." Jake walked back out to the driveway. "I talked to him before I changed out of my leathers. He said Lara spoke to her earlier in the evening, and Serena had promised her she would stay locked up tonight. Apparently she's working on another book. Ian was going to call her to let her know we're coming. If she's pissed off, well, she's in for a surprise. She's not really the client. Lara is. I'm not about to let her little temper tantrum keep me from doing my job."

Adam slapped his partner on the back. "Just keep talking that way, buddy. That's the attitude that's going to have her eating out of our hands."

"I'm sorry." Jake sighed heavily. "I just wish this case was a little more cut and dry. If she's doing this for publicity, you're going to get hurt again."

And he wouldn't? Jake was the badass, but there was a soft spot underneath that had been damaged in the past. It was up to Adam to gently push him toward the right outcome of this little mess. If Jake wanted to be the bad cop, Adam would let him play it that way. But only to a point. "Fine. But let's not call her very reasonable anger, with you I might add, a temper tantrum."

Jake's face remained closed. "Fine. I was an asshole. But we both know I'll be an asshole again. Let's go around and check out the back. She's got the front closed up, but she has windows everywhere. You want to bet they didn't secure the small windows?"

Jake looked at the small metal sign that proclaimed which security firm proudly protected the home. "No way. I know that firm. They secure the doors and large windows. They never tag the smaller ones."

Despite the fact that he didn't want to scare her, he always did like a little breaking and entering. It reminded him of those days in the Green Berets, going on covert operations. He'd been a different person then. He'd loved being part of a team. It was why he'd been happy to join McKay-Taggart. "Let's get going then."

Jake's lips curved up in a grin. "You know you would have made a good criminal."

"Absolutely." Adam followed Jake toward the back of the house, stopping at Serena's car. "Wow. Nice ride."

The little Audi A6 was a pretty car.

"Apparently writing has been good to her. Between this car and that house, she seems to be doing well." Jake got to one knee, his hand tracing the sleek lines of the car. "Although if it was parked in the garage all the time, no one would guess that she lives alone."

Adam could hear the suspicions underlying Jake's tone. Some people would do a lot to keep a lifestyle like this. Some people would do even more to move up. An odd line on the car's side caught his eye. It was a jagged white streak that looked wrong against the black of the car. "Is something wrong? Is that some damage?"

"Someone keyed her car." Jake showed him the thin line that ran across the passenger side of the Audi from the rear all the way to the front.

"Bastard. She didn't mention property damage this morning."

Jake got to his feet. "No. She said it was just threats. Looks like this guy is escalating at precisely the right time. Just as she thinks we've turned her down, something worse happens. Interesting. I want security cameras around the perimeter of this house."

Because he wanted to see if Serena had a hand in this herself. Adam didn't agree, but there was zero reason to argue with Jake until he had some proof. Jake was a "guilty until proven innocent" kind of guy.

Jake came to the backyard gate and gave it a tug. It didn't budge. "Good girl. She has a lock on it. Unfortunately, I can climb."

Jake hefted himself over the tall gate without a care. Adam planted his feet, pulled himself up, and followed. If this stalker worked out at all, he wouldn't have a problem.

Her small backyard looked like an oasis of calm. She had a lovely patio with sunny furniture and a little fire pit. The whole house was surrounded with old-growth trees—the kind that would be easy to climb and hide in.

There were five windows on the back of the house. Jake checked the largest two carefully.

"Sensors on these."

Adam inspected the smaller windows. The blinds were drawn. It could lead to a bedroom, but he would bet his money that this was a kitchen or a dining room window. He didn't see any wires or other sensors. "Here's our in. Are you sure we shouldn't just keep knocking on the damn door? We could easily prove this to her without giving her a heart attack."

"No." Jake shook his head as he pulled out the super sharp knife and duct tape he'd brought. Jake had a bag in the trunk of his vehicle filled with helpful items. "She needs to understand a few things. We won't always protect her in the manner she wants to be protected. You know how these things can go. She thinks because she's the 'client' that she gets to call the shots. And that will get her killed. I would rather have her pissed off and alive."

"And if she knows we're out here and she comes after us with a baseball bat, or worse, she shoots our asses?" Both were very reasonable scenarios. He'd just recovered from the last time he'd been shot. Without thinking about it, he put a hand over the scars on his gut. A single bullet had torn him apart. He was lucky to be alive. When he'd woken up and realized he hadn't gone into the light, he'd sworn he wouldn't let anything hold him back. He wouldn't give in to fear. He would be open to the possibilities. But when the possibilities included another round of surgery...

"She won't. If that woman owns a gun, then I can't read people. She's one of those 'gun control' nuts. Trust me, the only thing we might be in for is her cat meowing us to death." Jake worked quickly. It wasn't the first time they'd broken into a place to complete a mission. He passed Adam the knife as he tore through the duct tape. "Get to work on the glue."

It was a frighteningly simple thing. Jake made small handholds out of the duct tape while Adam cut through the glue that held the glass pane to the window. His knife was small and wickedly sharp, making quick work of the glue. In mere minutes, Jake pulled the entire pane out of the window and they had easy access to Serena's haven.

Adam decided to go first. Maybe she'd hold back when she realized it was him. He was pretty sure she'd shoot off Jake's junk the minute she had a chance. He lifted the shades, and sure enough, there was someone waiting for him. An enormous dog sat with wide eyes as though he'd just been waiting there for a playmate to show up. Adam got a big old kiss from the large mutt who seemed to have some form of doggy halitosis. He sputtered a bit, wiping away dog drool. "You were wrong about the cat. It's a really big dog."

Jake's low voice floated into the room. "He doesn't sound like he's growling."

The dog wasn't. His tail was wagging in a powerful thump, and he licked at Adam's face as though greeting an old friend. "Yeah, I think we can bet that this boy wasn't top of his class at security dog school."

The dog panted and did a couple of circles as Adam threw a leg over the sill and hauled himself in. The dog took advantage of his now fully exposed body to hop up, put his massive paws on Adam's shoulders, and lick at him enthusiastically.

"Well, at least we know you're going to find love in this house. It's a guarantee now," Jake said with a smirk as he, too, entered. "That dog is worth nothing."

But he put a hand out and greeted the enormous thing. Jake snorted slightly as the dog licked him, too. "I think this is a mix between a lab and a retriever. Do you think she walked in and asked for the biggest pussy dog she could find? Yes, boy, I called you a pussy. That's what you are. You should have already gnawed through Adam's leg. Yes, that's what good dogs do."

Adam had to admit it. Things weren't looking great for Serena Brooks. If he'd wanted to brutally murder her, he'd already gotten past her security system. He'd made friends with her guard dog, and so far, no one had shown up to clock him with a baseball bat.

Either Serena was very naïve or she wasn't that terrified.

His concern must have shown on his face since Jake slapped him across the shoulder. "There it is. I knew you could do it. I knew you could think with the other head."

"You're an asshole." His gut churned a little at the thought that he was wrong about Serena.

Jake shrugged. "Yep, but I'm an asshole who so far has managed to keep us in one piece."

There it was—that odd invisible tether that somehow kept them together. They had met their first day of basic training. Adam had felt the weight of generations of service on his shoulders. Jake had joined because he had nowhere else to go. Adam had come from privilege and Jake from poverty. And they had fit. Ten years, a war, several near-misses with death and countless women later, Adam couldn't imagine his life without Jacob Dean in it.

And he'd never forget the way his father had called him a faggot after they had gotten kicked out of the Army for sharing a woman.

His father would never understand. No one would.

Adam cleared his head and got back to the case. His father would never forgive him. Neither would his brothers. Jake was his only family now.

"Do you hear anything?" Adam asked. The house seemed perfectly quiet. Serena had turned off most of the lights. He was in a small breakfast area. Her kitchen was to the right. There was a bottle of wine open on the counter. Sauvignon Blanc. It looked like a decent year.

"At least she has good taste in wine," Jake noted. "Probably not the best idea to drink when someone is trying to kill you, though." His head came up. Jake gestured down the hall. *That way.*

And he saw her. She was in the living room. Her figure danced across the opening that led to the large space. She was actually dancing. And then she stopped, as though having a revelation. She was still for a moment and then a single fist pumped in the air and she began dancing again. Ear buds sat in her ears, connected to a small device hooked to her shirt.

Serena Brooks looked completely different than she had earlier in the day. Gone was the bulky sweater and loose fitting jeans. Her hair was out of its messy bun and flew out at odd, strangely sexy angles. In the soft light from her lamp, he could see that her hair wasn't a simple brown. It was threaded with blonde and red and dark brown, and there was a ton of it. Without the confines of a comb, the soft stuff seemed to go everywhere in a silky cloud. She wore red cotton underwear and a black tank top. Neither was inherently sexy, but on her the cotton clung to her every curve, accentuating her hourglass figure. Her breasts bounced, obviously free of confinement.

"What the hell is she doing?" Jake asked, his mouth slack as he watched her dance.

The dance wasn't some seductive siren call. It was odd and slightly awkward and joyous. It was the dance of a woman who was completely sure that she was alone. Adam relaxed a bit. She sure as hell didn't look like a woman who would ruthlessly plot her own stalking to get a little publicity. Maybe he was the naïve one, but damn, he didn't want to believe it.

"I got it. So simple. Why didn't I think of that before?" She started to sing. Again, it was probably not a thing she would do if she knew someone was watching. And Adam found her entirely adorable.

"She's insane." But there was a smile on Jake's face.

He had to see that Serena wasn't anything like Jennifer. Jennifer had been utterly perfect. She was an elegant female, never a hair out of place, even when she was in uniform. She always did the right thing and knew exactly what to say. She'd been ambitious, and she'd known how to get what she wanted.

Serena didn't even know the words to the song she was trying to jam to. And she played a terrible air guitar. But damn she had pretty tits.

"I could have killed her ten times by now." Jake didn't even try to keep his voice down. It was obvious that the music was far too loud for Serena to overhear their conversation.

"You need to get your head on straight and forget the violence," Adam tossed back, never taking his eyes off Serena. The big mutt had sat down in the middle of the floor between Adam and Jake, as though he belonged there. "Think about the other things we could have done to her by now. We could have her stripped, tied up, and part way to some sweet double penetration."

"Not a good idea, Adam." But his voice was tight, as though he was a bit uncomfortable.

It seemed like a perfect idea to Adam. She was unattached, obviously submissive, and in definite need of male attention and protection. They could handle all of her needs. They were a one-stop boyfriend shop. "I don't see why not."

Jake turned and shook his head. "Let me show you why not. In three point two seconds, she's going to be the one thinking about violence."

Jake strode down the hall just as she turned and finally opened her eyes at the precise right time.

Serena's pretty green eyes widened to the point of looking slightly painful and she screamed. It wasn't a girly scream. It was a full-on death scream that must have hit the Richter scale somewhere. The dog whined and ran to his mistress, his tail down but thumping. She pulled the ear buds out, grabbed her dog's collar, and started to run for the front door.

Jake was on her in an instant, moving almost faster that Adam could see. There was a reason his call sign had been Ghost. He moved like one. Jake wrapped an arm around Serena's waist and pulled her backward, lifting her feet off the floor. She dropped the dog's collar, and the poor boy just whined and turned in circles as though trying to figure out what to do. Serena kept screaming, her legs kicking out, her fists trying to find purchase.

Adam sighed. They were both drama queens. The whole scene could have been avoided if she'd simply answered either her phone or her door. Or Jake could have been a bit softer. Attacking her after breaking in was sure to make her angry. It might have been a better idea to simply break into her kitchen and cook her a nice meal. Then the whole breaking-and-entering blow could have been softened with a little pasta. He'd been taking some lessons from Sean. Cooking seemed like a good way to get a woman into bed. But no, the caveman had to attack in an attempt to prove he could.

He spied her half full glass of wine. The yelling was reaching a level that threatened to shake the walls. Yeah, he was going to need that. He picked it up and, without a single regret, took a long sip.

"Stop yelling!" Jake ordered. Adam recognized it as his big bad Dom voice.

"Let me go!" Serena screamed back. She seemed to be in excellent physical condition. No one could fight that hard and long without some serious stamina. He was impressed. And the Sauvignon Blanc wasn't half bad.

"You're both scaring the dog." Adam held out a hand, and the dog ran to him, cowering behind his legs. A Chihuahua would have at least made some noise.

Serena finally seemed to focus. "Adam?"

He winked her way. "In the flesh, sweetheart."

Jake's hold had made the tank top ride up. And he'd been right, the pretty girl wasn't wearing a bra. He got the slightest hint of nipple. Now that she'd calmed down a bit, she looked right in Jake's arms. She would be a sweet handful in between them. He'd never loved skinny girls. He wanted curves and boobs, and Miss Serena had plenty of both.

"What the hell are you two doing here? Motherfucker." She tried to pull away.

She also had a potty mouth. "Oh, I would watch the language, sweetheart. The big, nasty Dom doesn't like swearing. He just might spank you."

Serena stopped, every inch of that fair skin flushing in an instant. Yes. She liked that idea. He was going to have to read some of those books. Her laptop was open on a small desk in the corner. Her whole living room seemed to have been converted to a soft, feminine office. She'd been working, walking around her office and dancing. He wasn't sure how the dancing helped, but he'd liked it.

"Let me go, please." Serena's voice was hoarse from the screaming, but there was a tight control to it.

Jake hesitated. "Are you going to be calm now?"

"Yes," she replied, going completely still in his arms. "Now that I know you're not here to kill me, I think I can be calm. You aren't here to kill me, are you?"

Adam smiled before taking another sip. "Not at all. We're here to congratulate you. We're taking your case, sweetheart. We're your new bodyguards."

Chapter Five

Serena forced herself to calm down. Her heart was racing like a runaway freight train. She clutched the phone. Her bedroom was down the hall from where the two men who had invaded her home sat, but it still seemed a little too close for comfort.

"I want them gone." She peered around the corner and could see Adam sitting back, her traitor dog's head in his lap. She'd thought he was hot before in his perfectly cut suit. Now that he'd ditched the tie and jacket, she could see hints of just how cut his body was. And she'd felt for herself just how fit Jacob Dean was.

And how hard his cock could get. There had been no way to mistake the fact that once she'd started wriggling around on him, he'd responded. And so had she once she'd realized that he wasn't there to hurt her. She'd felt a deep pull on all of her girl parts. She needed to get laid. And not by someone like Jacob Dean.

There was a long sigh on the other end of the phone. "I don't think that's a good idea, sweetie. Ian wouldn't have assigned them if he didn't think they were the best men for the job. I know you don't know Ian Taggart, but he's an honorable man. I trust him. My brother thought he could walk on water."

Serena softened. She knew Lara's story. She knew how much

she missed her brother every day. "Why can't this Ian person babysit me?"

"Ian is the head of the company. He can't be with you twenty-four seven until this asshole is caught. And it's a bodyguard, not a babysitter. You are in danger. Don't you dare not take this seriously." Lara's sharp voice practically cut through the phone. When Lara loved someone, she could be fierce about it. It made her a hell of an agent. She viewed her clients as family.

"I am taking it seriously. I promise. I just wish they hadn't broken into my house and caught me in my underwear." That had been past humiliating. She'd ditched her PJ pants because the house had gotten warm. At least she'd managed to leave her tank top on. She really wished she hadn't taken off her bra though. She could just imagine what those two intensely fit men had thought of her cellulite and her saggy boobs.

Lara laughed. "Oh, no. Did they catch you doing that crazy dance thing you do when you can't quite figure out an action scene? Or did they catch you with the ménage dolls?"

She sometimes used dolls in order to get down the physicality of a love scene. She'd rapidly discovered that male dolls were deeply inflexible, so she had to use three ballerina dolls to make things work. Luckily, they were hidden in her desk drawer. "The dancing thing."

It made her weird. She knew that, but she'd given up on finding a man who would understand her a long time back. Her friends got that she thought better while singing and dancing. They ignored it when she talked to herself because she was working on dialogue and made crazy hand gestures. They didn't care that she non-sequitured her way through life because she had a million ideas going at once.

They didn't make fun of her.

"The dancing thing is cute," Lara assured her. "Ian told me that these guys know what they're doing. Adam Miles and Jacob Dean are former Special Forces. They worked with Ian's brother, Sean. He speaks very highly of them. They've been working in the private sector for five years. They're the best in the business. And this is only until we figure out who this asshole is. I promise Ian is working on that, too."

The cops hadn't done much. At least if they were paying these guys, they might actually look into it. She didn't have a problem hiring a security firm. But she did have a problem with Adam and Jake. "They're already making fun of me."

It was stupid. She was a twenty-eight-year-old woman. She shouldn't give a crap what people thought, but it hurt. She'd gotten the crap kicked out of her about a million times since she'd started writing erotic romance. She'd thought she could be happy and proud telling everyone that she was a published writer. Her aunt had asked when she was going to write a real book. Her husband had read it and promptly divorced her because he hadn't meant to marry a woman of her obviously low character. She couldn't even find writer friends outside of her genre. The one writers' group she'd gone to had asked her to leave because they didn't want her to tarnish the chapter's image. She was sick to death of being made fun of.

Lara's voice turned cajoling. Serena had to smile because she'd heard Lara use the same tone on authors who went all diva on her. "What did they do? Look, sweetie, guys don't understand romance. I know your covers are salacious, but they sell books. You can't expect some straight guy to get it."

"No, Lara. They started talking about Doms." She could still hear her ex-husband berating her for wanting to explore BDSM. He'd called her everything from a freak to a whore. The last thing she needed was two bodyguards who thought they could look down on her.

There was a long pause. "What exactly did they say?"

She felt her whole body flush. She looked around the corner to make sure they weren't listening in. Adam was still sitting in her desk chair, drinking her damn wine. He looked gorgeous. His dark hair fell perfectly over sculpted features. He spoke quietly to Jake, who she couldn't see.

"Adam made a crack about Jacob spanking me if I didn't watch my potty mouth."

Lara's laugh came over loud and clear. "Well, you can cuss a blue streak."

"He said the big bad Dom wouldn't like it. I'm sick of this shit,

Lara. I'm sick of men who make fun of me because I'm not some perfect little vanilla princess."

Lara sighed. "Okay, sweetie. I'll talk to Ian. I'm sorry. He's a good friend. I thought he could help. Have you talked to Storm about this?"

Storm was the Dom Serena had been talking with for a couple of months. She'd only recently met him, but he was an incredibly open man. Maybe she should talk to him. He might have some connections. She turned away and walked to the back of her bedroom. "I have a meeting with Master Storm in a couple of days. I'll talk to him."

"All right." Serena could hear Lara's tiredness. She wished she wasn't the cause of it. "I'm sorry. I thought it was the best I could do. Please don't throw them out. They really will protect you until we can get someone else in place. Just go to bed and don't talk to them."

She hated the thought that she wouldn't see them again. She really was an idiot. They were jerks who had thrown her out of their office, broken into her house, and made fun of her work. And she was hurt at the idea of them walking out of her life.

She really was a masochist.

She should probably talk to Master Storm about that, too.

"I promise." She felt her whole body sag. "I'll be a good girl. I really do appreciate it, you know. I just…I can't deal with it. I'm so tired of getting the shit kicked out of me for being honest. But I'll handle it while we find someone else."

"All right, sweetie. Talk to Master Storm. I'll talk to Ian tomorrow. I'll find someone who works. Hey, Brian just walked in. He says hi. You know he loves you, too."

Brian was Lara's husband and her partner. He handled the more mainstream clients. Serena wasn't sure he loved her. Sometimes she thought he could barely stand the erotic clients his wife had brought in, but he was still Lara's husband. "Tell him hi. I'll talk to you tomorrow, Lara."

She hung up the phone. She felt weary, too. She pulled her robe around her and took a deep breath. It was time to set the ground rules with her new bodyguards. She steeled herself. This time when she talked to them she wanted to at least sound like a professional.

"Who is Master Storm?" a low voice asked.

She shrieked like a five-year-old girl. Jake Dean had somehow gotten into her bedroom and behind her when she wasn't looking. "You have to stop that! God, you're going to give me a heart attack."

"He's good at that. It's one of his great life skills." Adam leaned negligently against her doorframe. Mojo sat beside him, their enormous bodies blocking her escape route. Mojo's tail thumped and his mouth hung open, tongue panting. At least her dog found them amusing.

They were both here in her small bedroom. It was the most straight-man attention this bedroom had gotten in years.

"Don't sneak up on me like that." She forced herself to look at Jake. Between the two of them it was obvious Adam would be easier to deal with. Jake was the hard-ass. She didn't deal well with hard-asses.

A single brow arched above his model perfect face. "I didn't sneak up. You weren't paying attention to your surroundings. You were far too busy telling your agent to fire us."

Adam's face fell. "What? But we just got here. Look, sweetheart, I know the whole breaking-in thing was scary, but we did have a point. Your security system sucks. And, in our defense, we did call and ring the doorbell. We can't do our job standing on your front porch waiting for you to finish with the dancing thing. That was adorable by the way."

She flushed. God, she hated the fact that a part of her wanted to believe he wasn't insulting her. His teasing tone was soft and cajoling. When he smiled, the most gorgeous dimples showed up on his face. Adam Miles was just about everything she could want in a boyfriend. He was charming and smart, and he came with a built-in alpha-male partner.

Stop right there, Serena Brooks. Your imagination is running wild. The world doesn't work that way.

"I don't think this is about the break-in. She said we were making fun of her." Jake's brows drew together in a serious expression as though he was working through a problem. "I didn't make fun of her. I told her to stop yelling. I have excellent hearing. I can't stand yelling."

And he apparently thought she was dense. "You know I wasn't talking about you." She turned to Adam. It had really hurt coming from him. She'd expected someone like Jake to think less of her for what she wrote, but Adam had seemed more tolerant.

"What? Me? Are you serious? How did I make fun of you?" He seemed to really struggle with the idea.

"You obviously read some of the titles of my books. Look, I get that you wouldn't read a book like that, but I won't listen to anyone denigrate the choices I've made in my lifestyle. You might not understand or accept it, but I will demand that you respect it."

Jake actually laughed. "The little sub thinks we have problems with BDSM."

Adam's eyes rolled. "Yeah, uhm, you do have some problems, sweetheart. How long have you been in the lifestyle? Or are you a little tourist who likes to rage against the machine?"

"I had to take off my leathers to come here. I was at a club called Sanctum." Jake's face had softened a bit. "Adam knows my limits. I don't like pretty subs spouting filth at me in anger. He has a smart mouth, but he would never ridicule you. Lightning would strike."

Adam smiled at her. "And the earth would shake. Seriously, we don't think that way. We're far too odd on our own. And I haven't read any of your books, but I would like to."

Jake's whole body went on wary alert. "We actually need to. From what I understand, this is about your books, correct?"

She was caught between relief and a dangerous joy. She believed them. They really didn't care. In fact, Jake seemed to be involved in the lifestyle. She didn't know many men outside the lifestyle who would use the term leathers when talking about a pair of pants. The thought of Jacob Dean in a pair of leathers, his cut chest on display as he nodded to the floor, silently requesting that she kneel at his feet, made her heart pound. About a million questions popped into her brain, but she forced herself to keep to the questions asked. "The man who's doing this seems to be familiar with my books. Like I said earlier, I thought it was a woman because this person seemed to take issue with some of my plot choices, but now I think it's a man. I don't think he likes my books very much. At first I thought he was your run-of-the-mill creep trolling the internet, but lately he's gotten uglier. He left me a text today."

"On your cell?" Adam asked. "Where is it?"

"My phone is on the bar in the kitchen," she said. The minute the words were out of her mouth, Adam took off.

She was alone with Jake.

"Now, who is this Master Storm?" The question came out on a low, ungodly sexy growl. "Is he your Dom? What the hell is he doing somewhere else when you're in trouble?"

"He's not my Dom. He's someone I talk to. I needed to do a little research. We've been kind of feeling each other out to see if he wouldn't mind training me."

One of the reasons she liked Master Storm was her utter lack of attraction to the man. She wasn't in danger of falling in love with him. If she was honest with herself, Master Storm was a bit of a puffed-up douche bag, but he did know D/s. She was looking for practical knowledge, not a man who made her heart pound in her chest—even when he wasn't sneaking up on her.

"I don't know this man. Where did you meet him? On the internet?"

"I'm not stupid. I met him at a munch. I found a flyer on a fetish lifestyle site, and it invited interested parties to come to a brunch at a local restaurant. First names only. I met Master Storm about two months ago. We've been talking on the phone about his philosophies."

"Have you been talking about what you need?" He was in her space, his big body taking up all the room. She wasn't even sure how he'd gotten so close. He was tall, at least six foot three, and he seemed to tower over her. His voice was still deep, but it had lost a bit of command.

It was hard to think when he was so close. She could practically feel the heat of his body. "Uhm, we haven't really gotten around to that. He thinks we should talk about his rules first to see if I can follow them."

"Drop him. He's not a Dom. He's a man who likes control but

not responsibility. He's testing you to see if you're right for him, but he isn't thinking about what's right for you. That should be his first and only qualification. A Dom should find what he needs, too, but what every good Dom needs is to do right by his submissive. If he hasn't even asked what you need, he's wrong for you." His eyes became hooded, and his gaze slid to the floor as though he didn't really want to look her in the eye. "You should talk to Ian Taggart. He owns Sanctum. He makes it his business to match well-meaning subs with good Doms."

She shook her head. The last thing she needed was to get more into Lara's friend's business. She'd done all right on her own so far. "Thanks, but I can handle it."

Now his eyes came back up, narrowing. "It's obvious to me you can't."

She was a little offended. He barely knew her, but he was making judgments already? "I didn't ask your opinion, Mr. Dean. But I'm curious. It's obvious you can't stand me. I get that a lot. What exactly is it you don't like?"

He crowded her just a bit, almost daring her to back away. Serena felt small and a little helpless against him. "I never said I didn't like you. You're a beautiful woman."

"But you don't seem to like me. You seem to like scaring me." He wasn't scaring her now. Fear wasn't what she felt.

"I did that for your protection. You need to know how vulnerable you really are. You aren't taking this seriously."

He said it quietly, as though he actually cared. It brought down her resentment level. It did nothing to bring down her frustration, but still, as she spoke she found herself doing so in a polite, respectful manner. "I don't understand. I did everything the cops told me to do. I hired a security firm to install an alarm system."

"It's not very good." He'd stopped moving closer, but she felt penned in, as though he'd herded her exactly where he wanted her to go.

Serena refused to give another inch. "How am I supposed to know that? I don't know anything about this stuff. I paid for it. I know Mojo isn't a good guard dog, but he was so sweet. I couldn't let them put him down. And I have a friend who comes over and walks the house and makes sure there's no one here before I lock myself up for the night."

"It's not enough. Unless there's something you're not telling me."

Humiliation washed over her. She knew what he was saying. "If you don't believe me, you should leave. I'll be fine on my own. I'm obviously just an attention-seeking whore."

He grabbed her elbow. "Don't call yourself that."

"Why not? It's what you were thinking. It's what the cops think."

He stared at her for the longest time. She stood there feeling ridiculous. Tears threatened. Why, oh why, couldn't she be tough like Lara and Bridget? They would just spit in this man's eyes and tell him to go to hell, but Serena stood there.

"You're really scared, aren't you? I require the truth."

"Yes, some man threatened to hurt me. It scares me. But I think you scare me, too."

His lips curved up. He wasn't as gorgeous as Adam. There was a starkness to his features that kept him from being beautiful, but when he smiled, his face transformed. "You're a smart girl. You keep on being scared. And when I said you were beautiful, I meant it. You're truly lovely, Serena. The only problem is I know not to trust a beautiful woman. Now be a good girl and get ready for bed. I'm going to sleep in the living room."

He stepped away, leaving her a little breathless—and a whole lot frustrated. She'd finally found a man who thought she was beautiful, and naturally he didn't trust her.

Adam strode back into her bedroom like he'd done it a thousand times. He looked at Jake. "You taking first watch? One of us needs to fix the window."

Jake nodded and without another word walked away toward the kitchen.

Adam rubbed his hands together. "Well, sweetheart, it's just you and me."

"What is that supposed to mean?" Serena asked, pulling her robe tighter.

"It means you're not sleeping alone tonight." He tossed his lean body into her comfy chair. It was an overstuffed piece of furniture covered in pink and green flowers. It had been her mother's, and though it didn't really go with Serena's contemporary style, she hadn't been able to get rid of it. She could still see her mom sitting there, watching over her.

Now Adam Miles made himself comfortable in the chair where Serena read every night. He looked far too masculine for the flowery upholstery, like a sleek jaguar stretched out for the night.

"I'll run a trace on the text tomorrow." He toed off his loafers and settled into the chair, his longish hair falling over his eyes and making him look years younger.

He was all soft seduction where Jake was one hundred percent alpha male.

"You won't find anything." It felt weird to get into bed knowing Adam intended to stay in the room with her. She hadn't slept with anyone in years. She and Bridget had shared rooms at conventions, but it wasn't the same. Even that had stopped since Bridget insisted on keeping the room sub-tropical at all times. "Do you need a blanket?"

He closed his eyes. "No. I'm good. Trust me. I've slept in far worse places. This is practically heaven."

"Like where?" The writer inside couldn't let that go. According to Lara, he was former Special Forces. She would love to hear his stories.

He yawned a little. "Another time, sweetheart. Go to bed. We have a long day tomorrow. You have to meet with Lara to talk about the book launch. You owe three blogs next week, so you should really get those done, and you haven't sent your editor back your line edits on *Their Sweetheart Slave*. Oh, and we have to meet with Eve. I scheduled that for the morning."

She felt her mouth drop open a little. "You looked through my day planner?"

"Oh, yes. And we're going to upgrade you to a PDA. Really, that day planner thing is a mess. Don't worry. I'll have you organized in no time at all. Consider it all part of the service." His eyes came open. "Don't hide anything from me, Serena. Jake and I are here to protect you. If that means violating your privacy, I'll do it, and I won't blink. You can choose to view it in that fashion or you can treat me like a personal assistant who also happens to know how to kill a man in two point three seconds and not leave a drop of blood. It's all in your point of view, isn't it?"

Adam Miles knew how to go for the throat. He might look softer than that caveman currently prowling her living room, but he was no less dangerous.

And she could keep them. For a little while.

Serena climbed into bed, certain she would never be able to sleep. She closed her eyes and for the first time in weeks fell into pleasant dreams.

Chapter Six

Jake punched the button to call the elevator, a weird feeling in the pit of his stomach. Serena was quiet, her pretty face a pale white. So very different from the vivacious woman who had woken up and fixed coffee. She'd been smiling this morning, as though her natural vibrancy couldn't be defeated by anything as inconsequential as two bodyguards in her house.

She'd made a pot of coffee, offered him a cup, and sat down to work, all that soft hair of hers tied in a knot at the top of her head. She'd been happy while she worked. She'd been a little insane. He wondered if she even realized she talked to herself. She'd muttered quietly as she wrote. Jake had found himself watching her, getting caught up in her enthusiasm, wondering exactly what was going on in that head of hers.

The morning had been oddly comfortable.

Until she'd seen her car.

Jake hadn't even thought about it. He'd assumed she had known about the long scratch.

"While you're talking to Eve, we're going to run a few things through our system." Adam had been the one to hold her while she cried over her car. Jake had held himself apart, preferring to spend his time on the phone with the police. Not preferring, exactly, but he had forced himself to stay away. "After we take a few pictures of the car and check for prints, I promise I'm going to make sure your car gets fixed. And we'll park it in the garage tonight."

She sniffled, the sound doing strange things to Jake's gut. "He'll just do it again. It's not really about the car. I mean, it is, but it isn't."

Adam reached out and touched her. Damn, Jake envied Adam's ability to just do what felt good to him. "It symbolizes something, doesn't it?"

She nodded, proving Adam, as always, was right on target when it came to reading a woman. "It was the first thing I bought after I really started selling books. You have to understand, my husband had divorced me. My parents are dead so I don't have support there. I had friends who sided with Doyle. They couldn't believe I would write a book like that. They didn't actually read it, just saw the cover. My first couple of checks were small. I managed to pay off my portion of Doyle's debt because, yay, we split that. And then after my fifth book came out, I got a check that was free and clear, and I bought the car of my dreams."

"It's a gorgeous car." Adam smiled at Serena, but his eyes sought out Jake's. Jake knew it was his cue to say something, anything.

"I like it. It's got a great engine. 3 liter V6." Yeah. That sounded good. He was really fucking smooth.

She turned to him, her eyes finally lighting up a little. "I wasn't thinking about the engine. I was thinking about the fact that Doyle never let me buy anything but a crappy sedan. We only had the one car. I had to take the bus to work. I had to take the bus everywhere."

He didn't like the sound of that. The bus could be dangerous. He would never let his sub take a bus if he wasn't there to make sure she was all right. And his wife? God, he couldn't imagine driving off in a car when his wife was forced to take a bus. What the hell kind of man did that?

The elevator finally dinged, and she started to walk in. Adam's eyes widened in a way that told Jake he wasn't doing something right. He leaned in.

"Escort her. Treat her like a lady." Adam's words were low, meant only for Jake's ears.

Jake wasn't exactly sure how he was supposed to escort her to the elevator. But he could make more of an effort. He'd sat up for what had felt like forever looking through her house. He'd found a stack of trade paperbacks she'd written. He'd picked up the first *Texas Sweethearts* book. He hadn't put it back down.

Serena wrote ménage, and not some crazy sex book where the woman simply slept with a bunch of men. She wrote about love. She wrote about love between one woman and two men who couldn't seem to live without each other. For the first time in his life, he'd read a book and seen a piece of himself.

He was dying to ask her if she'd been in the center of a ménage before. He just couldn't figure out a way to ask the question without seeming like a freak. Or a pervert. He'd already scared the crap out of her. He'd been a little surprised when she'd put a cup of coffee in front of him with a smile on her face.

"Uhm, what floor do you want?" That was polite, right?

Adam snorted but Serena smiled, a wide grin on her face. "I think it's the fifteenth floor. But you're the one who works here, so you might know better than me."

God, he was a dumbass. He was so much better when he was just killing something. He jabbed the button for his floor. "Sorry."

She pushed her glasses up. They made her look like a supercute librarian. "It's okay. I forget stuff all the time. And I'm sorry I made such a big deal about the car. I know it can be fixed. And that car has gotten me in trouble before. It's kind of why Doyle decided to sue my ass."

The elevator started to rise. He could smell her shampoo. Citrus. He loved that smell. He hadn't realized how much he loved the smell of citrus. "How did it get you in trouble?"

Adam beamed his way as though Jake was a toddler who'd just learned to say please. Jake was going to kick his ass later.

Her nose wrinkled as she confessed. "Bridget and I might have driven the car off the lot and gone straight to Doyle's place. We might have stopped in front of his mailbox where he was standing talking to some of his stuffy friends from the college. I might have shot him the finger and yelled that he made a huge mistake."

Jake couldn't help but smile. He totally understood the impulse. There were plenty of assholes he would love to shoot the bird at.

"He probably wouldn't have figured out I was making so much money if I had just left well enough alone. I kind of told him he was a dumbass for walking away from a slot machine just before it paid out."

"Yes, you probably should have left well enough alone," Adam said with a frown on his face.

But some things were worth doing. Jake understood that. "I bet it felt good."

The smile on her face heated his blood. She was getting under his skin. "Yes. It felt good. I would do it again. No matter what it cost."

"The cost could be half your income," Adam grumbled.

She seemed to shrink a bit. "It won't. My lawyer says it's just a ploy. He's being irritating on the off chance that I'll pay him to go away. My lawyer doesn't think he has a leg to stand on in court."

Jake thought about slapping Adam upside the head. She'd had a smile on her face, and now she'd shut down again. He glared his partner's way. Adam's eyes flared. Jake tilted his head.

What? Those wide eyes told Jake that Adam was going to be obtuse.

Stop fucking this up.

"Wow, you two are having a whole conversation with a series of small tics. That is deeply interesting." Serena watched them with wide eyes.

Adam shook his head, breaking up their little argument. "Now we've done it. We're going to end up in one of her books. Tell me something, sweetheart, how does your heroine pick which man she ends up with in your books?"

Jake suddenly felt better. He knew something Adam didn't know. Adam hadn't read one of her books yet. Adam thought she wrote a whole lot of sex and then ended her stories in a conventional fashion. But Jake was starting to learn there wasn't a lot that was conventional about Serena Brooks.

Serena turned to Adam. Her brows came together in

consternation. "What do you mean?"

Adam shrugged as though the answer didn't really mean anything. "I mean how does she choose between the men? I read some of the blurbs to your books this morning. I thought it was interesting. I've never seen a book like that. I just wondered how your heroines ultimately decide on who to marry. Do they tend to go with the meathead alpha male or the utterly reasonable, slightly metro hunk?"

Asshole. Now Jake did what came naturally. He slapped his best friend upside the head. "I'm not a meathead. But you are a metro douche bag. And Serena writes romance, idiot."

While Adam had holed up in her bedroom, Jake had used her computer. He'd read her website, checked out her reviews, Googled her. Amber Rose was known for happily ever afters. For everyone.

"What is that supposed to mean?" Adam asked. The tense set of his jaw told Jake that he knew he was in the doghouse.

Serena's whole frame stiffened as though she was just waiting for someone to kick her. "I write erotic romance. It's about love, not sex. Though there is a whole lot of sex. I write permanent ménages. I would never have my heroine choose. It would upset my readers."

The elevator doors opened, and Serena strode out, not bothering to look back.

"Dude, how was I supposed to know?" Adam's hands went up.

Jake felt a smug smile cross his face. Score one for the meathead alpha male. "Guess I'm just smarter than you."

They walked out. Jake could see that Grace had already caught Serena and was speaking animatedly. Sean's wife was practically vibrating. Jake was happy to see her. She would build Serena's confidence back up. According to Grace, Amber Rose was the greatest thing since sliced bread.

Adam stopped him before they opened the office door. "Are you seriously telling me that this woman writes about the type of life we want to live?"

It was almost too good to be true. A little of his good mood disappeared. Things that seemed to be too good to be true usually were. She could write it all she wanted to, but unless she'd lived the lifestyle, she didn't know a real thing about it. "Yes. I've only read the one. It was really nice."

He'd been surprised at how much he liked it. He'd expected to laugh and toss it aside, but he'd kind of gotten into it. The story of a woman returning to her small town after years of running had been compelling.

"Well, I'll just have to read two then, won't I?" Adam said before walking away.

Jake followed, his eyes never leaving Serena. Grace gave her a huge hug, and when her face turned up, Serena was smiling again.

Fuck. He was already in too deep.

* * * *

Adam had to hand it to Jake. When his partner decided to do something, he usually did it with the tenacity of a dog after a particularly juicy bone. If they had been battling it out for Serena's affections, round two would have gone to Jake.

Luckily, this was a tag team match, and the only opposition was a pretty brunette who had no idea how hot those damn glasses of hers were making him. She thought she could cover up with a shapeless blouse, but he'd seen her breasts. He'd watched the way they jiggled. He'd just known how nicely they would fit in the palm of his hand. He wanted to get her in a tight sweater. A V-neck would show off her breasts and give him good access when they were alone. "We should take her shopping."

Jake sighed. "Sometimes I think you've played gay too long."

They had played a gay couple before when undercover. It was a surprisingly good way to end up scoring a woman. "She should be wearing something that shows off her body."

A fierce scowl crossed Jake's face. "No. She's fine just the way she is. Don't try to change her."

It took everything Adam had not to fist pump. "You don't want her showing off. You don't want other men looking at her."

Jake was notoriously jealous when his heart got engaged. It was why Adam should have known it wouldn't work with Grace. Well, besides the fact that Sean would have killed him if he'd tried harder. But Jake had never connected to Grace the way he had with Serena.

Adam hadn't missed the way he'd backed her up in the elevator. It had allowed Jake to play the good cop for once.

Jake's jaw firmed stubbornly. "I don't think we should walk into the woman's life and start trying to change her, that's all. She looks nice in her own clothes."

She'd looked even nicer in that tank top and her undies. Serena Brooks had a nice round ass he'd love to get his hands on. She needed a good snug fitting pair of jeans. Adam didn't mind if other men looked at her. As long as they didn't touch, he wouldn't kill them.

Ian strode into the reception area. "You two. My office. Now."

"Crap. He's stopped using verbs. We're in deep shit." Jake scrubbed a hand through his hair. "I'm too tired to deal with a Big Tag fit."

Big Tag fits could range from a few words that were so cold they could freeze a dick off, all the way to the man actually putting a fist through a face. Adam had been the recipient of both. The bad news was Tag hit hard. The good news was he expected to be hit back.

Adam looked at Serena. She was standing there alone now that Grace had a phone call to deal with. She looked vulnerable, her eyes down. *Damn.* He actually didn't want to leave her there.

"Seriously? After one night?" Eve shook her head as she walked up. She was dressed to the nines in a perfectly tailored black business suit that made a stunning contrast to her chicly cut blonde hair. She gave him a wink and lowered her voice. "I know that look. It's the 'protective male' look."

"Well, we are supposed to be keeping her alive," Jake pointed out.

"Yeah, that's all it is." Eve sighed. "I read one of her books last night. Wow. If she's for real, I don't know how you're going to keep your collective hands off her. Ménage is her fantasy."

"I don't intend to keep my hands off her." Adam didn't. He would take it slow, but he liked Serena. Jake was attracted to her. Serena obviously was an open-minded girl. He wasn't going to let the opportunity go. How could they find the one they were searching for if they never took a chance?

"Yeah, well, ménage is our reality. A lot of women have the fantasy. They tend to run once real life sets in." Jake stalked off toward Ian's office.

"He's not going down easy," Eve said with a shake of her head. "How are his parents?"

Adam watched him go. "Still on the road, living like gypsies. The last time they came through town, he got the lecture on how killing people for a living brought shame to them all. His family is a wreck in the precise opposite way mine is. We run the whole spectrum."

"If I could get that man on a shrink's couch, I would."

"It wouldn't do any good. He's not going to forgive himself. He jokes about Jennifer sometimes, but he still feels the shame of getting kicked out. And then his mom tries to shame him for joining up in the first place. But nothing quite compares with being discharged the way he was. I should know." That single act had cost him his family.

"Adam, hundreds of soldiers have affairs every day. It's ridiculous that they discharged you."

"That's what happens to the unconventional." Maybe he should cut Jake a little slack. Maybe he should slow this whole thing down. Jake had his reasons to be wary.

"Adam?"

He turned and saw Serena standing next to him, gazing up with those green eyes that punched him in the gut every time he looked in them. Nope. He probably wasn't going to slow down. It was his fatal flaw, but he had never learned to slow down. Every time he got kicked to the fucking curb, he just bounced back. Maybe he was the masochist. "What is it, sweetheart?"

"Where should I wait?" She had a pen and small notebook in her hand. The minute she wasn't directly engaged with someone, she would sink back into her writing. Her secret world.

That wasn't happening right now.

Eve smiled. "You're with me, Ms. Brooks. I'm Dr. Eve St. James. It is so nice to meet you."

"I have to see a doctor?"

Adam felt a deep sense of satisfaction that she looked to him.

The question hadn't been directed at Eve. She'd instinctively looked to him for protection. Perfect.

He used his calmest tone on her, taking her hand in his. "Eve isn't a medical doctor. She's our profiler. She wants to ask you some questions that will help us figure out who this man is. We won't know a name, but we will have a type."

Her eyes lit up, and now she turned to Eve. "Seriously, you're a profiler. A real profiler?"

Adam stifled a laugh. He knew how to get Serena's motor running. All he had to do was introduce her to anyone who could answer a few questions.

"Absolutely. I used to work for the FBI, but Big Tag pays way better." Eve had a smile on her face, but there was a hitch to her words. Tag might pay better, but that wasn't the reason Eve had left the FBI. It wasn't the reason Alex had brought her on the team, hoping and praying that work could fix his ex-wife.

"That is incredibly cool. I write romantic suspense. I have a lot of law enforcement characters." Serena started to follow Eve down the hall toward her office. He'd been forgotten in the mad search for information.

"Adam!"

He rolled his eyes at Ian's bark. The boss was in a shitty mood. He strode down the opposite hall and entered Ian's domain. A stunning view of the Dallas skyline dominated the huge office. A heavenly smell permeated the air, reminding Adam that his only breakfast had been a granola bar. He was going to have to stock Serena's fridge. A man needed meat.

"God, that smells good." Adam eyed the container on Ian's desk.

"Don't you even fucking look at it." Ian sank into his chair, pulling the bowl toward him like a prisoner who only got one meal a day and would shank anyone who threatened to take it. "It's Sean's mac and cheese. I don't know what he does to it. It's like the best thing I ever ate."

"Sean is feeding you again?" Jake asked. As far as Adam and Jake knew, Sean still wasn't talking to his brother with anything but rude hand gestures and four-letter words.

Ian's face turned down. "No. Grace takes pity on me, though. If I have a relationship with my brother after this, it will be my sister-in-law's doing. I know I disapproved of the relationship, but, damn, I love that woman. Sean couldn't have done better. One day."

Adam knew what that meant. One day Sean would forgive him for that terrible night when Ian had been forced to choose between Grace's life and Sean's. He'd chosen his brother, and Grace had nearly died. Of course, it was the same night Adam had nearly died, too.

He'd gone through surgery, and when he'd woken up, he'd been surer than ever that he wanted to settle down. He'd wanted his life to start. He'd wanted a family.

"Would you do it again?" Jake asked.

Adam nearly did a double take. Jake never pried. Jake never asked questions. He kept to himself. Always.

Ian was quiet for long enough that Adam thought he would ignore the question entirely.

"No," Ian said, his voice a harsh whisper. "I would save Grace because that's what my brother would want. I get it. He loves her. That trumps what I need. I would do my damnedest to save them both, but Grace would come first." He took a bite of the mac and cheese. "But, god, the world would be worse without Sean. I don't even know what truffle oil is, but I love it."

"I wouldn't know," Adam said, wanting to try a bit. It looked amazing.

"Talk to Sean. Maybe he'll make you some." Ian continued to eat, not offering anyone a bite. He looked up as the door opened. "Took you long enough."

"You're in a piss mood," Liam said as he walked into the room carrying his laptop. The Irishman looked past tired. As far as Adam knew he'd been working around the clock. His accent was thicker and deeper than usual, a sure sign that he needed rest.

"Just tell them what you found out." Ian went back to his meal.

Liam sighed heavily and turned the laptop around. There was a grainy video paused on the screen. Serena sat at a long table with several other women, her hair in its bun and a different set of glasses on her nose. The timestamp date was for a year ago.

"This is your girl at something called 'Romance Fest' in Denver." Liam shuddered. "God, don't make me go to one of those things. There's enough estrogen in that room to make a man's balls shrivel up and fall off."

"You can cut the opinion portion of this lecture and get to the good stuff." Ian sat back, his eyes on the screen.

"What is this? Some sort of writer's retreat?" Jake asked, leaning over for a better view.

Liam shook his dark head and bit off a yawn. "I think they call it a reader convention. From what I can tell, a couple hundred sex-starved women get together with a lot of alcohol and chocolate and authors sell them books about more sex-starved women as sad-sack, obviously gay men walk around in very little clothing. No straight man would dress up in chaps when he isn't working on a ranch. Really, it's disturbing."

Ian grinned. "I'm sending him in as a cover model to the convention Serena is scheduled to appear at next month. God, I hope this case is still going by then."

"I'll die first," Liam vowed.

"Could you two just tell us what's going on?" Adam was getting a little sick of the banter. He wanted to see that tape.

"Fine. I think I'd rather just show you." Liam started the video. A voice off camera began speaking.

"My question is for Amber Rose. I was wondering how you manage to write your beautiful love stories when your personal life isn't what anyone would call a fairy tale? Please don't be offended. I'm asking because I'm going through a divorce, and I just get so depressed. How did you manage it?"

Serena's face had flushed at the original question, but she softened and leaned forward. "I'm so sorry to hear that. Divorce can be rough. I wrote several of my books before my divorce. I didn't actually get published until after my husband left me. Honestly, sending that first *Texas Sweethearts* book to a publisher was both for me and to show him, you know? My husband told me I was a talentless hack. He told me I was a pervert for writing about one woman with two men. I won't even go into what he said about BDSM. But I had to write. I had to write because this is who I am.

He'd already taken years from me. I couldn't let him take this, too."

The woman next to her, a pretty woman about Serena's age with jet black hair, leaned over and spoke into Serena's microphone. "And now her pencil-dick ex, who can't give away his crappy ass books, can live his vanilla life without his pervert wife's nice money."

The room erupted in laughter. Serena smiled and winked at the dark-haired woman. "Yeah, that's a nice bit of revenge. I got those first couple of checks, and that really helped my healing process."

"He must have been pissed!" Someone from the audience shouted.

Serena shrugged. "Yeah, well, he can be pissed. He's not getting my 'porn book' money, as he put it. I will make sure bad things happen before he lays a finger on it. And trust me, I'm a writer. I can come up with some crazy revenge stuff. We plot character deaths over lunch once a week. We could add my ex to the list of jerks we're going to kill off."

Liam shut the laptop.

Adam shook his head. "That doesn't mean a damn thing. We've all talked like that."

"Yeah, well, he did come after her money," Liam pointed out. "At least she hasn't killed the fucker yet. Tell her my services are for hire if she decides to off the asshole. I don't like anyone telling a sweet little sub that she's a pervert. He sounds like an asshole who doesn't want the responsibility of caring for a real woman."

"She isn't going to kill her ex." Adam was sure of it. She might talk big in a room full of supportive women. She might even kill his ass off in one of her books, but Serena Brooks was incapable of actually swatting a fly. Her dumb choice of guard dogs proved her soft heart.

"She doesn't have to kill him," Jake said. "She just has to make him look really bad. Maybe get him sent to jail. Then he couldn't come after her money."

Ian pointed his spoon Jake's way. "What he said. Dean, I always thought you were the muscle. You're the brains, too. What's Adam here for?"

"Fuck you, Tag." Adam turned to Jake, but there was no point in arguing in front of an audience. The morning with Serena had softened Jake up, and now all that work was gone with a five-minute video from a year before. It was time to turn to the case at hand. "Do you have anything beyond a couple of careless words caught on tape?"

"Touchy." Liam brought up a new document on his laptop. "Nothing special. Eve's got the duty of reading the books. I know she's paying special attention to the book where Amber Rose's heroine is stalked by her ex-husband."

Fuck. None of it sounded good. "How are her financials?"

"Healthy. But everything is connected to her books. She has deposits from her publisher and her agent. Almost all of her money is from those electronic books everyone loves these days. She sells almost everything online. She's a prolific little girl. In the two years since she started, she's put out almost fifteen books. Which explains the fact that she doesn't seem to date. She never leaves her computer."

"Being that isolated can do odd things to a person." Ian finished up his lunch. "She's obviously obsessed with her work."

"The same could be said of you." Adam felt fidgety. None of this had gone as planned.

"Do you have a list of her friends?" Jake asked. "I'm going out to talk to her ex-husband this afternoon. I could make the rounds."

Jake's tone had flattened. It was his professional voice, the one he used far too often these days.

"She's having lunch with a Bridget and a Chris tomorrow." Adam glanced down at the photocopied pages in his hand. They neatly detailed the rest of Serena's week. Her office came with a handy copy machine. If only all clients were so easy to deal with.

Liam had a ready answer. "Bridget Slaten and Chris Roberts. Both writers. And yes, Chris is a man. He writes romance as a woman, though. His pen name is Cherry Sparks. Who comes up with this shit? And Bridget writes as Dakota Cheyenne. Do you think they just go to a local strip club and ask for names?"

"So she's close to these other writers?" Adam asked.

"As far as I can tell, they're the only people she has regular contact with besides the police." Liam leaned against Ian's desk.

"Lara said Serena plays it close to the vest. She lost most of her friends from before the divorce. Bridget and Chris are clients of Lara's, too. They met at a party and have been tight for almost two years. Bridget took Serena under her wing." Ian passed two folders their way. "That's everything we have on those two and on the ex."

"You need to check into some asshole named Master Storm." Jake flinched a little as he said the name.

Ian stopped as though waiting for the punch line. "Are you fucking kidding me?"

Adam rolled his eyes. "She's researching BDSM."

"Did she find a Douchebag Dom site and ask for a mentor?" Ian asked. "Tourists. Bring her to Sanctum. It might be a good way to keep track of her. But she comes in on your leash, Jake."

Jake's head shook and the scaredy cat actually took a step back. "I don't think that's a good idea. She can come in with Adam."

"Adam doesn't have Master rights at Sanctum," Ian pointed out. "He's never completed the course."

There was a reason Adam hadn't completed the course. Ian taught it. He had to take Ian's shit eight to ten hours a day. He didn't need to go to a club and take some more. Ian was notoriously hard on Doms. But he liked the idea of taking Serena to Sanctum. It was a place where Jake felt comfortable. Serena would be thrilled to walk into an underground club. She would be forced to rely on Jake, and Jake would be forced to take care of her. It was perfect.

"Jake can have official control," Adam said. "You're right. It's a very good way to keep track of her and observe her behavior. You can watch her for yourself, Ian."

Ian seemed to consider the idea. "I'll watch her carefully. You can tell a lot about a sub during a scene. She wants to research BDSM? Push her limits. She'll learn quickly whether or not it's really for her. In fact, why don't I run a scene with her?"

"No." Jake practically barked his answer. "If she comes in with me, I'll run her scenes. No one touches her except me and Adam."

That was what he wanted to hear. When Jake turned into a possessive caveman, it meant he was engaged, whether he liked it or not.

"Fine." Ian sat back in his chair, and Adam suddenly realized that Ian had been testing Jake. *Sneaky, manipulative bastard.* "Make sure she's properly dressed. I don't allow tourists in my club."

Adam sighed. Little Serena would be in fetish wear and no shoes or she wouldn't get the knowledge she sought. She would do it. It would be far too much temptation for Serena. And he intended to make sure that Serena was too tempting for Jake.

"I'll handle everything," Adam promised smoothly as he got out of his chair.

"I just fucking bet you will," Jake said under his breath, his tone assured retribution.

Ian ignored them. "I'll let Eve know you're ready to pick up your charge. Somebody call and give me a report on how the meeting with the ex goes."

Jake held up a hand. "I'll do it. Adam's going to take her to the meeting with her agent."

"Liam, go with Jake as backup." Ian sat up, his body straightening. "And someone figure out who this Master Storm is. I need a last name, and it can't be Limp Dick."

Liam gave Ian a sarcastic salute. "Aye, aye, boss. I look forward to it. I don't get why everyone's all upset about the possibility that this girl is scamming her ex. He sounds like a fucker. I look forward to screwing with him."

Jake got up and sighed. "Great. I get the insane Irishman. My dream is complete."

"It's everyone's dream, boyo."

Despite Jake's anger, Adam was utterly upbeat as he went in search of Serena.

Chapter Seven

"Do you think this is your ex-husband?" Eve St. James asked.

Serena was deeply aware that there was so much more going on than a couple of simple questions. She was the one being profiled. Oh, Dr. St. James might say she was asking so she could get a feel for the man stalking her, but there was something underneath each question. McKay-Taggart Security obviously wanted to make sure their client wasn't lying.

In some ways, finally getting murdered would be a relief. She was totally putting "I Told You So" on her tombstone. "I think my ex would love to see me fail. He wants my money. I don't think he wants much more from me than that."

Eve's perfectly manicured fingernails tapped against the wood of her desk. "You were married for a long time."

Sometimes it felt like forever. Sometimes it was a blink of the eye and she could barely remember what Doyle looked like. But she could certainly remember what it felt like to have him toss her out of their home. He'd threatened it on many occasions, but actually having her things thrown on the lawn like trash had left deep wounds. Still, she wasn't going to lie to the profiler. "I don't think my ex would try to hurt me this way. The lawsuit is more his style. I don't think I know this person. I think this person is crazy."

Eve's mouth tightened. "I don't know about that. I've read

through some of the little notes he's sent you. It's odd. There seems to be a disconnect between the first Facebook notes and the latest e-mail messages. He gets much more violent. I would say this person is very creative, with a rich fantasy life that obviously disturbs him. Can I ask you a question?"

"I think that's what you're getting paid to do, Doc." Eve St. James made her a little nervous. She was perfect. Perfect clothes, nails, hair. It made Serena deeply self-conscious about her own imperfections.

Eve smiled slightly. "Have you thought about this man? As a character?"

She felt her whole body flush. If she lied and said no, it would be obvious. And if she told the truth, it would make her look all the more guilty. Catch 22. Story of her life. If she was going to be honest, she would go all the way. "If I were going to write this man as the bad guy in one of my books, I would say he came from a deeply religious family. Not because I have a problem with religion, but because it can sometimes warp a person's sensibility. I would say there was probably some abuse in his background. He's in pain, and he wants to share it. I offended him in some way. Either my books or something I did personally. I offend him on a deep level, something he would have a hard time even verbalizing because to admit it publicly would throw suspicion on his beliefs. He hasn't told anyone what he's doing, wouldn't tell anyone. This is intimate, possibly the most intimate relationship he has. He wants this to be just the two of us."

"He won't like the fact that you've brought someone else in."

"No." Her mind took over, the whole plot unrolling like a carpet being shaken out. "He wants this intimacy with me. He might hate me, but that's the only real emotion he's able to feel. He can pretend in the real world, but when the lights are out and no one is watching, hate is all he is. It's as important to him as love is to the rest of us. I'm the focus of his hate right now. He'll be offended that I brought someone else into our relationship. He'll step up the attacks. He's going to get violent."

Eve's perfectly manicured fingernails tapped against her desk. "I believe you're right. I think he will escalate. Adam sent me this morning's report. Your car was vandalized?"

Serena swallowed. She hated the fact that he'd touched her car. He'd been in her driveway while she'd been in the house. Had he looked into her windows? "Yes. We called the police but they told me to call my insurance company. They said it was probably kids. They aren't taking this seriously at all. It doesn't help that the lead investigator thinks I'm a kook."

Eve sat forward. "What do you mean? Who's the lead? Sergeant…Chitwood. I don't know him. We have some contacts, but I've never met him."

"He came out to my house about six months ago. My neighbors called the police. I'm afraid Doyle and I were having a little discussion about money. Domestic disturbance is what the officer called it. He took me seriously right up until he walked into my house."

"What changed his mind?"

She could still feel the humiliation of realizing that the cop had made up his mind about her. "I had some posters of my book covers up. My friends, Bridget and Chris, had made posters out of my e-book covers, and I was proud of them."

Eve's lips turned up. "They're a bit sexy."

They were salacious. They were over the top, but they were hers. "Sergeant Chitwood walked in and acted like I was the star of a porn film. Apparently he's not a big proponent of ménage in fiction."

"I don't think you'll have the same problem with your bodyguards. Adam and Jake are somewhat open-minded."

The door to Eve's office opened and Adam filled the space. He looked ridiculously scrumptious in a dark tailored suit and tie. He was a big-city hottie of the first order. Jake was almost his opposite. Jake Dean should be working a herd somewhere. She could see him in nothing but a pair of Levi's, lifting a bale of hale.

She really had to get her mind off those two. They were dangerous.

"Is she ready to go? She has a meeting with her agent, and we're supposed to drop by the police station. I got a call from my contact. He wants to take another look at the case. If we hurry, we can sneak in lunch."

He was her dream personal assistant. Gorgeous, stylish, sexy, and well-organized. The organization bit actually did things to her girl parts. Adam Miles would probably even be organized during sex. Teasing. Check. Oral. Check. Screaming orgasm. Check and check.

And Jacob Dean would just growl and pull her hair and tell her what to do.

Yeah. That did things to her, too.

"Serena?" Adam's voice pulled her out of that little fantasy. She spaced a lot. Her brain just went to crazy places. Unfortunately, it made most people think she was a complete flake. Eve had a quizzical expression on her face, but Adam smiled indulgently. He leaned in, whispering in her ear. "I would give a lot to know what you were just thinking about. It has your nipples hard."

She knew she should have worn a sweater or something. Her nipples were big. They weren't delicate and pretty. Her ex had told her she reminded him of a cow. She felt shame flood her.

"Hey." Adam got to one knee. "I was flirting. I wasn't complaining. I was happy about it."

He was so gorgeous. There was no way she could believe him. She turned back to Eve. "If you need anything else, please let me know. I want to help in any way I can, and I know that the first thing you're going to do is check me out to see if I'm some kind of whack job."

She stood, trying to make sure she didn't touch Adam at all. He was just doing his job, and one of the parts of his job was to make sure he controlled her. She was sure the flirting thing was all a part of Adam's game plan. She shouldn't take it seriously. No matter how much she wanted to. It would just put her in the position of playing another man's fool. She'd played her husband's fool for years and years. The fact that she'd stayed in a bad marriage shamed her. She didn't need to start a relationship with another man she couldn't handle.

Eve nodded, studying her thoughtfully. "I enjoyed our talk, Serena."

Sure she had. It hadn't been a talk. It had been a very polite interrogation. They still weren't sure about her. They still didn't believe and that meant she was still fucked because no one was going to put their lives on the line for a woman they thought just might be lying. "Thank you." She turned to Adam. Lunch wasn't a good idea. She had to remember at all times that he was the bodyguard, and she wasn't above suspicion. "I'm not really hungry. Let's get the errands done as quickly as possible. I need to get my word count in."

His face went blank as he nodded and politely gestured toward the door. "Eve, I'll talk to you soon."

Yes, she was sure he would. He would be on the phone with Eve asking whether or not his charge was an insane, publicity-seeking whore.

She managed to make it all the way to the elevator before he grabbed her elbow and turned her around. His hand bit into her flesh, making her deeply aware that he was there.

"You want to explain what that little scene was all about?" Adam asked, the words grinding out of his mouth. He pushed the button for the elevator, and his face evened out when he saw Grace Taggart walking by. The minute she was gone, his lips turned down and those glorious eyes narrowed. "Now, Serena. Explain."

The elevator dinged and before she could get a word out, he hauled her inside and jabbed the button that closed the door.

"Where's Jacob?" Serena asked. Were they leaving him behind? Had he gotten another assignment? Jake obviously hadn't wanted to take the case in the first place. Maybe Adam had drawn the short straw.

Adam reached out and slammed the button that stopped the elevator. "Jacob is going to talk to your ex-husband. Are you angry that it's me who's spending the day with you and not him?"

The words were cold, but there was hurt in his eyes. She softened. "No. Not at all. It's fine."

"Then why the cold shoulder?"

"Adam, I'm not giving you the cold shoulder. I just don't have time for lunch." And she didn't want to sit and talk to him and start to fall for him anymore than she already had. She knew her weaknesses. She wasn't such an idiot that she didn't know when she was in danger of falling for the wrong man.

He released the button, and the elevator started to go down again. "Well, I think you do. We're on my schedule now, Serena. We'll meet with Lara and then have lunch and then go see the Lieutenant. You'll be home in plenty of time to get your work done. If you fail to do so, it will be on you and not me."

She stared at him for a moment, but he was closed off now, his body language harsh. He was angry. She wasn't sure what she'd done. Why the hell did he care if she didn't want to go to lunch?

She was forever doomed to piss off the men in her life. Chris was the only man who didn't seem to get annoyed by her very presence, and he had zero interest in her vagina. Tears threatened to fall. What a crappy fucking day. And now she had to spend the rest of it with a man who wasn't happy with her.

The floors went by. Why the hell had Ian Taggart chosen the top floor?

Adam's fist came out, and he slammed at the button again, forcing the elevator to stop. "Why are you crying, Serena?"

She sniffled, hating the fact that she was losing control. *Damn it.* Why couldn't she be like Bridget? Bridget never cried. She told people to fuck off, and she meant it. Serena always cried and made herself look like a damn idiot. "I'm not."

"You are." He reached out and pulled her around. "Goddamn it, Serena. I might not be Jacob, but don't think you can disobey me. I'm in charge for now. You will mind me. You will do as I say, and I want to know why the fuck you're crying."

"I'm tired of no one believing me." She tried to pull away, but he held her tight. "Just let me go, Adam. I don't want to play these games. I want you to treat me like a client. I want you to have some respect for me or at least pretend to."

"Games? What the hell kind of game am I supposed to be playing?" Adam asked.

She was suddenly deeply aware that she was in a small space with a man she'd known for less than a day. A million and one scenarios ran through her head, most of them bad. "I think I'd like to go back upstairs now."

Adam stared at her for a long moment, and then his arms

dropped and he took a step back. His face became a polite mask. "Of course. I'm sure Liam can take over."

He pressed the button to release the elevator and then pressed fifteen. The elevator still continued on its way down. Adam cursed. "Sorry. It won't go back up until it hits the lobby. I'll get out then. You should be fine to get back to the office. Just tell Grace you need someone else, and she'll reassign you. Let her know I'm taking the rest of the day off."

He'd shut down, his normally animated face a complete blank. Despite her momentary fear, her heart ached because somehow she'd done this to him. She was always saying or doing the wrong thing. Awkward. She was awkward, and no amount of meaning well seemed to make up for it. The last few years had been easier for the simple fact that she'd lived them inside her head where she wrote the dialogue and the plot, and the good guys won and the awkward girl got the guys.

"Damn it, Serena. I'm giving you what you want. Stop crying. It's killing me." Adam stared at her but kept his hands in his pockets.

They were almost to the ground floor. Almost free. And she wouldn't see him again. She knew that beyond a shadow of a doubt. If she let the elevator doors close behind Adam Miles, he wouldn't smile or flirt or laugh her way again. He would avoid her, and she would never know what she'd done. He would be one more man who didn't like her, and she wouldn't know why.

She pushed the stop button and turned on him. The situation was fucked up, and she really couldn't make it worse. "What did I do?"

Adam's eyes went wide. "What do you mean?"

"I made you mad. I'd like to know what I did."

"I wasn't mad," Adam protested. "Well, maybe a little because it seemed like you preferred Jake. And then I realized you were scared of me, and I can't fight that. You have the right to feel safe. If someone else can do that for you, then I have to step away." He sighed, his body relaxing. "Serena, I was mad because I made reservations at a really nice restaurant. I planned your whole day around getting to spend a couple of hours alone with you. I was trying, apparently in a ham-handed way, to seduce you."

"You were?" God. The very thought made her head spin.

He flushed a little. "Yeah. Don't worry about it, sweetheart. You're not the first woman to turn me down. I suspect you won't be the last. Jake thinks I come on too strong. I don't mean to. I just tend to know what I want. I'm impatient. I didn't mean to scare you. I apologize. I promise Liam will do a good job. He won't throw himself at you. Of course, he'll also take you to Hooters for lunch, but he's a safe bet."

Suddenly, though, she didn't want safe. She wanted him. "Are you trying to seduce me because you think it will make me easier to control?"

Adam laughed, but it was a bitter little thing. "No. I'm trying to seduce you because I've had a hard-on since you walked into my office yesterday. I've been plotting and planning all day. When I slept in that chair last night, I decided to wine and dine you. I was going to make dinner for you tonight. Another thing you won't get from Liam, might I add."

She didn't want Liam. She wanted Adam and Jake. She'd spent two years with her head buried in the sand. Hell, it had been longer than that. Most of her life she'd simply let things happen to her. What would it feel like to take what she wanted? If she went in with a clear head, knowing it would end, maybe she could keep her heart whole.

She moved close to Adam. "You still like me?"

Adam sighed. "Serena, what is this about? How could I not like you? You're sweet and smart and funny. You're entirely lovable, baby."

That did it. Serena went on her toes and pressed her lips to his.

Adam took a startled step back. "Serena?"

God. Had she made a mistake? "I'm sorry."

He reached out and grabbed her, hauling her close. "You better be sure. You better think about this before you make a move on me." His lips curved up in the most deliciously decadent smile, but it was the tenderness in his eyes that pulled at her heart. "Don't tease a man who's already falling for you."

"Adam," she hated the insecurity in her voice. "I'm not dumb. I know I'm not some great catch."

He gripped her hips and pulled her close, letting her feel every inch of his cock. Hard. Thick. Deliciously long. She had to swallow. She had to force herself to take a breath.

"Baby, if you don't stop talking about yourself that way, I'm going to have to talk to Jake about punishment. Neither one of us will allow you to denigrate yourself. You're gorgeous and sexy as hell, and I can't wait to sink my dick in you. But I intend to be a gentleman for the time being because I don't want you to use me."

"Use you?"

"For sex."

Sex? Yeah, she wanted to use him for sex. What else was he talking about? "You don't want to have sex?"

He chuckled, his hands moving around her hips, skirting her ass. "Oh, I want the sex, but I don't want to get dumped by the smart, successful author because she sees me as a ridiculously hot piece of ass. I want you to get to know me. I want you to like me."

She was getting soft and wet. She liked him just fine. And he was talking like she regularly nabbed a boy toy for the night. "Don't be ridiculous, Adam. I haven't..."

Shit. She shouldn't go there.

He tilted her head up, placing his hand under her chin. It forced her to look into those baby blues that pulled her in every time. "Finish that sentence, Serena. And don't lie. Jake and I are taking you into a club soon. I would rather we spent the evening enjoying ourselves, but I can have fun spanking your ass red."

She flushed. She felt that heat from the top of her head right down through her toes. A club. Ian Taggart's underground club? She'd hoped that after a long while, Master Storm would be able to get her an invitation to one of the local play parties, but this was a real club, like the ones she wrote about. "Really?"

Adam leaned over, a smile on his face. He touched his forehead to hers. "All I have to do is find a place for you to do a little research and you're putty in my hands. Really, baby. I'm supposed to get you a collar and everything. Now finish that sentence."

The fact that he was so close and he understood what she wanted made it easier to be honest. "Adam, I haven't had sex in almost four years. Even before the divorce, Doyle lost interest in me. I'm not some crazy player. I'm not just trying to get into your pants."

"Well, I want to keep it that way, baby." His voice was lyrical, magnetic. His lips hovered above hers. "But I do believe in giving you a little taste of what I want."

His lips met hers, and this time it felt right. This time he was in charge, and all she had to do was be brave enough to follow. His mouth covered hers, rubbing their lips together. His hands moved in a restless pattern across her back and down her hips, finally cupping her ass and pressing her into him. His tongue licked along the seam of her lips, and she opened for him. How long since she'd been kissed? Forever. Like this? Perhaps never. Adam devoured her. He drank her down like a man who had been dying of thirst.

She softened, wanting to sink into him.

"Touch me, baby," Adam whispered. "Don't be shy. I want your hands on me. It's the best of both worlds. I'll let you play with me all you like, and Jake will tie you up. We can be everything you want."

The words were seduction in and of themselves. Everything she wanted. Everything she'd fantasized about. She could tell Adam her desires, and he wouldn't make her feel like a freak. She kissed him again, boldness taking over. She let her hands play along the lean muscles of his shoulders and down his biceps. Adam was cut everywhere. She kissed the strong line of his jaw, reveling in his scent. He smelled clean and masculine. His hair was just a little long. He looked like he belonged on the cover of a magazine, and he was offering himself up to her.

"That's right, baby. You explore to your heart's content." He took her right hand and pulled it down. "I think there's a part of me you missed."

His cock. She could feel it pressing against the fabric of his pants as though trying to get out. She cupped him, feeling his strength. What would it be like to ride that cock? Would she finally find the pleasure she wrote about? She'd come before, but never without the aid of something that required double A batteries. Adam didn't seem to need such aids. Adam seemed like he could handle the job just fine.

She kissed him again and wondered how it would work. Would he throw her against the elevator door or would he get down on the floor and let her lower herself on him inch by inch?

It was getting out of control. She kissed him, and somehow her hands were slipping past his belt, trying to seek out hot flesh.

And his phone rang.

"Shit." Adam kissed her again, hugging her with one arm as he reached for his cell with the other.

"That fucking better not be you in the goddamn elevator, Adam. Maintenance just called and said some asshole stopped the elevator and guess what? They started out on my floor. Are you fucking the client in the goddamn elevator five minutes after I told you not to fuck the fucking client?"

She tried to pull away, Ian Taggart's voice filling the elevator even though he was fifteen floors up.

Adam put the cell to his chest and gave her a reassuring grin. "He has a horrible potty mouth, baby. Don't worry about him." He brought the phone back up. "Well, boss, if you remember I did say I probably wouldn't try very hard."

"Goddamn it, Adam."

Adam reached out and started the elevator again. It dinged, and Adam put an arm around her and began to walk out like nothing had happened. "I'm joking, boss. You need to develop a sense of humor. We're on our way to her agent's. Someone else must be fucking in the elevator. Trust me, when I get around to fucking the client, it's going to be someplace more comfortable than an elevator."

"One of these days I'm going to fire your ass, Adam."

He clicked the phone off and slid it into his pants. "Come on. Let's get this meeting done so we can have a little lunch. I'm hungry."

Serena was, too, but not for lunch. She'd just developed a huge appetite for Adam Miles, but she wondered if it wouldn't be bad for both of them.

Adam smiled at her, a look she was starting to call his "don't worry about it" face.

But she was falling. And she was definitely worried.

Chapter Eight

Jake pulled his SUV up to the small bungalow-style house in a rundown neighborhood. Doyle Brooks hadn't fared as well as his wife in the last few years.

"Do we have a workup on this guy?" Jake sighed as he steeled himself for meeting Serena's ex-husband.

"Of course. It's me reason for living," Liam said, his accent thick. When Liam was alone, he preferred to let his Irish flow, but the minute they stepped outside the SUV, Jake knew his natural accent would be replaced with a flat, Midwestern cadence. It helped the Irishman blend in.

"Give it to me." He should have done this himself last night, but no, he'd been reading *Small Town Sweetheart* and wanking off in the shower, all the while envisioning himself and Adam as the men of the book and sweet little Serena as the heroine, Gabby. He was a dumbass. And Adam had been fucking her in the elevator. Damn him. He didn't buy that it wasn't Adam. Not for one minute. It had been there in the self-satisfied voice that had come over Ian's speaker phone. So much for taking her down together.

But then he hadn't given his partner a lot of hope that he would be amenable to taking her at all. And nothing that had happened today made him more likely to fall into bed with her. She was trouble. Sweet, sexy, hot as hell, submissive trouble.

"Am I talking for my own benefit here?"

Damn it. He had to get his head in the game. "Sorry. What did you say?"

"I could have said the sky was falling and my dick is the only thing holding it up and you wouldn't have noticed." Liam sat back, his deep green eyes narrowing. "Adam's not the only one crazy about this girl."

"Adam is the only one crazy enough to do anything about it. We don't even know if she's lying to us." He didn't think so, but he'd been wrong before.

"God, not again. I swear, just fuck her and get a ring on her finger and spare the rest of us. Sean nearly killed me last year. I had to watch Gracie twenty-four seven because he couldn't just get his shit together. You want my advice?"

"No." Jake didn't want anyone's advice, especially not "love 'em and leave 'em before he really even knows their name" Liam O'Donnell. It was like taking ethics advice from a politician.

"Good," Liam said, ignoring him entirely. "Here's my advice. It don't matter if the girl is a con or not. She's cute and sweet and obviously submissive. If you want her, take her. Spank her ass, fuck her until she can't see straight, and lay down some ground rules. No more fake stalking and no more of that pussy-Dom, BDSM-romance shit that makes women think they can walk all over us. That second bit is important."

Jake laughed a little. He could imagine what Serena would do if he told her to stop writing. His balls would need close-cover protection. But the rest of it was a bit intriguing. What if he could control Serena? They'd never tried a D/s relationship with any of the women he and Adam had lived with. What if he could come to trust her? "Stop with the love advice, man. Just give me the rundown on this asshole."

Liam pulled his tablet out. "Well, he's not the redneck asshole I suspected. It's far worse."

Jake knew a whole bunch of redneck assholes. He'd grown up around them. Hell, he still was one half the time. It was only through

Adam's influence that he knew about shit like gourmet food and what constituted a good suit. He didn't like the thought of Serena with a guy who spent all his time hunting. Serena seemed so delicate in some ways. "What is he then?"

Liam made a gagging sound. "He's a college professor. God spare me from intellectuals. He teaches English, for god's sake. Do college students really need a class in a fucking language they already speak? Me mother would roll over in her grave if I spent good money on an English class."

"Your mother probably would have been shocked that you could make it into college." Jake liked fucking with Liam.

"Me mother was pure IRA, boyo. Trust me, she wouldn't pay for anything that included the word English. Now, Professor Doyle teaches at a community college. North Lake. Damn me. He couldn't even hit the big leagues. No wonder he's jealous of his wife. At least she's doing something productive."

Obviously Liam wasn't big on higher education. "So he divorced Serena and moved out here?"

Liam shook his head. "Nope. This is the house they lived in. He kicked her out."

Asshole. "Is he still alone?"

"Nope. A grad student moved in with him about six weeks after he'd filed for divorce. Professor Doyle likes them young." Liam shoved the tablet back in his case. "He hurt her. You can understand that, right? From what I hear, she finally gets up the courage to do something she's wanted all her life and her husband tries to drive her into the dirt. What did that other girl on the tape say? He can't sell his own shit? What do you want to bet that asshole in there has a crap-ass novel he's been trying to sell for years? Some shit he thinks will change the world. He probably writes about morose yuppies and their sad-sack lives. He was jealous of her. He tried to stop her the only way a bully knows how. I'm just saying that if a woman wanted a little revenge against a man like that, maybe it's not so horrible."

Maybe not. And still, he needed to know the truth before he started anything with her. He couldn't walk in blind again. But he knew what it felt like to have everything he wanted dissected under a cruel microscope of so-called morality. He wasn't going to get to the bottom of anything if he stayed here. "Let's go. He seems to be home."

The car was in the driveway. Just one, like Serena had said. It seemed the good professor still made his woman take the bus.

Jake knocked on the door, Liam behind him.

A pretty blonde opened the door. She couldn't be past twenty-three. She was dressed in a sweatshirt and shorts that rode up her ass. "Hello."

"We're looking for Professor Brooks. We called earlier. My name is Jacob Dean. I'm with a firm called McKay-Taggart."

Her blue eyes went wide. "You're here about his ex-wife. Amber Rose?"

That was her pen name. Jake felt a deep need to correct the young woman. Amber Rose was a front. Serena was a woman. "Serena Brooks."

She turned her head as though watching for someone. When she turned back to them, her voice was hushed. "Don't tell Doyle about it, but I just love her books. I read all kinds of romance, but I just love erotic romance. Do you think she knows Eliza Gayle? That would be so cool. Amber Rose is good, but Eliza rocks, if you know what I mean."

Dear god, he'd found a groupie. "I don't, miss."

She chattered on. "I think it's horrible that someone is trying to hurt her. You should find this guy. It would be sad if she didn't write anymore. I have all her books on my e-reader. Doyle doesn't believe in e-books—like they don't exist or something. He's a little behind the times. But I read one because I was curious. He talks about those books all the time. I mean, he hates them. Doyle is just jealous because he can't get anyone in New York to buy his two thousand page book about single people in Manhattan. He has the grossest descriptions of venereal diseases. What's with that?"

Liam put an elbow in his side.

"Ginny, who is it?" A deep voice called out from the back of the house.

"It's the dudes who called earlier," Ginny screamed back. She scrunched up her nose. "Don't you tell him I read his ex's books. He thinks I'm all about the American masters. I need my thesis to pass muster. He's really good friends with my professor."

She opened the door and let them in.

Unlike Serena's place, Professor Brooks' home was a pin-perfect model of efficiency. Jake's heart clenched a little at the thought of messy, fun Serena being forced to keep everything perfect. There wasn't a book out of place or piles of notes scattered around. The home didn't look lived in. Though it was inexpensive, it was obvious the man who lived here aspired to much more.

Doyle Brooks walked into the living room. He looked the part of the upwardly mobile intellectual, dressed in slacks, a dress shirt, and a blazer. "Gentlemen, please join me in my office."

His office was a renovated extra bedroom refitted with dark panels and an enormous desk that looked about as full of itself as the man who sat behind it. There were numerous degrees and plaques hung neatly on the walls proclaiming just how smart and educated Doyle Brooks was. The man was only thirty. That meant he'd achieved many of those degrees while married to Serena. Serena, who had supported his ass while he went to school. Serena, who he'd dumped the moment she became difficult.

Poor little sub.

Introductions were made, and the professor seemed to take everything with a cool calm.

"So, Serena is still attempting to malign me." Doyle sat back with a sad sigh as though he didn't want to believe it, but knew it to be true.

"She's attempting to figure out who's stalking her, Professor Brooks." Liam's Midwestern accent was in full force. The Irishman stared at Serena's ex-husband with dark eyes, sizing the man up. Liam didn't have Eve's profiling credentials, but he'd spent years learning to read men and women. He'd had to. He'd had to learn who was going to try to kill him and who wouldn't. Just like Jake.

A little laugh puffed out Brooks' mouth. "No one is trying to kill her. I hate this. I really do. Serena used to be such a sweetheart, but she's playing some kind of game. We're in a little legal trouble, Serena and I, and she's decided to play dirty. Have you read the police reports?"

Yes, but now that he was sitting in front of Serena's ex, he could see what the cops had seen. A perfectly dressed, calm and reasonable man who could make his point in a manner they would understand. And Serena had most likely been a bit messy, a little mousy, and altogether awkward.

"I have," Jake replied. "I also know that Serena's been receiving some phone calls from you."

He'd listened to the one on her answering machine the night before. It had been filled with bile and vitriol. The harsh voice on the machine the night before bore little resemblance to the cultured, smooth tones of the man in front of him. Professor Brooks seemed to have two different personalities.

Brooks had the good sense to flush a little. "I shouldn't have left that message. It was wrong of me. I should have allowed our lawyers to handle things. Look, Serena and I have some matters to settle, obviously."

"Your divorce was finalized a couple of years ago," Liam noted. He had a notepad in his hand, looking to the casual watcher like an assistant.

Brooks sat up a little straighter. "Not everything was made clear to me at the time. My lawyer says this is a long shot, but I'm going to stand up for myself. I supported her while she wrote those...books, if you can call them that."

"That's what we usually call a collection of words forming a coherent story." Yeah, the professor was a pompous asshole.

"I don't know about coherent. What my ex-wife writes is pure pornography. It's clogging up the publishers so the real writers can't get through."

Liam cleared his throat. It was a clear "I told you so."

And he had. "Serena explained to us that you divorced her over her first book."

He took a long breath and sat back. "Well, what did she expect me to do? I had just gotten on at the college."

"Junior college." Liam seemed to feel a desperate need to keep poking the professor.

Brooks didn't acknowledge him. "A professor's wife is an important asset. She reflects on the professor. If I wanted to move up in my profession, I certainly couldn't be that man whose wife writes porn. And the acts she described." His nose wrinkled in distaste. "The book was filth. It shouldn't be out there. It made me sick and, quite frankly, some of it is demeaning to women."

That was ridiculous. Jake had read the same book. She used some rough language. She called a cock a cock. She hadn't used the phrase "honey pot" or "center" to describe a vagina. She'd called it a pussy. Jake found it refreshing. He didn't see how a woman choosing to explore her sexuality demeaned her. But this wasn't the time to defend Serena's work. "Where were you last night, Professor?"

The man seemed a bit startled. "I don't know that's any of your business."

"If you were at my client's home running a key across her car, it is most definitely my business." It was time to let this asshole know that someone was looking out for his ex. She wasn't on her own anymore.

The professor's fists clenched. "I was here grading papers. And no one was with me. Ginny was at class. The bus dropped her off after ten."

Liam gasped. "You let that little bit of fluff walk the streets alone? What kind of a man are you?"

"I'm a man who respects women. She isn't a child. She has a brain, and she can take care of herself."

Jake sat forward. He understood the man now. "I know men like you. You take and take and give nothing back and call yourself modern or some shit. You won't open a door for a woman because, according to you, it's insulting. I'm sure little Ginny in there is responsible for her own orgasm because you can't be bothered to give her one. You use every excuse in the book so you don't have to take responsibility."

He shrugged. "Well, I wouldn't want to piss off the feminists."

Jake stood. It was time to end this interview. It wouldn't go anywhere, and he knew at least one thing about the man. Jake didn't trust him. He would give Adam the go ahead to hack into every account the man had. It might take weeks to go through everything, but if this fucker had even written a nasty e-mail to her, Jake would take it to the cops. Brooks thought he could annoy Serena. Well, Jake had irritated some of the world's most deadly men in his time. Professor Brooks would be a breeze. Liam could keep an eye on the asshole for a few days, but talking to him was just pissing Jake off. "Serena Brooks is under my protection now. Do you understand?"

"I understand you sound like a meathead caveman."

Jake leaned over, using every bit of his military training to intimidate. A wave of pure predatory pleasure overtook him as the professor seemed to shrink right before his eyes. "Remember that. If you call her house again, I'll be back here, and we'll have a chat. I don't think you'll like how I chat. I don't use big words."

"You're threatening me."

He smiled, but Jake was pretty sure it wasn't a happy thing. "Look, Liam. All those degrees really made him smart." He backed off. "And as for Serena's books, they're good. I like them. I can see where you would want to divorce her. She made you look bad."

The professor's eyes narrowed. "You're fucking my wife."

There was the voice Jake had heard on the answering machine. Yep. The professor had a dark side.

"Not yet, he isn't. But he'll come around." Liam stood, gathering his things. He put a card on the professor's desk. "I want to make it easy for you to call and complain. Ask for Ian Taggart. He owns the company."

Doyle Brooks' face was a mottled red. He reached for the card. "Oh, Mr. Taggart will hear from me. Now, I believe I would like for you to leave my home."

Jake nodded. He had nothing left to say. He wished he could be there when Brooks tried to pull his shit on Ian. Liam was a bastard. Jake was happy to not be on the Irishman's bad side. He followed Liam out, wondering how hard it had been on Serena to live in this house. She wouldn't have been able to write in her underwear. She wouldn't have been able to dance around. She would have felt hemmed in. She had a deeply submissive nature. It didn't mean she would just let anyone walk on her. She'd proven that. She'd come out fighting. She'd followed her path. But it did mean she would more than likely attempt to please the people around her. Especially her husband. That shit bag in the office had taken advantage of her for as long as he could and then ground her under his overly pretentious loafer when he no longer had a use for her.

"You look like a man ready to take a chunk out of someone." Liam had a shit-eating grin on his face. "Remember my advice. Fuck her and get it over with. It's inevitable. Then you would have had every right to punch that bloody wanker in the face. That pussy wouldn't punch back."

Jake nodded to Ginny as he strode out the door. He hoped the young woman had enough sense to get out when she could.

He could hear Professor Brooks shouting at someone. God, he hoped it was Ian. The door slammed behind him, just as his cell rang. He looked down at the number.

"Tell me it's Ian giving us the go ahead to kill the bastard." Liam's Irish was back. And there was a grin on his face. He'd enjoyed fucking with the professor.

But Jake lost his smile. "It's Brighton." He slid his hand across the bar to answer the call. "This is Dean."

His police liaison sounded grim. "Hey, Jake. Did you take the Serena Brooks case? You know that writer you called about yesterday?"

Jake got a cold shiver that always went up his spine when the shit was about to hit the fan. "Yeah. I'm out at her ex-husband's place right now. What's going on?"

"You should come down to the station. The cop working her case found something. Do you want me to call her or would you rather do that yourself?"

Fuck. He didn't want to call her at all, but he didn't have the right to keep things from her. She had the right to know what was coming for her. "I'll do it. I'll be there in twenty minutes. How bad is it?"

"Well, it's more serious than we thought, or she's more clever. No idea, man. You need to talk to the detectives handling this case. I'll keep them here for you. I don't know about this, Jake. It gives me a nasty feeling."

Brighton was a cop with ten years in. Jake trusted Brighton's gut. Especially when his own was telling him this was more complex than it seemed. "We'll be there."

He hung up the phone and called Adam. The whole way to the police station, he couldn't help the feeling that everything was about to go wrong.

* * * *

Adam looked over the desk at Sargent Edward Chitwood. He was a quiet man with the sort of bland good looks that most people ignored. His desk was neatly appointed, complete with a picture of his perfectly bland wife and kids. In the family portrait, they were all smiling. The perfect American family. But Chitwood wasn't smiling now.

"Brass is not happy with you, partner." Chitwood's partner was a fit-looking man named Mike Hernandez.

Chitwood sighed. "I know, Mikey. It was stupid. It was also kind of instinctive. I had the thing in my hand before I really knew what I was doing."

"This is the letter you found?" Adam asked. He turned and looked back. Serena was standing at the vending machines. So much for his perfect lunch. She was going to have to eat chips and drink a soda. His gut was in knots. The minute they'd gotten Jake's call, she'd paled and a fine tremble had hit her. They had been forced to cancel lunch and leave her agent's office early. Serena's life was being completely disrupted.

Chitwood nodded. "Yes. I am so sorry to have to give this to her."

Hernandez looked over at Serena, his mouth a flat line. "I'd like to study her when she reads it."

He would be looking for anything that wasn't normal, anything that gave away the fact that she'd set this up herself.

"I'd like to point out the fact that she was with me when the note was left," Adam said.

Hernandez shrugged. "So she has an accomplice. Have you met those friends of hers?"

No. He was scheduled to have lunch with them tomorrow. Liam had already forwarded files on both Bridget Slaten and Chris Roberts. He hadn't read them, though. It was easy to see that at least one of the cops working her case thought Serena was a whack job.

He glanced back again. She had a green can in her hands. He could still feel her lips on his. She'd been so fucking sweet, her hands exploring his body with the awe of a woman on the verge of something amazing. He could still hear the hitch in her breath as he'd pulled their pelvises together. If Ian hadn't stopped him, he would have put his hand up her skirt and teased his fingers into her pussy, rubbing her little clit until she was shaking in his arms.

He wouldn't have fucked her. He wouldn't do that without Jacob. The last thing he wanted was for her to bond to only one of them. He'd been down that road, and it led to heartache.

The door to the division office opened, and Jake strode through with Liam in tow. He watched as Serena looked up and almost immediately took a step toward him. And then she forced herself to stop. Jake's eyes laser focused on her. His hand actually came up and then the big old coward put his hand back down. So close.

They said something, and Jake's hand finally came up and found her shoulder. It was an awkward touch, but it was there. Liam looked over and rolled his eyes letting Adam know he'd probably already figured the situation out.

"So, she has three bodyguards?" Chitwood asked, studying the scene in front of him. "That seems like a bit of overkill."

"It's just me and my partner, Jacob Dean. Liam is our backup. But I think Lieutenant Brighton would prefer you ran everything by me or Jake. We'll be with her twenty-four seven."

Hernandez whistled. "That must be costing her a pretty penny. She's way more loaded than we thought, Eddie. McKay-Taggart is one of those fancy security companies that handle really rich people."

Adam was getting annoyed with the cops. "She's very important to her agent. Now, I would like to know what's going on."

Jake walked up behind him, Serena at his side. There were only two chairs. Jake held out the remaining chair, offering it to Serena.

"It's all right. I can stand," Serena said.

Jake simply stared at her, and she sat down. They would have to train her to accept their courtesy. It went beyond mere politeness. It was their way of taking care of her.

"I would never sit while you were forced to stand," Jake explained. "And is this the only food you've had? A soda and some chips." He frowned Adam's way.

Adam held his hands out. His first instinct was to bark back at his partner, but he had to admit he was happy Jake seemed so invested in her well-being. "I had reservations. You're the one who called and told me to get my ass here."

"I saw a sandwich place across the street. Is turkey all right?" Liam asked, giving Serena a little wink. "Don't tell me no. Jake will Dom you to death. Just give in."

A little smile curved her lips. "Turkey is fine. With mustard. Thank you so much."

"I'll take the same," Adam said. "Except make it pastrami on rye and make the mustard hot."

Liam shot him the finger. "You'll be lucky to get anything at all."

Liam walked off. Adam might have to hope he got a few of those chips of Serena's. He turned back to the cops. "Now we're all here. Explain why you called us in."

Chitwood flushed slightly. He was very pale. Adam bet he burned all summer long. "It's my fault."

"Dude, I would probably have done the same thing," Hernandez said, slapping his partner on the back sympathetically.

Adam was just about ready to scream when the detective started to speak. "I went by to take the report on Miss Brooks' car."

Jake stood behind Serena, looking like some sort of protective bird of prey. "Why would you do that? We had an appointment to meet with Brighton at two o'clock."

"No one told me," Chitwood explained.

"He was taking care of his wife this morning. She's got cancer." Hernandez's face went grim. "His kids are off at college. He sometimes stays in when she has a bad morning. I cover for him with brass."

Adam was sorry to hear that. "If you didn't come in then how did you know anything had happened at all?"

"Mikey forwarded the report to me. I stopped by on my way in to work. I'll be honest. I would have done it whether I had known about the meeting with brass or not. I would have stopped by to take some photos. But I knocked on the door, and when I did, an envelope fell. It started to drop, and I did something stupid."

Adam closed his eyes. It was understandable, but didn't help their case. "You caught it."

A long huff blew from the detective's mouth. "Yep. So we're running it for prints, but you can bet mine will be on there."

"It's not a tragedy," Hernandez said.

It wasn't. It also wasn't optimal. "Do you have a copy?"

He didn't miss the fact that Hernandez focused in on Serena. While Chitwood grabbed a folder, Hernandez never took his eyes off Serena. She sat forward, obviously anxious about whatever was in that report.

"He knows where I live." Her tone was flat, fatalistic. "I hoped the car was a coincidence, but it wasn't. He has my home address."

Adam reached over and placed his hand over hers. "It's all right."

She shook her head. "I'm careful. I have a PO box. I never put my real name out there."

He knew how this asshole had found her. He'd checked up on her yesterday, and with one little piece of information, he'd found her real name and home address served up right on the internet. "You have an LLC."

Chitwood nodded. "I'm sure that's how he found you. The state requires all businesses to have a physical address. If he knows what LLC you publish under, it would be easy for him to look it up on the web and pull your actual address."

"God, I feel so dumb. Amber Rose LLC. Why the hell did I do that?" Tears were pooling in her eyes.

"You didn't know," Jake said. "It's fine, Serena. Not a lot of people think about it."

Adam already had a plan in motion. "I changed the address on her LLC this morning. I talked to a nice lady in the comptroller's office. We're going to use the physical address of the post office where her PO box is located."

She turned to him. "You did that?"

Adam shrugged. Some women might see it as meddling. He

merely saw it as taking care of a problem she didn't even know she'd had. "You were working. I didn't want to bother you. I explained to the woman that I was your assistant. She believed me since I had your passwords and all your information."

"You do?"

He nodded. "Yep."

He waited for her to get upset, but the hand under his turned and clutched at him. "Thank you. Whatever Lara is paying you, it isn't enough."

Adam breathed a sigh of relief. At least she was reasonable. "Now, let's take a look at this note."

Chitwood frowned but opened the folder. "You can't touch it. It still has to go through some more forensics, but as you can see, someone isn't happy."

Adam leaned forward. It was a single sheet of what looked like thick card stock paper. On it was the cover to Serena's latest book–*Their Sweetheart Slave*. The cover was vibrant, showing a western setting with the three lovers featured in the center of a field. A man with long, dark hair sat on a horse reaching down to a pretty brunette who stood beside a man adjusting his cowboy hat. And apparently cowboys in Serena's world didn't believe in shirts.

And someone had taken extreme offense at the cover. The men's faces were cut out and someone had written the word *WHORE* in bright red across the woman's body.

"This is the one that's coming out in a couple of weeks?" Jake asked. "Alexa, Caden, and Duke?"

Serena smiled up at him, her face glowing despite the circumstances. Jake couldn't have cut through the tension any better. "Yes."

Hernandez snorted. "You've read them?"

Jake stared down at the cover. "I've read one, but Alexa was in *Small Town Sweetheart*. She was Gabby's daughter. Duke was the alpha hero's long-lost brother. I kind of thought you were trying to get them together."

Adam vowed to catch up on his damn reading. He knew he should be thrilled, but he was a little jealous of the way Serena was looking at Jake like he was a conquering hero. He'd only proven he was literate. Adam could read, too.

He just hadn't imagined he would be reading something like *Their Sweetheart Slave*. "Where did they get the cover?"

"I posted it on my website the minute I got it. It's also on the publisher's site and several fan sites," Serena said. She stared down at the cover, her whole body still.

Jake put a hand on her shoulder. "What kind of knife did he use to cut the faces out? Or is that scissors?"

Chitwood pointed at the offending marks. "I think it's a knife. Note that the bottom of the marks are a little more ragged than the tops. That's where the cut starts."

Adam could see that now.

"I bet that's from a utility knife," Jake said. "Or a box cutter. Did you test the door for prints?"

Hernandez nodded. "The door and the storm door, though we're going to find the Keystone Cop's prints there, too."

Chitwood sighed. "I didn't know it was a crime scene until I opened the door and this fell out."

Serena took a long breath and looked back at the cops. "I don't understand any of this. Sometimes he or she or whoever it is seems like a disgruntled fan who's pissed about the books and other times…"

Adam squeezed her hand. He wanted to hear her instincts. She was the center of this. She was the one being stalked. Her instincts could be an important clue. "Go on. Finish the sentence, sweetheart."

She shivered a little. "Other times it feels more personal. Like this person hates me for who I really am. I'm scared of that person. I'm annoyed by the other."

Chitwood leaned forward. "Oftentimes these types of perps can have several mental disorders including schizophrenia and bipolar disorder. It's not surprising that this person is unstable. But then, I would suspect you probably have researched those disorders. I'm right in saying that your books contain an element of suspense, correct?"

She nodded, though she didn't light up the way she normally did when someone asked about her work. She seemed to understand that the cops were attempting to pin her down. "Of course. I had a character in *Sweetheart in Chains*. He was the bad guy. He had bipolar disorder. I understand the disease."

Adam really didn't like the look the cops exchanged. They were already filing her problems away as shit they didn't need to deal with.

"Send us the forensics report when you get it. I'm sure Brighton won't have a problem with it," Jake said. He held a hand out to Serena. "Come on. We can go across the street and meet Liam and have lunch over there. I don't think they need anything further from you. Adam, would you mind talking to Brighton? I need some air."

Serena stood and looked to Adam who nodded Jake's way.

"Go on. I'll be there in a minute." He didn't protest, though his stomach did a bit. Jake had a barely leashed air about him. He needed to get away before he said or did something stupid. Jake could be deeply patient, but when he felt an injustice was being done, he tended to get nasty. They still needed the cops. Finesse was called for, and that was Adam's middle name.

Serena walked away with Jake. What the hell had happened with her ex-husband to put Jake on edge like that? Whatever it was, Adam was grateful because Jake's hand came out as he opened the doors for her. He rested his hand on the small of her back, guiding her through. Protective. A little possessive.

Adam turned back to the cops. "I understand that you firmly believe my client is doing this to herself, but I expect you to investigate each and every incident. I'm having cameras installed today. I'm actually happy this asshole is getting close. We're with her twenty-four seven. If he comes close again, we'll get him."

Hernandez crossed his arms over his chest and sighed. "I hope you're right, but something feels off about the whole thing. I don't like the fact that it escalated just as we told her not to worry about it."

"It's not the first time we've seen something like this," Chitwood said. "I started working this division about a year ago, and I've already seen at least three cases where the ex-wife sets up the ex-husband. She was either looking for full custody or more money."

Adam felt his face heating with indignation.

"Miles? Hey, it's good to see you!" Derek Brighton's deep voice pulled Adam out of his fantasy where he beat the shit out of the two cops sitting in front of him.

It wouldn't do a lick of good. He forced himself to turn and smile because he genuinely liked the Lieutenant. Lieutenant Brighton nodded in greeting toward the detectives and then herded Adam away.

"Hey, how bad did they piss you off?" Brighton asked.

"They sent Jake running for the hills," Adam admitted, following the big guy into his office. He shut the door, happy to not have to listen to the cops anymore. "Can you get this case reassigned? They're totally prejudiced against her."

Brighton slumped into his chair. "I could, but you would run up against the same thing. Look, you work this job long enough and you get cynical about everything. You have to. Chitwood out there worked vice for ten years. He came over to this division because he was sick of hauling in hookers and he finds himself in the middle of some of the nastiest domestic disputes we've ever seen. And Hernandez, hell, he was born cynical. It didn't take five years as a cop for that one. This ain't the Army, buddy. Things aren't cut and dried here. Sometimes it can be hard to tell who the enemy is."

"What do you think?" Adam winced as he asked the question. He probably didn't want to know the answer.

Brighton sat back, his face turning thoughtful. He breathed out a long sigh before speaking. "If I was just going on instinct, I would tell you that girl is a natural sub and she's not capable of doing any of this. She would rather have positive attention. I would say she would actually go out of her way to avoid negative attention because she prefers to please the people in her life."

Brighton was a good cop, and from what Ian had told everyone, he was also a damn fine Dom. "That's what I think. Have you run that theory by your underlings?"

He snorted. "By straightlaced Chitwood and Mike goes-to-mass-four-times-a-week Hernandez? No. I haven't mentioned that I have BDSM training that tells me she's submissive. I can imagine how well that would go over. They're good cops. They'll handle the case and anyway, now that you and Jake are on her, I suspect you would rather handle things your way."

He was right about that. "Can I get everything you have? Even the stuff that's not in the reports?"

"I sent it to you five minutes ago. The techies hunted down the IPs the perp is using. Libraries. Nice. My tax dollars at work. The perp is using suburban library computers to contact your girl when he uses e-mail. We went out and talked to a couple of the librarians, but they don't really remember much. Apparently they're underfunded and busy."

But they might be talked into monitoring more closely. Computers at libraries were notoriously out of date. They wouldn't have camera functions he could turn on, but he could monitor them. It was a problem for tomorrow. Today, he had to deal with the security company and rearrange Serena's schedule. If she didn't get words on the page, she would feel crappy, and she had enough anxiety in her life right now. He'd had a little talk with her agent, who seemed to adore her. But Lara had made it clear that Serena's work was what had gotten her through the hard times.

The times couldn't seem much harder for her.

He thanked Brighton and promised to call if anything else broke.

He walked through the doors of the division and into the long hall. He had another problem. He was supposed to take Serena to Sanctum. That meant finding her proper clothes and preparing her. And prepping Jake to handle the situation, though he'd have to do that without Jake noticing it or he might get set on his ass.

His world had become a delicate web he had to navigate with thought and care. But if he managed it, he just might get everything he'd wanted. And if he failed, he could lose it all. Ian would be pissed. Jake would be furious. Serena would just go away.

He walked out into the sunshine and caught sight of them. Serena sat at one of the outdoor tables, her hair shining in the sun. She threw back her head and laughed. And Jake. Fuck all, Jacob Dean was beaming at her. He turned slightly, and his eyes found Adam. He nodded for Adam to join them.

Serena followed Jake's eyes and suddenly that smile lit up

105

Adam's whole world. She pushed her glasses up and and waved for him to come over. She pushed out the seat she'd saved for him.

He belonged there beside her.

He jogged across the street. Yep. It was a dangerous game he was playing, but if he won, he got a family out of it.

That was worth everything.

Chapter Nine

Two days later, Serena sat in her backyard, a mug of tea in her hand, her computer screen filled with words. It was barely five o'clock, but she'd doubled the word count she'd needed for the day.

It was simple. Adam had taken over everything else on the business end. He answered her e-mails, only forwarding the ones that needed her specific attention. He'd dealt with the security system and the plumber she'd had to call when the shower had conked out. He'd gone to the grocery store and stocked her kitchen. He'd sorted through her mail. All those little things that seemed to stop her in her tracks, Adam had taken over.

And Jake. Jake had become her shadow. It had been odd at first. He wouldn't say anything, but she could feel him there. It occurred to her that his very presence should be a distraction, and yet she found herself feeling so safe that the words flowed. For the first time in months, she could really sink into her story. Her new series, Happiness, Montana, was flowing like nothing she'd ever written before.

"You have an hour, sweetheart." Adam put a plate on the table. She glanced down. Sandwich.

"I ate lunch. Are you trying to make me fatter than I am?"

Serena asked the question lightheartedly. Adam seemed to feed her something every hour or so.

Jake growled in the background.

"You're pissing off the Dom, sweetheart." Adam winked down at her, pushing the sandwich closer. "Don't screw with him right now. He's already getting in his Dom space for tonight."

She caught her breath. Tonight. She was going into a club with them tonight. Just going into Club Sanctum would be an amazing thing, but going in with two hot Doms was more than she'd ever dreamed of.

They aren't your Doms, Serena. Slow that shit down, girl. They're being nice to you. They're getting paid to take care of you. You better not get used to this treatment.

She looked back at Jake who sat in one of her delicate-looking lawn chairs. Well, his enormous body made them look delicate. He frowned her way.

"Don't you forget it, Serena. I'm in charge tonight. I hear one word out of your mouth about your body fat and you're going to get very familiar with spankings."

He couldn't possibly know that she'd already played that scene with him a hundred times in her mind over the last several days. In each and every fantasy, Jake had been behind her, that big hand of his meting out punishment while Adam stood in front of her, pressing his cock to her lips, demanding that she suck him. She would be caught between them. She would have to take that big dick into her mouth even as Jake slapped at her cheeks. Heat would flow. She would feel it in her pussy. Every smack of his hand would send her higher, but she couldn't focus on it because she had to take care of Adam.

"Serena, dear, have we lost you?"

She flushed and couldn't miss the knowing smiles that passed between her bodyguards. God, they knew exactly what she'd been thinking. She took a sip of her perfectly brewed Earl Grey and tried to salvage her dignity. "I promise to behave very well this evening, Sir."

If Jake could find his Dom space, then maybe it was time to play the sub. She enjoyed the way Jake's eyes narrowed and he shifted in his seat. Maybe the sub wasn't without her power, too.

There was a little chime coming from Adam's phone. Jake's went off at the same time..

"Who the fuck is that?" Jake asked, studying the screen of his phone.

Adam held his toward her. "Do you recognize this guy?"

Serena leaned over and looked at the screen. It was still hard for her to believe, but she now had a security system that fed directly into her bodyguards' phones. Anytime the motion detectors caught anything bigger than a cat moving too close to her house, the security feed pinged their phones. It had made for some rough nights. Adam and Jake took turns sleeping in the room with her so she heard every time the system pinged. She'd never realized how many dogs ran around at night. And drunk teens. But she wasn't surprised to discover Mrs. Renfroe from next door stole her newspaper. She'd enjoyed watching the woman nearly have a heart attack when Jake had caught her.

But this wasn't a stray dog or a noisy neighbor.

"That's Master Storm. What on earth is he doing here?" She stood up and started for the house.

Jake was in front of her before she could make the back door. "Don't you dare."

He was a huge hunk of muscle blocking her way. "Jake, I know this guy."

"No, you don't," he insisted. "You've met him a couple of times. You don't really know him. And he doesn't have an appointment."

"Nope. I handle your schedule, sweetheart. I know for a fact he doesn't have an appointment," Adam said smoothly.

The doorbell rang. "You can't expect me to ignore him. He's been my contact with the BDSM world for months. He's helping me with research."

"You don't need him anymore," Adam said. "You have us. Ask us anything."

"No," Jake said, standing aside. "I think we let Master Storm in. Let's vet the guy a little. After all, some of this stuff started after you met him, right?"

There was no way in hell Master Storm was behind the stalking. "Don't be ridiculous."

The doorbell rang again, and Jake moved out of her way. "Invite him in. Let Adam open the door, though. You don't ever open that door."

She let Adam go first and then followed, feeling Jake right behind her. The men seemed to put her in the middle whenever they could. Even the night before when they had sat down and watched TV, she'd found herself comfortably squished in between their big bodies. It had been a nice, peaceful night. She'd enjoyed the last few days despite the specter hanging over her. Having Adam and Jake around had made her almost feel like she had a family again.

Adam punched in the alarm code and unbolted the locks. He swung the door open, and there was Master Storm, looking majorly pissed.

He was a lean man, roughly six foot. He dressed casually, his long, slightly graying hair in a ponytail, though she would bet he called it a queue or had some Asian term for it. He was a black belt in some form of martial art. He seemed to like to consider himself dangerous, but now that he stood next to Adam and Jake, he seemed less lethal than he had in the past. At one point in time he'd seemed mysterious, but now he looked small compared to her men.

Stop it. They aren't yours.

"Who are you?" Storm asked, his brows coming together in consternation.

Adam opened his mouth, most likely to say something sarcastic, but Serena stared him down. He unlocked the glass storm door and opened it.

"His name is Adam. He and his partner, Jake, are kind of my own little security force for the time being." She stepped back to let him in. He'd been patient with her, answering all of her questions, putting her in touch with some people in the lifestyle he knew. Despite his somewhat pompous manner, he'd been an asset.

He stepped inside, eyeing Jake and Adam but dismissing them like he would a waiter at a restaurant. "Would you like to explain to me why you suddenly need security?"

He was using that deep voice on her. It was funny, but suddenly she found it a little irritating. Jake's voice was deeper, and he'd been taking care of her. He was the one who checked out the house before she entered, who placed himself in front of her. He'd earned the right to use that voice on her. Master Storm had mostly just talked at her. Still, she owed him a bit of courtesy.

"I've had some trouble with a stalker," she admitted, showing him into her living room. It was usually covered in notes and papers, but Adam had neatly organized everything. Yet another plus he'd brought into her life. She was rapidly discovering just how much easier it was to work when she could find things.

His nose wrinkled up as he looked around. "Is this to do with those books you write?"

He didn't approve of her books, though not for the same reasons others did. She'd been disappointed, but he seemed to think romance was beneath him. He seemed to think that any book that featured BDSM should preach the lifestyle in intellectual terms.

"Yes, it seems I have an overzealous fan," Serena explained. "Won't you please have a seat?"

He stared at her. "Is that how you greet me, little one?"

"Excuse me?" Adam asked.

Jake put a hand on her elbow as though he knew what she had been planning on doing. "Don't you dare get to your knees."

She sighed. "It's nothing serious. He's just helping me with my form."

"I don't give a shit," Jake admitted. "You're not kneeling for him. You're not wearing his collar."

Master Storm laughed but it was a bitter little huff. "Well, now I understand what's happening, dear. I was a bit upset at the tone of our last two exchanges. I felt the need to come out and speak to you about it in person."

She was at a loss. Their last two exchanges had consisted of a phone conversation and a very pretentious lunch at a Japanese restaurant where she'd been forced to sit with her legs crossed for hours. When she'd tried to stretch, he'd explained that sometimes discomfort was good for the soul. It had seemed to her that discomfort just sucked. But she hadn't said it.

"Did I do something wrong?" Serena asked. The panic that

normally accompanied that question wasn't there this time. She wasn't terrified she'd made someone mad or done something awkward. She was merely curious. Days spent with Jake and Adam seemed to have had an effect. She'd learned rapidly she could be awkward around them and they just laughed it off. Well, Adam laughed, and Jake's normally stern face would turn up in a little uptick that let her know he was amused.

"You didn't do anything wrong," Adam insisted.

Jake sat down on her couch and tugged her down beside him.

Master Storm's brows rose over his gray eyes. "I thought you said he was your employee, dear."

She rolled her eyes. "Don't call him that. It makes him mad."

"She isn't paying me. Her agent is. She's my trial and tribulation. Little brat."

Somehow when Jake said it she got a warm, gooshy feeling inside. Like he was teasing her with affection. "I am so easy."

Jake shook his head. "She's not easy. Do you know what I had to do yesterday? I had to take her and someone named Bridget to lunch. Sounds great, huh? Easy. Eat a little Mexican food. Relax. Those two spent the whole time talking about how to murder their characters. And then they talked about three-ways. And four-ways. And five-ways. After three margaritas, I'm pretty sure they talked about how to work a goat in."

Serena giggled. "You thought it was going to be some boring discussion of the craft didn't you? You haven't even met Chris yet."

Jake's head shook. "All I know is you ran off like five families, and I had to run off a whole table of asshole men who sat listening to you."

Adam held a hand out, giving his partner a high-five. "They were wimps. All we had to do was flash a piece and they took off."

Serena felt her jaw drop. "You showed those men at the table beside us your guns?"

Jake shrugged, obviously comfortable with his inner caveman. "It did the trick." He turned to Master Storm. "Would you like to see my gun?"

"I don't need a gun," Master Storm replied. "My body is a weapon."

Serena could feel the whole room go on testosterone overload. If she didn't handle this, and quickly, Master Storm was going to get a demonstration of what the Green Berets taught their men. "I'm afraid I'm confused, Sir. I was under the impression you were happy with my progress in our last talk."

She'd thought she would get an invitation to a demonstration. She'd been looking forward to it, and then her world had cracked open.

"I was referring to the rather bratty tone of your last two e-mails. I asked you if you would like to come to my house to play this weekend, and I was told to play with myself, though you used rougher terms. I'm rather wondering if that was you at all, dear."

She turned to Adam.

"I actually told him to fuck himself. And that if he needed an ass to paddle, he should look in the mirror." He sat back without a single look of remorse on his face.

She took a long breath and nodded back at Master Storm. "Obviously I didn't send that e-mail. I had asked Adam to send me any mail that needed my direct attention."

"And I was to handle anything that didn't," Adam explained. "I did exactly what you wanted me to. I handled the unimportant things."

They would have to have a talk about that later, but for now she simply sent him her most stern look. It seemed to bounce right off him. He winked at her.

"I am so sorry, Sir. I apologize for any discourtesy." Just because Adam had decided to act like an ass didn't mean she couldn't save the relationship. After Adam and Jake were gone, she doubted they would have the time to answer her questions. She would be alone in her fictional world, and she would need Master Storm. Jake and Adam might not see it that way, but she knew how it would work. They were interested because she was the only woman available. They were being paid to be with her twenty-four seven. When they didn't have to be, they would find a woman in their league, and she would be out in the cold.

Master Storm finally sat down. He seemed to ignore the men in the room, his eyes focusing on her. "I'm glad to hear that, little one.

I have to admit I was more hurt by that e-mail than I would have expected to be."

Actually, that didn't help. One of the things she'd liked about Storm was the fact that he'd seemed relatively unmoved by her. The last thing she needed was to get involved with someone she didn't even like. She'd chosen Storm because she wouldn't get emotionally involved. And yet she couldn't quite say it to him.

"I'm sorry. I didn't send it, and obviously Adam and I will be having a conversation."

Jake sat forward. "Add me in, baby, because I made him put in the part about this guy being a complete ass. You do know his real name is Austin Stinchfield, right? I would have changed my name, too, dude. Though I would have picked something other than Storm."

Storm's eyes narrowed. "Serena, dear, one of the things about our lifestyle is we must decide to ignore those who don't understand us. And we must make hard decisions." He leaned forward. "Serena, you don't have to do this. I have a dojo. I teach several members of the Dallas Police Department. I can protect you. You don't have to put up with this. As a matter of fact, it would be best if you would get a bag and simply come back to my place."

Jake sat forward. "She's not going anywhere. This is a serious threat."

Jake's jaw had tightened, forming a dangerous line. Serena put a hand on his knee, silently begging him to let her handle this. They had already damaged her relationship with Master Storm.

"I thank you for the offer, Sir," she began politely.

Master Storm smiled, a deeply self-satisfied expression. "Good. Because I also wanted to discuss your books with you."

"I told you," Jake began, but Adam stopped him. They seemed to have one of those silent conversations she usually found fascinating. After a moment, Jake sat back. "Please feel free to have the discussion now."

Master Storm frowned. "I think this is best done privately. I don't like to humiliate my submissives unless I am forced to."

Humiliate? She felt her gut tighten. She didn't like the sound of that. Master Storm had told her he would read her books. He'd

114

shown an interest, and she'd thought that perhaps she could change his mind. After all, he was in the lifestyle. She was promoting the lifestyle. She knew that what she wrote was romance and not pure erotica, but surely he would see the value in it. "I'd like to hear your opinion."

She didn't want to, but it was better to know.

Master Storm frowned and settled back into the loveseat. "Fine. If you insist. One of the reasons I've decided to take on your training is so I can mold your writing career. You have some talent, but you are woefully wrong about most aspects of the lifestyle. There is no such thing as ménage with any permanency in BDSM."

"Oh, god, he's a 'one-true-wayer,'" Jake said on a groan.

Storm ignored him. "You place the emphasis on the submissive which only proves to me that you don't understand the meaning of submission. Submission is about service to the Dom, and the submissive finds her true purpose in serving and pleasing the Dom. The Doms in your books are far too easy on the submissives. I believe that if I train you, you will understand Dominance and submission more fully. I'm going to offer you a place as a full-time slave. I'll take a guiding hand in your work. You need to move away from the bourgeois romance angle."

"Really?" Yep. There it was. Humiliation. Adam's hand crept out, seeking hers, but she ignored it. He'd humiliated her, too.

Storm sighed. "It's all right, little one. You simply don't understand. You're taking a child's view of the world."

Serena took a deep breath, trying to banish those hated tears that had gathered again. "So you intend to take control of how I do my job?"

The Dom's face was a bland blank. "Yes, dear, that's what a Dom does. I will be in control of your work and your daily life. I already have a schedule planned for you. Your day will be highly regimented. I noticed that you seem a bit disorganized. That will stop. I will inspect your room, the house, and your work station on a daily basis. If they are not up to my standards, you will be punished in whatever manner I see fit. I have a whole contract already written out. I will need you to sign it, and then we can begin our work."

"You wrote the contract without her input?" Adam asked.

"It's obvious to me neither of you understands the relationship between a Dominant and his submissive. The submissive will either sign the contract or refuse. I am not going to negotiate."

"Which is precisely why Ian Taggart refused you a membership to Club Sanctum." Jake stared straight at the Dom. "I pulled your records when I discovered you were involved with my charge. Sanctum's counselor wouldn't clear you. She believed you would potentially abuse the power you took over your subs. I won't allow Serena to go anywhere with you. You should leave now."

Gray eyes narrowed and Storm's mouth turned down in a mulish frown. "I believe that is up to Serena."

"Convenient," Adam murmured. "She doesn't have any say until you need her to agree with you."

Storm leaned forward. "Those men at Sanctum are dabblers, Serena. They just play at D/s. You need to come with me. I can show you the way. I can free you."

By taking over her life. Maybe she didn't understand D/s at all. It had seemed so perfect, but Master Storm's way just seemed like a selfish thing. It wasn't what she'd wanted at all. She'd wanted someone who looked out for her. It seemed like Storm merely wanted a slave. Maybe that worked for some, and she wouldn't deny them their right to enjoy a lifestyle that worked, but once again it seemed there was no place for her.

Her ex-husband thought she was a pervert. The Master didn't think she was submissive enough. She was never right, and she should just get that through her thick skull. She'd seen BDSM as a place she might be able to fit in, but it was like everything else, she was either too much or not enough.

She stood. "Master Storm, I appreciate all of your patience with me, but I am going to decline to sign a contract with you. I think you're right. BDSM isn't for me. I will attempt to stick to writing ménage from now on. I wouldn't want to embarrass the community."

He frowned. "But I can teach you, Serena."

She shook her head and walked to the door. She just wanted to get it all over with. "I don't think so. Thank you, though."

He stood and stalked over to her. "I guess I really was right about you. You don't have what it takes to be my submissive. Good evening."

He walked off and with him many of her hopes. She hadn't hoped for him, but he represented what she had hoped for—a place to belong. A little community that accepted her. She watched him walk away. She hadn't fit into Doyle's academic world. She'd thought she would fit in with other writers, but it seemed she was either not successful enough or far too successful, depending on the view. Even among erotic romance writers she struggled to find a place. And now this door had closed.

She knew what to do. Sink into her work. The world inside her head was the only place that would ever accept her as she was. She should simply acknowledge and accept it and be done with trying to fit in on the outside. She closed the door and turned around.

Adam and Jake were both standing, waiting.

She sighed. Now she had to deal with them. "I think I'm going to go and work for a while."

She definitely needed to take a long step back from everything. Especially from them. They had come in and turned her world upside down, but they would leave at the end of this. They would go back to their world where they fit in and had a whole team who cared about them. She would be alone, and she shouldn't come to depend on them.

"Serena, I should have told you he'd written," Adam said, his voice tentative. "I'm afraid I didn't think he was good for you so I told him off. I was in the wrong."

"No, you weren't," Jake replied. "He is wrong for her. We just handled it the wrong way."

It didn't matter. She knew now. "It's fine. Like I said, I need to get some work done."

Adam crossed his arms over his chest, considering her. "You don't have much time. You've met your word count for the day. Why don't you go and take a shower? We're supposed to be at Sanctum in a couple of hours. Let Jake and me take you out to dinner before we show you around the club."

Wow. She was so not going there. "I changed my mind. I want to stay in. Please thank Mr. Taggart for inviting me, but I'll stay out of things I don't understand from now on."

She would focus on the ménage books. They were just her fantasy. She wouldn't be offending anyone by writing them. Well, no one who wasn't already offended.

"Stop." Jake's voice had gone completely still.

"What do you want from me, Jacob?" Serena asked, feeling past tired. She'd gotten too used to them. Pulling away was going to be hard. Having them around had made her realize just how lonely she'd been.

Adam got into her space. He seemed to like to do that. "We want you to yell at us. We fucked up. Me more than Jake."

"No, I high-fived you as you sent the e-mail off." Jake seemed determined to present a united front. "Serena, you have to see Master Storm was wrong for you. There is a faction of the lifestyle that truly believes their way is the only way and the rest of us are posers. They treat it almost like a religion when it isn't. It should be far more flexible. If you got involved with a man like that, he would have you believing there was only one way for a sub to get into that great dungeon in the sky."

And they thought she was an idiot. Nice. "I wouldn't have signed a contract with him. I would have walked away the minute he started to try to tell me what to write. I was curious, Jacob, not a doormat."

Though she probably seemed that way sometimes.

"Excellent," Adam said, taking her hand. "Then you can't be too mad at us. Sweetheart, you need someone to organize your life. You need someone to take care of you, not to try to turn your life into taking care of him. That works for some people, but it wouldn't for you. BDSM is about having choices and figuring out what works for a couple...or a trio. Don't let him run you off."

"I think I should just lay low until this whole stalker thing dies down."

Jake moved in front of the door that led to the back, an obvious road block. "He got to you. Don't let him spoil our night. Don't let him send you back into your shell."

She took a deep breath. "It's all right. I was just disappointed to find out what a douche bag he was. He was my only real contact."

Adam waved a hand. "Hello." He pointed at Jacob. "Real live certified Dom standing right there. I wouldn't let Ian bark at me for three weeks, so I don't have my shiny piece of paper, but I know a thing or two. And I think I've been doing a damn fine job of taking care of you. I've been topping you for days, and you didn't even notice."

That was ridiculous. Except it wasn't. She thought about the last several days. Adam had quietly taken over much of the day-to-day details of her life. He'd done it with a smile, pushing her to concentrate on her work. He'd started answering her e-mails, making her appointments, even answering her phone calls. He'd taken over, and she'd just been happy to not have to do all those things. It had felt natural. Adam had taken over the minutia, and Jake made sure no one got close.

They were topping her. And she kind of liked it. It had made her life easier, and she'd felt safe and cared for.

"See," Adam said as though he could read her mind. "It can work for you, but it has to be gentler than what Master Douchewad wants from you. That can work, too. But not on you."

She shook her head. "But I'm not doing anything for the two of you."

"Aren't you? Jake had a headache yesterday. What did you do?" Adam asked.

She'd noticed that he looked stressed. She hadn't really understood that he'd had a headache. She'd just followed her instincts. She rubbed his scalp until he'd practically melted into his chair. She'd been a bit surprised and deeply pleased that he'd allowed the contact.

"You made me feel better," Jake said. "You did what you could to take care of me. Hell, Serena, you went into the guest bedroom and pulled out mine and Adam's dirty clothes. You didn't have to wash them. We would have gotten them."

"I was doing a load anyway." She said the words, but they felt a little stubborn. At the time, she'd wanted to do something for them. She'd wanted to help them the way they were helping her. Maybe that was what a relationship really was.

"Come with us tonight," Adam cajoled, his hand on her arm.

"Let us show you that this lifestyle, like anything else, is what you make it."

Jake stared down at her, not touching her at all, but she still felt his heat. Adam's hand caressed her.

She could take the chance. She didn't have much to lose. She might learn a little something. Despite the fact that she'd told Storm that she would concentrate on ménage, she was still thinking about the fact that her latest book had BDSM in it. And apparently Ian Taggart was the ultimate authority in the DFW area. She'd heard of Sanctum. And she'd heard that they only admitted people who passed strict tests. She was being given a true opportunity to research. If she could keep herself separate, it could work in her favor.

Adam hovered near her. He was so damn close. And Jake. He was so perfect. Each called to her in their own way.

"Come with us."

She was just about to answer when the doorbell rang again.

"Damn it." Jake crossed the space, his hand going for the door. "If it's that jerk, he's going to see my gun. 'My body is a weapon.' Dumb shit. I bet my gun can take out his body really damn quick."

She turned, Adam's hand on her shoulder. He leaned in, his lips close to her ear. "Give us a chance, baby. We can show you a whole new world."

It was the right thing to say. It was exactly what she needed to hear. The world she was in was hard. It would be nice to have some place to sink into.

"Say yes."

She nodded. She didn't have anything better to do.

Jake turned back, a box in his hand. "It was a courier. Were you expecting some books?"

She shook her head. "No. I have to order prints. I haven't ordered any. I have a signing coming up, but Lara ordered those and they went straight to the bookstore."

"There's a return address." He carefully pulled off the label and started to open the box. He pulled out a book. She recognized it immediately. There was a sweet-looking blonde, her head turned submissively to the side, a hot Dom, and the cool as sin beta hero in a cowboy hat. *Sweetheart in Chains.*

"It's just your books," Jake said, passing it to her.

Serena picked it up. It was her book in trade paperback. Nothing out of the ordinary. She had a closet full of them. She flipped through and saw the difference.

Every dirty word, every pussy, cock, dick, fuck, and others, had been marked through. Someone had taken an enormous amount of time to mark through every part of the book that could be considered slightly controversial.

She flipped to the front.

Stop writing filth or my wrath will come down on you

"Someone sent you a copy of every book you've got in print." Adam held up a copy of *Two Men to Love*. He started to flip through it, and his skin flushed. She knew they were all the same.

Someone hated her. It was all too fucking much. Between Storm's criticism and this, she felt the tears begin. Too much. She'd just wanted to find a place, and she'd found so much rejection.

Jake put his arms around her. She was hauled to his chest as the sobs began.

Chapter Ten

Jake stood beside Adam, the soft throb of industrial music thudding in from the dungeon. He watched the women's locker room, waiting for the moment Serena walked out with Eve. He'd been damn happy Eve was around. He worried that if he'd sent Serena in there alone, she might never have come out.

"She's taking her time." Adam watched, too.

"She's nervous." And afraid. And a little heartsick. He'd held her while she'd cried, and most of his damn defenses were sorely in need of shoring up. The last several days with Serena had been hard. It had been hard to keep his distance, hard to not like her, hard to just be hard every minute of the day. His cock had made its decision. His cock didn't give a shit that this was a bad idea. His cock just knew that she was exactly his type and that her soft heart matched her curvy body. It was a dangerous combination.

"I went easy on her." Adam's mouth turned down. "I didn't leave her completely naked."

Jake turned. "Maybe I shouldn't have left you in charge of her clothes."

"Give me a little credit. I didn't want to scare her away. I left her a miniskirt and a corset."

Just like that Jake's dick jumped. His leathers suddenly felt too confining. *Fuck*. How the hell was he supposed to keep his hands off her? He had a hard time when she was fully dressed. What the fuck was he going to do when she walked out wearing next to nothing and looking like his wet dream?

Adam put a hand on his shoulder. He was still in street clothes. He had a job to do. "You can handle this. It's one very curious woman who is likely to also be deeply shy. You'll probably stand at the edge of the crowd the whole time."

Jake threw his partner a look. Serena could be deeply shy, but Jake had the feeling that once she got in the dungeon, her shyness would battle with curiosity, and there was no way shy won. Serena was too interested in everything. He'd watched her corner a waiter who'd mentioned he'd spent some time in Iraq. She'd had a million questions. She hadn't been too shy to talk to him.

"So, where's the client who no one here is fucking?" Ian stepped beside Jake, his massive body crowding the space. Ian was dressed for play in motorcycle boots and his leathers.

"She's in the locker room with Eve. I'm pretty sure Eve's not fucking her, either." Adam just had to push it with Ian.

Ian just smiled and one eyebrow cocked up. "Let's not be hasty. I might actually watch that show." He sighed. "So, I heard from Liam there was some movement today. I got a frantic call from Lara. She's really worried about this. She also said she got a call from a local TV station. It seems someone's smelling blood in the water, and they think it might make a good story."

A hard knot formed in the pit of Jake's stomach. This was what he'd been worried about. Serena didn't seem to want the publicity. She hadn't called the press. So who had?

"Cool it, Dean. Don't you know reporters routinely pump police for interesting cases?" Ian always could read his mind.

Adam jumped on that little fact like it was a lifeline. "Of course. It's an interesting story. Writer's private life mirrors her books. I can see a reporter wanting a piece of that. And I've checked her phone. The only people she's talked to are her friends and her agent. She's practically a damn nun."

Ian's face creased. "Yeah. See, that's what I want to hear. Of course, she's not exactly wearing a habit right now. Damn." He growled a little as Serena walked out. "There's no fucking way you don't fuck her. Goddamn it. I was happier when you two were playing gay."

Jake would never be able to play gay with this client. His cock jumped as he caught sight of Serena. To call the skirt she was wearing a mini was being deeply generous. It was more like a piece of spandex she'd wrapped around her luscious ass. It would be so easy to push it aside and bend her over. He could shove his cock deep without ever having to remove the thing. And her breasts looked like they would spill out of the corset. It was a vibrant red, her porcelain skin making a sharp contrast against it. Her hair cascaded down her shoulders. In her everyday life, she wore it in a ponytail or she would use a pen to form a loose, messy bun, but now the soft brown hair made a waterfall down her back. He could sink his hand into it and use the hold to guide her where he wanted her to go. He could force her to the floor, kneeling in front of him, that glorious mouth lined up to accept his cock.

"You look beautiful, Serena." At least Adam still had the power of speech.

"You look like someone's serving you up to a big bad Dom. Adam, did you forget to put the cherry on top?" Ian asked, sarcasm flowing.

Serena flushed.

"Not at all, boss. But little Serena there has a cherry of her own. It's not on top, if you know what I mean." Adam laughed, but the husky quality told Jake he wasn't unaffected.

Serena shook her head. "I don't know what you…oh, my god, you're talking about my bottom."

Ian laughed. "Look at the little sub blush. After reading some excerpts of your books, I would have sworn you didn't have it in you. You use some rough language."

Serena straightened up. Jake was just about to tell Ian to stuff it. She'd had a hard day, and the last thing she needed was Ian's comments on her books. But Serena frowned and took it straight to the Dom. "If you can't handle a little rough use, maybe you should stick to vanilla books."

Ian laughed. "Oh, I like a brat, honey. I like to eat them for lunch. Mind your manners, sub, or you'll find yourself over my lap. We'll see if you turn your bratty mouth on me then."

"Back off, Ian." Jake took her by the hand and pulled her close, half shoving her behind his body. He wasn't about to stand here and watch Ian flirt with his sub. *Fuck.* She wasn't his. Except she was for the night. He had her collar in his hand. Thin and delicate, it was a training collar. It was the only piece of her wardrobe he'd been responsible for, and he'd taken two goddamn hours to pick it out. Ian had been yelling at him to leave Serena alone, and now the asshole was staring down at her like a hungry hawk who'd eyed a particularly juicy bunny. No fucking way. A deep possessiveness took hold in his gut. "I told you no one else is disciplining her."

Ian shook his head. "This shit had better work out, Dean. I don't want a lawsuit. You make sure she's taken care of. And try to think with your brain and not your dick. Did she sign a contract?"

Jake could feel Serena behind him, her head peeking from behind his shoulders.

"I did, but they wouldn't let me take a copy with me. I should get a copy, don't you think?" Serena asked as though the man hadn't just threatened to spank her ass.

Ian stared down at her. "So I could see it written into your next book? I don't think so. Tell me something, Serena. Are you interested in the lifestyle because BDSM sells books, or are you interested for your own sake?"

"She's interested, Ian," Jake explained. "She's been trying to find a mentor. Unfortunately, she found Dom Douchebag."

"Yeah, I heard he turned out to be Stinchfield. I didn't like the way he handled the subs I tested him on. He showed no real emotion toward them. There should be more there than mere service between a Dom and a sub. There should be some excitement. Some emotion. He was very interested in service from the submissive's end. He wanted a total power exchange, but I didn't think he would handle that in a way that served the sub."

"I think you were right to turn him away," Jake admitted. "But it doesn't make me want to let you flirt with my sub."

"Our sub," Adam interjected.

"So you screen everyone?" Serena asked, her cheek against his bicep. "Do they sit down with Eve? Is there a form they have to fill out? Does everyone sign the same contract that I did? I have Jacob acting as my Dom. What happens if a sub doesn't have a Dom? Do you find one for her?"

"Down, sub," Ian barked. Jake had no doubt that if he wasn't standing between them, Ian would be towering over Serena.

"She's very curious." Jake felt an irrational need to defend her. "But she'll hold her questions for me."

Ian's eyes narrowed. "She can ask her questions, but I would rather she submitted them in written form, and I'll decide what I will and won't answer. There will be no negotiations about my answers. You will follow your contract and obey Jacob. If Adam has anything to say that is meaningful and helpful, you will obey him as well."

Adam huffed behind him.

Ian ignored it. "And if this works out and you prove you truly are interested in this, then we can talk about giving you greater access to Sanctum, and I'll speak with the other Doms and subs about talking to you."

"Really?" Serena asked.

Ian nodded. "Yes, really. I'm not some monster. Well, not most of the time. I started this club to help little subs like you. And, hey, those excerpts I read were hot. You might want to tone down the whole 'pussy Dom' crap, but otherwise, I know a lot of the subs here would love your books. Maybe you could do a signing or something."

Jake sighed. That would go an enormously long way to settling Serena down.

"I could totally do that. And I would love to talk to subs and Doms. I have a million and one questions. Like when did you know you were a Dom? What were your first indications?"

It was time to take control of his sub. "Serena, stop."

She had the good sense to go quiet.

Ian looked back at Adam. "Do you need backup?"

He shook his head. "I have it. It's a simple trace, and I need to go through the tapes I got from the libraries. I have hours of footage from the two libraries with CCTV. I think I found a way to use facial profiling technology to compare the two. I'm looking for some connection, and the time stamps should help me. It shouldn't be difficult, just time consuming. I could actually do it in the morning."

"Do it now, Adam," Ian barked and then walked away.

Jake turned and looked at Serena. "You're going to be trouble."

Adam's hand found her hip. They were crowding her, her half-naked body in the middle. "Which is precisely why I should stay. She needs two Masters. She's too much trouble for just one."

"Or we could all go home and you could do the job we're getting paid to do." Jake stared at his partner.

After everything that had happened today, how could he possibly be thinking about putting off the case? Jake had looked at those books, and they had turned his stomach. Whoever had sent that package had a deep need to hurt Serena. Every dirty word, every pussy, fuck, cock, cunt, even damn had been marked through. There was no note. No words on the page. The books had simply been cleaned of anything the reader thought of as filth. Nothing this stalker had done before had scared Jacob the way this little stunt had. The attention to detail had made his hair stand on end. How long had he sat at a desk with his marker, decimating Serena's books? How far would he go to hurt the woman herself?

He locked eyes with his partner, felt Serena tense beside him.

"I'll go get changed."

"No," Adam said quickly. "Stay. Enjoy the club. Have a good time with Jake." Adam leaned over and kissed her cheek. "I'll still be here. I set up my gear in the conference room. I can work from there so if you need anything at all, I can be here."

That was what Jake wanted to hear. The whole computer search thing was Adam's stock-in-trade. And tonight, Jake's job was to keep their sub's mind off all the bad shit. Client, he corrected himself. Client. She didn't belong to them. He had to remember that.

Adam winked at her and walked toward the conference room.

"We don't have to do this," Serena said after a long moment of silence. "We can go and help Adam. Or we could just go home. I know this wasn't your idea."

Jake took a deep breath and really looked at her. Despite the sexy clothes, there was still an air of innocence that clung to her. And there was definitely an air of self-doubt. Her husband had turned her away for wanting to be dominated sexually. She'd written down her deeply held fantasies, and yes, they involved sex, but more than that all of her fantasies involved true love and acceptance. She'd been looking for that acceptance for years, and if she didn't find it soon, she might stop looking altogether. It might occur to her that it would be easier to shove that part of herself away, to bury it deep down where it no longer mattered. He didn't want that for her. She was beautiful, and it went bone deep. He wanted her to be free.

"You don't want to play? I thought you would at least want to watch a few scenes." He still found it hard to simply say what he wanted.

She smiled, a wan little thing. "I want to try it all. I want the whole experience, Jacob, but I know you don't think of me like that. It's okay. We can just watch. I promise not to be too obnoxious with the questions." Her eyes trailed after Adam. The longing there made Jake jealous. "Adam said he would help with the rest of it."

Had he? How very fucking nice of Adam to offer to help with "the rest of it." Something nasty took root in Jake's gut. It wasn't fair. He knew it. He'd been the one who'd tried to push her away in the beginning, but living with her these past few days had made him draw close to her. He couldn't help it. He'd watched her, grown to care. And now Adam wanted him to stand beside her, watching scenes while he plotted and scheduled her training? Adam wasn't half the Dom Jake was. He wasn't as invested in the lifestyle, but he thought he would train the sexy little wide-eyed natural sub?

Fuck no.

"What exactly is the other stuff, Serena?" The words came out in a harsh grind.

Serena flushed, her fair skin pinkening prettily. She would look so fucking good draped over his knee. His cock settled into a deep, throbbing rhythm.

Her eyes slid away from him. "The protocol stuff."

He cupped her neck, his palm on her spine, forcing her gently to look up. He slipped the collar around her neck, adjusting it to a comfortable length. He touched the collar as he spoke. "I'm responsible for you. Not Adam. I'm the one with rights here. If you want to learn something about the lifestyle, you'll go through me. Let's start at the beginning. Show me how you greet your Master."

He couldn't resist. He knew he should just nod and walk her through the dungeon, but the temptation of seeing her kneel at his feet was too much. She bit into her bottom lip, looking around the area as though trying to decide if it was safe. But that wasn't her call.

"Now, Serena. On your knees. You want a Dom for the night? Well, that's my collar around your neck. You will obey me, or we'll do exactly what you said. We'll go home and sit and wait for Adam. Hell, we'll watch some incredibly boring TV and you can sink into your safe-as-pie vanilla life, and you never have to really know what it means to submit. You can just write about it."

A fire lit her eyes, and she fell to her knees. Yes, that was what he wanted. She wasn't thinking about the fact that her skirt was too short or that people might see her. She was thinking about him and proving him wrong. It wasn't the exact place he wanted her. He would rather she was merely thinking about pleasing him, but he would take it.

He studied her for a moment. She had the basics down. Her brunette head was bent submissively toward the floor. Her hands were on her knees, shoulders back. If she had been naked, her breasts would have been on full, glorious display.

"I prefer the palms up position, Serena."

She turned her palms up. "I read about it the other way."

"There are many ways to practice, Serena. It's something you and your partner decide on. I prefer palms up. I can't really explain why. It's merely what turns me on." And it did. She looked lovely, but there was a certain perfection that could only come with long training. "Spread your knees further apart."

She hesitated a second before moving her knees a fraction of an inch to the side.

"Wider, Serena." Jake was well aware of the impatience in his voice.

Serena huffed a little, and her knees spread further. The little skirt Adam had given her rolled up and showed off a spectacular view of something Jake was pretty damn sure Adam hadn't included in her clothing options.

"What is covering your pussy?" Jake asked, putting a hand in her hair. He tugged lightly, aware of the flush that stole across her skin. Her breathing had picked up, too. She was becoming aroused. He was sure of it.

"Underwear, Jake."

He tightened his hand in her hair and gave her a little growl.

"Sir," she corrected quickly. "It's my underwear, Sir."

"Did Adam include plain, white cotton underwear with your clothes for this evening?" Jake damn straight knew the answer to that question. There was no way Adam had included it. Adam loved lingerie. Whenever they had a woman, Adam would buy box after box of expensive lingerie and fetish wear to dress her. Jake would laugh and tell Adam he was looking for a Fuck-Me Barbie.

Her eyes got wide as though realizing she was in trouble. "No. He left something else. It was too small. It didn't cover me. It was a thong, and I don't really like those."

"You don't like thongs? Are you kidding me? Serena, pet, I've read your work. Tell me what Joshua Lake would do to a submissive who blatantly violated her Dom's orders regarding clothing." He would use her work against her, though in this case it really was proper training material.

That sexy lower lip trembled, making him want to kiss her until she couldn't move. "He would probably just tell her to not do it again."

She wanted to play it that way? He pulled her hair gently, forcing her to look him straight in the eye. "He's not a pussy Dom, Serena. You didn't write him that way. Of all the characters you've written, he's the most vivid, the most alive. He's your fantasy. Now you tell me what he would do."

Her breath escaped in shallow pants. "He would say I gave up the right to underwear at all."

Jake smiled, releasing her hair. "Excellent. We'll start there. Remove those panties. They offend me."

"But Jake, if I take them off, the skirt is so short people will be able to see me."

"That's ten swats."

"But I didn't know," Serena tried to argue.

Reality seemed to be setting in for the little sub. It was odd, but Jake found himself actually enjoying the push and pull. He'd spent the last several years with perfectly trained subs who got off on showing their bodies and displaying their pure obedience. But it hadn't been earned from Jake. And he also got that this was Serena's fantasy. Serena's fantasies weren't about everything going perfectly. Her characters had to fight. This would be a little fight, but they both could win.

"You didn't know your Dom would discipline you?" Jake asked. "That's another ten, by the way."

Her fists clenched. "I didn't know it would be you."

The words hit him like a bucket of ice cold water. "You thought it would be Adam. Of course."

She cared about Adam. She wanted Adam. Adam was the one with all the smooth moves. Adam cooked for her and took care of her schedule. Jake was just the meathead whose job was to throw his oversized body in front of any bullet that came her way. Yeah. He should have gotten that by now.

"I just thought Ian was making you do it because you did the course thing."

He heard the words, but his head was somewhere else. "It's fine, Serena. Come on. I'll show you around the club. Adam is going to be a couple of hours. We can look around, and then I'll take you home. What do you want to see first?"

He would be like a tour guide, polite, efficient, and uninvolved. His cock would just have to calm the fuck down. He turned to go, but she caught his hand. When he turned back, she was struggling to get to her feet. He helped her up. He would at least prove he could be polite. He wasn't some animal. Jennifer's words came back to haunt him.

You're just a dumb piece of beefcake, Jake. I was never going to marry you. I'm not going to spend my life with a grunt no matter how well trained he is. Adam is a man I could see marrying, but you ruined him. Now he doesn't even have a career.

He helped Serena up because she was Adam's girl. Not his. He wasn't going to fuck it up for Adam again.

Serena stood there looking at him, her big eyes threatening to pull him in. "I'm sorry, Sir."

He shook his head. "No, I apologize. I didn't get what you wanted. No problem, Serena. And just call me Jake."

It would be too hard to listen to her call him "Sir" in that breathy Texas twang of hers, not when it wasn't real. He didn't want to play with Serena. He wanted it to be real. He'd been an idiot, doing exactly what he'd promised Ian he wouldn't do. He'd been thinking with his heart and not his head.

"Tell me you're not playing with me."

Serena's soft words made him turn around. She looked small and fragile standing there in her miniskirt and corset, her bare feet on the carpet.

He sighed. "I'm not going to hurt you, Serena. I promise. No swats. Nothing at all. You need to stay by my side because you don't know your way around, but no one is going to touch you."

Her fists clenched at her sides. "Damn it, Jake, that wasn't what I meant."

He hated being cursed at, especially by subs, but she was the client and his best friend's crush. "Then please explain what you want, Serena. I'm here to meet your needs."

She shook her head. "I don't want this. I want it the way it was just a few minutes ago, but I'm scared. Not of you. God, Jacob, we need to work on your self-esteem. You're so gorgeous I have a hard time looking at you, but the first place your brain goes to when I talk is that I'm rejecting you. I'm not. I'm scared that this is going to be the best experience of my life and you'll just walk away afterward and never think of me again. That's what I'm scared of. And I think you'll spank really hard. I probably will cry and maybe scream and I'll make a fool of myself. But if you'll just tell me that this means something, anything, to you, then I'll be okay. Jake, I'm not asking for an engagement ring or a permanent collar, I just want to know that you like me, that this isn't something you're doing because Adam pushed you to it."

God, he was crazy about her. No other woman in the world

would have accused him of having self-esteem issues, but Serena just put it all out there. She laid it on the line and stood there waiting for his judgment. For his honesty. It was a beautiful thing.

"Serena, I don't know if this is going to go anywhere," he admitted. "You get that Adam and I share, right?"

She nodded. "Yeah, I don't seem to have a problem with that."

"It can be rough on a woman. And we haven't known each other for long."

"I know. But this whole lifestyle is about being brave enough to try, isn't it? I got the shit kicked out of me, Jake. My husband did a number on me. There's this piece deep inside that wants to hide and pretend I don't need anyone, but I need to be braver than that. I want to explore this with you. And all I really ask is that if you decide you don't want me, treat me with a little kindness, okay? I'm a big girl. I can handle it, but I want some kindness."

His heart hurt for her. He couldn't fucking help it anymore. He reached out and pulled her close, her hands on his skin for the first time. He wrapped himself around her as though he could protect her from all the shit coming her way. Kindness was the least she should expect from the men she shared her body with. Kindness, tenderness, affection. She was starving for them.

"I can handle the kindness, Serena," he whispered in her ear. Fuck, he wasn't going to be able to keep his hands off her now. No way. He just had to hold off until Adam could be around. But Adam had already had a taste. It was only fair he got a kiss, too. He nuzzled her ear, reveling in the little sigh she made. It felt right to be so close to her. He kissed her, his lips finding her cheek first and then the soft edge of her mouth.

The minute her mouth flowered open beneath his, he nearly lost control. She was so fucking perfect for him. He loved her curves and the way she practically melted into him. Her hands were tentative as they found his waist, but she gripped him, using him for balance. That was what he wanted, to balance her and make her the center of his desire.

He kissed her, licking a demanding path across her lips, telling her with a little growl what he wanted.

She sighed, and her tongue came out to dance with his. He took over, dominating her mouth, his hands tangling in her hair so he could move her the way he wanted. He hauled her close, wanting not a fucking centimeter of distance between them. His cock ground against her belly. He needed to get her higher. She was petite, small against him. He would have to shove her against a wall in order to get her to the right height so he could thrust his cock deep.

He started to maneuver her toward the wall when he heard heels clicking along the floor that led to the locker room.

"Should I get you a privacy room?" Eve's voice was a shock to his system. *Fuck.* He'd forgotten where they were. It wasn't like he hadn't fucked a couple of subs in full view of the dungeon, but he didn't just go at it in front of the locker room. What was he thinking? And he couldn't fuck Serena. Not without Adam.

Jake pulled away. His head was cloudy, but he managed to focus on Eve. She was dressed to kill in a perfectly tailored miniskirt and corset. It was rather like Serena's, but Eve was slender and her hair was perfectly done. There wasn't a thing messy about Eve. Hair, nails, and makeup all perfect. He was certain the five-inch stilettos on her feet were some designer who charged so much for a pair of shoes that Jake's eyeballs would bulge. So why was messy, plump Serena the one who called to him? Why did the sight of her bare feet turn him on? He held her hand in his. Her nails were short, and there were calluses all over her hands. She used them all day. She typed, and when she was plotting, she would get out a pen or a marker and write all over a notebook or her white board. He fucking loved her hands. He pulled one to his mouth and placed a kiss on her palm.

"Sorry," he said to Eve, holding Serena close. "I got carried away. And I forgot all about the discipline my sub requires."

Serena's face tilted up. She'd put her contacts in, and they made her eyes wide and open. He was just sadist enough to enjoy the little tremor of trepidation he saw there. "It was only twenty, right?"

"Who's getting twenty?" Alex asked, walking out of the men's locker room. His eyes fastened on Eve briefly before looking to the ground. "Certainly not Evie. She's requested fifty."

God, was that still going on? Jake felt for Alex. He was divorced from Eve, but she still came to him for discipline. As far as

Jake could tell they had no intimacy beyond the flick of Alex's whip or the slap of his paddle. Alex had told him once over way too many beers that it was the only way she would relate to him anymore. And he would take it because he still loved his ex-wife.

Jake slid an arm around Serena's waist. They were starting out, and with any luck at all, they would never get to the place Alex and Eve were in, longing and unfulfilled. "Just twenty, pet. But it will be more if you don't give me those panties."

Eve smiled, a little chuckle escaping her mouth. It was good to hear her laugh. "I warned her you wouldn't like the panties."

Serena nodded. "Okay. I'll go put on the thong thingee."

Jake gave that gorgeous ass a sharp slap. "Not on your life, baby. You gave up the thong thingee the minute you tried to circumvent Adam's wishes by covering your pussy with a piece of cotton. Now, you are either in or you're out. If you're not ready, march back in the locker room and change. We'll go home and we'll talk. If you are, take those fucking panties off, and remember that if I see you in them again, it will be fifty smacks, and they won't be erotic."

Her cheeks flared, and just for a moment he thought she would run into the locker room like a scared little rabbit. She took a deep breath and visibly steeled herself.

"Okay."

* * * *

Her hands shook a little as she reached for her skirt. It was absolutely the shortest piece of material she'd ever worn, but it was also a test. She realized that now. If she wanted the joys of the power exchange, she'd better be ready for the scary shit, too. Jake wanted her underwear. She wanted Jake. A plus B equaled potential orgasm, and she wasn't going to let a little thing like complete and utter humiliation keep her from making that math work.

She hooked her thumbs under the waist of her plain-Jane cotton undies and wished she'd given the butt floss a try. It was all her fault. Two seconds into the lifestyle and Serena Brooks was topping from the bottom. And getting her ass spanked. Jacob Dean was going to spank her ass, and she suddenly realized he wouldn't leave the skirt between them. He would more than likely push that spandex aside and lay his hand on her bare ass. It would sting at first, the heat flaring along her skin.

"Serena, this is not rocket science."

She looked up into his seriously impatient brown eyes. Jacob Dean was her wet dream Dom fantasy and here she was daydreaming. "Sorry, Sir."

He held out a hand, waiting for her to give up the offensive garment. She tried to pull the panties off while she held on to some semblance of dignity. She wasn't sure if she would have had the courage to simply haul up her skirt and pull down her undies if they had been alone, but she felt brutally conscious of the fact that gorgeous Eve St. James was standing beside her. And Ian's partner, who seemed to be Eve's Dom.

"That is not going to work," Eve whispered.

But Serena tried. She wiggled and squirmed until she had the panties to her knees, and she felt triumphant as she passed them to Jake and smoothed her skirt down. She'd done it. She'd gotten those panties off and she hadn't flashed her cootchie. Yeah. Topping from the bottom could be fun.

Jake took her underwear and proved he didn't have any problems with self-consciousness. He put them right up to his nose and took a long whiff. Serena watched, a little horrified and a little turned on.

"God, you smell so fucking good, Serena." Jake tucked the underwear in his pocket and frowned. "Now find your position."

"I told you it wouldn't work," Eve said with a sympathetic smile.

Damn it. He was forcing her into a corner. If she got on her knees and spread her legs, she would be open to the viewing public. And if she refused, she would hate herself. It was just a pussy. She'd written the scene a thousand times. A pussy was just a pussy, and it wasn't like hers was horrible looking. She'd shaved. Sure, it had been awhile, but she no longer looked like Sasquatch. She could do this.

"Serena, I'm waiting."

"What if I'm not pretty?"

He laughed, a surprised sound. "If you're not pretty, I'll give up my left nut. Seriously, Serena, if that's what you're worried about, then find your position and let me and Alex put your mind at ease."

"I can give you a girl's perspective," Eve offered with a smile. "I'm totally not into the girl-on-girl thing, but I know an attractive pussy when I see one."

It was ridiculous. It was silly. It was precisely why she'd written that first book, because it was also real. She suddenly felt freer than she had before, and she dropped to the ground, spreading her knees wide. She placed her hands palms up and felt the cool air of the room on her feminine flesh. She was open and bare and strangely powerful.

"Serena, you aren't pretty, baby. You're beautiful. Isn't my sub gorgeous, Alex?" Jake's words were like warm honey, heating her up and making her feel sweet.

"She is, indeed. It makes me want to see mine right there beside her."

"Alex," Eve began.

"Are you mine for the night or not?" Alex's tone turned icy and stubborn. "We have a contract, Eve. Just because I choose to not demand my rights doesn't mean they don't exist. I won't touch you. I just want to look. I want to feel like I actually have a sub for a minute. I'm feeling brutally jealous of Jacob right now."

Eve sank to her knees beside Serena.

"Is he going to catch you wearing underwear, too?" Serena asked.

Eve giggled, her previous irritation seeming to melt a bit. "I've been doing this a long time, Serena. I know no Dom wants his pussy covered." She stopped as though her words had made her flustered again.

"We have two lovely subs. And I think both their asses will be red tonight," Jake promised. "Now, I seem to remember that Alex and Eve have a scene to play, and Serena and I would love to watch."

Her first real live scene. She looked up, still a little nervous around Eve, but the cool, professional woman gave her a wink.

"I think you're going to love it here, Serena. Just do what Jake tells you. He won't steer you wrong." She patted Serena's hand.

A warm feeling of acceptance suffused Serena. She could belong here if she just opened herself to the experience. Jake reached out a hand and hauled her up as Alex helped Eve off the floor. Alex quickly let her go, but Jake pulled Serena close. Yes, this was what she'd been looking for all her damn life. She felt cared for in Jake's arms, and knowing that Adam wasn't far away made her heart beat faster. Two men. Could she keep them? Could she be enough for them?

"You did a good job, baby," Jake said. "I know that was hard for you, but you handled it beautifully."

But it hadn't been hard once she'd made the decision to trust him. She leaned into his strength. For all his hot body and gorgeous face, he was still a man who needed love and affection. She had so much to give if he would just take it.

He kissed her as though he could read her mind. "Come on. I know you want to see everything."

He led her through the doors and into the dungeon. She followed, ready to begin this new part of her life.

Chapter Eleven

Adam studied line after line of code, the numbers threatening to run together. He'd been at it for three hours, and all that time Serena had been running around the dungeon, her ass in nothing more than a strip of fabric. He wanted to see her in the pretty thong he'd picked out for her. If she had any idea all the filthy, disgusting lingerie he'd already scoped out for her, she would probably run. She would look gorgeous in something filmy and lacy, her cute little feet in some serious fuck-me heels.

But no. He was sitting in the conference room surrounded by computers instead of watching his sweet girl get introduced to kink.

He growled a little as the program kicked back out. Nothing. He didn't believe it. It was possible that Serena's stalker was really good with computers and was routing the e-mails through systems, but Adam doubted it. Why use a system in such close physical proximity to Serena? If the person was good, he or she would likely have bounced the e-mails all over the place. No. Adam was sure the stalker was using the libraries' computers in person.

The problem was, Adam wasn't happy with the facial recognition software that was on the market. He was playing around with the code, trying to make it better. The answer had to be here.

He had time stamps from two libraries that matched up with e-mails sent from their public computers to Serena's computer.

All he had to do was find the face that had been in both places.

"You still at it?" Liam asked, setting a cup of coffee down in front of him.

Adam ran a weary hand through his hair. "Yes. It's a lot of shit to get through. I got the delivery records. Surprise, surprise. This asshole paid cash, an address that turned out to be a coffee shop, and a fake name. Joshua Lake. Serena's big bad Dom."

"I think she might have a new big bad Dom. I saw the way Jake was looking at her." Liam sat down on the edge of the desk. "You two planning on double-teaming the girl?"

That was the plan. He actually felt a little bad for Jake. It wouldn't be easy for him to keep his hands off Serena. He would most likely end up with fucking blue balls. "We've been playing it slow and easy with this one. I like her."

Liam nodded. "I like her, too. She's an odd one, but I like her openness. I think Jake's in as deep as you are. Are you absolutely certain she doesn't have anything to do with this?"

Adam groaned. He was sick of this question. "Yes. I'm sure."

Liam held his hands up. "I'm not judging the girl. People can have a lot of reasons to pull a stunt like this. I ain't some perfect man. I don't expect a woman to be perfect either. I'm just saying that Jake's got a chip on his shoulder about honesty, and if he finds out she's been lying, it won't go so pretty for either of you."

If there was one thing Adam was certain of it was that Serena was scared of this person. She wouldn't be scared if she was doing it herself. "I'm sure about Serena."

Liam went quiet for a minute and then looked at the computer, his eyes squinting as he read the code. "I'm glad you're sure, man. I got a couple of things that bug me about this case. I read through Evie's profile. She's a bit confused, I think."

"She says this guy must be bipolar." He hoped somewhere out there the asshole was getting back on his fucking meds.

Liam's head shook. "She said she thought he must be since the notes and e-mails are so radically different. But I was actually thinking something else. I knew this girl back in Ireland. She had a—what do you call it here? You know, when a guy ain't got the balls to tell a girl he wants in her pants?"

"Secret admirer," Adam replied.

"I call them pussies. Anyway, this friend of mine started getting chocolates and then dirty notes. Not the bad kind. The kind that got her hot under the collar, if you know what I mean. So she was thinking that he was trying to play both sides with her. The notes with the chocolates were real sweet, all about love and how pretty she was, and then the other ones were just about fucking. Well, she thought she'd hit the jackpot."

Adam could see where this was going. "It was two guys, right?"

"Oh, yes. One was a boy who sat next to her in science class, and the other was his asshole best friend who had made a bet as to which one she would prefer. She told everyone she wasn't interested in either one, but she made arrangements to meet with the dirty boy after school let out. He was a dumb shit. Had to marry the girl eight weeks later. Now they have four kids, and he drinks too much. Really, he's living the dream. But my point is, she didn't know it was two men. She simply responded to the darker side of what she assumed was one man."

Adam looked up from his work. "How do you know she thought it was only one man? She could have figured it out. Someone could have told her."

"Because I was the dumbass kid who sent her the chocolates. She talked to me about it. She told me she liked the chocolates, but she really liked the bad boy side of her admirer." Liam's fingers drummed along the surface of the desk, his mouth frowning.

"You think this could be two people?" Adam hadn't considered it. It seemed far too coincidental. Some celebrities had multiple stalkers, but Serena wasn't well known.

Liam shrugged. "I don't know, but if I had to guess, I would say these are different people." He opened the folder and pulled out copies of the notes Serena had been sent. "This one likes to use the internet. And she talks about the work. She's mad about the characters. And quite frankly, she sounds like a nagging woman. When I picture this one, I see a shut-in who probably has multiple cats and gets more invested in fictional characters than in the world around her. The point is, she's pissed that her favorite characters didn't do what she wanted them to. She talks about that, not about Serena herself."

A good point. "But couldn't she have just gotten mad enough to hate Serena?"

Liam shrugged. "Then why keep going back to it? Look, there's a pattern. It's all about these characters in her new book until roughly two weeks ago. Then the really nasty stuff started. Then it shifts to attacks on Serena herself. The person who wrote those notes hates her as a writer and as a woman. The attacks get vicious and personal. And it feels like this is a man. Listen to the way he talks. He talks about her tempting men. He talks about sin and judgment. This person doesn't read her books. He hates them."

But Eve had explained how this could happen. "Look, if this chick or guy or whoever is off their meds, she could careen wildly. She could behave almost like two different people."

"You know I love Evie, but she's always looking for the most interesting mental problems. I think she's overthinking it in this case. She's looking for zebras when she should be looking for horses—two to be exact. It's two people you're looking for. Just think about it. I think you have two perps, one dangerous and one a whackadoodle who probably wants to talk Serena to death. The key is going to be catching the dangerous one while not getting distracted by the whack job."

It wasn't a theory he wanted to think about, but Liam made some sense. "I'll take that into account. You playing tonight?"

"I was, but then I got depressed. It hurts watching Alex and Eve. I didn't make it through the whole scene. It's going on right now." Liam sighed and stretched. "I feel for the poor bastard. Six years and she's still punishing him. I don't think she's ever going to forgive him for whatever the hell he did to her. And she sure as hell ain't close to forgiving herself."

"Shit. Is Serena watching it?" Sometimes Eve and Alex's scenes could get very rough. Eve usually ended up sobbing, and Alex got close to it. And yet they held on to the ritual as though it was the only thing that connected them anymore. It wasn't what he would have wanted Serena to see.

"Yes, she's there, but from what I saw it was quite tender tonight. I think she thought it was lovely." Liam's mouth turned down, and his eyes found the floor. "It won't scare her away, if that's what you're worried about. I just know that look in Alex's eyes. He's hurting, and it throws me off me game. I wish you buggers would stop the whole relationship thing. It's depressing to a man. I'm going to end up with Ian as my wingman. He's a terrible wingman. Half the time he scares the women away."

Adam snorted. Yeah, he didn't see Ian helping Liam pick up chicks any time soon. "Well, if you don't have anything to do, you could always help me analyze the tapes from the CCTV cameras."

Liam's eyes narrowed. "What are the CC's attached to? A women's gym? Inside a strip club?"

"Library in the suburbs." Adam didn't hold much hope that Liam was going to hang around.

"I'm gone." Liam was out the door before Adam could call him an asshole.

He turned back to his work. Two people. Fuck. Serena seemed to attract ménages wherever she went.

* * * *

Serena watched as Alex helped Eve off the St. Andrew's cross, tucking her beautiful body into a plush white robe that covered the delicate lashes across her back. The new ones, that was. Eve's back was a mess of scars, some old and white and ragged, and some almost surgical in their precision. She had to wonder if Alex had given her all of them. When the scene had begun, she'd stared at Alex, wondering what kind of a man he was.

"Don't look at Alex that way. He didn't leave those marks on her," Jake had whispered when she'd gasped as Eve had fully disrobed. "And any he gives her today will be faded by tomorrow. Don't judge until you've watched them, Serena."

And then the scene had started, and Serena understood what he'd meant. Alex was careful, so careful with her. He was a master with the whip. It was a four-foot singletail. He'd snapped the whip a couple of times before he'd started. The snick of the whip had

143

cracked through the air, but when the whip had flicked against Eve's skin, it had barely left a mark. Alex had stopped every ten strokes and requested an update on where she was. Eve would answer that she was green, meaning she was happy and ready for more. She'd been perfectly calm, her face peaceful with only the occasional grimace. Tears had finally started as she'd taken the fortieth lash, and she'd been crying openly at fifty, but she'd still told him green when Alex had asked.

"Will he give her aftercare now?" Serena asked. Eve shivered in her robe and seemed to be looking for someone. She moved away from the Dom.

Aftercare, she'd researched, was what lifestylers called the time after a scene, when the Dom took care of the sub's needs. It could be anything from cuddling to first aid. It was a time for the Dom and the sub to come out of their "spaces" and get back to reality, like coming down from a high.

"One of the other subs will make sure her welts are properly tended," Jake said with a serious expression on his face. "Eve won't let Alex perform her aftercare."

But he wanted to hold her. That much was clear. The big Dom's eyes were sad as Eve was led off by a sweet-faced sub. Eve was still crying, seemingly lost in her own world, and Serena suddenly understood.

"It's the only way she can cry, isn't it?" Serena asked, wondering what had happened that would put Eve in this position.

Jake frowned, watching as Alex coiled his whip and put it away. "She doesn't talk about it, but she had a case go bad. She was FBI and something happened. She won't talk about the scars around her neck, either. She and Alex had divorced years before, and he'd started working with Ian. Alex brought her on. When she first came here, she was so cold. Then she started doing this, and she got somewhat better. But I don't want to talk about them tonight."

"Should we find another scene?" Serena asked, looking around. There was so much she wanted to see. She wanted to watch a fire play scene. She'd read a book by Cherise Sinclair with a fire play scene, and it had sparked her imagination. And puppy play. She really wanted to see that. She wasn't sure how she could make that sexy, but she was willing to watch.

Jake didn't move from his place, merely stood staring down at her. "The scenes can wait. I believe I still owe you a little discipline. Spanking chair or my lap?"

"What?" She swallowed. She should have known he wouldn't forget, but she'd kind of hoped. Her eyes caught on a scene playing out in a corner. She had to stop and stare. Ian Taggart had one of the subs trussed up, and he was showing her the biggest dildo Serena had ever seen. It had to be bigger around than her wrist, and it might have been almost a foot long. "Holy crap. Is that an elephant penis?"

Jake huffed. "No, it's a large butt plug. It's for training, Serena. Jenna has been somewhat resistant to anal sex, but she swears she wants to try it. Ian won't fuck her ass until he's prepared her."

"For a horse? Seriously, Jacob, that thing is huge." And she was kind of curious as to what was going to happen. It was odd, but knowing that everyone here had a contract and that everything was consensual made it seem all right to watch.

Jake shook his head. "You're kidding, right?"

She turned back to Jake. "About how big that thing is? No. I am not. I think we need to cross that apparatus off the list."

His voice dipped low as he leaned in. "Serena, I'm bigger than that plug."

She stared at him, her mind completely off the plug now. She couldn't help it. She looked down at his leathers. "No way."

A big grin crossed his face. "Way. Adam's not far behind me. And from what I've seen, poor Jenna probably has another two steps up before she takes on Ian. I have no idea how he functions. He should pass out from having so little blood in his brain. Now stop worrying about something that isn't happening yet and answer the question. Bench or lap?"

She was nervous. She was excited. She was somewhat aroused. She was really aroused. And she was definitely interested in whether Jake was telling the truth or not. Her mouth kind of watered at the idea of it. How big was he? She'd only slept with Doyle, and it hadn't been that great. It had mostly been an exercise in futility and frustration. What if she was the problem? Doyle had always claimed that she was, and now he was sleeping with a perky little grad student. What if he'd been right, and she really was frigid? What if she disappointed Jake? What if this all fell apart just when it seemed to be getting good?

"Lap it is, then." He reached down and picked her up as though she weighed next to nothing. He made her feel so delicate.

"Jake, what are you doing?" She looked around, but no one seemed to care that she was being kidnapped.

He walked away from the stage toward the back of the dungeon. "I think we'll make this first punishment private. I want to get you out of that head of yours. I don't like it when you disappear like you just did. I have no idea what was going on inside that brain, but I didn't like the expression it put on your face."

A man in leathers stood in front of a small hallway.

"You need a room, Jake?" The big man handed him a key. "Five is free and fully stocked."

"Thanks, Glen. And if Ian asks," Jake began.

Glen shrugged. "I never see anything. I'm practically fucking blind, man. And I wouldn't stand in the path of true love. Ian's got a black heart."

Serena blushed at the thought, but Jake just thanked the man and started walking toward the room numbered five. Privacy rooms. For doing stuff. Sex stuff. Kinky stuff. Spankings. And sex. She was going to be alone with Jacob Dean. She was going to be half naked, and maybe totally naked, and then he would see her cellulite. God, why hadn't she thought about wearing some sort of girdle? What was she thinking? They had barely let her have a thong. Her panties were in Jake's pocket, hanging out for all to see. He probably wouldn't like her covered in a girdle.

"You see, there it is. You just went somewhere else when you should be with me." He set her on her feet and had the door open in an instant. He hustled her in and turned on the light. The room was like a little mini playroom. There was a spanking bench, a wall full of implements, and a big bed. A big, comfy-looking bed.

She was alone with him.

"What were you thinking about? Tell me now." He used that deep, dark voice on her. She found it almost impossible to resist.

Well, she was nothing if not honest. "I was worried about how

I'll look when you take my clothes off."

He shook his head and sat down on the bed. His muscular legs were spread apart, his arms going across that cut chest of his. "I'm not going to take off your clothes, Serena. If you thought I would take you back here and rip your clothes off, you're going to be disappointed."

She was, actually. And now she was embarrassed. That had been a big assumption on her part. She'd kind of thought that since Adam had made it plain he wanted her, that meant Jake wanted her, too. But how could she be sure he wasn't just playing a role? He'd kissed her. It didn't have to mean anything. She had to get it out of her head. This was what a lot of people did. They played. It wasn't serious. It was just casual sex. The trouble was she wasn't a casual type of girl. "Sorry. I just thought since we were alone that you would…"

Jake cut her off with a curt shake of his head. "Make it easy on you? No way. You're going to undress for me. Slowly. You're going to show me your breasts and your pussy and your ass, and then you'll lay yourself across my lap and you will accept my discipline. What are your safe words?"

He'd had them written into their contract. "Yellow and red." Yellow slowed things down, and red stopped them altogether. She was kind of worried that a big yellow light was in her future. She was confused, but that was probably more about her than him. She didn't have a whole lot of experience. All the men she'd dreamed about lately were in her books. They were safe.

"Why are you scared, Serena?"

"I'm worried that you won't want me once you see me naked, and I want for you to want me."

He smiled, a long, slow parting of his lips. "Excellent. I appreciate the honesty, baby. I can't tell you how much I love the fact that you don't play games. So I won't either. I find you intensely attractive. I have had a fucking hard-on since the day you walked into my office. Now, do as I asked and take off your clothes. You won't know until you try."

Be brave. It was what she preached in her books. It was time to take a page out of one. None of her heroines got what they wanted without learning to ask for it. She started to undo the corset, remarkably aware of just how awkward she was. She could still hear Doyle telling her she wasn't sexy. But when she looked up, Jake was smiling at her as though he found her awkwardness endearing.

"Go as slow or as fast as you like, sweetheart. I'll just enjoy the show."

She took a deep breath. She felt safe with Jacob Dean. Days of living with him had made her comfortable. She unhooked the first hook and then the second, her breasts spilling out. She laid the corset aside with shaking hands.

"Show me your breasts, Serena." His tone had gotten slow, his accent thicker than before. He was a southern boy.

She cupped them. They'd always seemed too big, but Jake's eyes ate her up. It made her nipples hard, her pussy wet, her heart soar. She could ignore everything except her heart. But he was engaging her, and it had been so damn long since she'd really wanted.

"Now get rid of the skirt. I want to see your pussy."

She didn't hesitate this time. She pushed the skirt off her hips.

"Very nice, baby." Jake's voice soothed her. She understood why he'd brought her here. He'd wanted the privacy because she wasn't thinking about anything or anyone but him. There was a small part of her that still worried about such trivial things as cellulite, but here, in this place with Jacob, it was easy to silence that minor voice.

The air was cool on her skin, but his eyes were hot. He raised his hands and made a little circle, silently requesting that she turn. He wanted to look at her backside. Her ass, he would say in his deep, gravelly voice. He wanted to look at her ass, and he wasn't expecting perfection. He was expecting curves and softness. He was expecting her.

She turned, confidence in her every move. He'd told her what he wanted, and she had zero reason to think he was lying. He'd been honest with her. He'd been hurt, and he hadn't trusted her. Now he wanted her, and he wouldn't hold back. They were an oddly matched set, both insecure in their own ways. She could feel him looking at her. She breathed in and let it happen.

"Very nice, baby. It's time, though. Come here and place yourself over my lap." He patted his lap.

It was time to be in or out. She knew what she was. She was in. She wasn't about to stop now. She wanted to know where this went and if it was the place for her. She'd dreamed of this. She turned and walked to Jacob. He held out a hand and helped her drape herself over his lap. Her ass was in the air, his knee across her torso. She wiggled a little to try to get comfortable, but Jacob put a hand on her back, and she stilled.

"Where are you, Serena?"

She smiled. "Green, Sir. I'm fine."

"I'm glad because I am absolutely green, Serena. I want this." His hand came down on her ass, the sound smacking through the room.

She squealed. She couldn't help it. That single smack lit up her flesh. Heat and a jangle of pain rushed through her system. Jacob's hand came down again. He struck twice, and then a third and fourth and fifth time. He moved around, never hitting the same spot twice. She squirmed on Jake's lap, and she felt his cock twitch.

"Where are you, baby? It's your first time. We can take it slow and easy."

She breathed in. The heat was sinking into her flesh, endorphins rushing through her system. Her backside hurt, but her skin was on fire, and it wasn't all pain. "I'm good."

"I need to hear the word, Serena." Jake's voice was calm, but she could hear the undercurrent. He wasn't an aloof participant. He was barely leashed, and his cock was a hard line against her stomach. She'd made him hard. She wiggled her ass a little and felt his cock jump. "Now, Serena."

"Green, Sir." She was completely sure now. She heard the fine edge to his voice, knew she was the reason he sounded that way.

His hand came down again, this time right on the crease of her ass. "Little tease." He smacked her again and again. "You like the fact that I'm hard and ready for you, don't you, baby? You like teasing the big bad Dom."

She squealed just a little because he wasn't holding back, and he wasn't playing politely. He didn't merely spank and get the whole thing over with. He seemed to sink into his role, reveling in her flesh. He slapped at her ass and then gripped it as though he could hold the heat in. He parted her cheeks, and from his primal growl, she thought he liked what he saw there. His hand would trace down the line of her spine before jumping out and slamming down again. He kept her on edge, waiting to see what he would do next.

"You're not thinking about anything but me now." The satisfaction in his voice let her know it wasn't a question. He spanked her, five times in rapid succession. She'd lost count, but he hadn't. She felt strangely relaxed. Her submission had somehow given her permission to enjoy this in a way she couldn't have before.

He stopped, frustrating her completely. His hand dipped lower. "I can smell you."

She breathed in, and the room smelled like sex. She was so wet, wetter than she'd ever been in her life. Jake's hand teased at the edges of her pussy, dipping in and retreating.

"Jacob, please. I've never wanted anything the way I want this."

"What do you want, Serena? Be very specific."

"I want you." She wanted him, and she wanted Adam, but Adam wasn't here right now. It was just the two of them, and Jake was so close. It seemed wrong to not get closer. She wiggled, trying to tempt his finger inside. It wouldn't be enough. She knew that. She would just want more, but anything was better than the slow tease he was giving her now.

He slapped her ass, once on both cheeks. "Don't you try to control this. This isn't yours to command. It's mine. And I asked you to be specific. What part of me do you want? Do you want this finger?"

A single finger played at her pussy, whirling around and sinking deep. Serena gasped.

"Is that all you want? You want me to finger fuck you?"

If she said yes, it might be all he did. He was forcing her to ask for what she wanted. He wouldn't let her off easy. It was a part of the exchange for Jake. He wanted to hear it from her. It also forced her to accept responsibility for her actions. It made her Jake's partner. "No. I don't want your finger."

She wanted more. She wanted everything.

He pulled his finger free. She whimpered, missing its warmth. She heard him suck the finger into his mouth. "Fuck, baby, you taste so damn sweet. Maybe you want my tongue. Do you want me to eat your pussy? Do you want me to lick your clit and suck it into my mouth? Do you want me to shove my tongue up your cunt and fuck you that way?"

She shivered. He smacked her ass again, but he was playing now. Her discipline was over, but the torture wasn't. The idea of Jake's mouth on her pussy lit a fire in her, but that wasn't what she wanted, either. Not now.

"Answer me." He slapped at her thigh.

"No. That isn't what I want."

"Tell me, Serena. Tell me what you want." He moved, pulling her off his lap. She found herself on her knees between his legs, looking up at him. His face was flushed, his shoulders squared. He looked so dominant and masculine that her eyes slid away. His hand came up, tilting her chin to face him. "You tell me what you want. Don't you mince words with me."

She was breathless. She'd never once felt so powerless and yet safe. "I want your cock, Jacob. I want your cock inside me."

"Fuck." He stared at her. "We shouldn't. I shouldn't. I'm not good for you."

He couldn't back away now. Not when she was so close. "Shouldn't I decide that? I told you what I wanted. I told you my requirements. I'm not asking for a ring, Jake. I'm not even asking for a collar."

He leaned toward her. "But if you keep this up, baby, that's exactly what you're going to get. You're going to get my collar around your neck. You're going to get my cock so deep in your pussy that you won't remember what it feels like to not be full of me. I'll be on you five times a day, and I won't ask politely. I'll take you because you're mine. I'll take your pussy and your ass, and I'll fuck that mouth of yours. I'll spank your ass when you get out of line, and sometimes I'll just do it for fun. I'll tie you up. I'll spread you wide. I'll parade you around naked because you will belong to me. Mine, Serena. Can you begin to imagine how fucking possessive I'll be?"

It might have scared her, just a little, but he had Adam to balance him. Adam, who took such tender care of her. Adam, who'd been topping her so gently she hadn't even noticed. There was a delicate balance between the two of them. Take one without the other and the relationship might fail, falling into outrageous possessiveness for Jake and overindulgence on Adam's part. But together, they were exactly what she needed, craved.

"I think I can handle you, Jake."

His hand sank into her hair, pulling lightly but with just enough bite to let her know he was serious. "What do you call me when I'm topping you?"

This was where Jacob truly enjoyed dominating. He wanted her submissive in the bedroom. She'd noticed that he preferred to remain in the background most of the time, silently supporting and protecting, but he wanted to be utterly in charge when it came to this.

"Sir. I am sorry, Sir. I can handle you, Sir."

"You think so now, but you better be sure, Serena. You better be fucking sure." His hands went to the ties of his leathers. "Take my cock out. I can't resist. I need you, baby."

The way he fumbled made her heart ache. He was nervous about sleeping with her? He was practically a Greek god, but the fine tremble in his hands marked him as a man, and that warmed Serena. She placed her hands over his and slowly untied his laces. She pulled back the leather and realized she wasn't the only one not wearing underwear. Jake's cock sprang free, and he hadn't been joking. He was huge, long and thick, and topped with a plum-shaped head. A drop of pearly fluid seeped from the tip.

Jake looked down at her, his face hard with desire. He nodded toward his dick. "Taste me."

She wasn't good at this, but suddenly that was okay. Jake would tell her what he wanted. He wouldn't lie there silently and then complain that she didn't know what to do. He would talk to her. She leaned forward and licked the drop of fluid. It was salty and tangy and elicited the sweetest groan from his chest.

"That's right, baby. Lick me. Lick my cock. Get me ready to fuck your little pussy. Get the Dom hard so he can make his sub howl."

She loved the dirty talk. It was almost as arousing as being skin to skin with him. She breathed in the scent of his arousal as she licked her way up his cock. She started at the base, where the stalk met heavy balls. She brought her hand up to cup him, playing and squeezing lightly as she ran her mouth along his dick.

"Suck the head."

She moved to the cockhead, pulling it into her mouth. She let her tongue find the deep *V* on the backside of his cock.

"Fuck, yeah, baby. That's what I want." His hands tangled in her hair, pulling her in, showing her what he wanted. "Deeper. I want to fuck your mouth, Serena."

She relaxed and tried to take him deeper. He filled her, fucking into her mouth in short strokes. She ran her tongue every way she could.

He pulled out suddenly. "I can't wait. Fuck it. I can't wait."

He stood and shoved his leathers off, tossing them to the side. He took her hand and gathered her to him. He twisted her around so her backside pressed against his front. She gasped when she saw the mirror. It was large and faced the bed. She had noticed it briefly when she'd entered, but now she could see that Jake had been watching. He'd watched as he'd spanked her and as she'd taken his cock in her mouth.

"Look at how pretty you are, baby. Look at those tits." He cupped them, his thumbs flicking at the nipples.

She looked different. She'd always hated her body, but she seemed to be a different woman. This woman was sexy, wanton, desired. Jake's hands were large on her body. He towered over her. His hand ran down the length of her torso to her pussy. There was no way to hide the glistening moisture that coated her femininity. Jake's fingers slid easily through her labia, parting the petals and forcing her clitoris to poke out of its hood.

"Your pussy is pretty, too." His eyes caught hers in the mirror, holding her in his dark gaze.

She was drowning, and she liked it. She pressed her pelvis up, begging him for more. He nipped at her earlobe.

"You're going to be so hard to handle." He turned her again, his mouth slamming down on hers. He forced her jaw open, his tongue invading. She wrapped herself around him, hands skimming the hard line of his muscles. He was cut everywhere. And strong. He was so strong. He dominated her with ease and yet his hands could be so gentle. They skimmed her backside, tracing her curves and making her skin light up. He moved her backward, her knees hitting the edge of the bed.

She found herself on her back, looking up at Jake. He stroked his cock. God, it was so big and it would be inside her soon. He reached over to the small dresser and grabbed a condom. He rolled it over his dick.

"Be sure, Serena. I won't be able to let you go."

She reached for him.

"I warned you. Don't you dare say I didn't warn you." He climbed on the bed, pushing her back, pressing her legs open. His cock was at the edge of her pussy. "Take me, Serena. Take me inside."

She groaned as that big cock began to force its way inside her. She bit her lip. Big. He was so big. His thumb found her clit, pressing against the little button. Pleasure began to swirl in her system combining with the feel of Jake fucking her in short, easy strokes.

"It's all right, baby. You're tight. You're so fucking tight, but you were made for me. You were made to take my cock." His eyes were half opened, head turned down. "Look at it."

He moved his hand out of the way so she could look down her body and see the place where his cock disappeared into her pussy. He moved his hips, pulling out almost all the way. She could see the length of his cock, covered in her juices. It was intimate, binding her to him in a way mere sex couldn't. Jake forced her to be in the moment, to bear witness to her own awakening.

He groaned as he pushed in again, gaining ground with each long thrust. Her knees were spread wide. He wouldn't accept anything less than her being fully opened and exposed to him. Sex before had been a quick thing. Easy on, easy off. Wham, bam, leave you frustrated ma'am. But this was something completely different. This was something like her fantasies. She could feel Jacob and not just his cock. She was connected to him, meshing into him until she forgot where she ended and he began.

"I want you to come for me." He pressed deep, locking them together.

Oh, she was so full. He stretched her, but she'd been ready for him. He'd made sure of it. He'd warmed her up with the spanking and played with her. He'd talked dirty and sweet. She accepted him for all that he was.

"Wrap your legs around me. God, Serena, you're so fucking tight."

She loved his weight on top of her. She was deliciously crushed into the mattress. He kissed her, holding himself deep inside, and she took the time to adjust to his size. She wrapped her legs around his waist, locking her ankles together. He drugged her with kisses, grinding his pelvis against hers, lighting up her clit. Over and over he hit it, bringing her close to the edge and then hauling her away. It was maddening, and she tried to move, to force him to fuck her, but he was too big. She was utterly powerless against his strength.

"You're going to get another spanking, baby. Don't you move. I'm enjoying this."

He was torturing her. She couldn't breathe. She was so close.

"How long since you had an orgasm?" His words came out in a deep rumble, as though he was trying to hold on to his control.

"I use a vibrator sometimes," she admitted. Why was he still talking? Was he trying to make her crazy? She tightened her legs around him.

"How long since you had an orgasm from a cock in your pussy?" He started to thrust again, little shallow moves that slid across some magical place deep inside. "There it is. There's your sweet spot, baby. How long since you had a lover hit your sweet spot?"

She gasped. It felt so good. Pressure was building. She felt like a bottle of champagne waiting to bubble over the minute her cork got popped. "I didn't know I had a spot."

Oh, but Jake had found it. He thrust up hard. "Your husband was an asshole. I won't make the same mistake, Serena. I'll make you mine, and I'll keep you."

And he was off. He didn't hold back. He fucked into her hard, hitting that spot and grinding down on her clit. Over and over he thrust, his face contorting with the effort. He was so beautiful to her as he worked over her body. She couldn't breathe. It was starting. Something amazing. Bigger than ever before.

"Say it, Serena. Say you're mine."

She could barely think, but she managed to say it. He needed to hear it. "I'm yours, Jake. I want to be yours."

He came off his leash. He pounded into her, and she went flying, the orgasm overtaking her, lighting up every inch of her flesh. Jake's gorgeous face contorted, and he thrust deep one last time.

He collapsed on top of her, sinking in, his mouth nuzzling her neck. "Now you've done it, baby. Now you're all mine."

She felt a smile start to cross her face, but then she caught sight of a man standing by the door. She screamed a little, her heart thumping in her chest.

"Sorry," Adam said, his face a polite blank. "I didn't think anyone could sneak up on Jake. He was always the one with the best hearing in our unit. Guess he was involved in other things. I finished up early. The rest of the programs can run overnight, and we should have an answer in the morning. I thought you two would want an update."

Jake sat up, his chest still heaving. "Adam, I am so sorry. I lost control."

"You never lose control, Jake. I know that about you," Adam replied.

Serena pulled at the sheet, covering herself up. She was suddenly very aware that Adam had watched them. At least he'd watched the last part. He'd been watching when she'd screamed out in Jake's arms. But wasn't that what he'd wanted? "I don't understand what's wrong."

Adam shook his head. "Not a thing, Serena. It's fine. I'm sure you'll be really happy with Jake."

"What?" Confusion set in. She'd been sure this was what Adam had wanted. He'd been pushing her together with Jake for a week. "I don't understand."

Adam smiled, but it was a bitter thing. "Oh, but I do, sweetheart. Good luck with him. He can be hard to handle. I'll let Liam know that he can take my place. Or hell, you can handle the whole op since you're the big bad Dom."

"Adam, calm down." Jake practically growled.

"You don't fucking top me, Jake. Screw you. Ten fucking years and this is how it ends." He opened the door and slammed it, the crash clanging through the room with a thud of finality.

"Why is he so mad?" All of the joy that had come with making love to Jake had fled. She was right back to feeling vulnerable.

"Because he's an asshole who wanted to be first. Get dressed, Serena. We have to find him, and you're going to have to convince him you still want him. He took everything we said wrong. Goddamn it. This is my fault. I knew I should have waited." He stalked to the bathroom and closed the door.

Serena looked at it and wondered if both doors hadn't just closed forever.

Chapter Twelve

Jake stalked down the hallway after Adam. He couldn't have gotten too far.

Fuck. Fuck. Fuck.

What the hell had he been thinking? He hadn't been thinking at all. He and Adam had talked about this. Begin as you mean to go. That was their motto. Start together and let the woman bond to both of them. But Jake hadn't been thinking about that. He'd been focused on Serena. He gripped her hand, a little afraid that if he let go, she might walk away. The happiness he'd seen in her eyes was gone, replaced with utter uncertainty.

Yes, Jake knew he was at fault. And he was still seriously considering beating the shit out of Adam when he found him.

"Hey, was I not supposed to send Adam back?" Glen asked. He'd been a monitor at Sanctum since Ian had opened the club. He knew all about Adam and Jake's proclivities. Jake couldn't blame him. It was what they did. They shared women.

"Don't worry about it. Which way did he go?"

Glen pointed toward the bar. Of course. Adam would head straight for the Scotch or the vodka or whatever the hell else was trendy this week. He was being an asshole.

"Maybe I should go change." Serena struggled to keep up with him.

He slowed down. Adam wasn't the only one making an ass of himself. Serena was unsure and scared, and she'd just had her first sex in years and what had her Dom done? Her Dom had shoved her into her clothes and made her race through the club.

He groaned and pulled her close. "Serena, baby, I'm sorry."

Her head shook against his chest. "It's my fault. You said we shouldn't do anything."

"No. It was bound to happen. And Adam will come around. He's just pissed, and he's pissed at me." *He better be pissed at me.* If Adam was mad at Serena, then they really would fight. He kissed her forehead. They should still be in bed. He should be cuddling her close. Hell, Adam should have tossed off his clothes and climbed in with them.

"I don't know about that," she said sadly. "I screw up a lot."

He tilted her head up. "No. Not this time. You were perfect, baby. Don't you forget that. And you're mine. Mine and Adam's. Don't forget that, either. Go and get dressed, and we'll take you home. I gotta warn you. He's going to want equal time."

Adam would most likely take more than equal time, but Jake was willing to give it. He'd fucked up. And he'd do just about anything to see Serena smile again.

She shook her head. "He doesn't seem interested now. It doesn't matter. I would really like to head home. I'm tired."

He held his temper in check. It wasn't directed at her. He kissed her again. "Serena, I meant what I said before. We're together now. I won't allow you to pull away because it got a little scary. Now go and change. We'll all talk when we get home."

She nodded, but there didn't seem to be a lot of hope in her eyes. She walked into the locker room. Jake turned and found his quarry. Adam was standing in the bar, talking to Liam. He was probably telling Liam how he could take over his assignment now that Jake had stolen the girl. Drama queen. *Goddamn it.*

Adam didn't even look up as Jake walked into the bar area.

"So you'll need to coordinate with Jake," Adam was saying.

"You, fucker. Do you have any idea what you just did to her?"

He knew he should start with apologies, but that sad look on her face was too fresh in his mind. She was in the locker room all alone because Adam hadn't been able to hold his own fucking feelings in.

Adam turned his face up. "I certainly know what you just did to her. Let's see. You fucked her. You claimed her. I believe your words were something like 'You're mine. All fucking mine.'"

Liam hopped off his barstool. "I am not getting in the middle of this. You two need to work this out. And Adam, I ain't taking your place. Not until Ian tells me to. This is a fucking job. This ain't about your love life. She's still in some sort of danger. Put your dick aside. You're getting paid to do a job. This is exactly why Ian told you to stay away from her."

He started to walk away. Jake got ready to lay into Adam, but Liam turned back.

"You two are supposed to be fucking partners. Fucking partners don't split because one partner did something stupid. You two better get your shit together. You have no idea what it's like to be alone. No fucking idea." Liam didn't wait for a reply. He stalked away.

Alone. Jake had been alone most of his life, even among his family. No one had understood him. He'd been that trashy Dean kid who hadn't lived in anything nicer than an apartment or Army barracks until he'd become Adam's roommate. Hell, a good portion of his life had been spent in communes or living in his dad's truck because his parents wanted to find nature or some shit. It might have been nice if his parents had paid a moment's attention to him, but they were far too busy finding themselves to deal with their kids.

Adam had taught him most of what he knew about moving through society. Adam had been his touchstone. Adam had been the first time he'd truly connected with another human being. He didn't want to sleep with Adam, but he cared about him deeply. He couldn't imagine his life without Adam. But now he couldn't imagine it without Serena, either.

"I am sorry, Adam."

"You knew how I felt about her." Adam sat back in his chair. He sounded tired.

"Yes." He probably wouldn't have moved forward if he hadn't known how Adam felt about her. It wouldn't have worked if Adam hadn't wanted her, too. "You've made it clear. And you've pushed me into her arms."

Adam's eyes narrowed. "And you damn well knew I should have been there. You want the upper hand."

Jake growled. "What fucking upper hand? You're the one who likes to play little mind games, Adam. I don't do that. I wanted her. She was naked. End of story. You're the one who pushed me to initiate her into D/s."

"That's your excuse?" Adam huffed the question out. "You were initiating her? I get put on the fucking back burner because I don't walk around with a crop in my hand twenty-four seven?"

Jake leaned over, getting into Adam's space. "She writes BDSM. What did you think would happen?"

Adam's eyes came up, narrowing. "She also writes ménage. I rather thought I would be invited to that fucking party. I didn't realize that Jacob Dean would take the woman I fell for as his sub. Ten fucking years, Jake. How many women have I been serious about? And you claim the one who might have worked. Ten years. Ten fucking wasted years."

Jake couldn't help it. He rolled his eyes. "You set this up. You pushed us together. Fuck, man, you dressed her yourself. I am sorry that I didn't wait, but it just happened, and guess what, I'm crazy about her."

"Yeah. I got that. And she's yours. I fucking got that, too."

"It was the heat of the moment. Goddamn it, Adam. You're acting like a child."

Adam threw up his hands. "Well, I guess that's just my fucking place, isn't it? It's my place to be the dumbass fuck up. It's my place to hang on to you and hope that the woman wants to lower herself to the fucking beta guy. You're in charge. I'm the metro douchebag who hangs on to your alpha-male coattails."

God, Adam's father had done a number on him. "She's crazy about you. If you'd been the one walking her around tonight, you would have been the one in bed with her."

He shook his head. "No. I wouldn't have. I would have waited for you. I could have had her in the elevator, and I didn't."

And that was the heart of the matter. Adam would have waited.

"I'm sorry. I can't say more than that. But you set her back tonight. I had her in a good place. If you had taken two seconds to think about her, you would have talked this out. Now her only sexual experience in years is coated in guilt."

He went ashen. "I wasn't mad at her. I was mad at you."

"She doesn't get that. Her husband had her thinking she fucked everything up, and you reinforced that tonight."

Adam stopped, that brilliant mind of his finally working through the problem. "But she said she was yours. I heard it. I know what I saw. I don't blame her. I didn't really get a chance, did I?"

He was like a two-year-old when he got this way. "No. You didn't take your chance. Did it occur to you to jump in bed with us?"

"No. It didn't." Adam took a long drink of the Scotch in front of him. "I understand rules and boundaries. When your best friend's girl tells him she belongs to him and only him, a decent man steps aside."

"Really? Have you told that to Sean?" Adam had spent plenty of time chasing after Grace even after she'd gotten together with Sean.

"That was different."

"Sure, it was different. That was Grace. This is Serena."

"You were in love with Grace?" A familiar voice broke through their argument.

Jake closed his eyes and wished he hadn't brought that up at all. *Fuck.* Serena had spoken the words. And she'd gotten ready far faster than he would have given her credit for. He turned and saw she was back in her frumpy clothes, her hair pulled up in a ponytail. She'd dragged her armor back on, and like a knight who didn't procrastinate, she'd come out for battle.

Adam flushed. "I was attracted to her. I was going through kind of a crappy time. I made a mistake. She's in love with Sean. She always was. She didn't want me."

Serena took a moment. Jake could see her mind working, and he was pretty sure he wouldn't like what she was thinking. "Grace is very beautiful. I can see where you would be interested. Can we go home now, Jake? Or do we have to wait for Liam?"

Jake gritted his teeth. Serena was the freaking author. Adam was the charming one. Neither one of them had a problem with communication. So why the fuck were they relying on him? He didn't even like to talk. He liked being the silent type because he never really had anything to say, but now the two people who meant the most to him were clamming up.

The two people. Serena had become important, maybe even necessary. Adam had fucking done this to him, and he wasn't about to let Adam screw this up now. If Jake let Serena walk away, it could be days before they hashed this out. Jake didn't want to wait days. He looked down at his sub. She was the weak link. She was the one behaving unlike herself.

"Ask him. You don't have any trouble asking people the weirdest most awkward questions that can pop out of your mouth. Ask him. Be brave. Be Serena."

She stopped, her eyes widening. "Be Serena? That's rich, Jake. Serena is a little mouse."

Jake scrubbed a hand through his hair. "No, she isn't. She's a fighter. She's a woman who didn't quit because her jerk of a husband told her to. She's a woman who fights for her damn place. She's a woman who doesn't stop looking for what she needs just because she finds some douchebags along the way. Damn it, Serena, I'm not cut out for this shit. I don't know how to argue. I would rather just punch things, but I'm asking you to be the woman I've spent days getting to know. That woman wouldn't let him off the hook. That woman wouldn't walk away. That woman would make him explain himself."

Adam stared at him. "That's the most words I've ever heard you use at one time."

Serena smiled up at him like he was a toddler who'd just done something good. "You are very good with words, Jacob." She went on her tiptoes and gave him a kiss, then turned to Adam. Jake was a little happy to see Adam had earned a frown. "Explain yourself, Adam."

Adam's face turned mulishly stubborn. "I don't think there's all that much to explain."

"I think there is," Serena shot back. "You put me in this position. You're the one who talked endlessly about how you and

Jake are trying to find one woman to share. You knew how I would feel about that. Were you lying? Were you just playing up to my fantasies? Did you find out I wrote about ménage and decide it was a way to control me?"

Adam's brows came together. "No. That's ridiculous, Serena. It's the truth. Jake and I have shared women for years. We really are looking for something permanent."

Serena's foot tapped against the floor. It was something she seemed to do when she got impatient. "Then why the big dramatic moment? Did you not expect me to sleep with Jacob? Does a ménage work differently in your world?"

Adam was beginning to look a little cornered. "Jacob and I agreed that we would work together."

"Fine. We screwed up. I wasn't given a schedule. You're good at that, Adam. Why don't you shoot me off a schedule of who I'm supposed to screw and when and in what position? That way I'll know." She turned on her heels and started to walk off. "I'm going home now. You two can hash this out. I can see plainly it has nothing to do with me."

Adam stared after her. "What the fuck just happened?"

Jake smiled. "I think the sub just took you down." He looked at his partner. "I am sorry. I didn't mean to hurt you, but it felt right to be with her. I wasn't trying to cut you out. She wouldn't let me. I was in Dom space. That doesn't mean I was tossing out ten years of friendship. But you seem really fast to. I have to change. Follow her. Whatever you plan to do about this, try to remember she's still in danger."

He turned and jogged for the locker room. He had a feeling Serena might take a cab if he didn't hurry.

* * * *

Adam watched Jake head off. How had he fucked things up so completely? He'd been happy when he'd found out they were in a privacy room. He'd taken the extra key from Glen and expected that he would walk in on a hot BDSM scene. He hadn't expected the tenderness he'd found.

Serena had been wrapped around Jake so perfectly that he'd just known there wasn't a place for him. The way she'd moaned Jake's name and promised that she was Jake's and Jake's alone had cut through him, slicing him to the bone. He'd been the one to recognize her. He'd been the one to try to get them all together. He should have been the one she'd clung to as he'd made her come. His gut had curled with jealousy.

And he'd made an ass of himself. Now Serena was walking away, and he had to stop her. He wasn't sure what the hell he was planning on saying, but he knew he'd better say it fast or she might try walking home. He took off for the front lobby.

She stood there, staring out into the dark parking lot. Her shoulders were hunched as though she was already drawing into herself. He'd done that to her. Jake was right about that. She'd been happy in the privacy room. She'd been passionate and uninhibited. Now she was busy putting up walls again.

He decided to start with the obvious. "Thank god. I was afraid you would leave."

She didn't look at him, simply continued to gaze through the windows. The street was dark, only a sliver of moonlight illuminating the world outside. "I'm not an idiot, Adam. I know that would be dangerous. I was just waiting for Jacob. The doors are locked and there's security. I'm safe enough standing here. I'm not going to throw myself out into the night just to prove a point."

She was standing right there, but she'd never been more distant. He'd put that remote look on her face. If he let her, she'd retreat completely. She had a whole world in her head. He'd watched her go inside, and he'd had to draw her out. If he played his cards wrong, she might stay there.

"Serena, I'm sorry about that scene." The words sounded dumb coming out of his mouth. He was smooth, damn it. He always knew what to say, but now the words wouldn't come.

She sighed, her mouth turning down. "I'm not. It's better to know now."

"Know what?" He wanted to reach out, but he doubted she would accept affection from him.

"That it wouldn't work. It's just a fantasy, Adam. It wouldn't work because people don't function like that."

"Why the hell would you say that?"

She laughed a little, but there was no humor in it. "Empirical data, as my ex would say. The first time I get really close to Jacob, you flip out. I would always be in the middle, wouldn't I? I would always be worried that I was paying too much attention to one and not enough to the other. It sounds like a dream, but I'm now realizing what a nightmare it could be."

He leaned against the window, trying to force her to look him in the eyes. "You were right the first time, Serena. I screwed this up because I'm just as insecure as the rest of the world. I heard you talking to Jake, and I suddenly wondered what the hell I can offer you."

"What are you talking about?"

She'd been so honest with him. It was time he paid her back. If this was going to work, she would have to know a few things about him. "I don't know what I can offer you. I worry that if you fall for Jake, you won't have any use for me."

"It doesn't work like that, Adam."

How little she knew. "Now I'm going on empirical data. It does work like that. I should know because the minute I proved to be a nuisance, I lost my family. I was never quite enough for my father, you see. I wasn't as strong as my oldest brother or as smart as my younger brother. And then I was useless. Serena, I don't have a family any more. My father and my brothers no longer speak to me."

She finally turned to him, concern written all over her face. She really needed a keeper. "Why?"

"Because I was given a general discharge from the Army. Do you understand what that means?"

"It means they found some reason to force you out, but you didn't do anything criminal. Who did you sleep with that you shouldn't have?"

"A woman who one of the commanding officers was crazy about. She was also a couple of ranks up from us. Me and Jake were Special Forces, but she was intelligence. She was more important, and she knew it. We were sleeping with her, but when we got caught, the charges were that we were sleeping with each other. Back then, don't ask, don't tell meant don't get caught."

Her jaw dropped open. "Your father thinks you're gay? Well, why don't you tell him the truth?"

Naïve little thing. "I tried, sweetheart. He was done with me the minute the story made the rounds. My family has a long and storied career of military service. A Miles has died in every war this country has fought since the War of 1812. He would rather I had taken a grenade to the gut in Afghanistan than get discharged. My brothers agree with him. They have their happy, vanilla lives, and they no longer acknowledge the pervert in the family."

"What about your mom?"

He wasn't sure his mom would have made a difference. He barely remembered her. She was a picture on a wall, a pretty woman who seemed so proud to be standing next to her officer husband. Would she have stood by him? He doubted it. "She died when I was five. Cancer. Dad remarried, but Justine didn't want to have much to do with us kids. We were all sent to boarding school. I didn't live at home after I was seven years old. I expected to have a long-term military career. Except I discovered I liked sharing. Apparently the Army isn't hip to what's hot in erotic romance."

Her hands came up to cup his shoulders. "Adam, I'm so sorry to hear that."

He took advantage. He pulled her in for a hug. He would take what he could get, and if her sympathy got his foot back in the door, he wouldn't feel a moment's remorse. "I never fit in, Serena. When I would go home, my dad would accuse me of being queer because I spent too much time on clothes or I liked to wear my hair longer than a buzz cut. Hell, the fact that I liked to read books made my father question my sexuality. Jake fit in better with my family than I did. I took him home with me on leave once and my dad asked why I couldn't be more like Jake. I was a fucking commando and I wasn't masculine enough for my dad. He accused me of ruining Jake."

"Your dad was an asshole." Jake stood behind them, dressed in jeans and a T-shirt.

"Yeah, well, it looks like it runs in the family." Adam took a deep breath and pulled away, looking down into Serena's eyes. "I fucked up. I can't top you the way Jake does. I don't want to. I prefer to do the small things. I'm not this badass Dom."

She looked up at him, her eyes warm again. She pushed back his hair, her fingers running through it with affection. "I don't want you to be. I want you to be Adam. I want you to plan my day and force me to eat something I didn't microwave. I want you both for different reasons, but I'm scared now. I'm scared that jealousy is always going to be here."

"I had a bad moment, Serena. I don't have many of them." He looked back at Jake. "Have I ever acted like this over a woman in the whole time we've been sharing? What would I have done if I'd found you screwing Grace?"

Jake moved behind Serena, trapping her between their bodies, proving that his instincts were always spot on. "You probably would have done a happy dance, but then I knew Grace wasn't the one for us. I can't say the same about this one. And I think that's the problem. You know she's right for us. You're worried she's going to choose between us and that you'll come up on the losing end."

"I won't choose." Serena's mouth firmed into a stubborn line, but Adam noticed that she didn't try to get away. She sort of snuggled in as though she knew it was exactly where she belonged. "I won't come between you two. Adam, you better make the decision. I can't handle another scene like that one. And I can't spend all my time worried that I'm pissing one of you off."

Jake leaned in, rubbing his cheek against her hair. "I think we can work it out. Now, can we take this home?"

Adam liked the sound of that. And he rather liked Serena's pretty little house. He had a house of his own purchased with trust fund money his father hadn't been able to touch, but Serena's house had character. He should start slowly moving his and Jake's things in. By the time the assignment was over, they would have firmly established themselves in Serena's life and her home and she wouldn't even realize it until it was too late and he'd put a ring on her finger and Jacob had put a collar around her neck.

Stealth. Stealth would win this particular battle. It had already worked with Jake. Adam looked down at Serena. He had some serious groveling to do. Luckily, he was good at it. He leaned down and brushed his lips against hers, happy that she didn't pull away. "I'm sorry, sweetheart."

She sniffled a little, but her smile was bright. "Okay. Don't do it again. I asked Jake to just be honest with me. I can handle a lot. I'm not fragile. I want honesty, and if you decide to leave, I want some kindness."

He wasn't going to leave, so that was an easy promise.

They broke apart, Adam taking Serena's hand. Jake opened the door to the club, and they all walked outside. The night air was slightly cool and the parking lot was darker than it usually was. When they had arrived, the whole thing had been lit up. Sanctum was a small club. It was also private. There was no neon sign pointing the way in. Ian had bought and renovated an old warehouse. From the street, it looked like an industrial space. The parking lot was blocked off to anyone who didn't have the code, but it was on the street. It would be easy to walk into. Especially if it was dark.

"Is the light out?" Jake asked, looking up at the streetlights. It appeared the whole lot was dark.

Adam looked up and down the street. It was usually relatively quiet at this time of night, but it felt dead silent now. Every now and then a car would pass, but they were on a side street. Ian preferred it. It was less conspicuous. Adam caught sight of the SIG Jake always carried. He reached into his shoulder holster and pulled his own. Something was off.

"What's going on?" Serena asked, her voice a mere whisper.

Even that was too much for Jake. He held his hand up in a single fist, silently telling Adam to go as quiet as possible. Jake pointed to himself and then made a circle with his fist. He was going to do a sweep, but he wanted Adam to remain here. Adam nodded then pulled Serena closer, his hand around her waist. He leaned over, putting his mouth to her ear.

"It's probably nothing, but you stay close to me. Jake is going to check everything out." Adam was well aware that his job was to protect Serena. If Jake caught sight of something funky, he would give Adam the signal to hustle her back inside while he investigated.

Adam had learned long ago to trust Jake's instincts. Those instincts had saved their whole platoon on more than one occasion.

Serena nodded, but stayed quiet. It seemed her instincts were good, too.

Jake did a perimeter sweep, moving cautiously and in complete silence. He checked behind every car in the small lot. He was meticulous, glancing inside every single one before stopping in front of Serena's Audi. It had just come back from the shop that morning, and she'd been so happy. Adam had convinced Jake to take it out. He hadn't been able to convince Jake to let Serena drive. Jake pulled the keys out of his pocket and opened the trunk. He shut it and then looked in the windows. Finally he gave the all clear.

"We're good?" Serena asked. It sounded as though she'd been holding her breath.

Adam gave her a little squeeze. "We're good. It's all right. We're just being a little paranoid."

Her hand was shaky when he reached for it. He held his weapon to his side, hoping that if she couldn't see it, she might forget that she needed an armed guard. He wouldn't. His blood practically boiled. He had to find this asshole so he never had to stand in a fucking parking lot worried about someone trying to kill his girl again. He checked his anger. Serena needed calm. She needed to know they were in control.

"Why don't you get in the back with her?" Jake phrased it as a question, but Adam knew an order when he heard it. And he agreed. If anything happened, he could cover her with his body. "I'll call Ian from the road and tell him to pay his maintenance company better. Those lights should be working."

Jake pushed the button and unlocked the door. Adam opened the back and moved to allow Serena to get in. She was almost through the door when he heard it. A hard rattle came from the backseat, the sound menacing, deadly. Without a second thought, he pulled Serena back, jerking her by her elbow. She hit the ground behind him with a thud and a little shriek, but Adam couldn't help her. He had to deal with the goddamn fucking snake that was rearing up in the backseat.

"Is that what I think it is?" Jake asked.

Adam couldn't answer. The snake reared, and Adam took his shot. The sound boomed through the night, but his shot had proven true. The snake's head was gone, and Serena's car would have to go right back to the shop.

And the stalker had just gotten more dangerous.

Chapter Thirteen

Serena shivered despite the warmth of the conference room.

"Here, sweetheart, drink this." Adam put a cup of coffee in front of her. Since the minute he'd killed the snake, he'd been all over her. Adam had carried her back into the club, though she'd protested that he'd already killed the snake and there probably weren't more in the parking lot. He'd sat with her, his arms around her shoulder, as Jake had called the police. Ian Taggart had shown up and started issuing orders to the staff, who had the lobby looking perfectly vanilla in under five minutes.

It was a good thing, too, since the police had shown up ten minutes later.

Someone had put a rattlesnake in her car. Someone had tried to kill her.

Edward Chitwood walked in, notepad in hand. He was dressed in a suit, but his partner looked like he'd been called away from home. He had his badge around his neck, but he was in sweatpants and a hoodie. He didn't seem happy to be here.

"Sorry to have to see you again like this, Ms. Brooks." Chitwood had been nothing if not ridiculously polite. He had an air of superiority, but he was always scrupulously courteous with her.

And he kind of gave her the creeps. "It's a bad situation."

"Yes, it is," Hernandez agreed. "And it seems to be getting worse. This is twice in one day. We barely got the call about the books someone sent you and then this. Someone seems to have it in for you."

He placed obvious emphasis on the word "someone," all the while pointedly looking at her.

Serena pushed the coffee away. She felt sick to her stomach. Just an hour before, she'd been in Jake's arms and the world had seemed a warm and happy place. Now she was reminded of its brutality.

"Did you check for prints on the car?" Adam asked.

The door swung open again and Jake entered, followed by Ian Taggart. Jake sat down on the other side of her while Ian Taggart loomed over the proceedings like a large predator waiting to decide who to eat for dinner.

"Of course we'll check for prints." Hernandez leaned forward, looking right at her. "Do you have any idea who called the press? There's a news van sitting right outside this place."

No wonder Ian looked ready to kill. *Damn it.* Ian Taggart seemed to be a man who enjoyed his privacy. He wouldn't like news crews lining up in front of his underground sex club. She was causing him an enormous amount of trouble. Would he drop her as a client? Would Jake and Adam hang around if no one was paying them to? How could they? She would need to leave town. She might have to change her name.

"Serena." Jake's harsh tone pulled her out. He gave her a faint smile and then turned back to the cops. "She does this thing where she kind of checks out when she's panicked. I think it's an author thing. They asked you a question, sweetheart."

Question. Yes, they had asked about the press. She wiped her eyes. The last thing she wanted was her trouble to be splashed across the papers. "I don't know. I certainly didn't call anyone."

Adam leaned forward. "She hasn't called a damn person. She's been in shock. I've been with her the whole time."

Chitwood waved him off. "Calm down, Mr. Miles. We're not accusing her of anything. Now, let me give you an update. We can print the car, but I don't know what it's going to tell us. The car came out of the shop earlier today, right?"

She nodded. "So anyone in the shop could have touched it."

Chitwood tapped his pen on the face of his notepad. "Yes. I hate to tell you this, Ms. Brooks, but it's going to be very hard to figure out who should or shouldn't have left a print on your car. The car has also been sitting in a parking lot in the middle of the city. That makes things harder than if it had been in your garage the whole time. I'm a bit confused, though. Did you say the car was locked?"

Jake sighed. "I went over this. I opened the car. I opened the trunk first, and then I unlocked the doors. Adam opened the back passenger side, and that's when we found the snake."

It seemed surreal. A snake. She'd never seen a snake up close where there hadn't been glass in between them. But someone had handled it. Someone had risked being bitten because it was more important to hurt her than to be safe. She felt so distant. She knew they were talking, but it seemed to come from far away.

"I'm just interested in how this person might have gotten around your car's security system." Chitwood wrote something on his notepad.

"I could do it," Adam replied. "I'm sure there are a lot of people out there with the technical skills. You cops have to deal with this crap all the time. You know a criminal with purpose can get through just about anything."

Hernandez stared a hole through her. "Or someone has a key."

She felt her face flush.

Chitwood stopped writing and looked up. "Does someone else have a key, Ms. Brooks?"

"No one else has a key," Adam said, and then he sighed. "Bridget or Chris?"

"Bridget is too disorganized. I left one with Lara. I sometimes lose things. I had two sets from the dealership and a valet key. I gave Lara the extra set. But she wouldn't do this. The only way she would touch a snake is on a pair of Manolo Blahniks." They couldn't possibly think that Lara was involved.

The two cops exchanged glances. She could tell immediately that they didn't believe her. They had decided that she was using them to further her career at the beginning of the investigation, and nothing had happened to deter them from it. They weren't going to change their minds until they had a body on their hands.

Chitwood smiled, an unctuous little expression. "That can certainly be cleared up with a simple phone call. Don't worry about it. I'll call her myself tomorrow. Now, we have animal control determining the breed of snake."

"It rattled. I think it's safe to bet it was a fucking rattlesnake," Jake said, his voice low.

"There are many different varieties of rattlesnakes, Mr. Dean," Chitwood pointed out. "I would like to know the breed. I would like to know if it's common or rare. Perhaps it was bought from a store that specializes in reptiles. There might be a money trail to follow."

"Of course, it could all be normal. You know we do have snakes in Texas," Hernandez said. "Sometimes they find their way into cars."

Serena shook her head. "I can tell you what kind it was. It was an eastern timber."

"You're an expert on snakes?" Chitwood adjusted his tie.

"I'm an expert on my own work," Serena replied, her voice a flat monotone. She was sure what she told them next would do nothing but confirm their suspicions about her. "In *Sweetheart in Chains*, I had a scene where the bad guy slipped an eastern timber rattlesnake into the hero's car."

"Shit," Jake muttered under his breath.

"I really kind of wish I hadn't written that particular scene now. Next time I'll make it a fluffy bunny. It seemed so exciting when writing it, but it was actually quite terrifying." She looked at Adam, who had come so close to that snake. He'd pushed her backward and taken her place. If he hadn't been there, she would have surely climbed in and been bitten, possibly multiple times. "Did I thank you?"

His hands squeezed hers. "No, but it's all right. You can make it up to me later." Adam yelped a little as Ian's hand came out and swatted him on the head.

"Forgive my employees, officers," Ian said. "They're the best in the business, but they can be a little unprofessional at times."

Adam frowned back at Ian. "Hey, I very professionally shot that snake."

"He did. He didn't girly scream or anything." Jake shot him a smug grin.

Adam's middle finger came up, pointing directly at Jake. "As if."

Jake shrugged. "I can still hear the screaming you did on that op in South America."

"I got caught by a twenty-nine-foot anaconda. Fucker broke two ribs and I still managed to finish the mission."

"And you still screamed like a girl."

"Shut up, both of you," Ian said.

Jake stood up. "I don't see why, boss. It's obvious they aren't going to help. They've made up their minds."

Chitwood stood as well. "That's not at all true, but we do have to look at all the angles. This isn't cut and dried. Usually in stalker cases, the stalker lets the victim know who he is. He wants the victim to fear him in particular. This is different. This person seems to have a point to make. He seems to want Ms. Brooks to understand that what she's doing is wrong. His words, of course. Now, I understand you're looking at the CCTV footage? Do you have anything on it yet? We couldn't find any matches."

"I'm playing around with the software, trying to refine it," Adam explained. "I should know if it works in the morning."

"If you get anything, we expect you to share it with us," Hernadez stood and stretched. "I know you guys are professionals, but it's obvious that you're personally involved. I don't want any vigilante justice."

"It might be the only justice we get," Adam said, earning him another slap on the head. "Damn it, Ian. Stop it."

"I will when you stop saying dumb shit in front of the cops." Ian walked to the door and opened it. "Officers, I thank you for your time. I assure you, the press has been dealt with. The news vans are gone. The only story that will run tonight will feature one of my employees and her encounter with a snake. It will be explained away as she and her boyfriend must have picked it up when they went fishing. If the station runs the story at all, it will be nothing but a minor, humorous story."

"You're very good at manipulating people, aren't you, Mr. Taggart?" Chitwood frowned at him.

"Remember that." Ian closed the door behind them. He turned back. "Those two are useless. They think she's working the system, and nothing is going to change their minds. Adam, how close are you to being comfortable with the CCTV shit?"

Serena took a deep breath. "You still believe me?"

Ian shrugged. "Serena, you're the client. I'm asking you right now. Are you playing some sort of game that's gone wrong? Did you start this and someone else is finishing it? Tell me right fucking now because it's the only way I can protect you."

It was the first time anyone had just asked her flat out. She really appreciated it. "I didn't have anything to do with it. I don't know what's happening. I'm really scared."

Ian Taggart's face softened slightly. "All right, then. Don't worry about the cops. This is our op. We'll take care of you." His eyes narrowed as he looked at the men in the room. "Besides, I get the feeling you're part of the family now. You fuck her, Jacob?"

Jake sat back in his chair, a little smile on his face. "Yep."

Adam frowned. "I haven't yet."

"Dear god, Serena, fuck Adam. He'll sulk until you do." Ian opened the door. "And keep me up to date. Liam's on his way with a new car. You two take her back to your place. Whoever this asswipe is, he knows where she lives, and he's getting more dangerous by the second. I'm having cameras installed around the parking lot. I'm sure the guests will love that, but it looks like someone cut the power to our lights. I don't like any of this."

"I can't go home?" Serena asked. Her laptop was at home. Her notes were at home. Her dog was at home.

"Give Alex your keys and the code to your alarm. He'll go and pick up a few things for you. You have a dog, right? Is it dangerous?" Ian asked.

"Not unless Alex is worried about having his leg humped," Jake shot back. "Tell him not to forget her laptop."

"Or her notebooks. Or her schedule. I haven't switched her over to a PDA yet. She's still writing shit down. And she needs her IPod with the purple ear buds. The white ones don't fit right, and she gets frustrated with them," Adam said.

He'd noticed that?

"And socks," Jake continued. "She likes her fuzzy socks. Her feet get cold."

Ian's brows climbed up his head. "Is there anything else Princess Serena needs? Would you like to pick out her panties for her?"

Jake and Adam managed to answer that one at the same time. "She's not allowed to wear panties."

Ian closed his eyes as if gathering the reins of his patience. When he opened them again, he sighed in obvious defeat. "Well at least I taught you something. Adam, I expect a call as soon as you figure anything out."

He walked out the door.

"Does everyone have to know about the panties?" Serena asked.

Adam shrugged. "I don't want Alex to waste time packing something you're not going to need. Panties are a privilege, not a right." He reached out and pulled her into his lap.

She didn't hesitate. She wrapped her arms around him, feeling safer than she had in an hour. Adam surrounded her.

"I can't go home." She knew she sounded forlorn, but she couldn't help it. It had seemed real before, but now it was super-HD-3D-Technicolor real. She couldn't go home. She had two men whose job it was to make sure she stayed alive. This was her life.

"It's all right, baby," Jake said, his hand in her hair. "We're not going anywhere."

She clung to Adam and prayed Jake was telling the truth.

* * * *

Adam took the bag from Alex's hand and stepped aside as Mojo trotted in. Alex had brought everything they needed, including the laptop he'd left at the club. It was still on and still running its program. Adam quickly went and plugged it in, unwilling to lose the data.

"That dog is useless," Alex said, a glimmer of a smile on his face as the big mutt wagged his tail. "He barked once when I walked in. I told him to stop it in a slightly deeper than normal voice, and then he followed me around with his tail between his legs. He's a sub dog. How did she find a sub dog?"

"I think like attracts like in this case," Adam murmured, petting the dog.

"Is she okay?" Alex asked.

Adam nodded. "Sort of. I think she's still in shock. Having her laptop will help. I really appreciate it, man."

"No problem." Alex stopped. "You're serious about this girl, right? Because Eve actually thinks she's a little fragile."

"She's not fragile. She's been through a lot." She was strong.

"I think Eve's worried about you hurting her."

"Why the hell would I hurt her? I'm trying to protect her." He defended himself, but he'd already hurt her once tonight.

"You throw yourself into these things without really thinking it through, and Jake can be like a cactus sometimes. I'm a little worried about what happens to her if this thing doesn't work out. This is her fantasy. She's been dreaming about this, writing about it. I'm just worried about what happens when the bubble bursts."

"It won't." Adam was getting a little sick of everyone warning him. He wasn't a kid. He was thirty freaking years old, and he knew what he wanted. He wanted Serena. He intended to have her.

Alex held up his hands in mock surrender. "Just make sure you let her down easy if the time comes. That's all I'm saying."

Alex turned and walked out the door.

"No one believes this can work." Jake stood in the kitchen archway, a glass of wine in his hand. It had to be for Serena. Jake didn't drink wine. He was a beer and whiskey kind of guy.

"Well, we know differently." Adam didn't like the hollow look in Jake's eyes. "I fucked up. You fucked up. Look at us. We're still fine. She's still here. It's going to be okay."

He had to believe that. He'd given up way too much to think that they couldn't make it work in the end.

Jake nodded. "She's still real quiet. I told her to take a shower. You need to go to her. You need to fix her. She gets in that head of hers and she won't come out."

She'd been silent on the way home, looking back out the window as her car disappeared. That car was going to be towed again, and she might not feel safe in it. It had been a symbol of what she'd accomplished, and now it was a reminder of how much life could suck. She couldn't go home. She was alone and vulnerable and probably wondering what else could go wrong. She needed to be reminded of what could go right. Gentle, sweet cajoling probably wasn't going to work.

"One of us needs to keep watch. I think she needs you more than me," Adam conceded. She needed a Dom. She needed someone who wouldn't take no for an answer when it came to her happiness.

Jake shook his head. "I had my time with her. Now you show her what we want. We want to share. Well, it's your turn, brother. Top her if she gives you trouble. It's what she wants. You can do it. She doesn't need a spanking. She just needs a firm push in the right direction to get her mind off all this shit and back where it should be. Me and Mojo will keep watch. Well, I'll watch, Mojo will likely lick his own ass. A lot."

Jake shoved the wine glass in his hand and practically pushed him toward the master bedroom. The house had five bedrooms. He and Jake each had their own. There was a large master they had set up for a relationship that hadn't occurred. He'd settled Serena into it and thought about how perfect she looked there. He would unpack her clothes in the morning and store them in the center dresser. There were three in the room, each one empty. But not after tomorrow.

For tonight, she didn't need clothes.

He could hear the shower running in the bathroom. He tried the door and found it locked, an irritating state that he wouldn't put up with. It was a simple turn lock, something to let a person know the room was occupied, nothing more. He fished a nickel out of his pocket, and with a quick turn, had the door open.

He'd gutted the bathroom when he'd bought the house. Gutted and enlarged it until it was a decadent paradise, and up until now he'd had no real reason to use it. He'd spent time on this space. A large Jacuzzi tub dominated the room, but Serena was in the glass-encased shower. Steam coated the shower and misted the whole bathroom in a haze. Through the fog, he could see her figure, her head against the tile, shoulders bent over. She let the water beat on her. Though he couldn't hear her, he would bet everything that she was crying.

Jake was right. She needed something else to focus on. He couldn't think of anything else he'd rather have her focus on than him. He pulled his shirt over his head and then went to work on his jeans. He tossed them to the side and walked to the shower. Very quietly, he opened the door. Serena turned, her eyes heavy.

"Adam. I locked the door."

"And I unlocked it."

She seemed to realize that she was naked. Her hands went to cover her breasts, but he caught them, stepping under the hot spray from the showerhead. The shower was large, built to fit three people engaged in more activities than merely getting clean.

"Adam, this isn't a good idea."

There was a weariness stamped on her face, but Adam couldn't give in. "Give me one reason."

"Because it won't work. Adam, if we don't catch this person, I might have to leave. I might have to change my name and run."

There was no way in hell he was letting her leave. "I'll catch him, Serena. You have to trust me. I'll catch him. I won't let anything happen to you, sweetheart. Jake and I will take very good care of you."

Her hair was wet, hanging down past her shoulders. He let go of her hands, but didn't move out of her space. He had zero intention of allowing her space for the next several hours. He let his eyes roam across her body. Round, firm breasts tipped with perky pink nipples had his cock jumping. He ran a hand from her shoulder to cup one deliciously decadent mound.

"Adam," she moaned his name. Her eyes half closed as she looked down his body. She wasn't thinking about the snake or the books or the fact that there was an asshole out there trying to hurt her. She was thinking about him. Jake was right. She needed this. Adam needed it, too. He needed it so badly. He needed her.

"Serena, this is my time. Jake had his time. This is about me and you."

"Is this how you want it?" Her eyes came up. She sucked that bottom lip between her teeth. "I don't know how it works. I've written a relationship like this a dozen times, but I don't know how it works in the real world."

He knew how he wanted it to work. "We don't really have to have any rules. Not that way. We won't be taking turns most of the time. We'll take you together. We'll lay you out like a feast fit for two men."

He wanted to feast on her right now. She was so sweet. He ran his hands down her body, discovering her curves. Her skin was soft and warm from the water. His cock nuzzled her belly. Yes, this was exactly where he wanted to be.

"What if I'm not enough?" Her voice shook a little as she asked the question.

"Oh, baby, that is the last thing you need to worry about." He groaned a little because he couldn't do what he wanted to do. He wanted to shove her against the side of the shower, spread her legs and let his cock slide deep inside her. But he needed to show her how much they both wanted her. He turned her around so he held her backside to his front. The hot water cascaded down her body. He put his mouth right to her ear, his voice low. "Do you want me to tell you all the ways I want you? I have to warn you, the water might go cold. The list is long."

He could see her lips tug up at the corners. "Why don't you give the highlights?"

"I want your breasts. God, Serena, do you have any idea what your breasts do to me? It makes me fucking crazy that you cover them up, but then I'm happy about it because I don't think anyone else should look at them." He plucked at her nipples again. "I want to suck on these. When Jake and I get you in bed, we'll each take a breast and suck on them until you can't stand it anymore."

She wriggled against him.

He let his hands drift up to trace the line of her lips. "I want this mouth, too. You say such bratty things sometimes that I feel the need to shove something in here."

Her tongue came out, playfully licking his fingers. "You're going to shove your fingers in my mouth?"

"See, bratty." He let her feel his cock along the seam of her ass. "You're going to get something way bigger than my fingers."

She sucked at his fingers a little. "I thought Jake was the Dom. You're not exactly talking like a vanilla boy."

He nipped at her neck. "I might not be the Dom Jake is, but don't you think for an instant that I can't top you. And there is nothing vanilla about me, baby. I'll fuck your mouth and your pussy and your sweet, sweet ass. Hell, I'll lube up those tits, press them together and fuck you like that. There won't be any part of you that I don't cover with me."

He ran his hands down to her pussy. She'd shaved as he'd asked her to. There was nothing there but hot, plump flesh. And she seemed to like it when he talked dirty.

"And what about Jake?"

He chuckled. "Jake will be filling you up, too. Tell me something, sweetheart, before Jake jumped the gun, how long had it been?"

"A couple of years, if you don't count vibrators." Her voice was breathless, catching as he explored her pussy. "I kind of do. I named mine. Though I admit that some nights I took Sam out and then got caught up in a TV show, and we just watched. So I might suck at sex since I couldn't even interest my vibrator."

God, she made him laugh. "I think your luck is changing, sweetheart. I don't think Jake had the same problem. He wasn't interested in anything but you. And I watched him at the end of it. I don't think there's any question at all that you're good at sex. Tell me something, did you enjoy your time with Jake?"

He started to gently rub her clit.

"It was amazing." Her head fell back, her body arching.

"Tell me or I'll stop rubbing."

She moaned a little but started talking. "I liked it. It was the best sex I've ever had."

He bit at her ear. "Serena, you're a writer. I expect a little more than 'I liked it.' Tell me how his cock felt. Tell me what he did. Did he spank you?"

"Yes. I disobeyed. I wore underwear."

Jake had been hard on her. "He didn't like the pretty little thong

I left? I'm surprised. I told him what I was doing. He was just looking for a reason to spank this pretty ass."

There was something about the way she hesitated that made him think he was missing something. "You did look good in the thong I bought you, didn't you, sweetheart?"

"I didn't put it on."

He stopped and withdrew his hands.

She turned, putting her hands on his chest. "Jake already spanked me."

She'd been through a lot, but he had to make a statement. "You didn't wear what I told you to wear."

She bit that bottom lip, obviously going for broke. It was cute, but it wouldn't work on him.

"Turn and face the wall, hands on the tile, legs spread wide."

Tears welled. "Adam, I'm sorry. I know it was wrong. Jake already spanked me. I'm still sore."

"I'm not spanking you. I'm doing something I planned on doing tomorrow, but now, because you openly defied me in the club with all our friends watching, you'll get it tonight."

"Oh, god, you're going to plug me."

He couldn't help it. He had to grin. "Yes, but how did you know?"

"I've written this scene, Adam. What if I don't want to be plugged?"

"Then we can end this right here and right now. I'll be as vanilla as possible, and you'll never know how it feels to have two men inside you because neither one of us will fuck your ass until you've been properly prepared." He took a hard line, but softened a little, smoothing back her hair. "The whole ménage thing is kind of dependent on anal sex. If you aren't interested, then we should rethink this. I really don't want to take turns. I would rather we take you together. I have my fantasies, too."

Her chin came up in a stubborn tilt, and she turned, placing her hands on the walls of the shower and spreading her legs. She leaned over, making her back almost flat.

"Will this do?" Serena asked.

It was an excellent position of entry. "For a virgin, you're quite informed."

She turned a little, a smile on her face. "I research."

"You researched anal sex?"

"Of course. So I know you're going to need lube. Don't try to convince me that water will work."

"Never, sweetheart." He stepped out of the shower and thanked god he was a deeply prepared man. He had lube and the plug he'd purchased just for her waiting in the drawer by the sink. He grabbed them both and stepped back into the shower. Her ass wiggled a little as she firmed her stance. He put his hands on the globes of that gorgeous ass. "Tell me how one researches anal sex."

He placed the small plug on her back just above the dimples of her ass. He opened the lube and parted her cheeks, viewing that perky little rosette for the first time.

"The normal way. I read. I watched movies."

He lubed up a finger and touched it. His cock jumped as she clenched. He rimmed her. He would have to go slowly, carefully. It was all right. He was a patient man. He was also deeply amused. "Sweetheart, the normal way to research anal is to take a cock up your ass."

"And that's how you researched it?" Serena's voice dripped with sarcasm.

"Yes, it is." He was suddenly damn happy he could answer that question in the positive. "I don't have Master rights at Sanctum, but every person with a membership has to pass a safety course. For the men who intend to engage in anal sex, that includes taking a plugging."

Her whole body shook. "So you and Jake?"

He circled her over and over, forcing the muscles to start to relax. Talking to her seemed to help. She'd settled down, the tenseness leaving her body. "Yep. And let me tell you, he whined the whole time. He's a goddamn commando, but one little plug up the old rectum had his eyes watering." He was sure everything he was telling her would wind up in a book. Jake was going to kick his ass. "And I'll go one better. Ian follows his own rules."

"Ian Taggart?"

He pressed his pinky finger in slightly, gaining ground. She didn't flinch. He was sure her mind was working through his words. "Ian Taggart wouldn't do anything to a sub he hasn't experienced himself. I might think Ian's an asshole of epic proportions half the time, but he's a good Dom. He takes it seriously. I take it seriously. Not the Dom thing, but sex. This is serious, Serena. It's supposed to be fun, but I want to take care of you, too."

Her laughter had died, a somberness taking over. "I think I would like that."

His finger sank into her ass, the muscles clenching around him. Fuck, she was going to be so tight. He wouldn't last long in the heat of her ass. He started to fuck her with his finger, slow and gentle. "I would like that, too. I've enjoyed this week. I like preparing your schedule and making sure you have what you need. How do you feel, Serena?"

Her breath came out in a ragged little burst. "Okay. It's weird. I don't know that I like it, but I don't hate it."

He pulled his pinky out, washed off in the shower, and got the plug ready. He pressed the tip to her anus and applied a little pressure, satisfied by the huff that came out of her. "This is the kind of sex that gets better with time. And a cock is different. Or so I've been told."

"You don't know?"

He stopped. "No. Despite what my father thinks, I've never taken a cock up my ass and have no intentions to."

"I was joking, Adam." Serena wiggled her ass, this time seemingly on purpose. "I have no doubt about your heteroness. I have no idea what your dad is thinking. You couldn't pass for gay if you tried."

He laughed a little. She was being incredibly sweet. He knew how he could come off at times. But he intended to make sure she never questioned his desire for her. "You say that because you haven't seen me try. Jake and I have gone undercover as lovers before."

She stood, obviously forgetting she had orders. "You and Jake?"

It was said with a breathless curiosity that had Adam smiling. "Yes. We've discovered it's an amazing way to get a woman in between us." He sobered a little. "It's also a good way to seem innocuous. When someone we've got under surveillance thinks we're gay, they get it in their head that all these muscles are about being attractive, not years of training. They discount that either of us could be dangerous."

Her eyes roamed his body, stopping on the freshest of his scars, a puckered, circular scar in the center of a neat, surgical one.

"It looks like someone didn't underestimate you." Her voice sounded small as though she was just understanding his job was dangerous.

"Oh, no, this is courtesy of a man who definitely underestimated me. He also got the jump on me because I was attempting to save Grace at the time." He caught her hand and brought it to touch the scar on his abdomen. She needed to understand. "This is who I am, Serena. This isn't my only scar. This was a bullet to the gut." He moved her hand to a silvery scar on his chest. "This I got in Afghanistan. If you look at my back, there's a knife wound from some close quarter fighting in Iraq."

She touched a small scar over his left brow. "And here?"

He smiled. "I was ten, fell down at boarding school. I think I was trying to climb over a fence I wasn't supposed to climb at the time."

"I don't care how many scars you have, Adam. I think you're beautiful." Her chin came up as though she was just daring him to deny her.

So sweet. She was beyond what he needed. She was practically perfect.

"I think you're gorgeous, sweetheart." He leaned over and kissed her, putting his mouth on hers, reveling in the way she softened under him. "Now turn around and let me do what I need to do. You want both of us, don't you? You have to know we won't take you until you're ready. We don't want to hurt you."

She nodded and turned back, finding her previous position. He could tell she was nervous by the tight lines of her body. She might have written this scene before, but she'd certainly never performed it. He was going to give her a whole new perspective. Helping Serena explore this side of herself would bind them all together. It would be the gift they gave each other.

She shivered a little. The water was still hot, so Adam chalked it up to nerves. He lubed up the plug. Once it was in, she wouldn't be nervous again. She would know that it was just a necessary discomfort, and after the first few minutes, it wouldn't even be terribly uncomfortable.

He pressed the plug to her rosette and began to work it in. He moved in little bursts, gaining an inch here and there and then pulling back, fucking her ass gently. Her back moved, her hands clenching, but she didn't protest or try to pull away.

"How are you doing, Serena?" He pushed the plug in, her anus fighting him, but slowly opening.

"I'm fine. I don't know if I like it."

He couldn't help but smile. He gained another inch, the plug beginning to sink into her bottom. "What if I told you it's an acquired taste, and once you've acquired it, you'll never want to go back. It's dark and dirty and so fucking intimate. You'll want one of us in your pussy and the other in your ass all the time."

Her breath shuddered out of her chest. "I hope so because I'm on the fence right now."

He sighed as the plug sank in. He pressed all the way in, the curves catching on her anus and holding the plug in place. The sight of the rosy plug seated deep in her ass made his cock jump again. Soon that would be a cock, and she would be full of him and Jake. But for now, he could still please her.

"Are you all right, sweetheart?"

Her head nodded. "Just do it, Adam. I can handle it."

"It's done. You're nicely plugged." He tapped the plug and watched her spine jump.

She stopped for a moment as though trying to judge the truth of his words. "Oh. I can feel that."

He tapped the end of the plug again, and she reacted by shivering and giving him a little moan. "See. Not so bad."

She stood and took a long breath. "It's not bad. I can handle it. I can." The smile that crossed her face had him grinning, too. Only his Serena would look at the act of taking a plug up her ass as a life lesson.

He reached for her hand and guided it to his cock. "Can you handle me now, sweetheart?"

Her eyes darkened as she looked down at her hand on his cock. She ran her fingertips over the head of his cock, making him shudder. Her fingers were like little butterflies on the flesh of his cock. It felt amazing, but he wanted more.

"Grip my cock, Serena." He hardened his voice. His style might be a little softer than Jake's, but he was still in charge.

Serena's hand tightened.

"Yes, that's what I want." He gritted his teeth. Fuck, she felt good and he hadn't gotten close to her pussy yet. Her hand ran from the bulb of his cock down to the base, exploring every inch of him. She had a little smile on her face, an expression of feminine power. He loved that look. It was different from the shy girl he'd met at first. This was what Serena could be when she was well loved. She would know her power, revel in it. He pressed his hips forward. "Harder, love."

She gripped his cock and squeezed a little, the firmer pressure giving him exactly what he needed. Her hand pumped as she tilted her head up, and he leaned down to kiss her. He let his tongue tangle with hers, inhaling her. He loved how soft she was. He loved her small hand working his cock, getting him ready to fuck her.

It had been awhile since he'd had sex and much longer since he'd made love with someone he cared about. Serena was everything he could want in a partner for him and Jake. She was smart and creative and needed both his care and Jake's dominance. And she needed their protection.

He pulled back. If he let her go a minute more, he wouldn't have the ultimate pleasure of sinking inside her.

"Adam?" Serena looked up at him. Her hair was so much longer when it was wet. It curled on her chest, tendrils clinging to her nipples.

He lifted her up and sat her on the shelf. Ostensibly it could be there to hold shampoo and razors, but Adam had had it custom made. It was deep and at the perfect height for shower sex. "Keep your legs spread."

He grabbed a condom and rolled it on as quickly as he could

before he stepped between her legs and lined his cock up. Her pussy was already a juicy, wet, glorious mess. He coated his cock in her arousal and pressed in.

Serena gripped his shoulders and looked down between them, her eyes round. Adam followed the sight and realized Jake had been up to his old tricks. Jake liked to watch his cock sink into a pussy. He'd obviously taught her the beauty of watching. It really was a lovely thing. Her pussy bloomed open, sucking his cock in and making a place for him deep inside her body. He groaned as her legs wrapped around his waist, and her head fell back.

"It feels so good, Adam." Her voice was a low moan. "So tight. It's like Jake's already here with us."

That's exactly what he'd wanted her to know, how good and full she could feel. And he loved the righteously tight feel of her pussy. The plug was taking up space, making her cunt into a vise on his dick. He pressed in, gritting his teeth against the pure pleasure of fucking her. He held them together. He was inside. He was finally inside her.

And he understood why Jake had said what he'd said. This was different. This was Serena.

"Mine."

"Such possessive men," she said with a breathy little sigh.

She had no idea, but now wasn't the time to explain that her life had changed. She would learn soon enough that now that she'd taken them in, she wouldn't be able to get rid of them.

Adam pulled out, the plug in her ass a sweet drag on his dick, making every inch a pure pleasure. He fucked back and then out again. In and out. In and out. The friction made his balls draw up and his spine curl. He didn't want to ever stop fucking her, but she was too tight, too sweet, too good. It wouldn't last, and he needed to make her come.

He reached down between them and fingered her clit, pressing firmly as he pushed his dick into the hilt. Serena's gorgeous eyes went wide, and she cried out as her pussy clenched down on him, her orgasm forcing his own. Wave after wave of scalding pleasure rocketed through him. He dragged air into his lungs as he held her close, coming down from the orgasmic high.

She held him, her legs still wrapped around his waist, her hands in his hair. "I think I have to clean up again."

Adam laughed, his spirits buoyed by her sweetness. "I think I can handle that, love."

Chapter Fourteen

Serena came awake, but didn't open her eyes, preferring to revel in her memories of the night before. Adam had been perfect. After he'd made love to her, he'd been so tender. He'd shampooed her hair and washed off her body. When the water had finally gone cold, he'd towled her off and then used a dryer on her hair. All she'd had to do was sip her wine and let Adam take care of her.

She'd been sleepy and ready for bed, and Adam had carried her to the bedroom after taking the plug out and promising a larger one next time. He wanted to fuck her with Jake. He'd whispered how they would take her over and over again.

Serena shifted in bed, snuggling down into the mattress. This was right where she wanted to be.

Adam had cuddled her all night long.

Where was he now?

She gave up the game. She couldn't stay in bed all day long waiting for one of them to come and make love to her, though she had to admit it sounded better than getting up and working. Really good sex could play hell on her career of writing really good sex. The problem was the real thing was way better than writing about it.

"Serena?"

She turned and felt a smile curl her lips up. Adam stood there, looking deliciously handsome. He was in his normal day wear. No sweats and T-shirts for her boy. He was in a fine-looking pair of slacks and a perfectly designed shirt. He'd left the tie off, but Serena was beginning to understand that meant they weren't going anywhere. If they had been, he would have put on a tie. God, she loved him in a tie.

She let the top of the sheet slip down, exposing her breasts. Before yesterday, she would have been deeply embarrassed. Now, she felt sexy and beautiful. She'd made love with two men. Not sex. It had been far more than that. She'd made love with them. Hell, she was falling in love with them.

Adam kept his eyes on hers. "Serena, you need to get dressed and come out and meet us in the living room."

She felt a little trepidation at his tone, but decided he was just being overly serious. Jake had chastised her the night before for being too cowardly. She was supposed to ask for what she wanted. This whole relationship thing was all about communication. "Why don't you come back to bed? Come to think of it, why don't you go and get Jake and we can start the morning right."

She wanted them both. It was her fantasy and it was so much more because these weren't some dream men. These weren't some men she'd created in her head. Jake and Adam were real. They were perfectly imperfect and that made them amazing.

Adam's eyes turned down, and Serena felt a real stir of trouble. "You need to get dressed and come out here. We've got something on the tape from the library you need to see."

Jake had been going over the footage from the libraries with CCTV. Adam had started it, and Jake had been planning on running the software to see if they could get a match. They were looking for someone who had been in both libraries at roughly the same time the e-mails had been sent. It might not give them a name, but they would have a face and a place to start looking.

Had they found the guy? Was the case over? Despite the fact that she would be damn happy to not have some asshole shoving snakes into her car, she really wasn't sure she was ready for them to leave. Would it even work?

Or was this just what they did?

"I'll wait outside for you." Adam turned and walked toward the door.

"Adam? Adam, what's going on?"

He paused at the door, and his shoulders rose and fell with his deep intake of breath. "Just get dressed, Serena. We know everything now. Just hurry so we can get this over with."

Well, that answered one of her questions. Apparently when the case was over, they weren't going to have anything to do with her. Her gut felt like someone had punched a hole in it. How could he have made love to her the way he had the night before and then stared a hole through her this morning? They knew everything. The case was over—at least their part appeared to be, and now he wanted to get the lame-ass good-byes out of the way.

Serena forced herself to move. It would have been easier if they were at her place. She wouldn't feel so out of her depths. She wouldn't be staring a long, painful process in the face. They were done with her, but she didn't have a car. Someone would have to drive her home. Should she call a cab? Or Bridget? She could call Bridget. She reached for her phone. She'd placed it in her purse before she'd gone to take a shower.

Her purse was gone.

Why had they taken her purse?

Calm down. Get through this. Maybe it's just the way Adam is. Maybe he's thinking that now that the case is over, you won't want them anymore.

Positive thinking. She always went to the worst-case scenario, and it might get her in trouble here. If she walked out there looking mopey and down and just assumed that they were done, she might make it come true.

Serena got to her feet and found her clothes, then decided on a different tactic. She needed to take a cue from Bridget. Confidence. Sometimes she thought Bridget got things she shouldn't just because she acted like it was due to her. And Adam and Jake hadn't said a thing that would make her believe they wanted this little affair to end. To the contrary, they had practically told her they wanted to live with her.

Adam had hung his shirt from the night before over the dresser. Serena put it on, buttoning it, but leaving a good amount of cleavage exposed.

She looked at herself in the mirror. Sex hair. She finally had sex hair, and she was going to leave it that way.

Whatever had put Adam in a crappy mood, she would just have to deal with it. That's what people in love did.

Oh, crap. She was in love with them. It was stupid. It was such a dumb mistake because it could never work, but she'd fallen for them both, and she would hate herself if she didn't try.

She took a deep breath. She was ready to find out who was trying to hurt her so she could move on with Adam and Jake.

Serena opened the door and wished she'd decided to be brazen some other time. Adam stood staring at her, not a hint of emotion on his face. His eyebrow quirked up.

"This is how you're going to play it?" Adam asked.

"Play what?" She was starting to get the really bad feeling that he knew something she didn't. "Is everyone else out there? I'm sorry. I thought it was just us. I'll put on actual clothes."

"It's too late for that." He reached out and grasped her wrist, pulling her forward. "Come on then, sweetheart. It's time to pay the piper for this little game you've been playing."

She dug her heels in and slipped a little, landing on her ass. Her wrist twisted in Adam's hand. Pain flared. "What are you talking about?"

His eyes, always so warm, held not a hint of heat. "Get up. I want to get this over with so you can leave."

Heat flashed through her body, humiliation making her skin flush. This wasn't about some small misunderstanding or his insecurities. He meant what he was saying. He meant every harsh word of it. He'd made love to her the night before. He'd treated her like a princess, and now that he'd had his fun, she was getting kicked out of the castle. He was the one who had played a game, and Serena was the loser.

"I'll grab my things. I need my phone so I can call Bridget to come pick me up. Is there somewhere I can wait?" She wasn't about to sit in the living room with them. She wanted to be alone. She still couldn't quite process what had happened, but the last thing she wanted was some big scene where they told her everything she'd done wrong and why she wasn't good enough for them.

His smile seemed brutally cruel. "That would be the easy way out, wouldn't it, sweetheart? I'm not inclined to give you an easy out."

He reached for her again, and she tried backing away. "Stop it."

"Stop what? Stop trying to do my job when all you can do is lie? Are you kidding me?"

"Is she giving you trouble?" Jake stood at the end of the hall, his handsome face frowning down at her. "Don't touch her, Adam. She'll probably sue us. Imagine the publicity she could get out of that. Poor little writer gets abused by her bodyguards."

"What the hell are you talking about?" She was sick of this. "Just tell me. Stop all this bullshit."

Adam started to reach for her again, but Jake's bark stopped him. "I meant what I said, Adam. You know what's going on. Don't touch her. She'll use it against you. Treat her like that snake last night. She bites and she's venomous. Now, Ms. Brooks, if you would care to follow me, I'll show you how I figured out your little scam. It might help for the next time you decide to run it. You'll be better prepared. If you don't care to know, then feel free to leave. I really don't care anymore."

He turned and walked away like he'd never held her and told her she was his. Being Jacob Dean's didn't mean much, apparently. He certainly hadn't cared enough to keep her for very long. One night. It appeared to be all she was good for.

"Would you mind telling me what I'm being accused of?" She struggled to her feet, trying to keep some small bit of dignity around her. She wasn't wearing any underwear because they hadn't given her any. She'd been playing by their rules, but she hadn't really realized it was all just a game. It had seemed so real. The words they had said had meant something to her. She'd been out of the dating scene for far too long, living in a world that only existed inside her head. Now she remembered why she'd retreated. The real world was brutal and unkind.

Adam didn't lift a hand to help her up, simply stood there as if her gracelessness was a burden. "You know what you did, Serena. You can stop pretending. We caught it all on tape."

Frustration welled. "Pretend like I'm an idiot."

He wouldn't have to pretend. She was an idiot who had fallen for their every kind word and probably well-practiced moves. How many women had they pulled the "woe is me, the world doesn't understand our needs" act on?

Finally there was a spark of emotion on his face. Unfortunately, it looked an awful lot like rage. "You set this whole thing up. God, I don't even want to look at you. I can't stand the sight of you. I can handle you pulling this shit with me. You know, if it were just me, I'd probably even forgive you, but you knew how Jake felt and you still played him."

Ah. They were back to the money and attention-grabbing fame-whore argument. Her hands shaking, she wiped at the stupid tears that kept falling. "I'd like to see this tape."

It wouldn't change anything. She knew she wasn't responsible, but she'd like to see what had caused this change. Maybe they had doctored it themselves in order to get out of a messy relationship. Maybe Adam had rolled out of bed with her and gone and exchanged notes with Jake, and they had decided she wasn't good enough in the sack to be their magical "one."

But she damn sure wanted to see that tape.

"Fine. Go change."

She wasn't about to let him tell her what to do ever again. She might not have ever been in a real D/s relationship before, but she knew one thing. She didn't owe the Doms anything now. They had broken the connection and quite brutally. They hadn't taken care of her, and that had been promised. They hadn't communicated with her, and that had been promised, too. She'd given them her submission and her body, and it seemed to her they valued neither.

"I don't think so. I'll see whatever this evidence is you have against me, and then I'll change and be out of your life. I take it you have my phone? Did you steal it after I fell asleep? You could have just asked. I would have given it to you." She would have given him anything. She had given him everything.

She was a moron who never learned, but they might just be the men who could finally teach her the lesson.

For the first time, he seemed a bit unsure, his eyes narrowing and his mouth becoming a flat line. "Jake asked for it after he figured out what was on that tape."

"Well, of course." His first loyalty would always be to Jake. She was just a girl they'd screwed around with. Deep down, she really did understand that. She'd just thought that they had let her into their tight circle.

But she would always be on the outside. Something was broken inside them, and she wasn't the woman who would be able to fix it. It had been foolish to even try.

"I can't get you to change?" His eyes were on the *V* of her shirt for a moment and then they slid away.

So, he wasn't completely unaffected. Not that it mattered. He liked breasts. He'd made that plain the night before. He liked her body, just not enough to treat her with the kindness she'd asked for.

"I thought you were in a hurry to get this over with so you didn't have to look at me anymore."

"I changed my mind. I think this can be more civilized if you're properly dressed." The words came out of his mouth in a harsh grind.

But she was done taking their shit. A cold place opened inside of her. She should have remembered that all she had were her friends. Bridget and Chris and Lara. They were the ones who would stick by her. She should have been happy with that and remembered that a vibrator couldn't break her heart.

But she could learn. "Well, it's obvious to me that none of this is going to be civilized and you change your mind an awful lot, Mr. Miles. So lead on. Let's get this scene over with."

She waited for him to move, but he seemed held in place, as though he couldn't quite figure out what he wanted to do or how to handle her.

She gave up and walked on by herself. She'd always been alone. They had just been a fantasy. The reality was that she was alone, and it was so much easier that way. She marched into the living room with her head held high.

* * * *

Jake paced. He'd been pacing all night. Lack of sleep and the horrible gaping wound in his gut were taking their toll. When would he learn? If something looked like it was too good to be true, it usually was.

Serena Brooks had gotten under his skin with her sweet smile and soft body and even softer heart.

The heart part had all been a lie. The tapes and her phone proved that beyond a reasonable doubt.

Once again, dumbass Jake had gotten played by a pretty woman. At least this one wouldn't cost him his career. It just cost him another chunk of his heart and a whole lot of pride.

Serena walked in the room wearing nothing but Adam's dress shirt. It hung down to her knees, and she'd left the top couple of buttons open so a creamy expanse of skin could be seen along with a tantalizing view of the round curve of her breasts. He fucking loved her tits. They were real, and they were so damn soft. He couldn't forget the little sound she made when he'd flicked at her nipples. She loved that.

Or had that been a lie, too? After all, she was very good at crafting fiction.

"I'd like to see the tape, please." She was so polite, but he could see that she'd been crying. And she held her right wrist up.

Had Adam hurt her? *Fuck.* He couldn't have meant to. "What's wrong with your wrist?"

"It doesn't matter. I'd like to see the tape."

Did she think she was going to get to control this? "Serena, I asked you a question. What happened to your wrist?"

Adam followed her into the room, a hollow look on his face. "I held it too tight, and she tried to get away. She fell down, and it sort of twisted. I'll get some ice."

He stalked off toward the kitchen.

"I can take care of it later. It's not that bad. If you need me to sign some sort of form stating I won't sue you for abuse of my person, I'll certainly sign it. I just want to get this over with so I can find another set of bodyguards."

God, she was going to play it out until the end. "I suppose the bodyguards make great window dressing, don't they?"

She simply stood there, waiting, not taking the bait. Her face cleared of all expression. There was simply a blank stare on her face as though he meant nothing to her. He was just something she had to get through so she could move on with her life. He hated her a little in that moment.

"Maybe you'll fuck the new guards, too."

Nothing. Not a response. Not even a blink. He wanted so much more. He wanted her to hurt the way he was hurting, but for that to happen, she would have to care about him just a little, and he knew for damn sure she didn't. Still, a little kernel of rage was stoking him on.

"You should shelve the innocent girl routine, though. Really, it gets old fast. The whole quiet and shy thing is a little boring, sweetheart. You would make a much better slut."

Her hand came out in a vicious arc as she slapped him right across the face. Pain flared and something deep inside was satisfied that at least he'd gotten a rise out of her.

"Show me the tape or I will sue all of you. Do you understand me? I won't stand here and let you talk to me like that. I know that I'm the one who put it in your head that I'm some sort of doormat, but I never did anything to deserve this from you. Now show me the tape."

Her voice shook. Everything inside Jake told him that she was being brave, that she was holding some well of sadness deep inside, and it was taking everything she had not to break down here and now. If he followed his dumbass instincts, he would pull her into his arms and promise her that everything would be all right, and he would take care of her and beg her forgiveness. But fuck it all, she couldn't explain away that tape.

"Here." Adam held out a bag of ice he'd rolled in a dish towel.

"I'm fine." Her voice was back to the flat monotone it had been before she'd slapped the shit out of him. "Give it to Jake. His face looks a little red."

Adam's eyes widened. "What happened? Holy shit. Did you hit Jake?"

"I took offense to him calling me a slut. I think he was looking out for you. He goaded me into smacking him. Now if I sue you like the greedy bitch I apparently am, he can sue me right back. Mutually assured destruction."

Adam's eyes closed, and he took a long breath before he opened them again. "Why don't we all sit down and talk this out?"

Serena shook her head. "That option is no longer on the table. It was off the table the minute you looked at me like a piece of trash this morning. There's nothing to talk about anymore, Adam. Just show me the tape and give me my phone and I'll leave."

It was exactly what Jake wanted. He wanted her out of his life. Except that the thought kind of made him want to vomit. The idea of not seeing her again was a gaping wound in his chest. He didn't really want her to walk out. He wanted her on her fucking knees in front of him, begging his forgiveness. He wanted to force her to work for it, and while he would never really forgive her, he would take her back into his bed because he was fucking addicted to her. He would screw her until she didn't have this hold on him, and then he would show her the door.

The trouble was he wasn't sure he would ever get over her. Serena Brooks had proven to him once and for all time that he hadn't been in love with Jennifer. He knew that now because he was sickeningly sure he loved Serena.

And he would just have to get over it.

He forced himself to turn and cue up the tape. Client. She was just a client who had lied and gotten caught. He had to think of her that way. He couldn't think about how good it had felt to slide into the silky heat of her body or how she'd wrapped herself around him, clinging to him like he was the only thing that mattered in the whole world.

Jake forced himself to use his most professional voice. "So you know we got the CCTV tapes from two of the libraries where the e-mail messages came from?"

She nodded, her eyes on the screen. "Yes, you were looking for someone who was at the library at the same time the message was sent. You have two libraries and two messages. If you find the same person at both libraries at the right times, you'll have a place to start."

Adam put the bag of ice down, obviously unwilling to fight with her about it. He sighed and switched the feed to the large screen. The black and white tape began playing. The important tape had come from a library in Hurst where the camera was on patrons both entering and leaving the library. "You can see that the tapes are time stamped, so we were looking at the hours before and after the e-mail was sent. It can be hard to catch faces, but I set us up with some really advanced facial recognition software. It looks for similar facial structures based on math. I set it to run before we went to bed."

He'd set it to run before he'd gone and fucked Serena's brains out. Now Jake wished he'd been a little less giving. He could have forced his way in. Adam would have let him. He could have had one more night with her.

"Here it is." He slowed the tape down.

"I don't recognize that person." Serena peered down, her eyes narrowing on the lone figure. The person, obviously female, walked into the library, a huge bag on her shoulder. She wore sunglasses, her figure hidden by a long coat. She stopped in the middle of the lobby and pulled out her phone. She pushed the sunglasses off her face. She smiled as she placed the call, her face turning right toward the camera.

Jake studied Serena carefully, and he felt a punch to his gut as her eyes widened and her mouth dropped.

"That's Lara." Her hand came up over her mouth, covering it. She shook her head. "You're wrong. This doesn't prove anything."

"She showed up at the Irving library, too." He held up her phone. "Would you like to know who she's calling here?"

Serena had gone stark white, all the color draining from her skin. "I'm sure it was me. It has to be, right?"

"You don't clean off your messages." Jake pushed the button and the message played.

"Hey, Serena, babe, it's me. Look, I know you're worried about the promo for the new *Sweetheart* book, but I promise you I have it all taken care of. I did exactly what you told me to. It's a little unorthodox as promos go, but hey, you're not exactly writing sweet

Regency romances. I think you're right. This will work. I'll set it all up. Talk to you later."

Serena's whole body seemed to droop. Her shoulders slumped, and her head hung a bit as though some force had been animating her and now it was gone. "You won't believe me, but that message was about a signing I'm doing at an adult toy store to promote the new book. I had to talk her into it. She thought it would be trashy, but I thought it would be fun. I even talked to a friend who makes naughty cupcakes. She's catering it. But it doesn't matter. I'll just go now."

She started to turn away. Jake didn't like the way she looked. He'd seen the same blank, glassy stare on victims of trauma. When he'd been in the service, he'd seen the exact vacant look in the eyes of men and women who'd just had their houses blown up by a bomb. It was as though they couldn't really process the horror of what had just happened.

She seemed a little dazed and unsteady on her feet. For the first time since he'd seen that damn video, he felt uncertain about just what he'd witnessed.

"Serena, do you need help?" He wasn't going to let her fall over no matter how angry he was with her. God, just looking at her was making his heart hurt, and for the first time he had to really consider the fact that he might have to forgive her. Really forgive her because she had become necessary. He started to reach out. She needed to get ice on that wrist.

"Don't touch me." She stepped away, her jaw clenching. "Don't ever touch me again."

"Serena, would you like to explain yourself? I'm willing to listen." Adam's voice came out on a shaky breath, as though he knew he was walking a tight rope, and he was pretty sure he didn't want to fall off.

"Listen? You're willing to listen? Fuck your listening, Adam because I've been listening to both of you, and I don't like a word I've heard." Her fists were clenched at her sides, her face a deep red. She was crying again, the tears running down her cheeks. She looked young and vulnerable and so fucking fragile in Adam's shirt and those glasses she hid behind. "You want the truth? I'm everything you've ever thought I was. I'm just a greedy slut. I used you both, and now I'm really upset that you found out because I haven't hit the *Times* yet and I was really hoping to hit the *Times*. If you hadn't found out, I was planning on faking my own rape and torture so I could move up on the best seller list. So congratulations to you both. You were right. I was always a wretched whore. Jake, you should go back to sulking, and Adam can go forth on his quest to find the perfect woman. It sure as fuck isn't me."

She turned, but Jake was faster. He moved in front of her, cutting off her retreat. "No, Serena. I think we're all going to sit down and talk. I apologize for what I said earlier. I was overly emotional. Now please sit down and let's discuss this."

"Shove your apology straight up your ass, Jacob. Or you could have Adam do it for you. He likes to be helpful."

Fuck, she knew where to shove a knife in. Jake watched Adam's face go a polite blank. It was the same look he'd had when his father had thrown him out. "Serena, I'm willing to admit I might have been hasty, but you have to agree it's compelling evidence."

"I don't have to agree with you. I have to go and get my things and leave."

"I'm not going to let you do that." Now that he was thinking a little more clearly, he had a few questions. He got the e-mails. He could even buy that Lara had paid someone to trash Serena's car. But the snake? Really?

Adam's cell rang. He pulled it out and answered it, his voice going to a quiet, professional tone.

"Let me go." Serena stared a hole through him.

He couldn't. He was panicking a little now. She couldn't lie to save her life and the whole "I'm a whore" speech had been one long lie. What if she was telling the truth? What if she had no idea? He'd just fucked everything up, and if he let her go, he might never see her again. Might? Hell, if he took his damn eyes off of her, she would be gone, and he couldn't let that happen. "No. Not until we figure this out."

"There is nothing to figure out."

But there was a whole lot Jake needed to figure out. He needed to know just how deeply screwed he was and how hard he would have to work to get out of the hole he'd dug. "There is and you know it. Serena, you are still under our protection."

"No, I am not. You're fired."

"You're not the client."

A bitter little smile crossed Serena's face. "No, Lara is. But guess what, Jake? She's fired, too. If you're going to keep me here, you're going to have to do it against my will."

He felt his whole body go on alert. She wanted a fight? He could handle a fight. "That can be arranged."

He'd wanted to tie her up since the moment he'd seen her.

"Jake, we need to take her downtown." Adam stood with the keys to the SUV in his hand. "That was Ian. He's got Lara in his office. He wants to talk to all of us."

Fuck, he'd dug a hole with Adam, too. Adam had wanted to wake her up and ask her about it. Jake had been the one to work him into a froth over the situation. And now he'd gotten Ian involved. Jake had called Ian after he'd listened to the message on Serena's voice mail.

What the fuck was he going to do if Ian put a stop to the op?

"Go and get dressed, Serena. And I swear to god, I will hunt you down if you leave this house. The alarm is on, so if you try to hustle out a window, I'll be on your backside before you can get to the gate, and I won't give a shit if you call the police later."

Her smile was a nasty little thing. "No problem, Jake. The cops think I'm a publicity-seeking whore, too. I think you're safe. Let me go change. I have a few things to say to my ex-agent."

He stepped out of the way, satisfied she wouldn't run.

Not now, at least.

She disappeared down the hall, and Adam stepped up.

"She didn't know about it."

"I know." Jake wasn't sure how the fuck he was going to get out of this. He'd been brutal, his past informing his present in a way that almost ensured he had no future.

"She's never going to forgive us." Adam turned away. "I'll go get the car ready."

He walked out like a man who had already given up. Serena was a woman scorned.

But none of that could compete with a man on a mission. He wasn't going to give up. Yes, he'd fucked everything up, but Serena was too important. He had a fucking future, and it was with her. He wasn't going to allow his past to hold him back one second longer. He stared down the hallway, something opening up inside him. For so long he'd been closed off, maybe for most of his fucking life, but Serena had brought in the goddamn sunshine, and now he craved it.

He'd screwed up, but he wasn't going back to the dark. He would have the life he wanted, and it was only possible with her.

He waited, a lion on the prowl. No matter what, he would have his prey.

Chapter Fifteen

Serena felt hollowed out, like someone had decided it would be a good idea to take an ice cream scooper to her insides. Or like one of those Russian nesting dolls. Yes. That was better imagery. She was like the largest of the dolls, a hollow thing who was only good harboring the smaller dolls which contained all of the great things about her. Someone had opened her up and broken her insides, and now she was a useless, futile thing.

Yes. That was good imagery. She could use that.

The floors ticked by, and she realized this was the rest of her life. Living inside her head. Deciding how best to put emotions to paper because that was going to be the only way she ever felt anything again.

Maybe she was the drama queen.

"How is your wrist?" Adam asked solicitously. He had been deeply polite, avoiding eye contact and anything that might be controversial. He was the bodyguard, and she was the client. There was nothing more.

"I'm fine." It hadn't been nearly as bad as she'd made it out to be. She doubted she would bruise. It was nothing compared to the ache on her insides.

Adam and Jake she could almost handle. After all, she'd known deep down that they wouldn't really stay. Men like them didn't end up in permanent relationships with women like Serena. They found trophy wives when they were ready to settle down. In some ways, it just spared her the pain for later.

But Lara was another story.

Jake pulled her arm into both of his hands. Serena tried to pull away, but he had her by the elbow and the palm, turning her forearm over and inspecting her skin.

"Stop it." She didn't want him to touch her. It felt too nice, his callused hands on her skin. It reminded her of how it had felt to be in his arms.

"No." He traced a finger over the light chafing on her wrist. "I think she's fine. On the outside. We did a number to her on the inside."

Adam simply watched the floors go by.

"He's going to be the difficult one," Jake said, his voice almost conspiratorial. What the hell was his game now? When she didn't reply, he merely carried on the conversation as though she had. "I know. I'm surprised, too. I'm usually the obnoxious asshole. I don't like this whole 'being the moderator' thing, but I guess compromise is key in this relationship."

"There is no relationship, Jacob. The relationship died about a half an hour ago when you called me a whore."

He shook his head. "I didn't call you a whore, baby. I mentioned that you would make a good slut. A whore takes money. A slut just loves sex, and you really like sex."

Asshole. When had he decided to try to get back into her good graces, and why would he bother? Was he afraid his boss would get pissed off? She was pretty sure Ian Taggart was about to tell her she was on her own. Lara had lied to him, too.

Were Bridget and Chris in on it? She didn't know if she could handle it if they were. She would really be all alone in the world.

"Can I have my arm back?" Serena asked.

His thumb made little circles over the pulse at her wrist, a tiny touch that threatened to send shivers right through her. It reminded her that she might not have loved sex before, but after Jake and

Adam, she was an addict. And she would just have to go cold turkey because she wouldn't fall for their line of bullshit again.

"Serena, don't make this hard. You know you want to forgive us. We were wrong. We were complete assholes, but you saw that evidence. Come on, baby, let's get through this meeting with Ian and then we'll take you out to breakfast, which is exactly what we should have done in the first place. It's what Adam wanted to do."

"It doesn't matter what Adam wanted. All that matters is what happened, and I won't ever trust either one of you again. So give me my arm back, and let's get this little farce out of the way so we can get on with our lives." After today, she might never trust anyone again.

Jake brought her hand up, kissing her palm. "I'm not going away, Serena."

"Great, so now I can have two stalkers. Oh, wait. One was a fake, so you can be my first."

He let go of her hand, but his eyes heated up in that dark, Dom, sultry, get-her-panties-wet way he had. *Damn him.* "I was your first in other ways, too."

He'd been her first real man-given orgasm, and it didn't seem like he would let her forget it.

The doors opened, and Serena walked out. At least Adam seemed to have given up the game. He didn't look her way or say anything that didn't need to be said.

Grace looked up from her place at the front desk, a bright smile on her face which disappeared when no one returned it. "Oh crap. They fucked up, didn't they? I knew something was wrong when Ian called us all in on a Saturday. He's in the back with your agent. Is everyone all right?"

Serena liked Grace, but she didn't need to plaster her problems across the walls for everyone to see. She gave Grace what she hoped was her best smile. "We're fine. I think the case is wrapping up, and that's a good thing."

Jake wouldn't let up. "We're not fine. We did fuck up. We accused Serena of lying and using us, and we were complete assholes and now she's not talking to us and it's shut Adam down emotionally."

Adam turned cold eyes on his partner. "Really? You want to go there?"

Jake shrugged. "We have to go somewhere, buddy. If you don't like how I'm handling this scene, then feel free to come out of your shell and take over. Trust me. I will be deeply relieved. You're supposed to handle the emotional shit."

Grace's eyes went from Adam to Jake and back again. "Do y'all need to see Eve first? She does group rate therapy, I think."

Jake smiled at the thought. "Not a bad idea. Can she schedule us in for this morning?"

Serena rounded on Jake. He wasn't giving her the option of keeping her humiliation private. "What the hell are you doing?"

He took her by the elbow and led her away from Grace. Adam stayed in his place, the only one who seemed to be behaving as he should. Jake kept his voice low. "I am trying to salvage what was a complete cluster fuck of a morning."

"Why? You're out, Jake. You don't have to worry about me. You don't have to protect me. Just leave it where it is, and we can both move on."

His eyes were steady on her. "I have zero intentions of moving on without you."

"That's not what you said this morning. I believe you said you couldn't stand the sight of me."

He softened a little, his voice lowering. "And after all that evidence, I was already trying to justify in my mind why I should keep you. I was already trying to figure out how to fix it or how to punish you so I could be okay with staying with you."

He was so frustrating. "Why?"

He started to say something and then his whole face closed off. "Because we're good together."

Not the answer she'd wanted. Not the answer she would accept. She'd hoped, just for a second, he would say the one thing that her stupid heart wouldn't be able to handle. *I love you.* She would have thrown herself into his arms and forgiven him with those three little words, but she was just convenient. He was Dominant. She was submissive. She was interested in a ménage. She probably looked like a pretty good deal to Jake now that he was sure she wasn't a lying, gold-digging whore.

"Let it alone, Jake. You want me to forgive you. Fine. I forgive you, but I can't forget that the first time you had the slightest doubt about me, you were ready to toss me to the wolves. I asked for one thing, Jake. A little kindness when you were done."

His face became as hard as granite. "I'm not done, Serena. And I'm sorry to shatter your illusions, but I'm not particularly kind, either. And you know what, you gave as good as you got, sister."

"What are you talking about?" She'd held it together.

He pointed back at Adam. "What was that crack about Adam shoving something up my ass? Do you know what that did to him? I know he's a big boy and he should be able to handle it, but god, Serena, you opened about a thousand wounds in that man that have never healed."

She glanced over. Adam wasn't talking to Grace. He stood there, his arms crossed as though he was just waiting for it all to be over. "I meant you two protect each other, and you were both pushing me out. I didn't mean it that way."

"I don't care how you meant it, Serena. It's how he took it. So can't we all just acknowledge that we said some stupid shit and move on?"

And what would happen the next time she screwed up? The next time she upset Adam? It was too much. She couldn't handle the drama. "I don't want this anymore. I think I'm saying my safe word."

He shook his head, disappointment clear on his face. "We aren't in the dungeon, so it doesn't count. I'm not giving up on this, Serena."

Ian walked in, his face stern and unforgiving. "Serena, will you please come on back to my office? We need to talk about something. Jake, Adam?"

The men nodded, and everyone started the walk to Ian's office.

Ian opened the door, and the first thing she saw was Lara standing at the window. She turned, and Serena almost took a step back. Her always perfectly polished agent was red faced from crying. She'd obviously scrubbed her face clean at some point, and Lara Anderson without makeup looked younger and much more vulnerable than Serena had imagined she could look.

Looks were almost always deceiving.

"Serena, I am so sorry." She started to take a step forward, but stopped when Jake moved slightly in front of Serena, his gesture clear. He would protect her. Oh, he would casually rip her heart out, stomp on it, and then decide, hey, he didn't mean it after all, but he would protect her.

Serena noticed Brian leaning against the back wall of the office. His arms were crossed, and he was practically vibrating with discomfort. Still, he gave her a tight smile when he noticed her looking his way. "Serena, hello. I would like you to know that this wasn't a publicity stunt the firm itself had anything to do with."

"Shut up, Brian. Can we talk about this like friends? Do we have to start in with the legal crap?" Lara asked, her eyes narrowing.

Brian flushed. His hair was conservatively cut, and he was dressed in a full suit, looking every inch the successful literary agent. According to Bridget, he wasn't particularly happy with his wife's new romance clients, but he liked the money they were bringing in. And now he seemed to be worried about a lawsuit. "You'll wish we'd brought our lawyer into this when Serena uses every fucking thing you say in this office to sue us for everything we have. She needs to know you did this, not the firm."

"I think we've established that Mr. Anderson doesn't like his wife's business practices." Ian took a long breath as he sat behind his desk. He looked right there, a king on his throne, deciding what to do about the peasants. "I take it Jake and Adam filled you in on what they discovered?"

Jake held out the nearest chair to Ian's desk. He sent her a look that said he would make a big deal out of it if she didn't sit down. Serena believed him. He seemed utterly willing to humiliate her at every turn. She sank into the chair and looked Ian Taggart squarely in the eyes. "Yes. I understand that this was all a publicity stunt cooked up by my agent. I know you probably won't believe this, but I had nothing to do with it. I deeply apologize for wasting your time and resources. If you would just send me the bill for the last week, I'll pay it."

She stood to go. She didn't need any explanations. Now it was all out in the open, and she would pay the piper and Adam and Jake could be out of her life. And she didn't need an agent. She would go independent. That way she wouldn't be forced to rely on anyone.

Ian's hands came out, steepling in front of his chest as he considered her. He let a long moment of deeply uncomfortable silence pass. Finally, Serena couldn't take another minute of it.

"So I should go now?" *Damn it*. That hadn't sounded sure of herself. Ian was staring through her, and for the briefest of moments, she wanted to drop to her knees and find a submissive position and hope the big bad Dom was satisfied with it.

"No, Serena. You should not go now. You should sit back down until such time as this meeting is complete."

She swallowed, but decided to make her stand. Independent meant she couldn't afford to be submissive to anyone. She had to be her own woman, able to stand up to someone like Ian Taggart. "I believe my business is through here. Like I said, send me a bill."

"Fine. The bill will be for half a million dollars." Ian's smile was a chillingly polite thing. "And some change. I'll get you an itemized list. You can leave a check with Grace."

"Fuck me," Brian said under his breath. "She's going to sue us for that, too. Goddamn it, Lara. I should never have let you bring in clients on your own."

"Shut up, Brian. I didn't ask you to be here," Lara hissed back.

Serena stared at Ian for a moment and decided he was serious. She'd had top-notch bodyguards around the clock for a week, and another agent had been pouring over her case. Yes. It could be half a million dollars. She didn't have it. Everything was in her house and her car and her business. If she drained her accounts, she might be able to come up with a little over two hundred thousand, but she also had to fight her ex in court. Her advances were small compared to the big New York authors. She made her money in volume. She would have to up her writing schedule. She would need to put out more books.

She would need a payment plan.

"Damn it, Ian. Let her off the hook," Adam said, frowning at his boss.

"But she's wriggling so nicely." Ian's expression didn't change.

"Sit down, baby." Jake nodded toward the chair again. "He's not going to charge you. He's being a prick."

It seemed to be a condition that was going around today.

Ian eyed his employee. "I am merely trying to set parameters, Jacob. And you know how I deal with bratty, impolite subs."

"I'm working on the problem," Jake said as she sank back to her seat.

Problem? She wasn't the problem here. "I am not his sub. I'm not anyone's sub."

Ian's eyes rolled. "And you didn't take my advice. Ms. Brooks, when Jacob called me in the middle of the night, waking me from a well-deserved sleep to tell me that you had tricked us all, I mentioned to him that perhaps he should take a step back and look at the problem from a place of intellect and not emotion."

"He told me to stop thinking with my dick," Jake admitted.

"And what did you do?" Ian asked.

"Oh, my dick is very stupid, boss. Practically moronic. But that's between the three of us."

Ian's head shook. "If only that were true. Now, your deeply inappropriate and messy relationship aside, can we get to the reason I called you in? It certainly wasn't to pass you a bill and send you on your way. Though I will take a check if you feel obligated."

"Ian!" Adam practically shouted.

Ian shrugged, a lazy movement he managed to make predatory. "Well, I didn't get this office by working pro bono."

"I'll take care of it, Ian. I'll make sure you have a check." Lara took a deep breath and stared back out the window.

Brian gaped her direction. "You're kidding me. You are not writing a fucking half-million dollar check so your client can fuck her bodyguards." He flushed and turned to Serena. "I'm sorry, Serena. I'm apparently not up on today's professional standards. This isn't the way my authors work. I really am sorry for what Lara did, but I can't handle this. No one seems to understand my reputation is at stake, too."

He stalked out of the room.

Lara shook her head, her eyes on the door her husband had just slammed. "Please forgive him. He isn't handling this well. And I'm serious about paying for the case. This is my fault, not Serena's. And you'll need to stay on the case, obviously."

Ian sighed. "Can't I make a joke? Seriously, you kill a few people and get a reputation and suddenly no one thinks you're funny anymore. Stop being a martyr, Lara. You fucked up royally. It doesn't mean I'm going to bankrupt you, and besides, it's not like Adam and Jake have hated their duties. They've likely had enough fringe benefits that they won't mind not getting their bonus."

Serena felt herself flush.

"Ian, watch it," Jake said.

"Now I'm the bad guy because I point out the obvious. Keep the relationship to yourselves. Lara, talk."

Lara nodded her head, taking a minute to compose herself. She finally brought her eyes to meet Serena's before she obviously decided it was way easier to talk to Ian. "She's absolutely my most talented client. I say that from a place of love and respect, and not just because I stand to make a lot of money off her."

"But you do," Jake said. He hadn't left his place by her side, but Adam had started to pace.

Lara nodded. "Yes. Yes, I do. You have to understand that Serena's books are wonderful, but they're also only reaching a niche audience."

"I'm writing ménage, Lara. You knew that when you took me on. It's not exactly mainstream and neither is BDSM romance. If you wanted someone who writes sweet, you should have passed on me." What the hell had Lara been thinking? She'd managed to scare the holy crap out of Serena, and she'd done it for money.

"You write gorgeous love stories. They just needed some publicity." She took a long breath. "So I decided to be your stalker."

Adam turned on her. "You terrified her. You could have killed her with last night's stunt. Do you know what she's been going through?"

Ian held up a hand. "She's not done, Adam. This gets so much worse."

A little thrill of fear went through Serena. She'd lost the men she was getting close to and her agent all in an hour. She still might lose her friends. What could be worse?

"I only sent the e-mails. I swear to you, Serena, I just sent the e-mails. I was planning more. I had a whole plan mapped out on my computer. I was going to send you the e-mails for a couple of weeks and then I was going to up the ante so to speak. I was going to have my stalker persona take out ads in local papers begging you not to get Alexa together with Duke and Caden. I even found a skywriter who would put it up over downtown. Imagine it. Writer gets stalked by her characters. The press would have loved it. It's inventive. It's guerilla marketing and I thought it would be best if you didn't realize it was a publicity stunt. You would have reacted naturally."

"Yes, she reacted very naturally to nearly being killed." Jake's voice was like ice.

"I didn't have anything to do with trashing your car or the snake. I talked about the characters, Serena. My stalker idea was about loving your work. I wouldn't say anything bad about you. The first time you got a message that didn't come from me, I called in Ian. I started this, but someone has picked up on it. God, Serena, I'm so sorry."

She started crying again.

What the hell was she doing? Lara had always been a maverick with her own crazy ideas. It was one of the reasons they had clicked. It was one of the reasons she'd been willing to take a chance on a writer like Serena. Lara had been the only agent who would even read her work. She'd been a steady hand, guiding Serena through everything. Hadn't she earned a little leeway?

It wasn't like Serena had never made a mistake. She'd made tons.

"Were Bridget and Chris involved?" She had to know.

Lara shook her head, talking through her tears. "God, no. I'm a little scared of Bridget, and Chris can't keep a secret to save his life. He would have told you three minutes after I told him. Serena, I know you have to hate me now, but you also have to listen to me. I didn't put a snake in your car. I talked to the cops earlier. Yes, I have your key, but I swear I didn't use it. I wanted some press coverage. I didn't want to hurt you. I would never try to hurt you. I thought it was a little game. I thought we would get some good coverage for the release of the new book and the signing. It was stupid. I'm willing to do anything to make it right."

So it wasn't over. It wasn't over by a long shot. There had been a moment's peace when Serena had realized that even though she'd lost so much, she'd been free from the threats to her life.

Now she didn't even have that. Someone out there still wanted her dead.

She turned to Ian. "So what should I do? The police don't want to hear about it. If they find out about this, they'll think even less of me. I could go somewhere else."

It might be the best solution. She could find a place where no one knew who she was. Her cousin had a little cabin in Colorado that might work. She could look for someplace of her own from there. She could disappear into the mountains and just sink into her work. She could forget Jake and Adam.

"No. He could find you, and then you would be all alone," Ian said.

"He wouldn't know where I went." The more she thought about it, the better it sounded. The cabin was peaceful, isolated. She could go for days without seeing a soul.

Ian lifted a single eyebrow at Jake. "Would you know where she would go?"

Jake nodded. "She would head straight for a place called South Fork, Colorado. Her favorite cousin has a cabin there. If I couldn't find her there, she has a friend in St. Augustine with a condo on the beach she could hole up in. And if she wanted to get really exotic, she would go to Sydney, Australia. She talks to a writer friend there all the time. They talk about her going there."

Damn him. It was exactly what she'd been thinking and just in that order. Was she really that transparent?

Jake smiled down as though he could feel her frustration and took a special delight in it. "It's best you stay here and under our protection until he's caught. We'll take you back to our place. Now that we know what to ignore, we can concentrate on the real stuff. We can have Eve work up a new profile based on what we know. Adam, what is Serena's schedule like this week?"

Adam looked over, his eyes skimming her before focusing on Jake. "It's a quiet week. She's meeting Bridget and Chris for lunch this afternoon. She has some blog appearances, but the only thing she has to do publicly is the party at The Velvet Room. It's where the signing is. I already approved the catering menu."

He had? When had he done that?

Adam answered as though he'd read her mind. "I asked you to look over it yesterday, and you told me it was up to me. We're doing an hors d'oeuvres menu including dumplings. You like Asian, so I fashioned the menu off that. And the red velvet penis cupcakes. We have complimentary champagne, and I talked two of my reporter friends into covering it. I found a dress for you from Neiman's, and you'll hate the shoes, but they're perfect. Christian Louboutin stilettos. They arrive this afternoon, and you should break them in. I hired a photographer because we can use it on future press releases. I left an itemized receipt of everything, but I managed to get it all for ten percent under budget."

God, he was a sexy man. How the hell was she supposed to go back to life without him?

Ian was smiling. "See, I should charge you for his organizational skills alone." He slapped his hand on the desk. "All right. This is how it's going to be. Lara, you're a dumbass, but I loved your brother. He saved my life at the cost of his own, and that means putting up with you when you're a dumbass. Do you want Serena alive?"

He looked over at Serena as though her whole life depended on what Lara said next.

"I do. She won't believe it, but I love her."

Ian shook his head. "I don't care what she believes. Trust me, I know all about keeping someone I love alive when they hate my guts. If you want her alive, I will make sure she stays that way."

It seemed stupid to ask if she got a say in that, but she kind of wanted to. Still. It was a stupid question. She didn't envy whatever girl ended up falling in love with that deeply obnoxious, totally hot man. Ian Taggart was both rock and hard place.

But she would take more control this time. "I would like to interview some of the bodyguards and figure out which one would work best."

Ian leaned forward. "Do you understand the meaning of half a million and counting? You'll take what I give you and be goddamn happy you're alive. And you'll give serious consideration to forgiving Lara because she gives a damn. Adam and Jake think they told me something I didn't already know. Lara came clean a couple of days ago."

"Then why the fuck didn't you tell us?" Jake asked, his hands on his lean hips.

"It was on a need to know basis, and you didn't need to know. I told Eve after she met with Serena." He pushed a file folder across the desk. "Here's her new profile. I had hoped to keep Ms. Brooks in the dark. She would have been happier not knowing. If it helps, I gave Lara a long and drawn-out talking to."

"He yelled a lot," Lara admitted.

Jake grabbed the file folder. "I'll look over this on the way home."

Adam stepped forward. "I think you should replace us."

"What?" Jake asked, staring at his partner.

She liked the way Adam was thinking. He was thinking with an obviously clear head. "Yes, what he said. I'll take anyone else. Give me the interns. Surely you have interns."

Ian's eyebrow arched in that way that let her know that she, too, was a big old dumbass. "No. Oddly enough, I don't have a bunch of interns willing to take a bullet for a client in order to get me to sign off on three college credit hours. You get Adam and Jake. If Adam prefers to quit his job because he decided to go against my incredibly good advice not to screw the pretty client, then you just get Jake. Or you can face this asshole all on your own. I hope you know how to deal with snakes, since we know he likes to use them."

Fuck him. He was right, and he had her in a corner. What was she supposed to do? Should she make the decision her pride demanded? Should she take on whoever the hell this guy was on her own? Or perhaps she could give everything up and skulk off for a quiet life?

She could handle it. She wasn't giving up anything else. "Fine. But I would like to be kept up to date. I want this settled as quickly as possible."

"And so do I." Ian stood. "Liam is looking into the situation.

He'll continue to be Adam and Jake's backup until such time as I need to send him to Europe or wherever Mr. Black decides to rear his soon to be chopped-off head. Did I mention I'm going to kill that motherfucker?"

Serena had no idea who Mr. Black was, but she was happy she wasn't him. Ian Taggart wasn't a man she wanted to cross. But he was also the man who had placed her in an awkward position. She was going to have to rely on the very men who had humiliated her.

She looked up at Jake, who seemed utterly satisfied with the situation. And then Adam, who wouldn't meet her eyes. Adam, who had perfectly organized her life right down to the food and wine she would have wanted. She hadn't had to think. She'd just written because she'd trusted Adam to take care of everything, and it was okay because he liked doing it.

Hadn't he? He'd told her he did. He'd seemed happy when he was doing it.

Had that been a lie, too?

She was brutally confused and beyond miserable. How would she survive another couple of weeks around them? Especially when Jake was being aggressive, and Adam wouldn't even look at her.

But she didn't have a choice. She could deal with them or she could be on her own. She wasn't too stupid to live. She might be too stupid to be happy, but at least she would be alive.

"All right." There wasn't another answer. She was in a corner. She looked up at Jake. He'd put her in a corner. He was going to find out that she wouldn't stay there forever.

* * * *

Adam drove through the streets of Dallas, his eyes on the road and his mind on the woman in the backseat.

"I'm fine, Bridget. It's all right." She spoke into her phone. He glanced at her briefly through the rearview mirror. She'd forgotten her sunglasses again. She struggled to find the prescription sunglasses she had. He'd specifically requested that Alex pick them up the night before. He'd placed them next to her purse when he'd unpacked her things, but she'd obviously forgotten them again.

When she had her next appointment, he would make sure she got the kind of glasses that changed in the sunlight. The sun in Texas was far too bright to go without UV protection.

He set his eyes back on the road. What was he thinking? She wasn't his to take care of anymore, and that hurt like hell. He'd fucked up, and he knew from previous experience that she wouldn't forgive him. A man really only had one shot with most people. When he screwed up, he was out.

"Bridget, I'm not hiding anything. God, has anyone ever told you you're a little like a bulldog? Fine." There was a little pause and then Serena sighed. "No. That didn't work out."

Serena jumped a little and held the phone away from her ear. Bridget was shouting, her anger clearly expressed. No satellite could possibly filter the rage that was coming through Serena's little cell.

Well, he had a fan in Bridget, at least.

"Serena, sweetie? You can put the phone back to your ear. It's Chris. I've taken Bridget's phone. She's going to scream somewhere privately now."

Serena put the phone back, and the conversation seemed to take a much more civil tone.

Jake turned in his seat. "Why are you doing this?"

Bridget wasn't the only bulldog in the world. "What? Driving? Well, Jacob, when a person wants to get someplace, he has a few options."

"Shut that shit down, man. Why are you acting like a closed-off asshole?"

Because he wasn't going to grovel at her feet. It wouldn't work. "Do you mind having this conversation in private?"

Jake shook his head. "We are in private. It's just you and me and Serena."

"Without Serena." There was no more Adam and Jake and Serena.

"Buddy, she doesn't seem to have any problem with talking in front of us. I'm just playing by her rules."

Sure enough, Serena was sniffling into her phone. "It just didn't work out. Fine. Okay. I did. Well, both of them. No. We didn't get to that part. They decided they didn't want me."

"Bullshit, Serena, and that's twenty for lying." Jake narrowed his eyes, attempting to Dom her from the front seat.

She looked up at him. "You can't spank me anymore."

"Watch me."

She went back to her phone call, though a little quieter now. "See, he's brutal. No. Yes. I didn't say I didn't like it, but I don't now because he's an asshole. Can't we just talk about this at lunch?"

"There's no lunch, Serena," Jake said. "We're going home."

"She has lunch with Bridget and Chris once a week. This was the only day they could do it this week. I coordinated their schedules. I made the reservation myself," Adam pointed out. He already knew her habits. He loved to be involved in the ins and outs of her daily life. He had no interest in being one of those boyfriends who went his own way ninety percent of the time and just came to his lover for a little sex. He wanted to be important to her. Hell, he wanted to be indispensable.

A fat lot of good that had done him.

"I always have lunch with my friends. It's the only time I get out." Serena had her hand over the phone, and there was a lost look on her face.

Adam understood. It was her routine. She found comfort it in. The rest of her life was a chaotic mess, and she wanted to be with the only two people in the world who hadn't let her down. It was just a couple of hours, and she would be safe.

Jake held his line, but Adam had known he would. "No. You're going to cancel everything. Including that signing."

"I can't cancel the signing."

"She can't cancel the signing. We have everything in place." Adam had worked his ass off to make sure that signing happened.

She frowned, that gloriously plump bottom lip quivering just a little. "But if I cancel the signing, then the terrorist wins."

He wanted to laugh. She was so damn funny.

Jake didn't seem to find it amusing. "And if I don't make you cancel it, then I let the terrorist gut you with a really big knife."

God, Adam wanted to keep her safe, but he was kind of on Serena's side on this one. What were they doing here if she couldn't even make a single appearance to promote her own work? "Aren't we supposed to be protecting her so she can go on with her daily life?"

Serena leapt right on that. She pointed to Adam. "What he said." She put the phone back to her ear. "Sorry, babe, we're trying to figure out if the reasonable asshole is going to win or if the guy with a two-by-four shoved straight up his ass will prevail. Yes, that's Jake."

Adam stifled a laugh, but Jake turned around in his seat. "Two-by-four, Serena? Sweetheart, that's nothing compared to the plug I'm going to shove up yours. You know what little brats who tease their Doms get? They get a nice fat ginger root shoved up their rectum."

She whispered into the phone. "Yes, he just threatened to fig me. No. He can't do that because he isn't really my Dom. No. Ewww. You can't watch. That's not research, Chris."

Jake looked back at Adam, sadly shaking his head. "You don't have any say in this, man. You already checked out."

Adam felt a little surge of anger. Jake had gotten him in this trouble in the first place. He'd been the one to get Adam really angry. If they had done this Adam's way, they would have climbed into bed with her and asked her about the situation. But no. Jake had to make a worst-case scenario out of everything, and now he wanted to shove Adam out? "I am still on this case. If you have a problem with it, take it up with Ian."

Jake wasn't the only one who could make a decision. Adam switched lanes and made the next right hand turn.

"Where are you going?" Jake asked, his voice tight.

"It's Saturday. It's almost eleven o'clock. I'm taking our client to her lunch date."

"Reasonable asshole won. But I think he won because he's driving. I'm not sure I'll be allowed out of the car," Serena informed Chris. "Yeah. I totally need one. Order a pitcher."

"No liquor, Serena," Jake barked. He turned his eyes back to Adam. "I need to know you're still in this with me."

"I'll keep her safe. I'll do my job." But he was already thinking about how much her smile lit up his whole fucking day. How was he going to keep his hands off her? Because she'd made it plain she didn't want him anymore. He wasn't going to beat his head against a wall. He'd been up front and honest about everything he wanted, and the first mistake he made she'd tossed him out without even being willing to listen to an explanation. He'd been down that road before, and he couldn't do it again.

"That wasn't I meant, man." Jake sat back, a long sigh coming out of his chest. "I need you, man. I'm not any fucking good at this. I can't save it on my own."

"There's nothing to save except her life. Let's do what we should have done in the first place. Do our jobs. She's the client. Nothing more." He kept his words quiet, but every syllable was an ache in his gut.

He looked back at her in the rearview mirror, and for the briefest of seconds, he'd seen a startled hurt on her face, her eyes flaring in pain. She shut it down in an instant and went right back to her friend.

She was the client. He was the guard. It was far past time to start doing his job. Guarding her life and his dumbass heart.

Chapter Sixteen

Serena nearly ran into the restaurant. Bridget and Chris were at their customary table in the back room of the small Mexican food place. When they saw her, they stood and walked to meet her, concern written on their faces.

Thank god she wasn't alone. Bridget rushed to hug her, pulling her close.

"Hey, sweetie. Are you all right? I know you aren't, but that's just something stupid I feel like I should say. I'm so sorry. We've both decided to fire Lara."

Serena sniffled. She couldn't seem to stop crying today. "Don't fire her. At least let's really talk about this before you guys make a decision. I haven't fired her yet."

She'd meant to, but things had moved so fast, and then she just hadn't been able to make herself say the words to cut the relationship off. Lara had looked so miserable, and the truth of the matter was she didn't have many people in her life who truly claimed to love her. She could at least give Lara a day or two.

"That's a rational thing to do. Too bad you refuse to give the same courtesy to your lovers." Jake was standing beside her with a grim expression on his face.

He was going to be trouble. Adam, at least, seemed to just want to get through the day.

"Hello, Bridget. You seem to have gotten rid of the extra chairs." Jake eyed the small table. Sure enough, the table for four had only three seats.

Bridget faced Jake and gave him her happy middle finger. "Talk to the hand, asshole."

"It's really more of a finger," Jake pointed out.

Chris was infinitely more polite. He held a hand out, though there was a stony, blank expression on his face. "Sorry, she's a little upset. We both are, actually."

Jake took the offered hand and gave Chris a bright smile. Way brighter than she'd ever seen him have before. It was a charming smile, a smile that made him sigh worthy. *Asshole.* "I can understand why, Chris. I hope you give us a chance to explain at some point. For now, we'll just take this table next to the three of you. I would give you a little more privacy, but obviously that's not a good idea. We both take her health and welfare very seriously and not just because she's our client. We care about her. I know you understand."

Serena wanted to vomit. Jake had figured out exactly how to handle Chris. He'd said he was the one who didn't know how to deal with people, but that had been another in a long list of lies. Well, she admitted, Chris wasn't just a person. He was in the lifestyle, and Jake had probably figured it out by taking one look at him. Chris was a big old bottom, and he was already smiling up at the big bad Dom.

"We could get another couple of chairs," Chris offered.

"No we can't." Bridget didn't even come close to being submissive. "The asshole table is that way. Come on, Serena. I ordered you a swirl. And you better remember where your loyalties lie, Chris. Just because Hottie McHot Ass walks in with his super metro hot best friend, and all those like muscles and shit, doesn't mean you get to turn into a pile of goo. We hate them."

Chris sighed, staring at Jake's chest. He was wearing a T-shirt, but it was easy to see that he was covered in amazing muscles. Jake nodded to Chris, and then Adam after him, as they made their way to the back of the room and settled down at their table.

Bridget slapped Chris across the chest. "What is wrong with you?"

Chris's mouth was hanging slightly open. She couldn't blame him. They looked just as good from the back as they did from the front. They both had amazingly hot asses.

"I…holy crap, Serena. You really did both of them?"

Bridget narrowed her eyes at him. "Yes, she did terribly slutty things and then they treated her like trash, so we hate them."

"I do. I hate them. But holy crap." Chris looked back over their way. "Did you see them?" He reached for Serena's hand and held it to his heart. "I'm so sorry, baby. I really am. Are you sure they're not gay? Because he seemed really gay to me."

Serena couldn't help it. She laughed. Chris thought every man with a half-decent body was gay, so Adam and Jake must have sent his faulty gaydar into a tailspin. "I assure you—one hundred percent not gay. At least they didn't feel gay in bed."

"So they could be gay." Chris sighed. "But really, we hate them."

"Yes, we hate them." Serena said the words. She just wished she could feel them deep down in her soul. She didn't hate them. She was still crazy about them, but she could never trust them again. She followed Chris and Bridget back to their seats where Bridget started talking loudly about all the men she would set Serena up with when she was ready to date again.

She was never going to date again.

She listened as Adam and Jake ordered lunch. She played with the straw of her swirl margarita. Bridget and Chris started talking about work, normal, everyday things. It was the same as every lunch before except she was a completely different human being.

How could she already miss them? They were sitting not five feet away, but they were lost to her as though they were gone, never to be seen again. She wouldn't see them again. Not really. She would move through the days, but she wouldn't really share them. Adam and Jake would be around, but more like accessories when before they had become essential. She'd come to rely on them far more in a week than she ever had her husband, and they had been married for years.

And someday soon, they would catch this guy. She knew they would. They would honor that promise. They would catch him and she would be safe, and they would move on. She would move on. Except she wouldn't. She hadn't moved in years, not emotionally. She'd worked on her career and put up barricades to everyone except her small group of friends. When Adam and Jake were gone, she wouldn't move on. She would simply move deeper inside herself until the only emotion she ever felt was typed out of her soul and placed on the internet for all to see.

"Honey? Are you all right?" Chris asked, reaching out and covering her hand with his.

She shook her head. "Nope. But I don't have another way to be right now."

He eyed her for a moment. "Are you sure about that?"

"Chris, you weren't there this morning. You didn't hear some of the things he said to me, and Adam hasn't said anything at all. Trust me. I know exactly where I stand with those two. I was a convenient lay."

"I don't know about that." Chris sat back, his eyes trailing to the table beside them where Jake and Adam sat. Their food had come, but neither seemed to be digging in.

"Well, I do. Men are jerks." Bridget leaned in as though ready to go off on one of her tirades.

"No. This is my turn." Chris didn't often use that sharp bark, but when he did, he meant business. Bridget sighed and nodded. Chris turned his gaze to Serena. "You know what Bridget is doing, right? She's going to agree with everything you say because she thinks what you need right now is a completely supportive friend, but I think what you need is someone to actually talk to. What do you want, sweetheart? I can sit here and cuss out men with Bridge or I can ask you some very specific questions."

She wanted to listen to Bridget wail because it would soothe her. She wanted them to simply tell her she was right about everything, but she simply couldn't. "Ask away."

"Serena, they don't look like two men who are eager to get away from you."

"Then you're not looking close enough." The words sounded stubborn coming out of her mouth.

"I'm watching them." Chris had a good line of sight to the table. "They both keep looking over here."

Well, she had the obvious answer to that one. "My life has been threatened numerous times. They're bodyguards. They're doing their jobs."

"I don't think so. They're worried and not about your life. Look, honey, I've been around a lot longer than you have. I know men. I can spot a playboy from a mile away. Neither one of those men even glanced at Bridget's cleavage, and she has the girls on full display."

Bridget shrugged. "It's true. I even opened another button when I found out they would be with you. No man can resist these double Ds. I hate to say it, but I think Chris might be right. They're either crazy about you or gay. The boob test doesn't lie."

Serena stared down at her drink. "You don't understand, guys. Think about it. They like to share a woman, and Jake is fairly hardcore when it comes to the whips and chains stuff. I'm completely open to both lifestyles. It's just easy. They couldn't really care about me and have acted the way they did this morning."

"Yes, because love is always rational," Chris said sadly. "I love my boyfriend, and we have said some of the most hurtful things in the world to each other. Sweetie, a man who is really passionate about you, who loves you to the core, can be deeply cruel when that love is threatened."

"All I asked for when we started this thing was a little kindness." It hadn't been that much.

Chris sighed. "There's nothing kind about passion. It can be, but you're expecting love to be one way, and it's not. It sure as hell isn't going to be with two men. You have two men with two hearts and two pasts to deal with. Have their lives been all sunshine and roses? You know we react the way we do because of what life has taught us. Ask yourself the question. What has life taught those two men? Did that factor into the way they reacted to some spectacularly bad news? Was what they did really unforgivable?"

Unforgivable? What did that really mean? But even if Chris was right, maybe she was simply too damaged to ever make this work. He'd talked about the way the past informed how a person dealt with the present. Her past had taught her that she made very bad judgment calls. She couldn't trust herself any more than she could trust them. She'd made the mistake of throwing herself into this when she'd known damn well it wouldn't work out.

But then that was just what she did. Nothing worked out how she'd planned. Even her writing career. She'd had visions of being acclaimed and beloved, but mostly she'd gotten scorn and derision from anyone outside the erotic romance community. And now someone took such singular exception to her work that she required bodyguards. Everything she did seemed to isolate her, to push her further and further away from the white picket fence and kids. She just couldn't see why her white picket fence couldn't go around a dungeon. And why couldn't there be two guys in her dream house?

Her fantasies were harmless. Why was she being punished for them? Why would any woman be punished for them?

Bridget took her other hand. "Hon, I know I can be a bit much, but even I can see you're miserable and it isn't all about the asshole who's sending you nasty messages."

"And a snake," Serena mentioned. God, she couldn't get that out of her head.

Bridget's eyes got wide. "A snake? In your car? Like *Sweetheart in Chains?*"

Chris turned a bright red. "He's pulling stuff out of your books and using it against you?"

Serena nodded. "Yep. Makes me wish I hadn't written all that creepy stuff. I think I'll give up the romantic suspense. The next time I write a stalker, he's going to leave fluffy bunnies behind. Living fluffy bunnies. I hope he hasn't read *Missing in Joy.*" What she'd done to her former FBI profiler character had been really awful.

Chris stood up and stalked to the next table, his hands clenched into fists. He stared down at Jake and Adam. "You tell me you're going to kill this guy. You better kill him, or I swear to god, I will."

When Chris went into protective mode, he went all out.

Jake looked up calmly. "I promise. I don't promise I'll do it quickly."

"We're going to take care of her," Adam said, finally looking at her. There was a hollow look in his eyes that she was pretty sure matched her own. "We'll take care of her whether she likes it or not."

Chris sat down at the table with her bodyguards and started asking all kinds of pointed questions.

Bridget poured Serena another drink. "They don't seem like men who are happy with the day's outcome. I hate that. I sound so reasonable, but Chris is in protect-his-women mode. So now I have to be the voice of reason. Yuck."

Serena felt a faint smile tilt her lips up. She loved Bridget. Reasonable or not. "I think they would have preferred to keep me in line with sex, and now they can't do that."

Bridget frowned. "Really? So they've been completely in control?"

Jake hadn't been. He'd lost it the night before. He'd taken her when he'd known he shouldn't. And Adam hadn't reacted like a man who'd gotten a woman under his thumb. He'd fought with his best friend because he hadn't been included in their deeply passionate time together. He'd demanded time of his own.

"No. It doesn't seem that way. I guess they could be playing a game with me, but I don't think so. It didn't feel like it at the time. It felt real, but this morning felt real, too." This morning had damn near killed her.

"I know. But that was inevitable. People in love fight." Yep. Bridget was being way too reasonable.

"They're not in love." They hadn't said anything beyond they would like to try a relationship. It was far too early to think about love.

"You are." Bridget let the words drop like a potential mine waiting to go off and blow up in her face.

Serena decided to defuse that bomb the only way she knew how. A little bit of truth and a whole lot of optimistic lying. "Maybe, but I can fall out, too. Hey, I thought I was in love with Doyle. I'm cured of that, and I was actually married to him."

She stood, stretching a little. She was sore in a way that

reminded her just how well they had used her body the night before. It had been years since she'd had sex, and she'd never had it the way they had given it to her. Hard and rough with an edge of real promise. Or she was just really good at making up fiction in her head and it had been simple sex, the act of two bodies coming together out of need and biology.

"I'm going to run to the bathroom." She needed a minute of quiet. She needed to get her head together. She wasn't going to cry in the middle of the restaurant.

Jake and Adam were already standing.

"I can surely go to the restroom alone," Serena said. Had she gotten to the point that she couldn't even have a single private moment?

Adam walked off, he and Jake exchanging glances.

"He'll check it out," Jake explained. "Bridget, would you mind coming with us? Is the bathroom completely interior? No windows?"

Bridget nodded, following as Jake started to walk toward the bathroom, Serena's elbow firmly in his hand. "It's small. Just two stalls. No windows. I'll go in with her."

Jake smiled back at her. "Thank you."

They got to the bathroom as Adam was exiting.

"It seems safe enough. No one is in there. Do you want me to stand outside the stall?" Adam asked, his jacket moving just enough to show a hint of dark metal at his side. His SIG Sauer.

"No," Serena said quickly. She couldn't think of anything worse than having to go into that bathroom with one of the men listening in. "No one's in there. No one can get in. I'll take Bridget."

"I've listened to her pee many times," Bridget said, still staring at that place where his gun had flashed.

Serena threw her a look, but Bridget just shrugged and opened the door.

The minute the door closed, she took a deep breath. Just being around them was hard.

"Holy crap, Serena. He has a gun." Bridget was staring at the door.

"He's a bodyguard. It's kind of part of his uniform." Serena looked down and found her hands were shaking. She wanted to walk right back out and beg one of them to hold her. She wanted to sink into their strength and let them surround her. She wanted to feel Adam's hands in her hair, hear his voice promising her that he would take care of everything. She wanted Jake to kiss her. When Jake dominated her mouth, she didn't think about anything but them.

But she couldn't do it. Even if they would let her, she wasn't sure it wouldn't simply lead to more heartache.

Tears formed in Bridget's eyes. "Why? Why is this happening? I don't understand."

At least she had Bridget. It was easy to hug her, to put her arms around her best friend and bring their heads close together. This woman was so dear to her. Bridget was brutally misunderstood because she didn't quite know how to filter her words. But deep down, Bridget was loyal to the core. She knew how to be a friend. She knew how to love. If everything fell down around her, Serena was one hundred percent sure that Bridget would still be beside her. "I'm going to be okay."

Bridget sniffled. Not many people understood just how emotional she could be. "You have to be. I don't know what I would do without you. I love you, Serena. I really do. I know they hurt you, but you have to listen to them. You can't take chances. You're too important. To me. To Chris. And no matter what this asshole is saying, you have a ton of readers who think you're important, too. Remember the signing we did where that woman thanked you because she read your books while she was going through chemo? You were important to her. He's just sick. You can't listen to him."

"I know," she said, though the tears just wouldn't come. She loved Bridget, too, but she felt horribly bottled up as though she simply couldn't let go. The tears were right there, but she blinked them back. Maybe one day she would be able to cry again. But not today. Today she would be strong. She would hold it all in until Jake and Adam were gone, and then she could wail all she wanted.

But now she would be strong.

Bridget released her, wiping her eyes. "Sorry. I'm just worried."

"I know. I would be worried about you, too, sweetie." She

crossed to the sink and ran some cold water. "Can we just hide here for a while?"

Bridget chuckled. "Well, I'm sure they'll come charging in when we've taken too long. I'll be right back."

Bridget disappeared into the larger of the two stalls. Serena stared at herself in the mirror. She looked tired and hollow. Just last night she'd sipped wine while Adam had brushed her hair. She'd felt like a princess. Was she being dumb? Should she just go out there and ask them if they could start all over again? Maybe it wouldn't work, but maybe it would.

"Dumbass," she said under her breath to the girl in the mirror. Not three hours after they'd ripped her heart out, she was looking for a reason to throw herself right back in the deep end of the pool.

The door to the stall was thrown open, and Bridget walked back out, her eyes wide and an envelope in her hand. "It was on the back of the door. I guess Adam just opened the door and made sure no one was inside. I didn't want to open it. I still don't want to. Oh, god. I touched it. I shouldn't have touched it."

Serena felt her heart flutter. Bridget held a plain white envelope in her hands, a piece of tape still sticking from the top. *Whore* was written on the front. Yep. That was probably meant for her. Without really thinking about it, Serena grabbed it. It was like pulling a bandage off. She wanted to just know. If she called Jake and Adam in, she might never actually see what the man who wanted to kill her had to say.

A couple of clipped news articles were attached to the single sheet of the computer-generated letter.

Please read the articles I have attached. You are ruining marriages with your disgusting words. You are tempting good men to do bad things. I love my wife, but I'm going to fuck you. You want it rough, bitch, then I'll give it to you good. You're a whore. You prove it with your words.

As you can see, I know your habits, so don't think you can hide away with your hired guards. I'll be patient. I'll wait and I will find you.

Whores don't deserve nice things. I've read your filth. You say it's your fantasy. I'm going to make your fantasies come true. All of them. Especially the nasty ones.

Serena felt her stomach turn.

The door to the bathroom opened, and Jake barged in. "Serena, we have to go."

She held up the letter. "He left this."

Jake's jaw firmed, and he grabbed her hand. "He did more than leave you a note, baby. I think he just burned down your house."

Chapter Seventeen

J ake tried to listen to the cops, but his mind was still on the ruined husk of Serena's house. The security cameras they had placed around the house hadn't helped. Jake had looked at the feed he'd received before the whole system had gone down and all he had was a vague shot of the back of a non-descript man in a dark hoodie and jeans moving outside the backyard camera. And then the feed had gone dead.

"Ms. Brooks," Edward Chitwood was saying, "obviously, this person is escalating."

"You admit this person exists?" Adam said, his bitterness showing through. He had paced the halls of the police station until the detectives had called them in. Adam had been the one who had hustled them all away from the crime scene. Jake had just stood there watching Serena's house burn, his whole soul in turmoil. Everything she had was in that house except for the small suitcase Alex had brought her the night before. Her whole world was burning down around her, and she wouldn't let him hold her.

At least Adam had been thinking. He'd gotten them out of there as quickly as possible since there was a crowd gathered around watching as the firefighters put out the blaze. Any one of them could have been the man who had started the fire. Adam had been smart enough to roll video from his phone of the crowd. They would analyze it later.

And Jake had just stood there watching Serena, feeling his whole soul falling apart. He had to figure out how to reach her. No matter what happened, he couldn't let her go. He knew that now. Even after all the shit he'd gone through, he couldn't let Serena get away. He hadn't been in love before, and it was so much more important than his own pride.

Chitwood frowned and leaned forward in his seat. "Yes, I think I understand that now. I, for one, don't think Miss Brooks would go so far as to burn down her own home to get a small amount of publicity. Speaking of publicity, the press is asking questions. It will be on the news this evening."

"Keep her name out of it," Jake said. The last thing he wanted was for the story to break. It might have been Lara's plan, but Serena herself had made it fail by refusing to play along. She'd called the cops and ignored the press. She'd guarded her privacy. It was the only damn thing she had left.

"At this point we're simply saying it was a fire. I wish we had a witness, but apparently there was a big block party going on at the other end of the street." Chitwood looked down at his report. "Tell me something, Mr. Miles, did you get anything off the CCTV tapes?"

Adam sighed and gave the cop a regretful shake of his head. "No. I'm still looking. It can be so hard to tell. Did your experts find anything?"

Their experts hadn't met Lara Anderson. She would look like just another woman walking out of the library, talking on her phone. Jake had found her on the other library's CCTV tape, but she'd had her face down in that tape, a scarf wrapped around her head. Adam had only identified her from her hand bag. There weren't many suburbanites walking around carrying Chanel. He and Adam had decided to not let the cops in on this piece of their investigation. They had the same tapes. If they didn't reach the same conclusions, it was their damn fault. Besides, it would only muddy the waters since Lara didn't have anything to do with this. He'd called Ian, and

Lara had been with him all afternoon, crying and trying to figure out how to help her client. If she was still working an angle, Jake couldn't see it.

"No. I think that's a dead end." Chitwood closed his folder and looked at Serena with now sympathetic eyes.

Jake wanted nothing more than to reach over and thread his fingers through hers. "Has the fire marshal determined how the fire was started?"

Chitwood sighed. "Well, we're sure it's arson, but there are protocols. He'll file his report in the next few weeks. We have a lot of evidence to sort through."

"Of course." Serena sat back, her eyes vacant. "I understand. Do you know how long it will be before the insurance adjusters can get in?"

Hernandez walked up behind his partner, his eyes narrowing. "It could be a while, Miss Brooks. Your insurance agent is going to want a full report. They don't just pay out because the house burns down. They need to make sure you have a legitimate claim."

Oh, Jake really wanted to punch Hernandez in the face. *Asshole.* He wasn't going to give an inch. "You know where to find her. If you have any other questions, call me. She's not going to be answering her cell phone any longer."

Chitwood nodded. "I think that's a good idea. It's very clear this person isn't going to go away. He seems to have a point to make. Tell me something, Miss Brooks. Have you thought about pulling back from work for a while? Maybe putting off the release of this new book? It might quiet him down."

Now Jake wanted to punch the shit out of Chitwood. "She's not putting off the release of her damn book. She hasn't done a goddamn thing wrong. She's trying to work in a legal profession, and she's not going to give in to someone who is trying to intimidate her."

Chitwood held up his hands. "It was just a suggestion."

Hernandez frowned. "It was a good suggestion. He's just trying to keep her alive. But, hey, if her little books are more important than her life, then she should go for it."

"Hernandez!" Brighton yelled from his office, his face red. "My office. Now."

Hernandez stiffened and then turned and walked to his boss' office.

Chitwood leaned forward. "Forgive him. He's very conservative. He's Catholic. He thinks your books are pushing the Mormon faith. I've tried to explain to him that your books have nothing to do with religion."

It was time to get Serena away from these people. He stood. "Thank you. Please keep in touch."

Adam stood as well, his entire body stiff. He looked like he was ready to throw a punch, but he seemed to contain it. "We should get our charge home. And her book is coming out on time. She'll be signing at the opening day party. I have some friends in the press who would love to know if the Dallas Police Department cares about stalking victims. I suspect I'll see you there."

Chitwood gave them the fakest of fake smiles. "We wouldn't be anywhere else. We are taking this seriously, gentleman."

"Serena." Jake turned and waited for Serena to stand. She did it, but she moved in a way that worried him. She moved, but there was no spark of life, no animation. She was like a zombie, shuffling along, going where he told her to go, doing what he told her to do. She'd completely shut down, and that was a problem.

She looked up at him. "I know I shouldn't, but could I go to the bathroom, please? I didn't actually make it to the one at the restaurant."

Chitwood stood, gesturing toward a female uniformed officer. "Leah? Could you escort Ms. Brooks to the bathroom? She shouldn't be left alone. Check the stalls before she goes in."

Leah, who was called Officer Nelson from her badge, gave Serena a smile. "Of course. Right this way." As they walked off, she leaned over, and Jacob could barely hear her words. "I heard you're a writer. That's so cool. Hey, do you happen to know Mari Carr? I love her books. What do you write?"

Adam followed the women, planting himself outside the bathroom door.

"So, are you coming out of your pout?" Jake asked because he was really sick of dealing with delicate moods.

"Fuck you, Jake. And yes, I'm coming out of my pout." He stared at the door. "I don't know what I'd do if she died. Look, I admit it. I want to run. I don't think this will work because I don't think she's going to let it work, but he torched her house. The least I can do is make sure this asshole goes down. I owe her that much."

"You're not willing to fight?" It was incomprehensible to Jake. How could he just let Serena go? A spark of anger lit him. "You got me into this relationship."

"And you got us out of it," Adam spat back.

Ah, there was the real reason. "I said I was sorry. I said a bunch of things I shouldn't have said. I took everything wrong. I was an asshole. But that doesn't mean I'm going to make the mistake of walking away now."

"I told you. I'm not walking away. I'm here. I'll do my job."

"Your job is to love her. It's both our jobs. Don't you see how this is going to go? If you both go to your corners, it's going to fall apart."

"It already fell apart," Adam growled his way.

Jake was past frustrated. "Then we fucking put it back together. Goddamn it, Adam. You know, maybe you're right. Maybe you should let Liam come back in because if this is the way you're going to be every time something goes wrong, then I don't want you in this relationship. I'm going to get her back, and I need a partner, not some whiny asshole who can't get over his daddy issues."

Jake hissed at the sharp shock of pain as Adam reared back and punched him right in the nose. *Fuck.* He hadn't forgotten how to hit. And it was the second time that day that someone he gave a shit about had popped him. It was a shitty, shitty fucking day. He felt his nose.

"I didn't break it." Adam leaned against the wall.

"Hey, is there a problem?" A uniformed officer stopped and stared at both of them.

"Yes," Jake replied, wincing at the pain in his nose. Adam hadn't broken it, but that didn't mean it didn't hurt like hell. "My partner is an asshole. But you know what? He's been that way since we went through basic together. It shouldn't come as a surprise."

"Ah, family matter. Well, my partner's an asshole, too, but what are you going to do? He's your brother, man." The cop walked off, shaking his head.

Adam was his brother. Adam was the only family Jake had left. His parents never thought to call. Jake had to find them if he wanted to talk. His brothers had all moved on. And Jake was Adam's only family.

"Are you going to forgive me?" Jake had to ask because suddenly he was a little worried about it. What the hell would he do without Adam? Adam had been his best friend for almost all of his adult life. He'd lived with Adam for most of that time. He'd come to just depend on the fact that Adam would always be there.

Adam was the one who planned out their days. Adam did all the little things that allowed Jake to do the big things.

They really were kind of an old married couple. Except without the sex. God, they needed Serena.

But he needed Adam, too. Somehow, someway, Adam had come to be more than just a friend. He was the odd other half of Jacob's soul.

Adam was just staring as though trying to figure out how to handle him. But Jake was done being handled by everyone. He'd made that bed by being a taciturn son of a bitch and allowing Adam to handle anything even vaguely emotional because Jake didn't want to deal with it. Adam had taken over with the women they shared. He'd taken over with their friends. All so Jake wouldn't have to wade into the big, scary-ass emotional ocean. God, he'd been a coward.

"Adam, I don't know what I would do without you, man. I really hope you can forgive me, because my life would suck ass without you, but I'm going after her with you or without you. You got me into this. You manipulated me until I fell hard for her. And I fucked up. But I won't back down. She's the one. She's the one for us, but if you're too chickenshit to try, then she can be the one for me."

Finally, a little smile curved Adam's mouth. It was his son-of-a-bitch smile, and Adam always used it when someone was challenging him and he decided to take it up. "You couldn't get her without me."

"I don't even want to try," Jake admitted. But he would.

"Jake, what happened?" Serena opened the door, and for the first time since he'd fucked everything up this morning, her eyes were wide with concern. "Your nose."

"He pissed me off," Adam admitted.

Serena walked toward him, her hands coming up, her whole body aflutter with soft, feminine concern. "He needs ice. Adam, how could you hit him?"

"After what he said to you, how could I not?" Adam asked.

Jake let his whole body sag. "I deserved it. I didn't even punch him back. I'm sorry."

Serena went a little pink. "There is no call for violence. We need to get him home. I think you're going to have a black eye."

Jake smiled at Adam as Serena moved around him. She put her hands on him for the first time since she'd slapped him. Her fingers smoothed across his arm as though she couldn't quite withhold comfort.

He followed her to the car, listening to her lecture on how friends shouldn't fight.

But he was going to fight. He was just glad he had his partner back. Now all they had to do was figure out who was trying to kill her.

* * * *

Two days later, Adam was ready to tear his own hair out.

"Do you want another cup of coffee?" Adam looked down at Serena sitting at his desk, her laptop open. She stared at the screen, but as far as Adam could tell, she hadn't written a single word in days.

"No, thank you." She didn't bother to look up, simply said as little words as she had to in that vacantly polite voice she used these days on anyone who wasn't her dog, her best friend, or her gay husband. He was beginning to think of Chris that way. He'd sounded very husband-like the other day when he'd threatened to cut Adam's balls off and make them the centerpiece of a lovely multimedia artwork he was planning in the near future.

Why did he bother to try? He'd tried because Jake had been so insistent, and for a couple of minutes that first night after they had fucked up so badly, he'd thought that she might forgive them. But by the time they had gotten home, she'd shut down again, and now she was polite and so distant he was pretty sure she didn't realize he existed past his function as her keeper.

And he was starting to get brutally angry with her.

They had done everything they could over the past forty-eight hours to make things up to her. They had treated her with tenderness and deep concern. They'd seen to her every need. When she'd mentioned she wanted something sweet, Jake had practically raced out of the house to get it. He'd come back with ice cream, and she'd sighed and told them she'd changed her mind and headed off to bed.

She was either punishing them or she was way more of a coward than he thought she was.

Or she was simply through.

He'd tried. He really had. He'd done just about everything he could. And it was all still failing. There was a knock on the door. He sighed and left her sitting there, staring at her blank screen. He crossed and looked at the security monitor. He had cameras pointed at several key points in and around the house. He glanced at the monitor that showed the front door. Liam stood there looking pointedly at the camera, flipping it off with a frown. Yep, he thought he should really set up Liam with Bridget. They seemed to speak the same language. Adam pushed the button that opened the door, and Liam smiled before walking in.

"You're both paranoid fuckers, you know," he said as he marched passed the foyer and into the kitchen. He set a bag on the granite island. "I just love being your grocery boy. Did I mention that I want a fucking case of me own?"

Adam started to unpack the groceries and tried to change the topic to something that wouldn't have Liam cussing.

"Did you look through the profile?" Adam asked. He'd been studying it for days, trying to figure out anything at all. But he'd wanted Liam to look at it. Liam had always thought there was something fishy about the case, and he'd been right.

"Sure. I have nothing better to do." Liam hopped onto the

barstool after plucking one of the bottles of beer free from its place in the six-pack. He twisted off the cap in a neat turn. "Eve and I talked about it last night actually. She's sure this is a man. She thinks he's likely been married or is married and feels his relationship is threatened by the fantasies Serena writes. It ain't easy to live up to the whole billionaire with the twelve-inch cock thing." He smiled slowly. "Well, it's hard to live up to the billionaire part, anyway."

The last thing Adam wanted was to talk about Liam's dick. "Fine, so he's pissed off that she makes him look bad."

Liam shrugged, taking a long swig. "It's more than just that. He's probably threatened by everyone. He's got a huge ego, but very little confidence. He's the kind of man who places blame everywhere but on himself. And we came up with something else, too."

Adam looked back at Liam. It appeared he and Eve were closer than Adam expected. He wondered what Alex thought of his ex-wife spending so much time with the handsome Irish Dom. "What did you come up with?"

Liam sat forward, intelligence evident in his green eyes. "I think she knows him, like he's part of her life. Maybe she's not real close to him, but she moves in his circles."

He hated to admit it, but he and Jake had talked about the same thing. "It's too coincidental."

Liam nodded shortly. "You got that right. Shit like this doesn't happen that way. He's taking advantage. He heard about what was happening to her and saw a way to make her hurt. Or he was introduced to her through the case."

That was the worst of all the scenarios he had run through his head. "I don't like the cops."

"And they say you're just a pretty face," Liam snarked. "I'm running some stuff on the cops. And I think we should take another look at the ex. Why don't you do that hacking thing you do? Get me everything. E-mails, those books he's written, hell, I'll look at his lesson plans."

It was a good plan and Adam wanted to take it further. "And Lara. I don't care what Ian thinks. She's suspicious. I'll get everything I can off the agency's computers, too."

Liam nodded. "Whoever this is, it's personal. He torched her house. The arsonist did a damn fine job, by the way. He was practically professional."

"Or he was actually professional and he was paid for his services."

Liam shrugged. "Could be. Chitwood and Hernandez interest me. You say they don't seem to like Serena?"

"They don't trust her. Hernandez seems to actively dislike her, and I have no idea why. She's as sweet as can be."

"She's a little doll." Liam smiled. "I actually like her quite a bit. You know how I feel about curious little subs."

"Hands off," Adam shot back. Liam was known for enjoying a lot of non-committed play.

"Sorry. She's a sweet thing. I think you both chose really well. I mean it. She'll be good for you."

Adam pulled Serena's favorite tea out of the bag. "I don't know about that. We're crazy about her, but she seems to be done with us."

Jake walked in, a towel around his neck. He was dressed for a workout. "I thought we'd agreed to try optimism. Hey, Li. How's it going?"

Liam grimaced. "I'm spending too much fucking time up Ian's ass. I'm telling you, if I get even a whiff of that fucker, Black, I'll kill him on principle alone. But we were talking about your girl. Adam seems to think you two are in serious trouble."

Jake leaned against the wall, his weariness evident. "She's a stubborn one. She hasn't really talked to us in days. We're trying to give her some space."

Liam laughed. "Well, there's your first mistake. Dumbasses. Don't ever give a woman a minute to think or she'll realize just how much better than you she deserves. Come on. You two are playing this like amateurs. She's been through hell. She needs a damn Dom, not some pussy boys who give her a bunch of choices she's not ready to make."

Adam looked to Jake. Maybe they were playing it all wrong. "She hasn't broken under our tender care."

Liam snorted. "You're letting her control this? She lost her house. She lost everything, and you're letting her be alone? Can't you see she's pushing some serious boundaries?"

Jake grabbed a water bottle, turning around and leaning against the counter. "We might have been a little rough on her when we found out about the whole Lara thing."

"Yeah, well, I would have had the same concerns," Liam replied. "And I probably would have made a complete ass of myself, too. But what you're doing now is worse. You're letting her flounder. Look, I don't think you two should have fucked the client, but you're obviously in love with her, so you're responsible for her. You should be in bed with her. You should be cuddling with her. I can't believe I just said that. Cuddling makes me want to vomit a little, but apparently women like it."

"She's not in a cuddling mood." Adam would love nothing more than to hold her, but each night she'd gotten into bed and turned away. Adam or Jake had stayed in the room with her, but neither had gotten into bed. Maybe that had been a mistake. Giving her space wasn't working. It was only making her worse.

"So get her in one." Liam hopped off his barstool. "She's curious. See if her curiosity is still in full force. You two have dumped every bit of training you have between you. She's an op. Where do you start?"

Adam knew exactly where he was going. "We assess our advantages and disadvantages."

Jake smiled, his eyebrows rising. "Her curiosity about BDSM is a definite advantage."

"And her absolute hatred of us is a definite disadvantage." He sighed. He was doing it again. He wasn't going to win Serena back by moping. "She doesn't really hate us. She's mad, and she doesn't know how to come out of it."

"So we show her."

Adam went through his mental checklist of everything he had to do for the day. He had case work to do. He had some organizational work to do. He needed to call the caterers and the owner of the adult toy store where the signing was on Saturday. He needed to run background checks on everyone who was attending the event. And now he needed to set up a scene at the club.

Yeah, that would be the best part of his day. His dick twitched at the thought of getting inside Serena again. He'd only had one night, and it hadn't been close to enough.

"I'll take the hit," Adam said. "I'll call Ian and see what we can do."

"You're a brave man." Jake slapped him on the back in a brotherly gesture. "I'm going to run out to the store where the signing is and see about the security. If I don't like it, she's not going."

Adam groaned. "Don't tell her that, man. We need her in a decent mood."

Jake shrugged, obviously leaving that part to Adam. Jake and Liam walked out, talking about the case, and Adam was left to handle the cleanup.

He sighed and picked up the discarded bottle. At least he was good for something.

Now he needed to make sure he was good for Serena.

Chapter Eighteen

Serena sat in the back of the car wondering just why she was here.

Damn it. She knew why she was here. Because she wanted to be here, but she intended to make sure they didn't realize exactly why she was willing to go with them. Because she couldn't stop thinking about them. Because the very idea of being forced to spend a night close to them made her heart start to beat again.

"You okay back there?" Adam asked. He'd slid into the driver's seat.

Okay? She was anxious. She was on the edge. She was restless. "I'm fine."

They were ruthless bastards who knew just how to get to a girl. They knew that to get to a girl, a man went for her curiosity. This might be the last time she got to go into a real-life club. The whole debacle with Master Storm had made her realize it wasn't exactly safe looking for someone to shepherd her through this world. Maybe putting up an ad on a social networking site wasn't the best idea.

Then there was the fact that she wanted one more night with them. She knew it couldn't work out now, but they had more to teach her than just a couple of spankings and some great sex. She wanted to know what it felt like to be between two men. Just once. It was the fantasy of her lifetime, and they were her fantasy men. She would take the experience and hold it close. She would write about it forever, long after they were gone and had a new woman.

If only she could figure out how to make it happen without giving too much of herself away.

Adam pulled up to the front door. Sanctum was an unspectacular building in a decent part of town. Nothing about the structure screamed hot sex club, but the man who stalked out the front door did that all on his own.

Liam was dressed in leathers and a pair of boots, and nothing else but a smile. He opened the door to the back of the car and held his hand out. "Your escort has arrived."

She couldn't figure out what bugged her about the gorgeous bodyguard, but something was off. He was hiding something, and she found it fascinating. If she was going to write him as a character, he would have a tragic past that clouded his future. He would be in hiding. And just like that she figured out what bugged her.

"That isn't your real accent, is it?"

The Dom looked at her, his eyes widening and then his Irish flowed. "Fuck me, the girl is good."

She smiled. There he was. "You don't look Midwestern." The flat cadence had never gone with the rest of him.

"The girl also already has an escort." Jake got in front of Liam, reaching in to take her hand.

Liam, for all his hotness, didn't get her heart racing the way Jake did. She didn't try to pull away. It had been made very clear to her that this trip to Sanctum was dependent on her very good behavior. She allowed Jake to help her out of the car.

"Ian wanted to make sure we didn't have a repeat of last time," Liam explained as Adam drove off to park the car. Adam and Jake had made it plain they didn't want that either. Security inside the club was very good, but they intended to drop her off and pick her up at the door. They had gone over all the protocols. She was to be close to one of them or Liam at all times. She wasn't allowed back into the car until Jake or Adam had checked it out and came to get her. She would then be escorted on the short walk from the club to the car by not one, but two men.

This was her life now.

"Hey," Jake said, squeezing her hand lightly. "It's going to be okay. Come on. Ian's supposedly working on punishing some of the subs. It should be fun."

"He's got his six footer out," Liam said with a wink her way. He was so different with his real voice, lighter, more at ease.

Jake hustled her to the door. "The six footer scares the crap out of me. I can't handle it."

They were talking about a whip. Ian intended to use a six-foot whip on some poor sub's backside. Or if the sub was a total masochist, he could be intending to use it on some lucky sub's backside. It was all in how a person looked at it. It was what she loved about the lifestyle. It was utterly open to what a person needed.

She needed Jake and Adam. Why did she have to need them? Why couldn't she just come out of her damn corner? She let Jake lead her inside. She was already dressed for the evening in a miniskirt and a bright pink tank top. And absolutely nothing else even though she'd explained to them she wasn't having sex. They had been adamant about no bra and no underwear.

And she was kind of hoping to have sex.

Serena groaned inwardly. She couldn't stand this indecision.

"I'm going to drop my keys and shirt off in my locker. Can you keep an eye on her?" Jake asked Liam.

Liam grinned down at her, waving Jake off. "Sure thing."

"Eyes on her, Li. No hands." Jake sent him a dark look before he walked toward the lockers.

Liam gave her a sexy smile and leaned against the front desk. "So, you're enjoying playing with the boys, are you?"

That felt like a loaded question. "I'm not playing with them. We had a brief affair, and now it's over."

"It doesn't look like it's over for them. They seem very serious about you."

Yep, this was more than a friendly conversation. "I was convenient."

"Do you want to see just how convenient you are? Do you think a man would try to kill his friend over a convenient lay? Trust me on this one. Adam damn well deserves this." Liam reached out and put a hand on her waist, pulling her close, her chest bumping against his.

"What are you doing?" Serena asked, her wide eyes taking him in.

"Proving a point. I'm about to make you deeply inconvenient." He leaned over, and before she could protest, he brushed his lips against hers.

She had a brief shock of recognition. Liam was intensely hot. He was insanely sexy. He had those deep green eyes and shockingly dark hair, and that accent that melted her female parts. She felt a moment's curiosity. She hadn't been kissed very often. She'd had a few boyfriends, but Doyle comprised the majority of her sexual experience.

It was different to kiss Liam. She viewed the experience from an intellectual standpoint even as Liam molded his lips to hers. He didn't use his tongue. She might have protested that. There was an almost lackadaisical interest coming from Liam. She felt oddly safe with him.

And while the man knew how to kiss, she really didn't want him to kiss her. Because she belonged to someone else. She belonged to Adam and Jake. Adam and Jake were the ones who moved her. She wouldn't have been thinking if she'd been in their arms. She would have been living that kiss.

Suddenly, it felt brutally wrong to be in Liam's arms. She started to push against him, but she didn't need to. She fell back on her ass as she was shoved out of his arms. Adam didn't play the gentleman. He didn't scream or ask what had happened. He didn't reach out to lend her a hand. His eyes were dark as night as his fist came out.

"Now, Adam, I was just making a point," Liam said, holding his hands up in a placating gesture.

Again, not a word passed Adam's lips. He struck out, his fist flying and catching Liam directly across the jaw. The Irish Dom cursed.

"Fuck all, Adam, you know you deserved that. Sean would high-five me." Liam had a shit-eating grin on his face.

Adam simply launched his body at the other man and rammed

his knee in his gut, causing Liam to grunt in pain.

"What the fuck is going on?" Jake asked, offering Serena a hand up.

Serena wasn't sure how to explain. She was watching two men fight. It was oddly quieter than she had expected it to be. Liam obviously decided he didn't like the way Adam had nearly kneed him in the groin and had stopped taunting him, obviously preferring to pay him back. He kicked out, trying to catch Adam. They were really fighting. Over her.

Well, Adam was fighting over her. She rather thought Liam was just fighting.

"Serena, I asked you a question." Jake glared at her, forcing her attention back to him.

"Adam didn't like something Liam did and so they started fighting."

Jake stared down at her. "What the fuck did he do? Tell me now."

"He kissed me." She couldn't think of a lie, and she was worried what he would do if she did lie. He liked to spank her, after all.

Jake nodded, and for the briefest of moments, she thought he would be reasonable about it. They didn't have a commitment. They weren't boyfriend and girlfriend. Or was that boyfriends and girlfriend? It didn't matter because Jake's moment of reason was deeply short lived. He turned and jumped into the fray. He punched Liam right in the eye.

"Goddamn it." Ian walked into the lobby, a fierce frown on his face. Alex was beside him. Both men were dressed in leathers and looked like a calm in the storm. *Thank god.* Someone could break this up.

Ian waded into the throng and pulled Adam up by his collar. Alex got a hand on Liam.

"You three need to calm down," Ian ordered, his deep voice blatantly military. Serena had no problem envisioning him handling a unit of elite soldiers. Or really mad Doms.

Alex held on to Liam's neck and then suddenly punched him straight on the nose. Liam shouted out, cursing.

"What the fuck?" Liam held his bloody nose.

"That was for Eve," Alex said, his shoulders set. He turned and walked away.

Liam held his hands up. He turned and looked at Ian, his eyes wide with apparent shock. "What was that about? I've never touched Eve."

"He knows you've been spending time with Eve. He suspects you're sleeping with her." Ian gave Adam a little snarl. "Don't fucking try anything else. That means you, too, Jake."

Jake gave him a mulish stare. "He kissed my sub."

"She doesn't have a collar on," Ian pointed out. "Get a collar around her throat and we'll talk. And you," he turned to Liam, "need to stay away from Alex's wife."

"Ex-wife." Liam frowned. "And I'm not fucking Eve. Not even close." He grinned Serena's way. "Though I will fuck that one."

Both Jake and Adam started for him again. Ian hauled Liam behind his own enormous body.

"Back off," Ian commanded. "He's being an asshole."

Liam crossed his arms over his chest and looked over at Serena. "There you go, dear. That's your answer. You're very inconvenient now. They're risking their jobs, and their jobs are pretty much all they have. You're being brutally stubborn. You're hurting all three of you. Come out of that corner, Serena. You don't really want to be there anyway." Liam backed away. "I'm going to clean up. You three better figure something out or it's going to be over."

He walked away. Ian practically had steam coming out of his ears. "What he fucking said. I'm sick of this shit. I have a sub to whip."

He stalked off, and she was left with the two men who had completely turned her life upside down.

Adam seemed to calm a bit. He straightened his clothes, a white dress shirt and his leathers. There was a scratch on his face, but otherwise he seemed to have fared well. "Come on then, Serena."

She felt rooted to the ground and deeply unsure. "I think we should probably talk about this."

"And I think someone is due a bit of punishment," Jake said harshly.

"Punishment?" Why the hell did that word make her pussy clench? Punishment meant they would put their hands on her. "I didn't do anything."

"Did you or did you not sign a contract when we first brought you into this club?" Jake asked. His face was set in hard lines. She had the sudden desire to get on her knees in front of him.

"You know I did." Ian wouldn't let her in without signing a contract. It stated that Jake would act as her Dom, and he would be responsible for her behavior. It covered all sorts of things like confidentiality and how she should behave. She felt her face fall. It had also made it plain that according to all rules of this club, she belonged to her Dom. She stared up at Jake. This wasn't her fault. "He kissed me, not the other way around."

"You weren't fighting him," Adam said. He seemed calmer now. "You were still in his arms. I know you, Serena. You would have fought him if you hadn't wanted it."

"I didn't want it, damn it. I was just curious."

Jake's smile held not an ounce of humor. "You know what curiosity did to the kitty cat. I think you're about to find out what it does to your pussy. Now, Serena. Or we can go back home and go right back to you sitting in front of the computer getting absolutely nothing done."

Adam put a hand on her shoulder. "Serena, aren't you curious about this?"

She was. Damn it. And it was just punishment. Punishment that might lead to sex. Sex that might lead to something else. No. She wasn't going to go there. She wasn't going to start planning a future with them. She was done with that. But she could have another night. Maybe a few more nights.

She dropped to her knees, trying to find the proper position. She wasn't going to deny it. She wanted to explore with them. She'd written about this lifestyle, studied it, and dreamed about it. Letting go of this chance because she knew it couldn't work with Jake and Adam seemed wrong.

She was nervous and so confused she couldn't see straight. She wasn't in a place to make any kind of decision, but she could have this. Just for a little while.

Jake's hand came out, forcing her chin up. "I'm not going easy on you tonight."

She didn't want him to. She wanted this experience. She wanted to ache and burn and to come like she never had before. And she wanted it with them. "Yes, Sir."

There was no way to mistake what that one simple word did to Jake's cock. It strained against his leathers. She remembered just how good that cock felt deep inside her body. She'd never felt so connected as she had when she'd made love to Jake and then again with Adam. For those brief moments, she'd been truly intimate with another human being. She'd felt more alive than ever before.

Was she making a terrible mistake? Maybe. But she couldn't just jump in again with her whole heart. Her body was another story.

"You're not going to give me an inch, are you?" Jake asked, his face losing its harshness. A cloud of sadness descended over him. "Adam is right. You're never going to forgive us."

"I forgive you." They were easy words to say. She didn't really have to mean them.

"I told you," Adam said, his voice deep.

Jake turned to Adam, and they had one of those silent moments she always envied. They seemed to be able to speak to each other without saying a word, as though some event long ago had connected them in ways few others could understand.

Jake finally looked back down at her. "This is all you'll give us?"

"It's all I have to give." She was still aching on the inside. She'd handed them her heart and gotten back a mottled mess. She just couldn't get past that moment when they'd rejected her. It would happen again. Potentially over and over again. Doyle had asked for a divorce three times before he'd finally gone through with it. Each time she'd allowed him to talk his way out of it. He was sorry. He'd said it in the heat of the moment. He hadn't really meant it.

But he had. Even if they hadn't meant it this time, they would in the future. She couldn't risk it. Not again.

"I'll take it." Jake took her elbow and helped her up. "All you want out of this is a D/s relationship. Do I understand you correctly?"

Serena latched onto that thought. A D/s relationship wasn't a love affair. It didn't have to involve anything except an exchange of power. Some D/s relationships didn't even involve sex. She sure as hell didn't want that, but a D/s relationship didn't necessarily have to end when the case was over.

Jake was a Dom. Adam was invested in the lifestyle. What if she could become their sub? They could come together for play. She could keep them in some small way.

"Yes, Sir. It's what I always wanted. I went looking for a Dom, if you remember." Serena kept her voice carefully controlled. "My life has been out of control for some time. I think I need this. I know I would like to try it."

"And if I say no? If I won't top you?" Jake practically growled the question.

If he wouldn't, she would probably just shut down that part of herself or keep it where she should have all along—deep in her books. Words couldn't hurt her. She simply shrugged. "Then there's no point in me being here, Sir. You should take me home."

Adam laughed, a bitter little sound. "Well, I can see I'm not needed here. I thought she was interested in ménage, but she seems to only want a Dom."

Why did he have to be so fucking sensitive? Most guys would follow her around and wait for a chance to shove his dick in, but no, Adam had to make a scene. Of course, most guys wouldn't wake up every morning, make her coffee and make sure her schedule was perfectly detailed and ready. He'd actually laid out the right clothes for her activities the last few days. She didn't have to think about the little things with Adam around. But she did have to deal with his ego.

"I would prefer two Doms."

"I'm not a Dom, Serena."

"Really? Because you seem to have control of my day. You control my schedule, my clothes, what I eat and when I eat it." He'd taken over just about everything, and her life was so much better for it. He'd even started feeding her dog. "I would prefer if you stayed, Sir. I am interested in ménage. From an intellectual viewpoint."

Adam's boots came into view. And then she hissed a little as he tugged on her hair, forcing her to face up to him. "Intellectual? You're full of shit, sweetheart, and if I thought for a second that you weren't lying to yourself and to both of us, I would walk away. But I happen to have a ton of frustration, and it would help me enormously to take it out on your sweet ass. I might not have Dom rights in this club, but don't you fucking think for a second that I can't top you. Now get on your feet."

Serena rose, Adam's hand on her arm, supporting her. That was what he'd become, her support, while Jacob was the bulwark against all the bad things that could come her way.

Except for just a minute, he'd been the bad thing.

Fuck all. She was so damn torn. Still, she couldn't help herself. They called and she followed.

"Take off your shirt." Jake crossed his arms over his chest.

She felt the world tilt just a little. "What?"

His eyes narrowed. "I said take off your shirt. I'm your Dom. I want to see your breasts. I want to show them off because in this club, those tits belong to me. I think they're beautiful, and I want to see them. So take off your shirt or use your safe word and we'll go home."

He was pushing her, and she wasn't going to take it. Well, not that way. She wasn't going to let him shove her away. She remained mulishly silent, but she pulled at the bottom of her tank top. It was just some skin. Every woman in the place had breasts. It wasn't anything that hadn't been seen a million times before.

With shaking hands, she passed Jake her shirt. Her breasts were exposed, the nipples tightening in the cool air of the club.

"Better." Jake turned her to Adam. "Should we start her punishment now?"

It hadn't already started? Ian walked by, his eyes trailing toward her. He was looking at her breasts. He was a magnificent specimen of a man who could likely get any woman he wanted, and he was looking right at her breasts. The barest hint of a smile turned those gorgeously sculpted lips up and then he winked at her as he strode by.

Holy crap. She was half naked and it actually felt sexy. An ache started, low in her gut.

Yes, this was a little bit of torture, but she felt more alive than she had in days.

Adam stared down at her, ignoring everything else around him. His hands went to his pockets. He came out with something she knew well, but not from actual experience. Nipple clamps. Two tweezer clamps connected by a little chain. Adam dropped to his knees, handing Jake the clamps. He leaned forward and sucked a nipple into his mouth.

Serena gasped. She started to stumble, but Jake was behind her, his strong arms holding her up.

"You let him get you ready. Don't fight him. Don't you fucking fight your Dom." Jake's breath was hot on her ear.

And Adam's tongue tortured her nipple. He sucked and bit and laved it with affection, the sensation going straight to her pussy. She fought to stay still. It was so hard, but she loved this. She was surrounded by them, their heat sinking into her skin.

Adam didn't let up. He ravished her nipples, one after another. People walked by, and Serena didn't care. Adam's arms wrapped around her waist, holding her close while Jake balanced her. She could feel Jake's erection nestled against the cheeks of her ass. She let her head fall back against his chest as Adam switched nipples. He teased one with his tongue while rolling the other with his thumb and forefinger.

And then he pulled back, looking at his handiwork. Her nipples strained toward him, standing straight up at attention. He held his hand out, and Jake passed him the clamps.

She whimpered a little as Adam attached them, carefully turning the screw.

"They're barely tight enough to stay on." Adam touched the chain that hung between her breasts. "You'll be wearing these for a while, so I can't get them too tight. Yet. But I'll work you up to a real burn. Jake, we're going to need a plug and a little privacy. I'm not done decorating this sub."

"I have just what we need." Jake kissed the nape of her neck. "I ordered a privacy room and had it stocked."

She was utterly out of breath. "I thought we were going to

watch Ian."

Jake growled a little. "I think we've seen enough from our team tonight. You can become acquainted with the whip at a later date. Tonight, you're going to get the crop."

She had to force herself to breath. The idea of Jacob's crop hitting the flesh of her ass made her heart pound.

"You're being punished for more than just kissing Liam." Adam's hands were on the chain that ran between her nipples. The pressure was very light, barely there. She wondered when they would turn the screw again. When Adam turned the screws on her clamps, would her nipples pool with blood and become deeply sensitive?

She'd written the scene so many times, but now it was real. Now it was visceral. They owned her body. It was a deep exchange that went beyond sex. It was about far more than a mere orgasm. It was about bonding. It was about being able to trust and depend on another.

She wanted that so badly. She couldn't have it in the real world, couldn't trust it, but she could pretend it was real here. Maybe, if she was lucky, she could keep the relationship where it should have been all along. A D/s relationship. A mentorship of sorts. No promises beyond the ones they made in a contract.

Jake pulled a collar out of his pocket. He must have had it on his person or kept it in his locker. It was a leather collar, thin and feminine, with a delicate silver ring on the front. He held it out, showing it off before he nodded to Adam.

Adam crowded her from behind, his thick erection rubbing against her backside. She shivered a little as he gathered her hair and held it up. With a solemn formality, he clasped the collar around her neck.

"It's just a training collar. You can relax. It's not a commitment. You don't seem to want that."

She wanted it more than anything. She just knew how much it meant. Doyle had committed. Her father had committed. Both had walked away when it became easier to do so than to stay. She knew she could be difficult. She lived in her head most of the time. It had been that way since she was a child. She could stop writing, but she couldn't stop those voices in her head. Doyle had never understood that her inner life didn't take away from her care for the outside world. It was just a part of her.

Jake and Adam would get tired of her remoteness in the end.

"I don't want it. I just want the training." The words sounded flat to her own ears, but he seemed to require an answer.

"If all you want is some real-life experience for those books of yours, then you shall have it." He turned, every muscle rigid. "Follow. Don't look the other Doms in the eye. It's rude. Keep your head down and don't speak unless you're directed to. Any infraction will cost your ass five swats. I'll pull your skirt up and spank you publicly. If you aren't ready for that, I would behave."

Adam's face was a careful blank as he took her elbow and started to walk her into the dungeon. The privacy rooms were to the side, but Jake walked past them, his long legs eating the distance between the entryway and the raised stage where a pretty sub with long, black hair was being strapped to a St. Andrew's cross. Her naked flesh was on full display, her shoulders relaxed as she allowed Ian to tighten the cinches at her wrists and ankles.

A second woman was already secured. She was a brunette with a curvy backside. Her head was thrown back as though simply waiting for her punishment to begin. There was a hushed air of expectancy that ran through the dungeon. A small crowd stood, almost all in some sort of fet wear. Serena took it all in. There was enough leather to start a mega store. Most of the women had on skirts and bustiers, but several wore nothing at all. There were Doms and Dommes with their submissives, both male and female.

What were they like in their everyday lives? Her mind raced with the possibilities. Were they powerful in their own ways, each seeking a bit of peace that came with submission? Did they crave it because the stresses of responsibility ate away at their souls? Or were they like her? Did they need permission to let go, to trust in any circumstance?

"She's gone again." Adam looked down at her, a ghost of a smile on his face.

Yes, she'd done it again. "I apologize."

"I wasn't mad," Adam said, his hand coming out to sweep

against her cheek. "I just wish I knew where you went. I envy you."

"Why?"

"Because there's a whole other world in your head. I've been reading your books. I'm not a huge romance fan, but I know a good story when I read it. I know that you sink into every book. In that head of yours you've already lived a hundred lives, seen things, felt them in a way the rest of us can't. I wish you would understand that I know how precious a gift that is. I want to protect it, to nurture it. I want to take care of the little things so that beautiful brain of yours can have the adventures it was built for."

He really knew what to say to her. "You would get tired of it after a while. You would think I was ignoring you."

He shook his head. "I would know I was in there somewhere. I would read what you wrote at the end of the day to find out about the stories you weave about me. You would be writing about me. I would make sure of it. I would love you so long and so well that you would have to write about me."

Jake didn't look her way. He kept his eyes on the stage, but there was an intimacy to his voice that gave away the fact that he wasn't entirely unemotional. "And I would force you to come out of it from time to time. I would keep you with us. We could keep you grounded, Serena. You don't have to hide all the time. I get that you love your work. I want you to. But you can love your reality, too."

Her reality was horrible right now. Her reality was someone trying to kill her and the men she loved being far away from her. She knew it was her choice. She knew she was being stubborn, but she couldn't quite reach out and grab them. "You'll pardon me if I don't enjoy real life right now."

Jake looked down at her. "I didn't mean enjoy, Serena. Enjoy is a lazy word. I know your life sucks right now. But your reality is you have a family around you. It might not be the one you wanted when you were six years old and had a child's dreams that everything would be perfect, but it's a family all the same. Bridget and Chris have been calling for days, and you're ignoring them."

She wasn't ignoring them. She just didn't know what to say. And she didn't want them hurt. "I think they should stay away from me for a while."

"Adam." The name came out of Jake's mouth like a sharp command, and Adam seemed to know just what to do.

"First turn of the screw, sweetheart," Adam said, his hands going to the clamps on her breasts. He turned the screw, her nipples peaking as they were tweaked.

She whimpered a little. Yeah, she felt that. "What was that for?"

Jake leaned over and whispered in her ear. "First off, I didn't ask you a direct question, so that's five, though we'll count this as a warning and leave it for the privacy room. The next time, it will be right here in public. Secondly, I'm attempting to do exactly what you just hired me for. You don't want me as a lover. You want a Dom. Well, a Dom's job is to correct the behaviors in his sub that cause her trouble and heartache. To instill discipline. You're pushing away your friends. It's going to cost you a couple of people you can't afford to lose. You will call them in the morning. You will reach out to them. Permission to speak, but keep a civil tongue."

Oh, that permission to speak shit was bugging her, but Jake had that superior look on his face. The one that told her this was what she got from the pure Dom. Not a boyfriend. A hired Dom. Damn it, she hadn't meant it that way, but she wasn't sure how to fix it. "Jake, what if this guy decides to hurt me through my friends?"

Adam turned her to face him. "Would you dump Bridget if she was in trouble?"

"Never." Bridget and Chris were her lifelines. And she would be devastated if they didn't let her help. If this was happening to Bridget and Chris, she would want to be there, standing right beside them. "I'll call them tomorrow."

"Excellent. Ah, Ian's ready to start." Adam turned her back to the stage. "Our little sub is finally thinking a bit."

"Good. I wasn't certain she was educable. She's very stubborn."

"I think she can learn. I also think she'll require an enormous amount of punishment."

Neither man looked at her, their object lesson clear. This was how they treated a submissive they had been told specifically to have no attachment to. She'd told them it was what she'd wanted.

She didn't know what she wanted. Ian was on stage saying all sorts of formal protocol stuff that would probably be really good for her next novel, and all she could think about was how miserable she was. And how she didn't know what to do about it.

Ian held out his whip, presenting it to both subs who kissed it reverently before he stepped back. His muscular arm flipped back, and there was a cracking sound that split the air around her.

"Does this do anything for you?" Adam asked. His arm wound around her waist, hauling her close so his mouth was right against her ear. She was nestled against him, back to front. One arm stayed around her waist, but the other was on her thigh, creeping up toward her unprotected-by-panties pussy.

Yeah, that did something for her. It made her breath quicken, her pink parts pulse. She was half naked in a club full of other naked people watching a seriously hot dude whip two women, and one of the sexiest men she'd ever seen was cuddling her close, his hand hovering above her pussy.

"Yes, Sir." The scene was interesting, but more than anything, she was interested in the arm around her waist and his breath on her ear. She cuddled close to him. Yes, her pussy was fluttering, but she really wanted to feel close to him, to both of them.

Jake was suddenly in front of her. His hand went to the chain between her breasts. "Then why are your eyes half closed? You aren't watching the scene at all. I thought you were curious. I thought you wanted to learn about D/s."

He pulled at the chain, and Serena felt her eyes water. Her nipples flared with a brief pain that turned to almost unbearable erotic stimulation.

"I do, Sir." But she wanted to learn it from them.

In the low light of the dungeon, Jake looked harsh and unrelenting. "I think you're more interested in an orgasm than you are in the lifestyle, little tourist. Do you know how we handle bratty tourists in this club? We show them the truth. By the end of the night, you'll either be in or you'll be out. I bet you'll be out. I suspect you won't be able to handle it."

He was challenging her? Well, she could be pretty stubborn herself. "Fuck you, Jake."

Adam chuckled low in her ear. "Now you've done it."

Jake picked her up, tossing her over his shoulder like a sack of potatoes. Her whole world upended as he stalked out of the dungeon toward the privacy rooms.

Serena went limp in his arms. He was right. She would know after tonight exactly what she could handle.

Chapter Nineteen

Jake's cock was throbbing, but it was nothing compared to just how angry he was at her. He pushed through the door to the privacy room. He'd reserved a different one than the room they'd first made love in. He couldn't go back in there. It wasn't the same. This wasn't about making love. She didn't want to make love to him. She didn't want a lover.

All she wanted was a damn Dom.

Well, he could be that for her.

He set her on her feet, well aware that he was on the edge of his control. His eyes went to the clamps on her breasts. Adam had been a pussy about those clamps. They were barely hanging on. If she wanted a BDSM relationship, she was going to have to get used to her role. He was the sadist. And she was the masochist.

Brusquely and as impersonally as he could, he tightened the screws.

Her eyes dilated, those green orbs huge in the low light. Well, at least one of them had their roles down. Little Serena liked a bite of pain. Yeah, he could give that to her.

"The red room?" Adam threw him a glance. "Really?"

The red room was known as a torture chamber. It was slightly larger than the other privacy rooms and boasted a whipping bench and a sawhorse, a multitude of hooks in the walls and the ceiling, and a whole wall of never used before impact play toys.

"She said she wanted a BDSM experience. I'll give her one." The first night they'd made love had been personal, intimate. He'd used his hand and then made love to her with the only thought being their mutual pleasure. It hadn't worked. It hadn't bound her to him. Days of lavishing affection on her hadn't worked. All she wanted was his harshness. Perhaps it was the only thing of value he had to give.

"Hold out your hands." He picked up a shiny pair of handcuffs from the table. He'd thought about buying a kit for her, selecting everything himself. But she didn't want that.

She obediently put her hands out. Her face was closed off, her stance shutting him out even as she was on display for him. He pressed the cuffs around her wrists, snapping them on and tightening them. Still not a look from her. She simply stared at the handcuffs, probably cataloging the experience for some future book.

"Take off the skirt, then turn around and place your hands flat on the sawhorse." The cuffs had enough give that she could make do.

"What are you going to do?" Serena asked.

Adam groaned. "I'll handle it." He sat down on the edge of the bed, the only softness in the whole room. He hauled Serena over his lap, pulled her miniskirt up, and gave her five quick slaps. Serena's legs kicked briefly and then she sagged down.

So fucking submissive. Why couldn't she see that they could be more than this?

"You have a safe word, Serena. You have a safe word and a slow-down word. Use them. This is not going to go well, love. Both you and Jake seem to want to tear each other apart tonight." Adam's hand soothed across her pinkened flesh.

Serena said nothing at all.

Adam sighed and set her back on her feet. "Then you should do as he says."

Serena turned and leaned over the sawhorse, placing her palms down on the surface and lowering her back. She didn't move to push her skirt down. It pooled at her waist, the only bit of clothing he'd left her.

He was fine with it. It gave the whole scene a little edge of brutality. If he ordered her to take it off, she would be naked, utterly vulnerable, all of her soft skin there for his pleasure. She would look far too open and trusting when he knew damn well she was closed to him. Well, at least her heart was. She was perfectly willing to open her legs for him.

He went to the toy rack and selected a new anal plug, this one larger than the itty bitty thing Adam had shoved up her ass. If she wanted a Dom, then she was going to find out that the Dom she'd selected enjoyed fucking submissive little assholes. She would learn to take his cock up her rectum. He washed the toy, scrubbing it with impatient hands and lubing it up.

"Jacob, maybe you should have a safe word, too."

Adam was starting to get to him. "If you don't like it, feel free to leave."

Adam sighed as he stared at them both. "You were the one who told me to be patient."

"I'm giving her exactly what she wants."

"She doesn't know what she wants, Jake."

"Fuck you, Adam," Serena said.

"Or she's too stubborn to admit what's good for her." Adam smacked her ass another five times, his hand swinging in an arc, leaving pink flesh where he slapped her. He took a deep breath in. "You know this is classic brat behavior. She's topping from the bottom. I can smell her pussy right now. She's trying to get what she wants without giving anything up for it."

"My ass is on fire, Adam. I think there's an exchange here." Serena didn't move, but her sarcasm seemed to be flowing nicely.

Adam grimaced, but did what needed to be done. Ten smacks this time, the last one right between her legs. "Keep your mouth closed, Serena. Unless you have something sweet to say or want to use your safe word and save us all a lot of heartache."

The little brat had nothing to say to that. God, he was still waiting for her to turn and ask him to kiss her, to hold her. He was still waiting for a forgiveness that wasn't coming. He'd ruined everything with a few careless words, but he knew himself well. He would fuck up again. He could be cruel. He could try, but if she put him through hell every time he was an idiot, then he would spend the rest of his life walking on eggshells.

Maybe she was right. Maybe this was the only way they could be together.

"Hold her cheeks apart for me." This wasn't happiness, but fuck it, he couldn't help himself. If this was all she would give him, he would take it and be everything she seemed to think he was.

Adam's hands caressed the cheeks of her ass briefly before pulling them apart, revealing the rosette of her ass. Jake's cock jumped in his pants. He wanted to take her there. He wanted to take her in every way it was possible for a man to have a woman. He wanted to fill her up, to know she was walking around with his semen deep inside her body.

Fuck. He wanted to get her pregnant. If she was pregnant, they would be tied together more tightly than any contract. Even if he managed to get her to sign a pure D/s contract with him, she could always walk away. He couldn't hold her. He was very aware that his time with her was limited. When they found her stalker and she was safe, she would leave and likely never speak to them again, or their only contact would be in this club with him as her distant Dom.

But a child would force them all together.

He pressed the lubed plug to her ass, the idea playing in his brain. Serena would be beautiful all big and round and full of child. His kid. Adam's kid. It didn't matter. The baby would be theirs, and they would have to find a way to function as a family. She would need him. She would need Adam.

Serena gasped, the little sound going straight to his cock. He rimmed the rosette of her ass with the plug before starting to push in.

"Breathe out, love," Adam instructed her. "Flatten your back. Let the plug slide in."

Adam. Adam was the sweet one. Adam was the one she already needed. Adam took care of her everyday needs. Jake was just the muscle who was there to take any bullet that came her way. Who the fuck was he kidding? Serena already knew the score. He was good for this, for research, for fucking. He would never be able to sit down and talk about books with her the way Adam did.

Something nasty took root in his gut. If he did get her pregnant, she still wouldn't want him around.

He pressed the plug in, forcing himself to be careful when all he really wanted to do was throw the fucking plug away and shove his cock inside. The plug finally moved, burying itself deep.

"See, that wasn't so bad," Adam said, his hand tracing up and down her spine.

Adam got to be the good guy. Jake was always put in the bad guy role. It was his place on the earth. He grabbed the crop off the wall.

"No count is required this time, Serena. You're getting fifteen for disobeying orders and protocol. Another ten for cursing me."

"But Adam already spanked me."

"And another five for questioning me." She really didn't understand the way this was going to go. "You wanted two Masters. Adam gave you his punishment. It's time for mine."

She was stubbornly silent, her ass in the air.

There was a little feeling of relief. He'd thought, for a moment, that she would tell him to leave. That he could lose both her and Adam in one moment.

But it had passed. And she still wanted the dark art he could teach her. Without a warning, he struck, bringing the crop down on her ass.

Serena yelped, her whole body shaking. Her cuffed hands held on to the sawhorse.

"No sound, sub." He struck again, bringing the leather crop down on the pale flesh of her ass. He couldn't help it. The sight of his mark on her just did something for him. She wouldn't bruise. He was more careful than that, but the pink line would be there for a day or two, marking her as his sub. Two and then three more times, he brought it down, spreading the pain across her body, waiting for it to flare and sink into her bones, heating her from the inside out.

"Test her, Adam." He needed to know if it was doing what it was intended to do. If she wasn't getting hot, if pain was all she felt, then he would walk away now with the full knowledge that he had nothing to give her.

Adam's fingers disappeared between her legs. He came back up, sucking those fingers into his mouth, licking up her juices. "She's a ripe, juicy peach, my brother. She's enjoying this."

At least one thing was going right. She did want a Dom. He wished she wanted more, but he could do this.

He kept count in his head, forcing himself to bury his unwanted emotions. He'd tried for days to be the patient, loving man he thought she wanted. He'd tried to talk to her only to have her shut down. He'd dealt with the insurance agents while Adam had handled her business. And she'd sat staring at the computer screen, shutting them both out.

She'd given him one way to reach her, and even that she'd put limits on. He needed to take some control back. He needed to begin as he meant to go, and that meant establishing boundaries. Walls between them that would guide their behaviors.

He worked her over with an unrelenting hand. And still she didn't cry. When he was done, Adam helped her stand and her face was red, but not a tear fell.

He'd tried to push past her walls, but they were too high to ever climb over.

"Are you all right?" It was a question he asked every sub. The answer was clear, but she lied again. One more wall.

"I'm fine, Sir."

"Then get on your knees." Even though his heart felt like it was going to shatter, he still fucking wanted her. He opened his leathers, setting his cock free. "There's a way to thank your Dom for his discipline. Should I spell it out for you?"

Finally, she cracked a smile. "I think I know where this is going. Thank you, Sir. The discipline was enlightening."

It should have been a bonding experience. It should have been deep and emotional and transformative, and he was pretty sure she was simply storing the memories for later use.

"Give me your hands." He unlocked the cuffs and set them aside. He would love to see her in full bondage. He adored the cuffs. If she was his, he would carry them with him always so he could bind his little sub whenever the need arose. If she was truly his, she would find herself cuffed and fucked in the oddest of places, the experiences creating a bond between them.

But she wasn't his, and seeing her in those damn cuffs made his heart hurt. He should have stuck to rope.

Adam was right about the emotion in the room, but he was wrong that it went both ways. Jake was the only one who was getting torn to shreds. But he would have some compensation.

"Suck me. Take my cock and swallow me down. Everything I give you." His unruly cock didn't care that his heart was aching. It wanted one thing and one thing only—Serena. He was a little worried he would never want anyone else again. Serena had spoiled him for all other women.

Adam helped her to her knees. "Clench your cheeks, love. It's hard at first, but you can do it."

She smiled up at him as she settled in. "Will I get punished if it comes out?"

"Yes, I think the big bad Dom there has an endless need to punish you tonight," Adam said, pulling her hair back. "You should do what he says. You should eat that big dick up. I think you should serve both your Masters."

Adam got to his feet and freed his own cock. Serena's eyes lit up, looking from Jake to Adam and back again. She licked those fuck-me lips of hers and then leaned over, her tongue sucking Jake's cock inside as she palmed Adam.

Pure, white pleasure suffused him as Serena sucked him. She was awkward at first, working her mouth around his cock, trying to find a rhythm.

This was how it should be, the three of them together. But he'd screwed it all up.

He closed his eyes and let the heat of her mouth wash over him. Her tongue whirled around his dick, encasing him in pleasure. The tension made his every muscle hard. She sucked him in long passes, and then moved to Adam, squeezing Jake with her hand.

He watched as her mouth closed over Adam's cock. He'd been told it was perverse, but fuck he liked watching. He liked watching and knowing he wasn't alone in pleasuring and taking care of a woman.

Serena switched back and forth, sucking them both in turn. She licked up and down Jake's cock, pulling him up so she could kiss and tongue his balls. They were so tight, waiting to shoot off.

Adam groaned as she sucked him, and then Adam's head fell back as he came in her mouth. Serena obediently swallowed everything he gave her and then turned those big green eyes on Jake. She looked so damned pleased with herself. They were her tutors. She was a student who thought she was going to get an A. There wasn't emotion in her eyes, just self-satisfaction.

Well, she wasn't finished yet.

He tangled his hands in her hair. "I'm going to fuck your mouth, Serena. Are you going to let me?"

"Yes, Sir." She was already leaning forward, obviously eager to do her duty.

He shoved his cock in, letting his need to dominate take control. It was the only fucking control he had. He pushed in, listening to her breathe through her nose, finding the rhythm that was right for both of them. He pushed in, gaining ground each time. Her mouth was small, but she seemed determined. Her tongue whirled, stroking the underside of his dick with a force, lighting him up. He felt his balls pulse, his spine tingle.

She was everything he wanted in a woman. Smart and creative and able to handle them both. But she didn't want that. All she wanted was this, the power exchange. He tried to hold it off. He fucked in and out, pulling and pushing, taking everything she gave, but it felt too good to last. He couldn't take another second. He drove to the back of her throat. She swallowed around him, and he was lost.

His come spurted out in jets, white-hot pleasure shooting through his body.

He came down with a little crash. Serena was licking him clean, her tongue lavishing him with affection. It was a sweet sight. His woman on her knees, giving him her love.

But it wasn't love. She was in subspace. And he wasn't close to Domspace. All his dumb ass wanted was to tell her he loved her and take her to bed. He wanted to get her between him and Adam and never let her go. After they'd loved her senseless, they could gently move her toward marriage and a family.

He wanted to be her slave.

He pulled his cock out of her mouth, forcing himself back to reality. She didn't love them, wouldn't welcome the declaration. He would just make a fool of himself, and he'd done enough of that. He needed to stop and think for two fucking seconds. He wasn't willing to give up, not exactly. But they all needed time. They'd jumped in with both feet and forced a situation. Serena wanted a Dom. They could give her two. He would wrap her up in a contract and slowly start wearing her down.

But he couldn't tonight. Tonight he was too raw on the inside. He should never have brought her back here. He shouldn't have laid a hand on her. He should have watched the demonstration, and then they all should have sat down and talked about it the way he would have with a sub he was training.

He needed things on the proper footing.

"Thank you, Serena." No more endearments. He had to take it slow. For her. For himself. And for Adam, too. If Jake let him, Adam would just fall to his knees. They'd tried that already. It was time to try a bit of toughness.

He tucked himself back in and took a long breath. "Pull your skirt down. Adam, we should probably get the clamps off her. She's had them on for a while. Let's see if we can catch the next punishment scene. I want to be out of here by eleven o'clock."

"What?" Serena sounded a little dazed, her mouth slightly open as she obviously tried to catch her breath.

So she'd thought she could get everything she'd wanted? Well, at least he hadn't lost every damn battle of the night. He would win this one. "Serena, I had no intention of satisfying you this evening. You had a safe word, and you agreed to punishment. I haven't agreed to sex."

She shook her head as if trying to clear it. "I don't understand."

It was said with a flat cadence that bugged the hell out of Jake. "Serena, this was punishment. Intercourse would be a reward. You haven't earned it. You wanted a D/s relationship. Here it is, sweetheart. Now clean yourself up so we can get to the rest of the night. Leave the plug in. You can remove it when we get home."

"All right." She took Adam's hand, but the minute she was on her feet, she turned away. "I'll take the clamps off myself, please. Could I have moment to myself? I'd prefer to clean up in private. And could I have my shirt back? I promise not to misbehave again."

It wasn't an unreasonable request. And it would be easier for him to not stare at her breasts all night. "You can wear your shirt. But allow Adam to take off the clamps. It requires some finesse."

"Please, Jacob." The request came out in a little huff, a breathy plea.

"Don't blame me when it hurts like hell." She wouldn't even let them take care of her.

He stalked out the door, Adam hard on his heels.

"What the holy fuck was that?" Adam asked, pulling on Jake's arm. "Dude, why didn't you just beat the shit out of her? It would have hurt less."

And his night was complete. Adam was pissed again. "We talked about this. We're supposed to show her what a D/s relationship is like."

"You're never that harsh with a sub. Never."

He'd never had his heart ripped out by one, either. "I was perfectly polite. She disobeyed. She was punished, and quite frankly, I went easy on the punishment. She's just mad she didn't get multiple orgasms. It's what she really was looking for. Well, I don't intend to be the stud she puts out to pasture the minute this mission is over."

Adam leaned against the wall, his whole body sagging. "It's not going to work, is it? She wants us. I know she does. But if she won't let herself care, then it can't work. I thought she would break down during the punishment. I thought she would finally cry, but she's further away than ever."

And there was no way to reach her.

She would walk out, her shirt on and her armor up. They would go through the motions and then in a day or a week, she would dismiss them and get on with her life.

He would be left behind again.

What the hell was taking her so long? He wanted to get this cluster fuck of a night over with. He walked to the door, ready to tell her to get moving, and then he heard it. He heard the one thing he couldn't bluster against, couldn't fake his way through.

She was crying.

Jake opened the door, every thought of leaving her destroyed by that one tiny sound.

* * * *

Serena unhooked the second clamp and managed to not scream. Yep. He'd been right. It hurt like hell when the blood rushed back into her nipples, but it couldn't possibly hurt more than him dismissing her utterly.

She held her aching breast and was grateful they hadn't given her a bra. It wouldn't matter now. She could put on a parka and still feel naked.

For just a few moments, though, she'd lost herself in them. There had been a little while where nothing had mattered except pleasing them. She'd forgotten everything else. She'd gotten to her knees and looked up and they'd both been standing there. It was everything she could have wanted. They'd been so beautiful together, their cocks straining toward her like two delicious treats. When she'd had those hard cocks in her mouth, she'd felt powerful. That was the glory of submission. She'd found it on her knees. When she'd swallowed Adam and then Jake down, she'd forgotten anything else existed except them. She'd been ready to do just about anything to hold that feeling.

And now she knew that it had all been a lie. She didn't have any power at all.

And she'd asked for it.

A little sob escaped her mouth. She couldn't help it. It was all so wrong, and there was no damn way to fix it.

Her nipples hurt and she had a stupid plug in her ass, and she was just so stupid to even try. Why had she even tried? She stumbled a little to the bed. She needed to put her shirt on and straighten herself up. She needed to find a way to be calm again. She wanted to go home.

She didn't have a home anymore.

Tears streaked down her face. It was too much. Far too much.

"Baby." Jake's voice was softer than it had been all day. The bed dipped as he joined her, and his arms wound around her body, encasing her in his heat. "Baby, I'm so sorry. I didn't mean to make you cry. God, Serena. Please, don't cry."

He sounded tortured. She'd done that to him. She had no doubt.

Adam knelt on the side of the bed, his gorgeous face a watery mess because of her tears. "Don't listen to him, love. You cry now. You need to cry. Let it out. Let us hold you."

Jake's lips were on her cheek. "Please, Serena, you're killing me. Please."

Everything was gone. She only had the moment. She was far too weak to not give in. She turned her head just the tiniest bit, and Jake's mouth met hers. Heaven.

She grabbed on to the feeling. Jake's lips molded to hers, forcing her mouth open and dominating her in the sweetest way. His previous coldness seemed to have fled and heat took its place. Jake's tongue surged in, sliding against her own. He moved her, pulling on her hips until she was close to him, chest to chest. Her chafed nipples brushed against the smooth skin of Jake's chest.

Adam's hand wound in her hair. The minute Jake let her breathe, Adam took control. Adam held her head in his hands, making her feel safe and surrounded. He kissed her over and over. She felt Jake move off the bed, heard a drawer open and close.

"Serena," Adam's voice played across her skin. She loved the way he said her name, like a reverent prayer. "Baby, let me love you."

She wanted it. In the moment, she couldn't think of anything she wanted more. She opened her arms to him, pulling him close. Adam kissed her, feathering light kisses across her face. He brushed against her nose, her eyelids, her brow. He worked his way back down, brushing against her chin and her neck until he reached her breasts.

"I would have done this when I released the clamps. I would have replaced the pressure from the clamps with my lips, baby. I would have made you love them." He sucked a sensitive nipple into his mouth, making Serena gasp with the sensation. Her flesh flared with pain, and then his tongue soothed her, sucking her in gently. She whimpered. If the night had proven nothing else, she was sure now that she was genuinely submissive. She'd gotten so hot when Jake had smacked her ass with his crop. Her pussy had gotten so wet.

She was heating up again, and it wasn't entirely physical. She needed them.

She wrapped her arms around Adam's neck, reveling in the way he pulled her in. His tongue laved at her nipples. He licked her and then sucked the nipple in. Serena let her back bow, her head falling into Jake's shoulder.

"Forgive me." He took her mouth, playing lightly as he balanced her. He didn't give her time to think, didn't wait for an answer. He simply tilted her head back and kissed her with all the passion that had previously been missing. She let it all go. She cried even as she kissed him back.

They surrounded her, four arms winding around her body, making her feel safe. They fell back on the bed. Somehow Jake ended up holding her, her back to his front. Adam stripped the tiny skirt off her, and she was naked, but it was all right this time. There were no more harsh looks or dismissive words. This time they were with her.

Adam tossed the skirt aside and then went to work on his leathers. His cock sprang free again, obviously ready for another round.

"We're here for you, baby," Jake whispered. "We want to be here for you. We don't want you to worry. We want to build a whole fucking life that's about protecting you and taking care of you. The Dom thing is for play. This isn't play."

"We're not playing, Serena." Adam's eyes were deeply serious as he crawled back on the bed.

Jake's feet tangled with her own, spreading her wide, making a place for Adam at her core. Adam bent over, almost reverently placing a kiss on the mound of her pussy.

"This is my life, Serena. It can be our life."

And it sounded amazing. Two men to love. Two men to take care of her, to protect and surround her. But she couldn't just jump back in. Not when two minutes before they had been walking away. "Please, do I have to make a decision tonight?"

Adam kissed her pussy again before getting to his knees. "No, love. No decisions. Just this. The three of us together."

Jake caressed her breasts, his cock pulsing at the base of her spine. "This is how it should be."

Adam rolled a condom over his straining cock. She was ready, more than ready. She'd been wet and soft since Jake's crop had taken her to another place. But she needed more than just a cock. She needed them.

Adam lined his cock up, and Serena wrapped her arms around him, bringing him close. She was pressed between them, Adam's weight anchoring her to Jake's body. No space between them. She didn't want any.

"Love, you feel so good." Adam started to thrust, working his cock in a little at a time. "The plug makes you so tight."

"When you're ready, you'll have us both deep inside you. We'll make love to you at the same time. We'll fill you up with cock. You won't want to go back to just one man. You'll be addicted to us." Jake's husky words sounded like a prophecy.

She whimpered at the amazing fullness, but she was worried Jake was wrong. She was already addicted to them, and she had no way out of it. If they left, she would long for them forever.

Adam thrust in and pulled out, setting a rhythm that had her breathless. They were right about the plug. It tightened her and made her aware of every inch of his cock as he thrust in.

Jake's hand snaked down between them. "Let go, baby. Let go. We'll be right here to catch you."

His fingers found her clit, and he pressed down, making circles in time to Adam's thrusts. All the while he whispered how beautiful she was. He kissed her cheeks and her hair, telling her he couldn't wait to be the man fucking her.

The whole world melted away. Nothing else mattered but this. Her trouble seemed so far from her now. There was only this moment and these men.

Adam thrust up, hitting that magic place deep inside her just as Jake pinched her clit, and it sent her over the edge. Serena went wild, pressing up, trying to milk every minute she could. She pushed up and then back, pretending it was Jake inside her, that they were both balls-deep within her body.

Adam stiffened above her, grinding down and giving her his orgasm.

They all fell together in a delicious heap of arms and legs and sweet sweat that bound them together.

"I'm right where I want to be," Adam whispered, his cock still inside her. "Finally."

Jake buried his face in her neck, inhaling her scent. "He's right where I want to be. And he better vacate my spot because it's my turn, baby. You wanted a ménage? Oh, we can give you one. We can give it to you all night long."

Serena let her fears go for a little while and settled in for a long night.

Chapter Twenty

Adam thought about killing the man in the doorway. He could do it remotely. The asshole was just standing there, ringing the doorbell. It would be a simple thing to grab a rifle and snipe the fucker from the second floor.

Unfortunately, Liam was there with Grace and Sean, and Sean would throw a fit if Liam managed to bleed on Grace.

Tranquilizer dart. He might have some somewhere. Liam wouldn't bleed, but he would die if Adam got three or four of the suckers in him. Yeah. That was a plan.

"You going to let them in?" Jake asked, looking at the security screen.

"I was thinking about killing Li." Jake would probably help.

Jake huffed out a laugh and hit the button that opened the door. "Kill him inside, please. And don't let Grace see you." Jake slapped him on the back before starting down the hall. "You know we probably wouldn't have ended up in bed with Serena without Liam's help."

A fat lot of good that had done them. Serena was sleeping with them, but they weren't any closer to getting a commitment out of her. Any time he would ask, she got that blank look on her face and would mumble something about staying in the now. The now was precarious and kind of sucky. He wanted a goddamn future. He was starting to worry that Serena didn't share his plans.

"She'll come around." Jake was suddenly the optimistic one.

He could hear Liam talking to Sean as they gathered in the front room. Adam kept his voice low. The last thing he wanted was Liam to hear they were still at odds with their woman. The Irish fucker might decide to help out again, and then Adam would be forced to cut off his so-called friend's junk. "How can you be sure?"

"Because she stopped asking about a contract." Jake gave him a little nod. "I made the mistake of being impatient the other night. I'm still on the edge. I'm deeply aware that she could walk out any minute and we might never see her again, but she's still here, and as long as we're in her bed, we have a shot. And something else hit me. She's writing again."

She was still in front of her computer for eight to ten hours a day, but at least she was typing something now. She'd rewritten one of the love scenes of her latest ménage romance. She'd included the word sore at least ten times.

"And she's complaining again," Adam admitted. He couldn't stop his grin. "She was mad about the plug, man."

They had spent the last week settling into a quiet routine. Serena worked. Adam did research on his computer, and Jake punched stuff. Mostly the bag in the workout room. Jake also forced Serena to go on daily walks with Mojo, both he and Adam at her side. Jake had also started training Serena, though not in the way Adam knew he would have preferred. Jake was training her in self-defense, teaching her how to take care of herself. At night, they would eat dinner together and watch a movie or some television, and then they would go to bed, spending hours on filthy, nasty, beautiful sex.

Adam had watched Jake and Serena going over basic self-defense moves the day before. It had struck him that Jake was teaching her so she could defend herself in case they weren't around. He hated the thought, but he had to face the possibility because even with the sex, no one talked about the future except one small event. Serena had been taking a bigger plug every day, stretching her ass to accept anal sex. And she was complaining mightily.

"She said it was an elephant plug. I had to spank her to get her to take it," Adam said.

A broad smile crossed Jake's face. "She likes the spanking. She mouthed off to me three times yesterday so I would spank her. And the fact that she's making jokes again gives me a little hope. The old Serena is in there. We just have to pray we're still close when she comes roaring back to life."

That was the problem. Adam wasn't sure they could keep the relationship going once Serena didn't need their services any longer. And sooner or later they would catch this guy and have to deal with a world where they weren't on top of her twenty-four seven.

"Are we getting ready to go?" Serena asked, coming up behind them. She was wearing the dress he'd picked for her, a lovely blue and green wrap dress that hugged her curves and showed off her breasts. It was beautiful, but professional. And her legs looked amazing in the four-and-a-half-inch Louboutin heels. He'd seen her last night in those fuck-me heels and nothing else.

"Shouldn't you wear a sweater or something?" Jake asked. The caveman didn't seem to appreciate Adam's eye for dressing their gorgeous girl. Jake's eyes fastened on her chest. "Maybe a turtleneck?"

A slow smile spread across Serena's face. "You like?"

"He's worried everyone will like, love." Adam winked down at her. There was no way he would put her in a turtleneck. "But what he forgets is we have guns. You can look as beautiful as you like. Let everyone look. We'll just shoot the first guy who touches. And the second. And so on." He took her hand and led her into the living room where Liam, Sean, and Grace had gathered. "And there's the first one I'll kill."

Liam rolled his eyes. "Are we still on that mess, now?"

Sean grinned. "Ah, karma. I love karma."

"I didn't kiss Grace." Adam grimaced. "Well, not much anyway."

Serena sent him a dirty look. Jake put an arm around her waist.

"I never kissed Grace." Yep, Jake seemed proud of himself.

Luckily, they had a job to do. "Serena, if you don't mind keeping Grace and Sean company, we need to talk to Liam before we head out."

Suspicious eyes stared back at him. "Don't you mean you need to decide if we're going at all?"

Jake kissed her forehead and backed away. "Yep. That's what we mean."

He walked into the kitchen without another word. Adam followed. He rather hoped Liam's report on the security details for the event would cause them to call the whole thing off. He knew Serena wanted to do the signing. He'd helped plan the event, but now that he was actually facing the fact that she would be out in public, he was a little nervous.

Sean followed right behind Liam. "You guys are not leaving me out there. They're going to talk books and sex. And the books are about sex. Who knew women were so damn chatty about sex? Men don't do that. We just look at a girl, announce we did her, and everyone moves on."

Yeah, it was simpler that way.

Liam shook his head. "You're all full of bullshit. In the last couple of months, I've had to listen to the three of you talk about your feelings more than a damn talk show. I swear you've all grown vaginas."

Sean didn't seem to take offense. "Nope. We're all pussy whipped. I like being pussy whipped. It means that pussy belongs to me. You've just spent too much time around college girls in hot pants looking for tips."

"I like hot pants. No one used to wear hot pants back in Ireland." He sighed as though thinking of something lovely, probably whatever nineteen-year-old he'd done the previous night. "More women should wear them."

"Dude, if you're thinking about Eve in short shorts right now, stop it. You cannot go there. Alex will kill you. He won't do it fair. He'll wait until you've forgotten all about him and then stab your ass in a back alley one night," Jake said.

"I'll have to stay out of alleys then, won't I?" Liam asked, his back coming up. And then he sighed. "I'm not sleeping with Eve.

I'm just spending time with her. It's innocent."

But almost nothing was innocent when it came to Liam and women. "You're playing a dangerous game, man."

"I'm not playing at all. And fuck you. You're trying to pull me into vagina talk. I won't do it. I don't have feelings. None at all. And I'm keeping it that way." He frowned and sat on one of the barstools. "Now, on to actual business. I checked out the security for the toy store. First off, have I mentioned how much I fucking love America? That place is amazing. It's like a grocery store except with porn. You can get anything there. I was eyeing a very nice flogger. I met this sub the other night at Hooters…"

"You're talking about feelings again," Adam pointed out, deeply wanting to avoid listening in on Liam's sex life.

"No, I'm talking about being horny. That ain't a feeling. It's a simple state of being."

"It's his usual state of being," Sean supplied helpfully.

"Like I was saying, it's not so bad. There's two points of entry, both guarded with alarms and cameras. No windows. It really is a box, though a nicely decorated one. The main floor has fairly clean lines of sight. I advised the owner to place the table where she'll be signing those books in the back, so she's got a wall behind her. As for the cocktail party, as long as we're in the same room, we should be fine. We can use metal detectors. The owner sells impact toys. No knives. I've already talked to the police, and they're sending the two detectives and a plainclothes who'll join the party. I think your girl's little party is a go."

Not what he'd wanted to hear, but at least Liam was thorough. Adam slid a look Sean's way. "And you're letting Grace come?"

"She wouldn't miss it. She loves Amber Rose. She thinks those books brought us together. I would say they probably helped." Sean sighed and opened his coat, showing off a shiny SIG Sauer. "I'm coming out of retirement for the day. This woman means a lot to my wife. I won't let some shitbag hurt her. And I think she means something to my friends."

Jake nodded somberly. "She does. She means the world to us. We just have to convince her of it."

"I think Grace might be helping out with that even as we

speak," Sean replied.

Liam let his head hit the bar. "You're back on feelings again. Can someone shoot me?"

Adam laughed. This was way better than shooting Liam. Torture. The Irishman deserved it. Well, just a little. He looked at Sean Taggart, his commanding officer in the Army, his friend and mentor, the man who seemed to be forgiving him. "Thanks for coming along, Sean. We would love to have the help."

"Feelings make me vomit." Liam's head came up. "Do we have time for a beer?"

"No drinking before work," Jake announced.

Liam frowned. "But I'm on e-mail duty. I get to sit here and read four hundred and fifty of Doyle Brooks' boring rants against undergrads and all the people who don't appreciate his genius. God, just let me kill the pretentious fucker."

They had been going through every bit of information Adam had managed to hack from Professor Brooks' computers and the computers from the Anderson Agency. They had all been taking turns going through them and all the information they had been able to find out on the two detectives.

Jake shook his head. "No beer. No killing Brooks until we get some shit on him. Now, let's get ready. We leave in twenty minutes."

Adam was going to count the minutes until they could snuggle down beside Serena, and she would be safe and sound again.

* * * *

"Are you sure you don't mind?" Grace Taggart asked.

Serena had to smile as she took the books from Grace. She might be a little jealous of the lovely woman since it seemed Adam had previously had a thing for her, but she was so sweet it was impossible to hate Grace. And she was a fan. That made up for a lot of ill will in Serena's mind. They were all there. All the *Texas Sweetheart* books and *Three Riders, One Love* and the rest of that series. Yes, Grace Taggart was definitely a fan.

"Most people just buy the e-books," Serena said, sitting down on the couch as Grace handed her a pen. She opened the first book. *Small Town Sweetheart*. She'd labored over that book. She'd put so much of herself into it.

"I got through many lonely nights because of those books. I guess I would really like to thank you for that."

Tears pricked at Serena's eyes, and she had to fight to maintain a modicum of professionalism. She hadn't started writing thinking she would find people like Grace. She'd started writing because it filled a void in her life. It was one of the universe's great miracles that her work had managed to fill the void in someone else's life. "Thanks. That means a lot to me."

"So you can't let some jerk scare you out of writing."

She signed her name with a flourish. Well, she signed her fake name with a flourish. Sometimes she wondered who was more real—Serena Brooks or Amber Rose? Last night, Serena had been the real one. Serena had been the one locked in Jake's and Adam's arms. "I won't. I'm not even going to let him scare me out of going to the signing."

Grace smiled and then took a long breath. "And you also shouldn't let some jerk scare you out of having a great life with two amazing men."

The conversation had taken a turn for the deeply personal. It seemed her men liked to talk. "Well, I guess you know Adam, Jake, and I have been having a little fun."

"No. I know Adam and Jake are falling in love with you."

What the hell was she supposed to say to that? "I wouldn't say it's that serious. We haven't talked anything long term. It's just a little fling."

The sympathy that hit Grace Taggart's hazel eyes made Serena want to flinch. "Oh, sweetie, some man did a number on you, didn't he? You're divorced?"

"Happily," she forced herself to say. She hadn't really loved Doyle. She'd thought she was in love, but she'd been too young.

"Honey, no one is happy to get divorced. Not really. The marriage might have been hell, but almost everyone mourns at least the loss of the possibility it represented."

She'd been barely nineteen and the possibilities had been a

whole wide future. "Well, I only know that the reality was a man who threatened to walk out on me any time something went wrong. The whole marriage was one long fight where I had to give in to him or lose the relationship. I finally found something I wanted more than that marriage. I found writing. I don't think I'll ever get married again."

It was easier this way. She could just live for the moment and know that it could all end tomorrow. It was the truth. Nothing was certain, so why should she pretend it was?

"My husband died. I was pretty sure I wouldn't marry again."

"But you had a happy marriage?" There was a huge difference there. Grace's husband hadn't meant to leave her.

"For the most part. There were whole parts of myself I shut off because I didn't think my husband could handle it. And then I found Sean. I'm too old to start over. I told myself that like a hundred times. But it doesn't work that way, at least it doesn't have to. I'm forty-one. I should be a grandmother, but here I am having another baby, and I think this one is going to keep me young, like Sean does. I thought that loving Sean would be the stupidest thing I could possibly do, but it turns out to be the joy of my life."

"That's wonderful, Grace." It was a lovely story. It just didn't have anything to do with her.

"Why won't you give them a chance?" Grace sat back, her hand on her round belly. "Tell me if I'm intruding."

"You're intruding."

A slow smile slid across her face. "I might be now, but if you let yourself, we would be such good friends. So I'm going to claim pregnant-lady rights and plow through anyway. I'm going to say a few things because I love Adam and Jake and because I love you, too."

Serena shook her head. "You don't know me."

"Oh, but I do. You've been a voice in my head for the last few years. It's like that with some authors. When I was really lonely, I had your characters. And I learned a lot from them and the woman who wrote them." Grace put her hand on the stack of books that represented Serena's life work. "This woman is strong. This woman doesn't let the past rob her of a future. This woman reaches out with both hands and grabs what she deserves. This woman knows how to love and how to fight. I pray for my friends that this woman isn't a work of fiction."

Serena stared at her books, her life's passion. But what did her life mean if all her passion was spent on words? Her marriage had been a failure. Did that mean she should be alone for the rest of her life or simply exist in the moment because future hurts were too much to contemplate?

"Serena? Are you ready?" Jake stood in the doorway looking handsome in a dark suit and tie, the jacket of the suit in his hand. He had a leather shoulder holster on, his gun in plain sight, reminding her that she needed a bodyguard.

Was she ready? She probably wasn't ready for any of this. She wasn't ready to make a decision about anything.

"Baby?" Jake stared down at her. "You okay?"

She shook her head. He was asking if she was ready to go to the signing, and she was sitting here asking enormous life questions. Questions she still didn't have a damn answer for, but Grace Taggart was making her think. She'd been obsessed with this signing for months and now all she could think was that it would be nice to get it over with because she had a lot of thinking to do.

"I'm ready." She stood, her focus caught on the books. Was she just fiction? Or were those books her training wheels, her way of getting ready to do what it took to be truly strong, to take the risk to really love again? Her voice was steadier this time. "I'm ready."

Jake took her hand and led her to the car.

* * * *

Jake really wasn't ready. He looked around the small store and realized he wasn't ready to put her in harm's way, and he damn sure wasn't ready to let her go.

"So, this is where our illustrious author chooses to sign her books?" Detective Hernandez held up a vibrator in a box. "Well, we know what the books are about, at least."

Jake had had just about enough of the detective. He turned to Detective Chitwood. "Maybe we don't need Dallas PD here. This asshole obviously has a real problem with my client's work."

Chitwood motioned Jake over and kept his voice low. "Please, Mr. Dean, give him a little leeway. I'll talk to him. He's going through a bit of a rough patch at home. His wife seems to have found herself, so to speak. She started a new career, and she's leaving him behind. And she loved romance novels. Not like Amber Rose's, but Mike is lumping them all in together. I'm afraid he thinks his wife got unrealistic expectations of what to expect from books like that."

"I don't care about his marriage," Jake said frankly. Yeah, he would give Hernandez another look. They hadn't found anything, but Adam would have to look deeper. "I only care whether or not he does his job. And I got the feeling you didn't approve of Serena's career, either."

Chitwood shook his head. "I don't get it, but I don't particularly care one way or the other. It doesn't matter what she does for a living. She deserves to be able to make that living without fearing for her life. I took an oath, and I intend to honor it. My home life is hard right now, too, but I won't let it affect my ability to protect her. Speaking of, I got the profile you sent over. Excellent work. Your profiler seems very capable."

Eve had been the best the FBI had to offer until a case had taken a terrible turn. "So, you agree that this is someone she knows?"

"I'm not sure. I certainly think the perpetrator believes she's committed a great wrong that touches the stalker's life." Chitwood frowned and stared at his feet for a moment. "I know what you think."

Jake simply waited for Chitwood to prove he wasn't as dumb as he'd first looked.

"You think it's me or Mike. Given that the violent threats occurred after the police were called in, and given our response, I would logically put us both on a list of suspects. I think, after today, that we should recuse ourselves and let this whole case start over."

Chitwood was saying all the right things. But that wouldn't make Jake back off. "I think that would be a good idea."

A little smile played on the detective's lips. "Of course, it would be exactly the right play if I wanted to throw you off the scent. Feel free to have us followed, Mr. Dean. We are exactly what we come off as, a detective looking forward to retirement and…dear god, Mike, put that down." He shook his head back toward the racks where Hernandez was studying an enormous anal plug. "A detective looking toward retirement and his idiot partner. That's all you'll find."

Jake wasn't so sure about that, but Adam hadn't found anything on either man just yet. He'd already known Hernandez was separated and living at the *Y*, which could make any man cranky, and Chitwood's wife was fighting cancer. Still, Chitwood was described as deeply religious, his church's website posting some strong warnings against what they called the pornography of the world.

He would keep an eye on both. He felt much better about the plainclothes officer they had brought with them. She was a young woman with a bright smile who didn't seem at all offended that she was working in a toy store. She'd laughed with Grace about something before she'd started doing perimeter sweeps.

"Where's the agent?" Adam asked, coming in from outside. There was a line of readers, almost all women with stacks of books. It was a bit of a madhouse outside. Ian himself was handling the security, and surreptitiously taking pictures of everyone for later research. If the stalker was here, they would at least have a picture to go from.

"She's in the back." Jake pointed to the door that led to the owner's office and the large room which she used for storage. Jake had walked through the room, making sure the one door to the outside was locked up tight. There was a DPD officer standing guard outside. The officer had been very helpful, opening the door for Lara and Brian as they carted in books and boxes. Lara was in the quiet back room, unpacking books and merchandise. "I saw Chris helping her out, though he stated he was doing it under protest and that Lara was still on probation. And the other guy was down there, too, though he mostly seems to just be frowning at his wife."

"Brian Anderson?" Adam frowned. "I was told he ran the mainstream arm of the business and didn't particularly like having to deal with the lower-end clients."

Chris stopped in front of them, a large stack of *Their Sweetheart Slave* in his arms. "Are you talking about Brian? He kind of hates us. Oh, he tries to hide it, but I overheard him saying that Lara ruined their reputation as an agency when she brought us in as clients. You know we erotic romance authors are responsible for the fall of Western civilization."

"Then why's he here?" Jake asked. "He wasn't on the list, but Serena cleared him."

"Well, even a snob likes cash. I think Brian finally realized that genre fiction pays the bills, Jake. Can I call you Jake now that you're back in our girl's good graces? By the way, I meant the whole 'cutting your balls off' thing if you hurt her again. I'll just be mentioning that right up to your not wholly legal wedding day, which I assume is coming soon or I'll have to do the whole 'cutting your balls off' thing and I really don't like that. It's messy."

Jake rather liked the man Serena called her gay husband. "You're preaching to the choir, man. We've told her how we feel."

Chris's eyes narrowed. "All right then. It's just a matter of time." He sighed. "Back to the salt mines for me. I have to drop these books off and then help him in the back room. When is the champagne coming out?"

It seemed to be a rhetorical question because Chris walked toward the signing table.

Jake didn't like last minute changes. Not one bit. "Keep an eye on both the Andersons."

She'd burned Serena once. Jake intended to make sure she didn't get a second chance.

"Okay," Adam agreed. "And we haven't, you know."

"Haven't what?"

Adam looked toward Serena, his eyes softening. "We haven't told her how we feel. We've told her we want her. We've spanked her ass red and made her come, but we haven't said those three little words."

I love you.

God, he hadn't told her he loved her.

"But we do," Jake said solemnly, looking to Adam.

A bright smile crossed Adam's face. "Fuck yeah, we do."

Jake looked across the room where Serena sat at her little table. The table was for the signing that would begin after the cocktail reception. She looked so damn pretty. Despite the fact that he would prefer those lovely breasts of hers weren't on display in this type of a gathering, he had to admit that Adam had done a spectacular job of dressing her. "So, what do we do? Take her out to dinner after this thing and explain something she should have figured out awhile back?"

Adam leaned against the wall and watched her. "She's not deeply self-aware. And she's completely gun shy. I think we'll have to tell her more than once before it sinks in. We just have to make sure she doesn't run once this case is over."

"Well, I have some ideas on that front." Jake was good with handcuffs. He would just lock Serena up.

He knew one thing. He wasn't going to let her go. He would try everything he had to if it meant keeping her close.

Jake looked out the front windows. There was a crowd waiting. Mostly women, although a few seemed to have dragged husbands along. And there were a few men who seemed to be alone. Yeah, he wanted to check those men out.

"Not long now," Adam said, checking his watch.

Not long at all. Jake was going to count down the minutes until he could get Serena home and safe and they could start telling her exactly how they felt.

Chapter Twenty-One

"So, you're just sleeping with them now?" Bridget asked, pulling out pens and laying them on the table.

Serena could smell the hors d'oeuvres as the caterer began sending out staff to make the rounds. Any minute now the doors would open, and she would see if anyone had shown up. But all Bridget seemed to be able to think about was Serena's sex life.

Love life. It was a damn love life because she was in love.

"I don't know. I think I'm falling for them," she admitted, playing with her water bottle. She wasn't about to tell her best friend the full truth. That would mean admitting she'd already fallen for them both and wasn't sure how to handle it.

"Think? Really? You have to think about it?" Chris put down a big stack of the new book on the table. "There's more where this came from. Lara brought three cases. And a box of the last book, just in case. I'm going to go and get that and then I'm done being their errand boy. Don't they know I'm here as the eye candy for many lonely women? I thought it was in my job description. Gay best friend, also does male modeling and writes books. Nowhere in there are the words 'pack mule.' Nope. Uh uh. And Serena, you need to think about this. Those men give a damn, otherwise they wouldn't put up with the two of us."

Serena watched as Jake and Adam talked. "What do you mean?"

Bridget smiled. "We've been putting them through the besties test. Adam was dumb enough to give me his phone number and then he was annoyed enough to give me Jake's."

"We've been calling every day demanding updates and making a general nuisance of ourselves. It's just a little test. Men like those two will put up with very little crap from people, and yet they've been perfectly pleasant with the two of us," Chris confided.

"Jake did hang up on me when I asked him if he could help give my cat an enema." Bridget shrugged. "I might have overplayed my hand. But before that, he came over and installed a new security system. And he was nice enough to take his shirt off. Well, I was smart enough to turn off the air conditioning and get the place to like a hundred degrees before he came over. Damn girl, that man is fine."

They hadn't said a word to her. Neither man had said anything about helping out her friends. "Maybe they're just really nice."

Jake turned, his face in a deep scowl. Nope. He didn't look nice in the least. And she realized she was being stupidly stubborn. They did care. She just wasn't sure it would last. Jake's fists clenched, and he started talking through his earpiece. The doors had opened, and a flood of people came through.

"Maybe you're just dumb," Bridget said with a frown. "I say that because of the hot ménage men who seem to really care about you and also because I've listened for weeks about how no one will show up. Look, it's a mob, Little Miss Pessimism."

"Wow." She sat down and put on her author face as the first fan showed up.

Chris winked her way. "I'll be back in a bit, darling. Come on, Bridge, help me haul the books up. Our girl looks like she's going to need them."

Bridget and Chris walked off, and Serena began talking to her readers, sinking into one of the most rewarding parts of her job. Grace Taggart took the chair beside her and started making sure the books she signed had all the promo materials in them. Her handsome husband hovered close. Serena was pretty sure she'd caught a glimpse of a gun under his suit coat. She'd heard he was an aspiring chef now, but once he'd been Jake and Adam's CO in the Green Berets, so that made him a badass who could cook. Yeah. There was a hero in there somewhere.

But first she would have to write a story about Jake and Adam. She just prayed it had a happy ending.

* * * *

The party went on all around Adam. Soft music played, and Serena laughed and talked to a crowd of women who obviously adored her. She was oddly in her element, smiling and laughing, her shy nature fading away.

His girl was going places, and he meant to be by her side when she did. There was an optimism inside Adam that hadn't been there before. He and Jake were finally, completely on the same page at the same time. Now they just had to bring Serena along. But they would do it. They had been a great team for a really long time.

There was a little buzzing in his ear as Ian relayed a message that had Adam fuming. Adam touched the device in his right ear. "Are you fucking kidding me? I'll be right there. Guess who's standing outside, waiting to get in? Master Storm."

And the hits just kept coming. Any minute now, Serena's ex would show up and then the whole gang would be here.

"Are you kidding me?" Jake asked, his face becoming a stony mask.

"I'll handle it. You keep watch on our girl." Adam looked over where Serena was laughing at something a reader had said. Sean was across the room watching her as well.

"If you kill him, you better call me out to help," Jake said as Adam stepped outside. Ian was right by the door, vetting anyone who walked in.

Adam looked at Master Storm standing outside the building and felt a cold rage nearly split him in two. "You want to explain why you're here?"

The man gave him a slight smile. "It's a public signing, Mr.

Miles. Yes, I can do research, too. I know all about you and...your partner. Tell me, does Serena have the whole story on you? Does she know how you were thrown out of the Army? Bad business, that. I thought she should have all the information before she made a decision."

Adam had zero intention of allowing the man anywhere near Serena. "Serena made her decision. She chose to stop seeing you. You need to leave. You won't be allowed inside."

"Then I'll wait until after the event, but understand this, Mr. Miles, I will see Serena. I made a mistake in walking away the other day. Poor Serena doesn't know what she wants. She needs a guiding hand, and I won't allow you to come between us. I have decided one thing, if it makes you feel better. Serena should be allowed to write whatever she likes. I realize now it fills a void in her."

He'd studied up on this asshole. Oh, he'd had a file on him a mile wide about twenty-four hours after first meeting him. "I think what you need is an influx of cash. The martial arts business ain't paying the way it used to, is it?"

His face went pink. "I have no idea what you're talking about."

"Your business is in trouble, and you just figured out how much money Serena makes off those books of hers." Adam really wanted to shoot the fucker in the gut, but Ian was watching. Ian would get upset if he had to hide a body. Even though, apparently, he was really good at it. "She's not going to sign over her checks. Go away."

"I'm not going away, you motherfucker. I worked that girl for months, and I'm going to see my goddamn payoff."

Storm reached for the lapels of Adam's jacket, but Adam was way faster. He had the barrel of his gun securely between the motherfucker's eyes before he could grab Adam. Adam held onto the front of Storm's shirt, balancing the man who suddenly seemed like he wanted to get away.

"Adam, is there a problem?" Ian asked. As usual, his boss was cool, calm, and collected. He merely watched as though waiting to see if Adam would really pull the trigger.

"Did she tell you about the stalker?" Adam asked.

It occurred to Adam that if Storm really wanted Serena under his thumb, a good way to do it would be to scare her senseless. It would have sent her straight into his arms, his house, that fucking contract he'd wanted her to sign. How far would this man have gone?

"No. She didn't say a word. I swear I didn't know about it until that day at her house." The deep Dom voice was gone, and he looked at the gun, his eyes nearly crossing. "I didn't know anything."

"Adam, I don't think he did this." Ian shook his head shortly, disdain dripping from his every word. "I believe you'll find the man has peed himself. Not exactly the tough type. I think he'll probably leave Serena alone from now on. Besides, according to Liam's report, he was out working the night of the snake attack and out of town when her house burned down."

"Her house is gone?" Storm's eyes went wide. "Someone's really trying to kill her? I thought it was a little joke."

Adam groaned. The idiot really had peed himself. He let his grip go, and Storm fell on his ass, scrambling back. "Get out of here. If I see you around her again, I'll use this."

Storm scrambled away.

Ian sighed. "Damn, I was hoping it was him. He's an asshole. My heart kind of lit up when I realized he was in line. No one ever lets me kill people anymore. I miss it."

Adam looked out at the parking lot, a man catching his eye. He stood very close to Jake's SUV. Too close. The man was average height and looked rather fit, but he was wearing a dark hoodie, and it was warm outside. The hood was pulled over his head.

Adam watched as he stopped and seemed to say something into his cell phone. There were four stores in the small shopping center. The Velvet Room was the largest, but there was also a convenience store, a Laundromat, and a used book store. Twilight was rapidly approaching. He'd wanted this to be done before dark, but the crowd that had entered the store looking to talk to Serena had been larger than expected.

Adam kept looking at the man in the hoodie. Ian put a hand on his arm, his eyes looking down at his phone.

"Do you have this? Liam says he might have found something.

You had put out traces on a whole bunch of people in her life, and he wants to talk about a couple of them. Do you want to talk to Li or watch that ridiculously suspicious man?" Ian gave him a hopeful look. "Because I can take care of that asshole."

No way, no how. If there was any chance this was the guy, Adam wanted a shot at him. "You go talk to Liam, boss. And send Jake out here." Jake wouldn't want to miss the fun if this went the way he thought it would.

"All right. I'll put Sean on the front door. There's a uniform at the back door, and Officer Sims is keeping close to Serena. She hasn't seen anything odd yet. Just a bunch of women. Did you know some of them cried when they met Serena? What the hell's up with that? I don't get women. I'll be back."

Adam watched, the tension building, a little thrill running through his veins. Yes. Something was going to happen. He wasn't sure what, but it would happen. Every instinct in his body told him to go still and wait.

The door behind him came open. Jake was at his side. "What's going on? Everything seems quiet inside."

Adam merely nodded toward the parking lot. He was fairly certain the man hadn't seen him. There was a line of trees between him and the The Velvet Room. But Adam could definitely see him. He kept talking on his phone and inching closer and closer to the SUV.

"Shit. He's got something in his hand. What is it?" Jake asked, squinting in the early evening light.

"No idea, but the minute he drops it, I'm on his ass."

"He's roughly the same size as her ex-husband. I can't see his face." Jake's voice was a low growl, the sound of a predator waiting on a particularly juicy meal. "Fuck, I hope he has a gun."

If the asshole had a gun, they would be perfectly justified in killing him if they managed to get him to pull it. Then Serena wouldn't have to worry about anything except how soon they were getting married. Because he wasn't giving up, and he sure as fuck wasn't giving in to her fears.

"Come on. Move." Adam said the words like a prayer, his hand already in his jacket. The weight of his SIG was familiar and comforting. But if they moved too fast, they might spook him. Adam wanted this guy to make a move.

The man in the hoodie turned one last time, his eyes glancing across the parking lot as he slid his phone in his jacket. He was right next to the SUV. Then he did it. He pulled the windshield wiper up and placed an envelope under it.

"Go," Jake commanded, his voice low.

Adam touched his earpiece and spoke quietly, his calm voice at odds with his racing heart. A fierce joy threatened to overtake him. Fuck, he did like the chase. He moved from behind the trees as he spoke. "Ian, we're chasing down a suspect. You might want to send the cops out now. This could get ugly."

Ian's voice came over the radio. "Will do. Make sure it looks like self-defense, boys. Have some fun."

Jake moved beside him, silently stalking across the parking lot. The man in the hoodie turned, saw them, and did exactly what Adam hoped for. He took off running.

Adam sprinted across the lot, Jake going for the opposite side so they tracked him no matter which way he went. He heard the man curse and try to turn, but he fell down in a heap, his foot making hard contact with a parking lot barrier. There was a loud thud as the man hit the ground face first.

Fuck. He wasn't going to get a chance to shoot the asshole.

"Keep your hands on the ground." Adam trained his weapon on the back of the man's head.

Hoodie guy's fingers splayed against the concrete as though he was trying just about anything to prove he wasn't armed. "Dude, I'm just a courier. What the hell is going on? Someone call the cops."

"That's not her ex," Jake said, his gun trained on the man, too.

"You got him?" A loud voice split the air across the parking lot. Detective Hernandez.

"Yes, he's secure. Could you check the envelope he left on the car?" Adam asked. Something was still wrong. "Turn over, very slowly. I'm very impatient today, and if you make one wrong move, I'm likely to pull this trigger."

Jake watched as the man began to roll over, his body flinching in obvious pain. "Where is Ian going?"

"To talk to Liam. I guess he wanted a little privacy. Or he wanted to buy a drink." Ian had walked off in the direction of the convenience store. In the distance, Adam could see Liam's car pulling up. Liam jumped out and started toward the store. "He found out something about our friend here."

"Dude, I told you. It's a job." The man had turned over, and Adam could safely say he'd never seen the man before. And he was younger than Adam had pegged him. He looked like he might be twenty-five.

"Who paid you and what were you supposed to do?" Jake asked.

The young man's hands had taken the brunt of his fall, they were covered in scrapes and cuts from the pavement. "I was just supposed to put that envelope on the SUV with the license plate he gave me. He told me to try to make sure no one saw me. And I had to do it at 5:30 pm. I don't know why. And he didn't tell me how many people would be around."

"Hey, there's just a blank sheet of paper in here," Chitwood said, walking up behind them. He'd put latex gloves on his hands.

Hernandez was behind him, a quizzical look on his face. "It's addressed to Amber Rose, but there's nothing in it. What is that supposed to mean?"

Adam didn't like the feeling in his gut. Wrong. Very wrong. Something about this whole thing was starting to read setup. "Who hired you?"

The young man went beet red. "I don't know. I work for a courier service. They gave me the job. I thought it was like a proposal or something. I don't know anything. I had to call back because I forgot the plate number on the car. Do you think I'm going to get fired?"

Adam touched his headpiece as he turned. He wasn't going to waste another minute. Serena was in trouble. "Sean, I need you to get eyes on Serena right now. Jake and I are coming in." He waited for the reply. "Sean? Sean, can you hear me?"

"Com's not working." Jake took off running for the store. Adam ran after him, praying they weren't too late.

* * * *

Serena shook her fifty-first hand. Or something like that. She was desperately trying to remember names and faces. Chris leaned over and whispered in her ear.

"That's Regina Moore. She runs one of the largest erotic romance blogs on the web. Smile and tell her how much you love her site." Chris had been utterly indispensable. It seemed to Serena he knew everyone.

"Regina, hi." Serena shook her hand. "Thank you so much for coming. I can't tell you how much I love your site."

The older woman beamed. "It's a labor of love, dear. And I think you'll find a great review for the new book in next week's posting. Lara was kind enough to make sure I got an advanced copy. I loved it. I can't wait for the next one. Where is Lara, anyway?"

Lara was in hiding. Serena was going to have to deal with her. She just wasn't sure how to handle it yet. There was a big part of her that wanted to forgive and forget, but could she really do it?

"She's around," Serena said. "She's been doing all the background work."

Which was really not at all like Lara. Serena had been to many conventions with Lara, and her agent was usually a whirlwind of activity at these things.

"Serena?"

Serena turned. Brian Anderson stood in his dress shirt and tie, a sad expression on his face. "I think I'm going to take Lara home. You have enough books. All the promo is out, and the party seems to be going well. Is there any way I can get you to come in the back and say good-bye to her? I can't get her to come out here."

Serena sighed. Lara had taken a real chance on her. Lara had been a sympathetic ear. Lara had been her guide into the business world of publishing. And Lara had set this party in motion. She should at least make an appearance.

"Please, Serena, if it gets out that you and Lara are on the outs, it could really hurt business. She's trying to sign another up-and-coming author. And she knows she did something stupid." Brian stared down at her, his eyes strangely emotional. She'd heard he and

Lara were having trouble, and this situation couldn't have helped. The least she could do was make a goodwill gesture.

"All right. I'll get her to come up here." She moved toward the door to the back room. Maybe the relationship was salvageable, maybe it wasn't, but she couldn't make the decision now, and she owed Lara at least the chance to talk it out. She glanced over at Chris. He was in a deep discussion with a reviewer. Bridget had gone out to get a drink. Adam and Jake were nowhere to be found.

Grace's husband Sean walked up, his earpiece in his hand. "Something's wrong with the coms. Don't go anywhere."

She wasn't sure where she would go. It was her party, after all.

She opened the door to the back room and stepped in. "Lara? Why don't you come on out and join the party?"

The door closed behind her. She turned around. Brian was standing in the doorway, blocking the way. A little chill went through Serena.

"Where's Lara?" Serena asked. She didn't like the nasty suspicion creeping across her spine.

Brian's eyes looked cold and predatory in the dim light. "She's in here somewhere. Maybe you should check the bathroom."

"Tell her I'll talk to her later. I have to get back to the party." It was too quiet here, and something was wrong with Brian.

Brian didn't move out of her way. He stood there, six feet of fit male blocking the door. And then she saw the gun. "Don't scream or I'll shoot you right here, and Bridget won't have a chance to live. You want your friend to live, right?"

"Bridget?"

"Look behind the boxes, Serena. Or should I call you Amber? Amber is the one who ruined my life, after all." He pointed the gun to the left toward a stack of boxes. "Go on. She doesn't have a lot of time left."

Fear clawed at her. She took a step back and looked to her left. "Bridget!"

Bridget lay on the ground, her dark hair covering her face. She'd been wearing a white maxi dress, but Serena was horrified to see it was covered in bright red blood. Was she dead? Her friend? She couldn't be dead.

Serena dropped to her knees and reached for Bridget's hand. It was still warm. The blood was coming from a wound in her abdomen, right above her pelvis.

Bridget's eyes fluttered open. "You have to run. He's crazy. I think Lara's dead."

"Move away from her, Serena." Brian's voice was low and cold. "I can put a bullet in her, too. The silencer works quite well. Get up and move toward the back. We're going to get in the car or your friend is sure to die. Right now, she's still got a shot. One of those bodyguards is going to charge in here soon."

Serena got the message. If she went out that door, Bridget might have a shot. If she didn't, Bridget was dead.

"Don't go," Bridget said. The words were said on a low moan of pain. Bridget was loving and loyal and so talented. The world would be dimmer without her unique energy.

"I'll go." Serena stood and started toward the back door, her legs shaking. The heels were hampering her movements. "Is Lara alive?"

There was a low chuckle from behind her. "No, Serena. Lara is dead. I stuffed her body in the bathroom to be found along with a note from your so-called stalker. Open the door. My partner is outside."

If she got in that car, she wouldn't get out of this alive. And she really wanted to be alive. It was so clear now that she was facing that gun. She wanted to live, and she didn't want to waste another single minute being afraid. Maybe it would all end up going wrong, but she wanted to try.

She opened the door and got ready to run. She fumbled with the doorknob as she stepped out of her shoes. She couldn't run in them. She would have to go barefoot.

"Open the door, Serena," Brian commanded. "Get a move on. I can shoot her from here."

Bridget was so still. Was she dead already? Serena thought she saw her chest move up and down, lightly breathing, holding on to life. Chris would find her, or Jake and Adam would come looking and discover Bridget. She still had a chance. And Serena would have to take hers.

She took a deep breath and threw the door open wide, ready to run. She stumbled over a body. God, there was another body. The uniformed officer lay on the concrete, the back of his head a bloody mess. Serena struggled to her feet.

"Hello, Serena." Doyle stood in the alley, a gun in his hand. "Time to finish up this marriage."

Chapter Twenty-Two

Doyle reached out and pulled at her arm, hauling her close to his body. She felt the press of hard steel against her side. Brian stepped in front of her, a small ball in his hand.

"Open wide, bitch," Doyle said.

Serena tried to scream, but Brian forced the ball gag in her mouth. He pressed, shoving her back against Doyle.

"Did you kill that cop?" Doyle asked. "We didn't say anything about killing a cop."

She struggled but her jaw was forced open. Brian secured the gag. "He's still breathing, but he'll have a hell of a headache. And he didn't see me. All he'll know is someone hit him from behind and then he woke up to a bunch of dead bodies and one survivor—me. I have to go take care of the loud bitch. I don't think she's dead yet. It will be my pleasure to put that arrogant cunt out of her misery."

Bridget. They were going to finish off Bridget. Serena tried to kick back, but Doyle had her around the neck. He squeezed, cutting off her air.

"Don't fight me, Serena. I don't want to kill you just yet. I have to make this look really good." Doyle started to drag her toward the car. "We have a special place set up for you. You know all those times you wanted me to be a pervert who hurt you? You're going to get your wish. I'm going to torture you. I've been reading up on it, and I think you were right all along. I'm a bit of a sadist, dear. And you're righteously disorganized. Did you know I'm still the beneficiary on your life insurance policy? And I recently learned you haven't filed another will. I told you I would get what belongs to me. And no one will suspect me. I'm with Mother, you see. We're having a nice long talk at her place in Tyler. Yes, Mother always hated you, Serena. She's happy to help."

He'd shoved that damn ball gag in so far. She struggled to breathe. Panic was threatening to overtake her. He started to pull her toward a car she didn't recognize. It wasn't Doyle's sedan, and Brian drove an SUV. They had obviously been planning this together.

She tried to look around the alley. It backed up to another building, but she didn't see windows or doors. It was quiet in the alley with only two cars parked there and a large trash container. Once they got her in the car, it would take less than thirty seconds to get to the street. Royal Lane was busy. They would disappear very quickly, and Adam and Jake wouldn't be able to find her.

How was this happening? Just a few moments before, everything seemed open and bright. Now Lara was dead, and Bridget was dying and all because her ex-husband wanted her money. And she hadn't thought about her will in years. It had been a small thing. They had signed a form Doyle had printed from a legal site on the internet. A very simple will. But it would probably hold up in court.

And they would make it look like the "stalker" had killed them all.

"You think you write great books, sweetheart, but I always was the truly brilliant one. And your so-called agent is an idiot. She gave us the perfect plan. I even bet your filthy, piece-of-crap books will sell better after you're dead." He looked back toward the building. "What the fuck is taking him so long?"

Serena went limp, forcing her every muscle to drag.

She sure as hell wasn't going to help him.

"Hey." Doyle stumbled, trying to hold on to her. "Fuck, Serena. Get up. You're going to get in the car or I will kill you right here."

Tears clouded her eyes as she made her decision. She wouldn't get in that car alive. She might end up being his victim, but she wasn't going to play this his way.

Jake had taught her a few things. God, why had she been so stubborn? The weeks she'd been with Jake and Adam had been the best weeks of her life. Adam had taken care of her, proving to be a true partner, bolstering her where she was weak, and Jake had been a real Dom. A real Dom taught his sub to be strong when she needed to be.

"I said get the fuck up." Doyle stood over her, that nasty gun pointed right at her head. His feet were planted on either side of her hips, and he stood staring down at her like she was a piece of trash he needed to remove so his life would be lovely again.

Go for the soft spots, Serena. Self-defense doesn't have to be about strength. It can be about smarts. It can be about using your opponent's weaknesses against him.

Serena gathered every bit of strength she had. A punch, Jake had told her, shouldn't stop at the target. A punch should be sent straight through.

"Get the fuck up, bitch. Do you not understand English?"

Serena fisted her right hand and drove up, trying to punch her ex-husband's balls straight into his gut. She punched with everything she had.

Doyle gasped, his whole body doubling over. Serena pulled the gag out of her mouth and tossed it aside.

Serena took advantage, turning and starting for the street. "Help! Help me!"

She screamed as loud as she could as she ran. If he shot her in the back, then that's what happened, but she wouldn't let him take her away. She wouldn't let him abuse her more than he had. And he wouldn't get away with it. Jake and Adam would figure it out. They wouldn't give up. They wouldn't stop working the case because their client was dead.

They wouldn't stop because they loved her.

"Help me!"

Serena ran toward the street. She ran with everything she had because she had something to live for beyond the characters in her head. Real life was harder and real love was scary, but it was worth every pain, every piece of heartache, and it was worth fighting for.

She heard the shot that meant the end of Bridget's life. So much for Brian's silencer. Pain lashed through her, but she kept running. She couldn't stop. Her feet were being cut by rocks on the pavement, but she ran.

Almost there.

Almost there.

There was another shot, and Serena felt a sharp pain in her side. She fell, her knees buckling as she hit the pavement. Blood. There was blood at her side and a terrible burning sensation.

Almost there.

She tried to crawl. *Almost there.*

Something hard hit her back.

"Not this time, Serena. You don't get away this time." Doyle held her ankles and flipped her over, forcing her to look at him. He aimed the gun at her head. "This time I win."

Serena tried to fight, but she was afraid this time he was right.

She closed her eyes and thought about them. God, she wished she'd told them.

I love you.

Her last words, whispered only in her head.

I love you both so much.

* * * *

Ian caught up to Jake and Adam as Jake hit the door to The Velvet Room. His heart was pounding in his chest, but he forced himself to remain cool. Panic wouldn't save Serena.

Liam was right behind Ian. "It's the agent's husband. And Serena's ex. After Lara confessed to Ian, Adam hacked her account. I've been reading e-mails for days."

Jake looked around the room. So many fucking people. Where was Serena? Liam kept talking.

"Lara kept the records for the whole company when it came to submissions. Did you know that Doyle Brooks submitted a book to Brian Anderson last year? I took it a step further and hacked into his account. They emailed back and forth, nothing too suspicious, but it got me thinking. I don't think this is about some crazy person. This has always been about money. Lots of money."

"Where the hell is she?" Adam asked.

"Save the explanations, Liam. We need to find her." Jake knew they were right. He felt it in his gut. The cops were questioning the kid who had been hired. A diversion. Brian Anderson had needed a diversion at precisely 5:30. He'd gotten it. All the manpower had been chasing down some dumbass kid.

Sean walked up, a small black box in his hand. "Cell phone jammer. It was in a box of books. Mine's still struggling. There must be more than one."

"Where's Serena? And where's her agent?" Jake kept his voice low, but he felt like shouting.

"Do a sweep," Ian ordered, sending Sean and Liam into immediate motion.

Chris Roberts moved from the crowd, a glass of champagne in his hand. The worried look on his face didn't match his usual laid-back style. "What's going on?"

"I need to find Serena, and I need you and Bridget to stay away from Brian Anderson." Jake didn't need to worry about the man using Serena's friends as hostages.

The glass dropped from Chris's hands, and he went a stark white. Without a word, he turned and started for the back of the building.

Adam took off after him.

Something very bad was going on. "Clear the room," Jake ordered as he jogged past Ian.

Adam tackled Chris before he made the door.

"Stop," Chris protested. "You have to let me in there. She went with him to go get Lara. God, I watched her do it not three minutes ago. I let her go."

Jake understood the man's desperation, but they had to play this smart. "You stay here. Get to Ian. Tell him what's happening and that I need men to move around to the back of the building. I need every exit blocked, and I need the cops to put an APB out on Brian Anderson and possibly Doyle Brooks. Do you understand? As a precaution, call an ambulance and more cops. We have a potential hostage situation. I need this done as quickly as possible, and I need you to stay calm. Get to Ian. He's the big guy who's probably scaring the crap out of everyone right now. Tell him Jake sent you. He'll listen."

Chris nodded and allowed Adam to help him up.

"Three minutes is a long time," Adam said, his jaw clenched.

"And our girl is smart. If this really is about money, they might not kill her here. They need it to look good, and that means getting away." Jake prayed he was right. "Okay. You take my six."

"On it." Adam moved behind him. When they hit the back room, Adam would guard his back.

As quietly as he could, he opened the door and moved through in a firing stance.

"Dumb bitch, do you know how long I've wanted to do this?"

A masculine voice chuckled. The back room was littered with shelves and stacks of boxes. He couldn't see who was talking, but he was almost certain he recognized the voice. Brian Anderson. He pointed to the southwest, where the voice had come from. Moving on silent feet, he stalked through the warehouse-like room toward the voice.

"Fuck you, Anderson. You're not going to get away with it. Someone will figure it out."

That wasn't Serena. Bridget. *Fuck*. How was Bridget involved? She sounded hurt, her voice resonating with pain.

"I'm smarter than you, smarter than my dumbass wife who had to go and fuck up my business. I used to be respected. Now we're a laughingstock. No longer. I'll get Lara's money and Doyle will take Serena's. Good-bye, Bridget."

Jake found the right row of boxes. He sent Adam to the other side with a quick nod of his head. They'd worked together most of their adult lives. Jake didn't even have to look to know Adam was doing what he needed to do. With Adam backing him up, Jake could simply move into place.

Brian Anderson stood over Bridget, a knife in his hand. The

knife was a medium-sized kitchen knife, and it looked like he'd already used it on her. He prayed Chris had called that ambulance because they were going to need it. But even as he moved into place, one question pounded through his gut.

Where was Serena? He didn't see her. Where the hell was she?

If she was dead, he would tear through them all. Brian, Doyle, that motherfucker who had been planning to use her. He wouldn't stop until they were all buried in the ground.

"Put the knife down." He didn't really want Brian Anderson to put the knife down. He wanted to shoot him, but he needed to know where Serena was first.

Anderson gasped and started to turn to run, but Adam had cut him off.

"Jake?" Bridget's voice was a tortured moan. "You have to save her. I think he took her outside. I couldn't see. I…please help her."

Jake never took his eyes off Anderson, who was visibly shaking. At least Bridget thought Serena was alive. "The cops are on their way, Bridget. So is an ambulance. You just hold on. You're going to be able to testify against this asshole."

A sad little laugh came out of her mouth. "That would be good research, right?"

"I can't go to jail." The knife in Anderson's hands shook as he looked from Adam to Jake and back again. "I didn't do it. It was Doyle."

"We just caught you red-handed, dumbass," Adam explained. "Now tell us where Serena is and you might get off with attempted murder."

"He won't. He killed Lara. He killed his wife. He'll go down, and thank god we're in Texas." Bridget sounded a little drunk. "Death penalty, buddy. Enjoy your rape time before they shove a needle in your arm."

Jake cursed because he saw the minute Anderson made his decision. He turned to Adam and hefted the knife. He took a single step before Adam pulled the trigger. The knife hit the floor with a clatter just seconds before the agent's body slumped down.

The door that led inside opened, and Ian stormed in, his Glock at the ready. "Serena?"

"Bridget. And apparently Lara's here somewhere, but I don't think she made it. I'm sorry." Jake started for the back door. Bridget had said they took her out the back.

"I am, too." Ian knelt by Bridget. "Go find your girl."

Jake's blood nearly froze when he heard a muffled scream. "Help me!" a feminine voice was calling. Serena.

Adam kicked the door open, and Jake followed him into the alley. Serena's shoes had been kicked off in the doorway.

"To the right," Adam said.

Jake stood beside his partner. Serena was halfway down the alley. She was laying there, her brown hair all that Jake could see of her face.

A man stood over her, his back to Jake, but Jake had been in the military and then private security for far too long to not recognize the stance. Jake couldn't see the gun, but he knew what was happening. Doyle Brooks was going to win over his wife the only way he possibly could.

Jake raised his gun and fired, Adam doing the same.

Doyle's body jerked and then he fell to his knees, the gun dropping from his hand. He fell on top of Serena.

Adam got to her first, calling out her name and dragging that bastard's body off hers.

Jake dropped to the ground. She was bleeding. God, there was so much blood. How much of it was hers? He touched her face, terrified of moving her body. "Serena, baby? Baby, are you okay?"

Adam checked Doyle Brooks to make sure he was gone and then joined Jake, his hand cradling Serena's. "Serena, damn it, you can't die. Tell her, Jake. You're her damn Dom. Order her not to die."

Her lips curled up slightly. "I love a bossy man."

Her eyelids fluttered, and she went limp.

Jake heard the sirens coming and prayed they weren't too late.

Chapter Twenty-Three

"**I**'m ready to kill someone. Get me a fucking computer." Adam paced, his stomach in knots. Five hours. It had been five hours since the ambulance had taken Serena away, and all anyone would tell him was that she was okay.

Okay? She'd been fucking shot and assaulted and terrified, and all he knew was that she was "okay."

Sean and Grace sat across from Jake, Grace leaning into Sean's strong body. Eve and Alex had come as well, the whole of McKay-Taggart huddling together like a group of survivors in a life raft.

"You can't hack into the hospital," Jake said, his voice weary. He sat back, his head against the couch. They had retreated back home after the cops refused to give any information about Serena's whereabouts. According to the hospital, Adam Miles and Jacob Dean weren't "family" and therefore weren't welcome after visiting hours.

And then there was the fact that killing a man, even in the line of duty, required an enormous amount of paperwork.

"We should be out there looking for her." Adam couldn't quite come to terms with the fact that he wasn't allowed to see her or even know how she was doing. Not family. She was his whole fucking heart. "And I can hack a system. I can get in there and change her records to read that she's married to one of us."

"And if she doesn't want to see us?" Jake's eyes came open, his words forming a potential truth neither had been willing to discuss.

What if Serena wanted more time to figure out what was happening between the three of them? Could he accept it? Did he really have a choice?

Liam and Ian walked out from the kitchen. Ian's face was set in deep lines. Adam felt for him. He'd lost a lot. Ian had lost friends and family, and Lara Anderson was just one more person who was now gone forever from Ian's life.

"I'm sorry about your friend's sister," Adam offered. Words didn't mean a damn thing now, but he wasn't sure what else to do.

Ian's face was a careful blank. "I am, too. Despite her problems, Lara was a nice lady. She really did think she was helping Serena. It just turns out she gave her husband what he thought was a perfect cover for murder."

Jake sat up. Mojo had taken a spot at Jake's feet the minute he'd sat down, the dog trying to comfort the man who had become one of his masters. Jake's hand idly played through the dog's fur. "Go over it again. I don't know that I've fully processed this. So Doyle tried to get Serena's agent to rep his book?"

Liam shook his head. "No, Doyle tried to get Brian Anderson to rep his book."

Eve turned toward Jake and Adam. "Brian ran the mainstream arm of the business. He'd spent years trying to build his reputation on strong literary fiction. But he'd never had anything higher than a mid-list client. Then his wife decides to try her hand, and a few years later she's bringing in the majority of the money."

Adam could complete that thought for her. "But with what Brian Anderson considered low-quality writers. Serena and Bridget and Chris. And from what I overheard at one of their lunches, Lara was trying to expand by bringing in more romance authors."

Liam took a seat next to Sean and Grace. "Poor, snobby Brian couldn't catch a break. And neither could Doyle Brooks. I checked cell phone records. They started talking about three months ago. They talked for hours, several times a week. When Brian found out about the publicity stunt Lara was pulling, he must have thought he'd died and gone to heaven."

Grace's eyes were wide as she looked at Adam. "They were the ones who sent the violent notes and keyed her car?"

"And burned down her house." Killing them once hadn't been enough. "All in an effort to lend credibility to the fact that a stalker was really after Serena."

"Why make a move today?" Jake asked. "Why didn't they wait until things died down a little? Eventually we would have relaxed our guard a bit. I mean if they had backed off for a month or two, we probably would have thought the whole thing was over."

Ian took a long breath. "I can answer that. Lara told me she was filing for divorce next Monday. She was going to leave Brian and take all of her clients with her. Her clients were the only thing propping the agency up. At some point in time, he convinced Doyle Brooks that they could kill both their spouses and make some cash in the meantime. Serena had never updated her will. And there was a life insurance policy still in force on her for a half a million dollars. Doyle would have made a lot of money."

"So they knocked out the officer we'd placed outside the door, and then Doyle would have taken Serena after he'd shot or stabbed Brian Anderson in some non-lethal way to make it look like he was just another victim. I'm sure we would have found Serena's body in a few days and both men would have alibis. And with the money he would have made from the policy Brian had on Lara, he intended to find some real clients, I would bet. Hell, he might even have written a book himself. There would have been a lot of press. I'm sure there still will be," Jake pointed out.

"Writer gets stalked and nearly killed by agent." Alex huffed out a little laugh. "Yeah, it's going to make the national news. And Serena is about to get a lot of attention. Don't be surprised if her books go crazy after this."

Did she know that? Did she realize she was about to get bumped into another stratosphere? Would she need two difficult bodyguards now that she had just about achieved her dream?

They hadn't made things easy on her. Adam had been moody and emotional and Jake had been a hard-ass, and they hadn't had the chance to say it.

I love you.

Was he going to have to go to a signing to see her again?

The chime on the security system rang.

"I'll take care of it," Liam said, heading toward the front of the house. "Let's hope the reporters haven't figured out your address."

Adam looked at his partner and knew they were thinking the same things. They were wondering where she would stay and who would take care of her. She was a grown, smart, capable woman, but everyone needed people to take care of them, to see to the little things. Would she come back for her computer or send someone to get it?

"Hi."

Adam turned and his heart flip-flopped when he saw Serena in the doorway, a tired smile on her face.

Chris gave them all a little wave. "I drove her over. We managed to get by the press. They were all over the hospital. I smuggled her out the back."

"I'm sorry about that," Serena said. The polite tone of her voice set Adam on edge. "I know you would have preferred to drive me, but it was so crazy up there, I didn't want to add to it."

Adam's eyes ate her up, but he held his ground. Was she here to get her things? *Damn it.* He wasn't going to let her leave without a fight.

Jake had gotten to his feet. "They let you go? What did the doctors say?"

She looked so fragile standing there next to her friend. "The bullet grazed my side. No surgery. It only took three stitches. They were more worried I'd gotten a concussion, but the scans didn't show anything. I waited so long because I needed to make sure Bridget was okay. And I checked in on the officer who was hurt. He did have a concussion, but they say he'll be all right. I need to find a way to thank him."

"You will." Grace walked to Serena's side. "Is Bridget all right?"

Serena nodded, relief etched on her face. "It was close, but she's going to be okay. The doctors say Ian probably saved her life.

He held her together with his own hands until the EMTs got there. I can't thank you enough."

Ian simply sighed and started for the door. "You're welcome. I'm glad your friend is all right. I just wish I could have saved Lara."

Ian walked out, the door closing behind him.

Sean grabbed his wife's hand. "Little one?"

Grace nodded toward the door. "Go after him. Eve can give me a ride home. Your brother needs you. Put aside the rest of it for one night."

"He won't talk about it, but I can buy him a drink." Sean looked to Liam and Alex. "Come on. Let's take the boss out for a beer."

"I'll take the pregnant lady home." Eve put a hand on Adam's shoulder. She went on her toes and kissed his cheek. "You three should talk. Good night, Serena. If you need me, my door is always open."

Eve and Grace said their good-byes and left for the night.

Chris sighed. "And I need to get back to Bridget. She should be moved out of ICU in a couple of hours. I think I convinced them to let me stay the night with her. She doesn't like hospitals. I don't like cots, but my hatred of discomfort is overcome by my love for my girls."

"How did you get in? They wouldn't even tell us what room she was in. The cops had to tell us she was still alive." Adam had been frustrated for hours.

Chris smiled brightly. "Oh, they let me in to see my sisters."

"So you lied?" Jake stood staring at Serena even as he spoke to Chris.

Chris hugged Serena gently. "Nope. I just think society places far too much importance on blood and not enough on love. Night, my sister. I love you. I'll call tomorrow, and don't you worry about a thing. I'll take care of Bridget, and we'll handle Lara's arrangements later."

Tears dropped down Serena's face as she nodded Chris's way. "Love you, too. I'll come by tomorrow."

Chris left and they were finally alone.

Serena knelt down to pet her dog. She hugged Mojo, her face

stroking his fur. "I really am sorry about the whole hospital thing. I thought it was best."

She thought it was best to keep them from her when she was hurt? Adam took a step forward. She'd been shot, but all he wanted to do was make sure she was tied up so she couldn't leave.

"Your ride just left." Jake was unmoving, his big form straight and solid.

A faint smile crossed her lips. "I kind of hoped I had one here. Or two. I guess I was really hoping for two. If I don't have two, you should tell me now so I can catch Chris. I'm afraid I'm not good at compromise. I want you both. I want everything."

A surge of hope filled Adam. "Serena, you be sure. You be sure this is what you want because I won't ever let you go."

Jake finally moved, walking toward her. "She's not going to change her mind. She's finally figured it out. And she should know there's going to be some punishment for keeping us out of the hospital."

Now she simply smiled, her face lighting up. God, that smile lit up his whole fucking world. "I thought I was keeping us all safe, Sir. Should I call you Sir outside of the club?"

Jake put a hand on her head, his eyes softening at the contact. "No. I like the way you say my name. But, Serena, there is something else you're going to call me. You're going to get everything you want, but you have to call me and Adam by special names."

Oh, Adam knew just what name he wanted. And he wanted to share the name. "Husband. You're going to call us husband, Serena."

"I can't think of anything better." She closed her eyes, seeming to revel in Jake's touch. Even as her eyes were closed, she reached her hand out, calling to Adam. He didn't hesitate. He took her hand, threading his fingers through hers. Connected. This was what he'd wanted for days, for weeks, for long before he'd met her. He'd longed for the woman who could accept the man he was inside, the freak who needed Jake to be complete, the soldier who had to protect, the lover who wanted to take care of her.

"I love you, Serena." He said the words like a benediction.

"I love you, baby." Jake's smile could be heard in his voice. Satisfaction and contentment oozed from Jake. Peace. That was what Serena offered them both. A family. They were going to be a family.

Crystal tears dropped on her cheeks. "I'm glad because I love you both. When I thought I might die, all I wanted was one last moment with you. I won't check out again. I was scared, but I'm not anymore."

His heart opened. He hauled her into his arms, right where she should always be. "There's nothing to be afraid of. Baby, we'll never leave you. We might fight and be stupid, but this is forever."

She looked up into his eyes, but kept a hand on Jake, too. She was the glue that would keep them together, always. "And I'll be distant and lost in my work, and you both have to know that every hero I write for the rest of my life has a piece of you two. They always did. I was just waiting for the real men."

He kissed her, taking care of her, holding her gently. "What did the doctors say?"

His cock was aching, but if she couldn't handle it, he would just hold her. He and Jake would just cuddle her between them.

Her lips played against his. "The doctors said I need my men. Adam, Jake, I need you tonight. I need you both."

Adam caught Jake's eyes and saw the desire for Serena there. He knew it mirrored his own. Jake nodded, and Adam's heart rate sped up. It was time to claim their woman.

* * * *

Serena went up on her toes, pressing her lips to Adam's, her hand reaching out to Jake's and pulling him in. She needed a hand on both of them. When she'd thought she was going to die, the only thing she'd really regretted was not letting them know how much she loved them.

She'd allowed her fear and bitterness to rule her for far too long. They all had. She'd chosen wrong before, but it didn't matter. She got to choose again, and this time she chose them. She'd been given a second chance, and she would be damned if she didn't take it.

Jake's free hand tangled in her hair. When she came up for air, he gently directed her his way, his mouth covering hers. Adam's kiss was soft, playing along her lips, meltingly smooth. Jake dominated. His tongue took over. She'd never been kissed the way Jake kissed her, like he could inhale her. She didn't need to breathe when Jake kissed her. She could survive on his kiss alone.

Adam didn't waste time. His hands were on the straps of her dress, dragging them down. He made quick work of her bra, freeing her breasts. While Jacob plundered her mouth, Adam got to his knees and worshipped her breasts. Serena whimpered as his tongue teased her nipples, tightening them and making her ache. He sucked the tip into his mouth, biting down gently. It sparked heat through her whole body.

Jake released her mouth, taking a step back. "Adam, stop for a moment."

Adam stopped sucking, but his tongue licked at her. "Don't want to. I don't think I'll ever stop."

Jake chuckled, the sound dark and sexy. "We have a very long time with our little sub, and I want to start things off right. Since she's going to make us crazy in our daily life, the least she can do is cede control in the bedroom or the club or the elevator up to our office or anywhere else we can think of to make love to her."

She had to smile. She was pretty sure when it came to thinking up inventive places to have sex, Jake could match her. And she'd been dreaming of that elevator ever since Adam had kissed her there.

She sighed as Adam kissed her breasts one last time and then got to his feet.

"You're right. I think after what she put us through, she probably needs to be a little submissive tonight." Adam took Mojo's collar and led him out. "Time for bed, puppy. I don't think what's about to happen in here is suitable for your innocent doggy eyes."

Mojo followed him out.

Just a hint of trepidation crept up her spine as Jake watched her with dark eyes. Those were his Dom eyes. They were dangerous and hungry and promised all manner of delicious torture. Yeah, she liked his Dom eyes.

"You understand what you did?" Jake asked, his voice deepening. That voice got to her, too. There was a hard edge to every syllable that seemed to flavor the words with decadence.

"I should have called." She didn't move to cover her breasts. Days ago she would have felt vulnerable standing there with her breasts exposed while he was still dressed, but now she felt oddly powerful. It was right to be naked in front of them.

"Oh, you should have done more than called. You should have moved heaven and earth to make sure we could see you."

She sighed. She'd known they wouldn't understand, but she really had been trying to protect them. "Jake, there were reporters waiting on the ambulance. I don't know how they found out, but apparently it's a really good story. I didn't know if you should be exposed to that. You work undercover. Do you really need your face plastered all over the newspaper?"

He shook his head as Adam walked back into the room. "I don't give a damn. If I can't work undercover, then I can't. You are more important than any job."

"She put us through hell so we wouldn't get outed by the papers? What does she think is going to happen when people find out she's married to two men?" Adam asked. He turned to her, a scowl on his handsome face. "Because there is going to be a marriage out of this. You're marrying me. Jake lost at cards."

"I want a rematch. I'm pretty sure Adam cheated."

"Ah, romance." She couldn't help the smile that crossed her face. It was going to be an adventure with them. There would be trouble, but she would stand fast. "If that's all the proposal I get then yes, I will marry you. And I want Jake's collar. I want a ceremony and everything."

"You'll have it, baby," Jake promised. "Now take off your clothes and present yourself. I'd like to get the punishment part of the evening over with so we can get to the good stuff."

Her whole body trembled in anticipation.

"Take it off slowly, Serena," Adam ordered.

They were just standing there, watching her undress, waiting for her to follow their commands. It might have been different if the exchange hadn't been equal, but they gave her everything they had.

Adam took care of her, lavishing her with attention and affection and easing the strain of her days. And Jake was her warrior, teaching her to be strong, opening his heart where it had been closed to all but her.

It was an odd family they were forming, but she wouldn't have it any other way. She had them both, each stronger for their reliance on the other. They were halves of a whole, accepting what they needed, making it easy for her to accept them both.

Slowly, a little awkward at first, she pushed at the waist of her dress. She winced a little as she reached the bandage at her side.

"Stop." Jake said, moving in. He touched the white gauze pad that covered a patch of skin just above her right hip.

She wasn't about to let them put her on bed rest over that tiny wound. "It's fine, Jake. It's nothing. Like I said before, it's a little scratch."

He looked back at Adam as though asking his opinion.

Adam pulled the bandage slightly off, examining the wound before closing it up. "We'll be careful with her. We'll be gentle. And it doesn't affect what we should do to that gorgeous ass of hers. She's not fragile, Jake. She's wickedly strong. I heard she damn near took off her ex's balls. They were talking about it at the station house. The medical examiner said his balls were the size of a grapefruit."

That had been a horrible moment, but Jake had been with her in spirit. "I punched him."

"Good girl," Jake said solemnly. He kissed her forehead. "We're going to continue those lessons, baby. I want you strong."

She was strong. So strong. She hadn't known just how strong she was until she'd been in that moment and she'd known she would do anything to survive. "So stop bugging me and let me take my punishment."

He tweaked a nipple, causing her to gasp. "Such a brat. Get rid of the dress, and then I want that ass in the air."

She was so glad she wasn't wearing underwear. Not that she'd been given a choice, but now it was simple to push the dress off, hand it to Adam, and turn. She leaned over, placing her palms flat on the coffee table and raising her ass in the air. No more worrying about cellulite or those extra pounds. There was no place for that here. There was only the exchange between Dom and sub, a promise of safety and the freedom to explore.

"God, I love that ass." Jake's hands stroked her cheeks. "Are we ready for this? For taking her together?"

Adam chuckled. "I'm a boy scout, buddy. I've got lube and condoms, and she's taken the large plug with such grace. I promise it'll be a tight fit, but she can handle us."

"I don't know about grace, Adam. I think I took that plug with a whole lot of complaining." It had been rough. That plug was huge and still not quite the size of her men.

Jake slapped her ass, the sting a promise of things to come. "Your opinion is not required right now, baby. And this pretty ass was made for us. It was made to take a cock. But not just yet. You require a little warm-up session. Adam, I believe we'll start with a count of twenty."

She nearly screamed when both smacked her ass at the same time.

They counted aloud and, aside from the first stroke, took turns spanking her. Jake would slap at the fleshy part of her ass, and Adam would match it on her opposite cheek. They would strike and then hold their hands over the ache, allowing the warmth of the discipline to sink into her bones. She loved it. She was a freak, and she wouldn't be any other way. She needed this the way some women needed a glass of wine at night. She relaxed into her position, that erotic mix of pleasure and pain causing her muscles to melt and everything to fall away. Nothing in the world mattered except this. Tomorrow she could begin to process all that had happened. And she wouldn't be alone. They would be there to talk her through it, to hold her while she cried, to kiss her senseless when she couldn't think about it a second longer. Their love would be the blanket she wrapped around her soul when the bad dreams came.

Yes, she was vulnerable to men like Doyle and Brian, and yes, the world could be a crappy place. It invaded and encroached on the good things in life, but here, she was safe. Here, she was the queen, choosing them over and over again.

Her mind floated while they counted out her discipline. She was almost disappointed when they finally spoke the word twenty.

"Test her." Jake's hands traced the cheeks of her ass. She wondered if he was getting hard looking at the flesh made pink by the flat of his hand.

A finger slid through her pussy. Adam. "Oh, she's our kinky girl. She loves this, Jake. I think I might have to suffer through Ian's class after all. I never wanted to really dominate a woman before, but I think I want to be her proper Master."

"You never really loved a woman before," Jake said quietly.

"No. I fooled myself. But this is real."

"This is real."

She didn't say anything because she understood that this was something that would be just for them. They had an intimate relationship, too. It didn't include sex, but it was a form of love. She would be the center of their world, a way to express their caring for each other by sharing a wife and building a life.

It was a beautiful thing to be.

An arm wrapped around her middle, gently bringing her up. Jake lifted her into his arms, taking care with the wound on her side.

"Time to move to the bedroom, baby." He walked through the house, making short work of the distance.

She loved the master bedroom. She loved that it was big enough for the three of them. It had all the trappings of a normal marital bed. Dressers for clothes and containers for watches and wallets. Three in a row, with hers in the middle. Like they would sleep. Like they would walk together. She would always be in the middle, surrounded by their affection.

"Tell me those are good tears, Serena." Jake looked down at her as he placed her on the bed. "I never want to make you cry again. I need to know you forgive me."

For saying a few words in the heat of the moment? It seemed so far away now. It had been a foolish fight in the first place, and one they might have again. Trust would grow between them, but there would always be insecurities and tiny jealousies. It wasn't the fact that they were in a ménage that made it so, Serena knew. It was the fact that they were human and in love. They would fight and make up and fight again. It was inevitable in a passionate relationship. "I forgive you, Jake. Now, and the next time, and the time after that."

A smile curled his lips up. "I'm glad you recognize that I will fuck up again."

She touched his hair, so soft despite the hardness of the style. "We all will. And it'll be okay."

His lips hovered over hers. "It'll be okay."

He kissed her, but it was a sweet promise of emotion and passion and years of both ahead.

"Hey, my turn." The bed dipped, and Adam climbed on. He'd gotten out of his clothes. Seeing him naked just took her breath away. He crawled toward her, those broad shoulders coming into view.

Jake winked down and then got off the bed, leaving her to Adam.

He growled a little as he kissed her. "Get used to this, baby. I'm calling in some vacation time for me and Jake. We're going to start the honeymoon early. Now get on your knees. I want to taste you while Jake gets your pretty ass ready."

Oh, she wanted that, too. She wasn't sure there was a better feeling in the world than one of her men tasting her pussy like it was a particularly juicy piece of pie. She rolled to her side and got on her knees, lifting her ass in the air. Adam slid between her legs, his own dangling off the edge of the bed. She could feel his hot breath hovering under her pussy. His hands were on her hips, pulling her down.

A low moan escaped her mouth as Adam licked her pussy. He delved inside, sucking at the petals of her sex, pulling in one and then laving affection on the other. Pleasure bloomed across her skin, lighting up her nerves and making her so vibrantly aware that she was alive.

She'd survived. She was here with them, and she would never leave again.

Adam continued to lash her sex with pleasure as his hands parted the cheeks of her ass.

"I have to use a little lube, baby." Jake's voice skimmed across her back as he placed a soft kiss at the base of her spine. "Just relax. I'll be inside you soon. God, I can't wait to be inside you."

Adam licked at her clit, a slow drawing of tongue across flesh, as Jake worked the lube in. Serena was caught between the soft work of Adam's tongue and the erotic jangle of Jake's fingers rimming the rosette of her ass. So much sensation. She closed her eyes, trying to ride the wave.

"She's so tight. She's going to feel so good." Jake's finger opened her up, fucking in and out in a gentle motion. "Don't fight me, baby. I want in."

She tried to relax, but Adam fucked her with his tongue, spearing up inside her before moving to her clit and suckling. She couldn't take it anymore. She went over the edge, Adam's mouth sending sparks of pure bliss through her system. She shook and cried out as the orgasm flooded her.

And then they were moving. Before she'd even come down from the high, they were adjusting, getting into position. Adam rolled out from under her, getting up and stroking that big cock of his before he rolled a condom over it.

"Come on and ride me, love." He spread out on the bed, offering himself up.

Jake gave her a hand, helping her move over Adam's body. She gripped his muscled hips with her knees and braced her hands against his chest. He was so hard everywhere, a delectable man feast for her pleasure only.

"You look like you could eat me up," Adam said, his hips moving under hers. "I'll let you later. Later I'll fuck your mouth and find that soft spot at the back of your throat. I'll give you everything I have, but for now, I want this."

He pulled at her hips, impaling her on his cock. He was so big, she had to work her way down, forcing him in, inch by amazing inch. He filled her until she wasn't sure where Jake would fit.

"This is where I want to be all the time, Serena." Adam twisted his hips up, lighting her from the inside out.

She'd just come, but she was sparking all over again.

"Put your chest against Adam's, baby. Give me a little room to work." Jake's hand pressed on her back.

She let her breasts rub against the steel of Adam's chest. Adam kissed her, his tongue playing with hers as Jake pressed his cock at the rim of her ass.

She whimpered a little as he started to push inside. It wasn't pain, but it wasn't pleasure either. That cock working its way in was dominance in its purest, most erotic form. She softened, willing herself to take him, to give him what he wanted because he'd held up his end of their bargain. He'd taken care of her, loved her, tried his damnedest to protect her, and he'd offered up his soul to her. She flattened her back, wanting nothing more than both men inside her body, taking the pleasure that belonged to them because she'd made it her gift.

"Fuck, she's tight." Jake's cockhead finally slipped past the ring of muscles guarding her asshole. He held himself there for a moment, making Serena crazy. She felt so opened, bared to them both.

"Please, Jacob." She was going to die if they didn't start moving. She was caught on the precipice of something she'd never felt before, not even from them.

"Hush, baby. I know what I'm doing. Give me a second. This feels so beautiful. Do you know how happy you make me?" He pressed in, filling her with his dick.

She forced herself to obey him, to remain still. He'd given her nothing but pleasure. Even this was an odd mix of discomfiting fullness and intimacy. She felt pinned and trapped in the sweetest way possible.

Jake pressed forward until she could feel his balls against her. All the way. Both of her men were as far as they could go.

"Can you feel him?" Serena asked.

Adam's smile lit up his face. "Yeah. You're so tight this way. I feel him sliding against me. There are no words for it."

But she could think of a few. Heaven. Joy. Perfection.

"Are you ready, baby?" Jake asked.

She'd been ready for this forever. "Oh, yes."

Jake pulled out and Serena felt her fingers sink into Adam's chest. So good. It had been hard to take him, but the slow drag of his cock out of her ass caused her to flare with sensation, nerves firing off in pleasure.

While Jake pulled out, Adam pressed up, grinding his pelvis

against hers, hitting her clit.

And they were off. They found a pounding rhythm, a song made by their bodies, kept in perfect time.

Serena gave herself over. She was their beloved plaything, pulled and pushed and brought to the brink again and again. Their cocks slid in and out, pumping in time, until she wasn't sure where the sensation was coming from. She just wanted more. Every way she moved was a new feeling, her ass lighting up or her pussy pushed to the edge.

Adam pressed up again, and she couldn't hold it off a second longer. She let the orgasm take her. Serena wailed it out, unable to hold the sound in. She pushed back, taking Jake in and then forward to extract the maximum pleasure Adam's cock offered.

Jake shouted behind her, the hot wash of his orgasm filling her ass. A second later, Adam joined him, pumping up until he had nothing left to give.

She fell forward, utterly exhausted and completely happy.

"You okay, baby?" Jake asked, settling in behind her.

Adam snuggled close. "Were we too rough?"

"You were perfect."

Jake sat up, his hand moving to the nightstand. When he came back, he reached for her hands.

"Do it, buddy. This way she can't run again." Adam grinned.

Cool metal pressed around her wrists. Handcuffs. "Guys, I'm not going anywhere."

There was a deep look of satisfaction on Jake's face. "Nope. Not ever again. And I just might keep you chained to the bed for our whole honeymoon."

He kissed her again, and then Adam had his turn. She couldn't move her hands, but suddenly those cuffs seemed like the most beautiful jewelry she'd ever worn.

Chapter Twenty-Four

Serena hung the phone up, her head reeling a little.

"Who was it?" Chris asked. He sat beside Bridget on the patio with a margarita in his hand.

All around them, the party continued on. Her wedding party. She was married. She and Adam had gone to the justice of the peace, and she and Jake had solemnized their union at the club the night before. She had a wedding ring on her finger and a small gold collar around her neck, and her men had presented her with one more gift. A set of golden handcuffs to bind her. They had broken those cuffs in the night before, the perfect end to a perfect day.

Now all their friends were here, drinking and talking and wishing them well. Jake's parents and brothers had even come in. They'd been thrilled Jake was involved with someone creative.

Adam's family had declined her calls, but he hadn't seemed to care.

She looked at him, laughing at something Sean said. This was Adam's family. This was her family.

And she had both a new name and a new title.

"It was Maureen."

Jake passed her a fresh margarita. "The new agent?" He

motioned for Adam to come over. "What's wrong?"

Maureen Childress had taken over Lara Anderson's clients. She'd been friends with Lara and had tearfully asked that she be able to assist Lara's closest authors. She'd been a rock, handling everything she could from her New York office.

Bridget leaned forward, only wincing a little. She'd lost her spleen and dumped her boyfriend, but she was already on the mend. "Is she fielding those damn reporters again? Tell them to fuck themselves. Your personal life isn't their story."

"Down, Bridget. Don't pull your stitches. You don't want to screw up your date with the EMT guy tomorrow." Chris put a hand on hers.

Bridget smiled. "No, I don't. That man is so sexy. I swear I'm getting some hot man ass out of this whole 'getting sliced up by a psycho' thing. I have to admit that I understand why the press is sniffing around. Writers get screwed by their agents every day, but we actually almost got murdered. It's a hell of a story. God, this business sucks."

Chris shook his head. "And she wouldn't be anywhere else. She's already twenty thousand words into a book about an assault survivor and the team of doctors who save her."

"And fuck the hell out of her," Bridget said with a grin. "Mega ménage. Oh, and the doctors are also super-secret billionaires who happen to be werewolves. If I can work a secret baby angle in there, I'll hit all the tropes. God, I really love being a writer."

Adam frowned. "You're not allowed to write mega ménage, Serena. You're a traditionalist."

Yep. She slept between the two of them every night. Very traditional. "I'm also a *New York Times* bestselling author. *Their Sweetheart Slave* hit the E-list."

Sure, it had taken the publicity from the whole stalker debacle, but it had happened. A wistful sadness struck her. She wished Lara was here to see it.

But then she was wrapped in their arms, congratulations flowing. Adam and Jake kissed her and then started to bring out champagne for everyone.

Serena laughed, getting caught in the moment. She was

surrounded by this mish-mashed family she'd managed to find.

And her happy ending was just waiting to be written.

* * * *

Hours later, Liam O'Donnell sat in his office, watching, waiting for that one little signal. He wasn't sure how it would come. E-mail. Internet alert. Phone call from a source.

But he knew it would come. He would find Mr. Black, the man who had almost killed Sean Taggart. The man who had gotten away with treason. He would find him, and he would make him pay. He pretended not to care, but then he pretended about everything. He'd lied for so long, he often wondered if he would recognize the truth about himself if he found it.

But Mr. Black was another story. He stood beside Ian in his quest to take the fucker down. All it required was a little patience.

"You're still here?" Eve stood in his office doorway. "I thought you would be home after the party. It was lovely, wasn't it?"

It had been nice, but not for him. He was a predator, and he always felt out of place in celebrations like the one in Adam, Jake, and Serena's honor. Still, it was his job to make sure people in love got to stay in love. He'd given up his right to happiness long ago on another continent. Now all he had was the hunt and offering up his protection to the people who were happy. Mr. Black had almost taken that from Sean and Grace, too.

"It was a great party." The computer pinged, an e-mail coming through. Probably nothing, but he checked anyway.

"Do you want me to set up for a session?" Eve smiled a little.

A single picture came on the screen, cloudy and grainy. A still from a CCTV, but it got Liam's blood pumping.

Mr. Black—aka Eli Nelson—sat at a small table. Liam wasn't sure about the restaurant, but he knew the city well. The mighty Thames was behind Black's body, St. Paul's Cathedral in the distance.

His heart constricted a little. Too close to home, but he would be there overnight.

"Not tonight, Evie." Liam stood. "Tell Ian to get me on the next flight to London."

His time had come.

* * * *

The McKay-Taggart crew will return in the next exciting installment in the *Masters and Mercenaries* series...*A Dom Is Forever*.

Author's Note

I'm often asked by generous readers how they can help get the word out about a book they enjoyed. There are so many ways to help an author you like. Leave a review. If your e-reader allows you to lend a book to a friend, please share it. Go to Goodreads and connect with others. Recommend the books you love because stories are meant to be shared. Thank you so much for reading this book and for supporting all the authors you love!

A Dom Is Forever
Masters and Mercenaries, Book 3
By Lexi Blake
Now Available!

A Man with a Past...

Liam O'Donnell fled his native Ireland years ago after one of his missions ended in tragedy and he was accused of killing several of his fellow agents. Shrouded in mystery, Liam can't remember that fateful night. He came to the United States in disgrace, seeking redemption for crimes he may or may not have committed. But the hunt for an international terrorist leads him to London and right back into the world he left behind.

A Woman Looking for a Future...

Avery Charles followed her boss to London, eager to help the philanthropist with his many charities. When she meets a mysterious man who promises to show her London's fetish scene, she can't help but indulge in her darkest fantasies. Liam becomes her Dom, her protector, her lover. She opens her heart and her home to him, only to discover he's a man on a mission and she's just a means to an end.

When Avery's boss leads them to the traitorous Mr. Black, Liam must put together the puzzle of his past or Avery might not have a future...

* * * *

"I want you." She wanted him so badly. She just didn't trust that he could possibly want her.

"No, you don't, but you will." He stepped back and tucked his shirt in. "We're going to do this my way. We tried yours and it didn't work, so I'm taking control. I should have done it in the first place. If I thought you had some, I would tell you to change into fet

334

wear, but you don't happen to have a corset and some PVC hiding in that closet, do you?"

"I don't know what PVC is," she admitted, her heart aching a little. "I don't think this is a good idea, Lee. I don't think I can be what you need. I'm not experienced, and what experience I have wasn't very good. Don't get me wrong. I loved my husband, but the sex wasn't spectacular. I think I'm just one of those women who can't be sexy. I was trying to please you, but I couldn't."

Even in the dim light, she could see him staring, assessing. "And I think you're one of those women who can't stop thinking long enough to let her body take over. Look, Avery, the sex you've had happened with a kid. Was your husband older than you? More experienced?"

She shook her head. They had both been virgins.

"Then you have no idea what it can be like. I look at sex differently than most people. It's an exchange, and it should be good for both parties. I don't want you to spread your legs and let me have you because you want someone to hold you. If you want me to hold you, ask me. I want you to spread your legs because you can't wait another single second for my cock. I want that pussy ripe and ready and weeping for a big dick to split it wide and have its way. I want your nipples to peak because I walk into a room and you remember every dirty thing I can do to them. I want you to want me. I can make you crave me. I don't want some drive-by fucking that gets me off and I forget it five minutes later. I want to fuck all night long. I want to feel it all the next day because my cock got so used to being deep inside your body. If that's what you want, then get dressed in the sexiest thing you own and agree that I'm the boss when it comes to sex." He turned and walked out. "I'll give you five minutes to decide. I'll be waiting in your living room. If you really want me, you'll dress exactly how I've told you to dress and you'll present yourself to me for inspection. And Avery, no bra and no underwear. You won't need them."

The door closed behind him, and she had to remember how to breathe.

She wasn't sexy. She wasn't orgasmic.

But what if she could be? Lee hadn't been right about

335

everything, but he had a few points. He'd told her he wanted to be in control and then she'd tried to make all the decisions. He had more experience, but she'd decided she knew best. She hadn't listened to him.

He wanted control. He wanted her to really want him. She didn't understand, but if she ever wanted to understand, she had to try.

She'd taught herself how to walk again. That had been an enormous mountain to climb. Why was she so scared of this? She'd faced worse, but she was cowering in her boots over not wearing underwear and a bra? She'd lost so much. Was she willing to lose this, too?

What was she really risking? She might look dumb. She could end up with her heart broken, but at least she would have proven it still worked.

She'd come across the ocean to change her life—to have a life. What was life without a few risks?

She got her phone out and sent a quick text to Adam letting him know she was home and who she was with so if she was serially murdered, at least they would have a starting place for where to find her body.

But she was going to do this because she felt safe with Lee. And because she wanted to finally understand what it really meant to want someone.

Thieves

A new urban fantasy series by Lexi Blake

"Author Lexi Blake has created a supernatural world filled with surprises and a book that I couldn't put down once I started reading it."

Maven, The Talent Cave Reviews

"I truly love that Lexi took vampires and made them her own."

KC Lu, Guilty Pleasures Book Reviews

Stealing mystical and arcane artifacts is a dangerous business, especially for a human, but Zoey Wharton is an exceptional thief. The trick to staying alive is having friends in all the wrong places. With a vampire, a werewolf, and a witch on the payroll, Zoey takes the sorts of jobs no one else can perform—tracking down ancient artifacts filled with unthinkable magic power, while trying to stay one step ahead of monsters, demons, angels, and a Vampire Council with her in their crosshairs.

If only her love life could be as simple. Zoey and Daniel Donovan were childhood sweethearts until a violent car crash took his life. When Daniel returned from the grave as a vampire, his only interest in Zoey was in keeping her safely apart from the secrets of his dark world. Five years later, Zoey encounters Devinshea Quinn, an earthbound Faery prince who sweeps her off her feet. He could show her everything the supernatural world has to offer, but Daniel is still in her heart.

As their adventures in acquisition continue, Zoey will have to find a way to bring together the two men she loves or else none of them may survive the forces that have aligned against her.

Thieves:
Steal the Light
Steal the Day
Steal the Moon
Steal the Sun
Steal the Night
Ripper

Addict
Sleeper
Outcast, Coming 2018